IN ANOTHER WORLD'S SUN

IN ANOTHER WORLD'S SUN

DANIEL CROMPTON

Halo
PUBLISHING
INTERNATIONAL

Halo Publishing International
7550 WIH-10 #800, PMB 2069,
San Antonio, TX 78229

First Edition, February 2024
ISBN: 978-1-63765-552-8
Library of Congress Control Number: 2023924737

The information contained within this book is strictly for informational purposes. Unless otherwise indicated, all the names, characters, businesses, places, events and incidents in this book are either the product of the author's imagination or used in a fictitious manner. Any resemblance to actual persons, living or dead, or actual events is purely coincidental.

Halo Publishing International is a self-publishing company that publishes adult fiction and non-fiction, children's literature, self-help, spiritual, and faith-based books. We continually strive to help authors reach their publishing goals and provide many different services that help them do so. We do not publish books that are deemed to be politically, religiously, or socially disrespectful, or books that are sexually provocative, including erotica. Halo reserves the right to refuse publication of any manuscript if it is deemed not to be in line with our principles. Do you have a book idea you would like us to consider publishing? Please visit www.halopublishing.com for more information.

To my wife, Danielle Crompton, the woman who believed in me every step of the way. You were the rock at my side. Thank you for everything, my love. I could not have done this without you.

I'd also like to thank each and every one of you for taking the time to read my book, stepping out of your own world and into mine, if only for a little while, and joining me on an adventure.

Contents

Chapter 1 — A New Beginning in Another World's Sun

The day was bright and warm. I closed my eyes and leaned on a nearby wall, enjoying the feel of it on my skin and wishing I could take it and wrap myself in it. Cool air blew, bringing with it the scent of cut grass and other smells of summer. With a large smile on my face, I stopped for a few minutes to take in the feeling. Life wasn't great, but this moment was good, and that was all I could ask for. Living moment to moment is important when your life consists of getting yelled at by an abusive prick of a father who did his best to remind you that you were trash and nothing but a sponge soaking up his money.

I pushed off the wall and kept walking down the street, both hands in my pockets. I was five foot six and scrawny—I never could gain a pound in my life. I weighed all of 130 pounds; my ribs could be seen easily, and they weren't part of a six-pack either. I had short, buzz-cut sandy hair that was uneven and looked hastily cut. I wished it were longer, but my father always buzzed it while telling me it was a waste of money to get haircuts when we could just do it at home. I am an American guy, born and raised in the projects of a state that had turned its back on me after labeling me a malcontent.

I turn eighteen tomorrow and can finally leave that hell-hole legally. I didn't tell my father any of my plans; he would probably find some way to sabotage them. He loved guilting me into doing things for him, telling me that I was all he had and that he had broken his back caring for me all these years. Truth was, if anyone even cared to notice, it would have been called an abuse case long ago, and I would have been taken away from him. But no one cared.

The one time police were called when my father was heard screaming at me through the paper-thin walls of the house we were in, I had run out and begged the police to help me. Never in my life had I seen the contempt run so deeply in someone's face as they looked at me. They were disgusted by me. It was an awakening I had not been prepared for, one that left my soul shaken.

After all these years, I was going to wait till he was drunk out of his mind, and then I would walk out the front door and never come back. I was taking with me the only thing he'd taught me—how to survive without needing anyone, even him. It would have been nice to have friends, but I didn't need the looks of hurt or pity I knew I would get if they saw the way my father was.

I smiled softly; my freedom was close at hand. I was just walking aimlessly, biding my time until I had to go home—

he was drunk right now. In an endless stupor that would usher in a numbing headache in the morning, he would take it out on me as if I were the one who had held the bottle to his lips and made him drink. I shook my head—useless.

I turned the corner while I was walking, lost in my thoughts, and almost tripped over a homeless woman sitting on the sidewalk. I almost said something to her about moving from that spot before she got hurt, but I held my tongue. There was no point in talking with homeless folk; they didn't listen half the time, and the other half they got nasty and tried to fight.

I moved aside and started walking away, but then I saw small hands reaching from the woman's lap. The woman was asleep, but the small child in her lap was awake. Her small blue eyes gazed up at me helplessly, her jaws outlined with the classic signs of starvation. I almost choked while looking at her. The girl's eyes pleaded; she wanted food. I knew that. I didn't have anything; even worse, I had no money. My eyes began to water as I felt more helpless and lost.

"Please, sir. My mommy, she's so hungry. She can't even stay awake anymore," the little girl said weakly.

The mom's eyes opened as she heard her daughter's voice; she looked up at me and saw my eyes watering. She apparently sensed that I was going to cry. The lady curled her child into her chest to shush her, smiled apologetically at me, and said, "She is worried about me. I am grateful that she cares for her mother so. Don't you cry now, child. I won't have that; don't you worry. Take care of yourself now, boy; I have been through worse. I always survive, and my babe will too."

She looked so confident and sure of herself it made me want to believe her. I nodded and turned, hurrying off. I needed to get away from those eyes, those pleading eyes that felt as if they were looking right into my soul. I wanted to help the woman and child, give them anything at all. I felt as if I needed to do it, or I wouldn't be able to live with myself. So I walked, almost ran, to the nearest grocery store. Hurrying in through the front door after pushing on the handle, I took a moment to think about how the place needed an upgrade to get a set of those new, fancy sliding doors.

I started wandering around almost aimlessly. *What do I take? They need something.* Feeling flustered, I rubbed my head and groaned. Walking down an aisle, I bit my lip nervously while eyeing a package of bread on the shelf next to me. I didn't have enough money to buy it; I was dirt-poor. My mind flashed to the woman with her daughter in her lap. The thin, gaunt face looked up at me with only kindness in her small eyes. I ran my hands through my hair, groaned, and picked up the bread. I started walking around the store, looking at other things and trying to seem as if I were there just for a shopping trip.

I felt my own stomach rumble a little and shook my head. I had to focus on the task at hand; I was going to get this bread to that mother so she would have something to eat, at the very least. I started walking to the exit and stepped across the threshold, home free. I started smiling till a hand landed on my shoulder, stopping me short.

The grip on my shoulder was as solid as steel and almost strong enough to hurt. I turned, looked up, and saw the hard glare of the store's security guard. I sighed, and my head dropped as my heart plunged into the pit of my stomach.

"Kid, what are you doing? I have been watching you since you slunk in here, dripping sweat and looking nervous a half hour ago," the security said, his voice cold and hard.

My mouth dried up, and I almost choked on nothing at all. I looked around as I mumbled an apology and tried to think of some way out of this situation. I started to hand the guard the bread, but the little girl popped into my head again, those small, kind eyes in that hollow head. I jumped back hard, ripping myself free from the guard's grip, turned, and sprinted from the store. I heard the guard yell for me to stop, but I just kept running from the store and out onto the street. I just needed to make it back into the neighborhood and disappear among the broken-down houses.

My feet pounded the sidewalk; I felt as if it were a bad dream in which, no matter how much I moved my feet, I gained no distance on the guard. I heard him behind me. *Why is he so persistent? It is just bread, man, come on.* I took a left, headed into a building, and pounded my way up the steps. At the top of the building were some boards that spanned the distance between adjacent buildings. They were easy to cross and would definitely help me lose the guard. He looked too big to make it across the narrow pieces of wood.

The building was quite a few stories tall, and I finally made it to the top, breathing heavily. I slammed my shoulder into the door; I could hear the guard a flight or so behind me. I ran to the edge of the building and cried out when I saw the planks several stories down on the ground. They must have been knocked loose by someone who was tired of the local kids crossing on them. I turned and felt my heart leap into my throat as I saw the guard reaching out for me. I tried to take a step back on reflex, but found there was nothing to step back on. My head swam with vertigo as I began falling backwards.

The guard was getting farther away; his eyes didn't look so cold and hard now. Those were replaced by fear as he lunged for me, missing my outstretched hand by inches. I watched him as I fell; his eyes opened wide as I got farther and farther away with each passing moment. Within a second, he was gone from my view; replacing him was the side of the building, a solid and uncaring brick wall that passed me as I toppled downward.

Many things went through my head as I fell. *Is the bread worth this? Is it worth my life?* The windows went past me at an almost impossibly slow rate. I could see everything moving so slowly now, I felt as though, if I tried, I could count the bricks as they went past me. I closed my eyes, waiting to hit the ground. The sudden impact on my back from slamming into the ground was so fast and hard that I bounced off the ground before hitting it again.

I wanted to scream as I felt and heard several of my bones snapping at the same time. I opened my mouth to do just that, but no sound came out. The strain from trying to scream hurt so bad that I coughed. Coughing felt as if there were a hot knife being dug around in my chest and ribs. I felt tears stinging my eyes, but I was too weak to even move.

The guard came out and knelt next to me with tears in his eyes. "Kid! Kid! Come on, man, hold on! Ahhh, hell!" he cursed loudly as he fumbled with his phone, called for an ambulance, told them about what happened and where, and hung up. He grabbed my hand—which wasn't broken, thankfully—and held it. I almost felt like crying; it was the most warm and nice contact I'd had in a long time, and it felt good right then especially. I looked at the guard and coughed again, this time noticing the flecks of blood on the guard's face after I did so. The guard didn't even bother wiping it off; he seemed too worried about me to even notice.

I was going to die; I already knew that. Something inside of me told me it was my time. I started feeling tired and kind of fuzzy. The pain was starting to slip away, which was nice. My chest didn't hurt anymore, which was a blessing. I heard the sirens getting closer as they mixed with the sound of the security guard's prayers. I smiled. *Someone is praying? For me?* I closed my eyes once more and felt the warmth of the sun on my skin. I found I had no regrets; I would do it again. I wanted to help people. I wanted to help that lady and her kid.

Ah, I have one regret after all. Just one. That poor girl.

I died there with the guard holding my hand and, as the guard noted later, a smile on my face and a tear in my eye.

***

"Ahem. Eric, would you open your eyes, please?" a voice asked me.

The voice came from in front of me, and I almost couldn't believe I could hear it so well. I opened my eyes and found that I was sitting in a chair across from an older man who was holding a scroll. Apparently, on Earth, my story had ended, but my soul had gone on to sit in a chair across from a peculiar old man.

He looked up at me and then back down again. "Young man, you have died. Fallen from a building."

I slowly nodded and looked down at my hands, wringing them together. I really died then, no second chance or miraculous survival that would lead to changing my ways.

I looked up at the old man. "Tell me, Grandpa, who are you? What am I doing here?" I asked curiously. I bit my lip, tugging at it as I waited nervously for his answer.

The man set his scroll down and leaned back in his chair. "I am a god. I deal with accidents and mishaps and weigh your soul," he said as he leaned forward, grabbed at the air in front of him, and then leaned back again, holding a small orb that glowed blue. He fiddled with it and then held it up to the light, before setting it on a scale he summoned. The scale tilted back and forth a few times before it found that my soul was light.

I cocked my head to the side as I watched and wondered if where the scale had stopped was a good thing. The god tutted a few times before leaning in, grabbing the soul, and throwing it back to me. I lunged forward to grab it, letting out a loud yell as I watched it fade into nothing.

"Oh, don't worry about that; it went back to where it needed to be, Eric."

I leaned back, groaning. It felt as if my heart were dropping out of my chest.

"Tell me, Eric, what kind of life would you like to have?" the god asked me curiously.

"I think I would like a peaceful life. I've had enough of people. Maybe just sit around or take up farming," I answered slowly.

I had always wanted to grow my own food, to see what I could make with my own abilities. I had always had a great love of cooking, and so had lamented my lack of cooking paraphernalia; I had wished for a large gas stove with six burners.

But in reality, I had a small electric stove and an air fryer—only the necessities in our home. The fryer was a luxury that I'm sure had been stolen or found in the garbage.

"It's either that, or make things like potions and drinks in my next life," I said.

The god sitting across from me smiled and listened. He nodded and looked at his small scroll as he adjusted things, presumably trying to get things as close as possible to what I wanted. "Would you like to be an adventurer? A king? A conqueror of man, or perhaps one of the elfin race?" the god continued.

I scratched my jaw, considering what I wanted, and then explained to him that I wanted to be a human and that I would love to keep my own memories as well.

Glancing up from his scroll—which from across the table appeared to be a random assortment of glyphs, geometric symbols, and ever-changing shapes—the god asked me if there were things that I would like to change about my body.

I wanted to be a bit taller, perhaps around six feet. I certainly wanted my hair back and requested that it be a darker brown. I also wanted better musculature, to look more like an advanced weight lifter. I had always been on the malnourished side; no matter what I tried, I never gained weight. I wanted to be able to eat whatever I wanted and retain a muscular physique.

The god told me that he would alter my physical body so that I had to eat just enough to live and not the excessive amount bodybuilders had to consume. Unless I underate I would never lose my physique. I certainly planned on making plenty of food in this next life with whatever means I had.

Thinking more about things I definitely wanted, I scratched my chin. Finally, I snapped my fingers. "Could you also give me an observation ability? I have seen those in shows and think they're pretty cool," I said excitedly.

"What is that?" the god asked.

I explained to him that an observation ability was triggered when looking at an item or creature; details I did not know about what I was observing—for example, if a food is toxic or edible—would make themselves known to the person with the observation ability.

"Is there anything else that you would like?" the god asked me.

I nodded as I rubbed my hands together and remembered how the sun felt that final day I spent on Earth. "Can you make magic for me? I want the ability to take light and solidify it. To make structures and even weapons from it. I want it to be something I can be creative with."

The god muttered a few times and nodded before he threw his scroll into the air, where it exploded, creating a large cloud of smoke.

I raised my eyebrow as I watched. "That seems a little dramatic, don't you think?" I asked.

He turned to look at me and rolled his eyes. "I have been doing this since the beginning of time, I will have you know. I won't have you judging me for it either," the god said. He then harrumphed and turned away from me. "I have also added an ability for you. It will act as a mini map; at least, that is what I believe they are called," he said.

I nodded and thanked him. Having a map would be great, especially if I didn't have to carry around a physical one.

"You will have to fill the map in, of course. I can't just give you a whole-world map! That would ruin the adventure and be boring. You can add to the map by walking around and visiting areas you haven't been in before," the god added.

He looked back at me, closely, after he stopped feigning a grumpy demeanor; I could almost feel the sadness in his eyes. "You have had a rather painful life, Eric. I can't even imagine what it was like for you. Abandoned on the streets when you were born and raised by a man who did nothing for you but guilt you into doing things for him. Only to have him beat you whether you did them or not. You still loved him for most of your life, as only a child can love the one who raised them. The tree remembers, but the axe forgets. The man was always going on about how he found you on those streets and saved your life. The truth, however, is so much worse, Eric. The man killed your parents and kidnapped you."

I leaned back in my seat as my heart rose into my throat; I felt choked. *My whole life has been a lie?* I clenched my hands and looked up. I couldn't even comprehend a different life than the one I had, but I still felt cheated. "I was taken? If I wasn't dead, I would—" I stopped my threat midsentence. It didn't matter; I was dead anyway.

I had stolen food to feed a sick, homeless woman who was very weak and had a daughter who was starting to grow so thin I could see her bones through her skin. I had wanted to help any way I could. Something for which the man would have smacked me on the back of my head.

"People can stick up for themselves. No reason to help anyone but yourself. You hear me, Eric? Other people's presence isn't needed; keep to yourself!" the man said.

It was advice I regularly ignored. I wanted others to be happy and to be happy with them.

The god shook his head and added, "People say I have plans for everyone, but really the only thing that I have done since the beginning of time was create the Earth and the stars and the heavens. Other than that, life made itself from amazing conditions. From the smallest of cells all the way to the space whales."

I looked up quickly, my mind imagining a whale floating through the stars, and almost let my imagination take me away. "Did you say space whales? Are they in the universe where I am going?" I asked excitedly.

The god smiled and explained that the universe I had been in was overwhelmingly infinite and that the largest species that inhabited it was the space whale that swam through space. It was actually more closely related to plants; it fed by soaking in the radiation and light from the stars that it passed along the way.

Listening to him speak, I sat back with growing fascination as he explained that the section of the universe that he was talking about was hundreds and trillions of light-years away from Earth; it was a place where physics didn't really matter, and space there reflected the ocean on Earth. Whales swam through space; the stars were brightly glowing starfish. There were all manner of space fish as well. The god went on for a while, excited to talk about what he had made. I could have listened to him talk for the rest of eternity, but he slapped the palms of his hands on his legs.

"That's enough of that; we have to get on to ushering you into your own universe now," the god said while smiling and leaning back in his chair. He reached to his side and picked up a cup that was filled with a steaming drink.

I sniffed the air and found it filled with the scent of peppermint and something sweet, possibly honey.

The god sipped at it slowly and let out a content and happy sigh. "Everything has been set up for your new life, Eric. I really hope that you enjoy it. I made this world after you humans started creating your shows and your games. It takes a lot of inspiration from those things. I love what your people have come up with; I am never bored when I watch over your people," he said.

I was excited already. I was being sent to a world based on games and shows? I couldn't wait to see what it was going to be like when I got there. I hoped it was a better life than the one I had just lived; I wanted to have fun and live for myself in this new world. I looked to the god who seemed to be waiting.

He turned to me and told me to lean back and close my eyes. I was to keep them closed for three seconds.

I complied and started counting slowly; when I reached three, I slowly opened my eyes and started looking around. My eyes slowly grew wider with wonder.

Chapter 2 Another World's Forest

I was sitting in a forest on a fallen tree. Looking around me, I took in the breathtaking view of the trees. Some were enormous; they made the redwood trees back on Earth look like saplings. Others were small as twigs and so tall that they reached up into the sky. I took a deep breath and inhaled the scents of the decomposing leaves and soil around me. It was amazing how wonderful the air smelled—no pollution or chemicals in the air.

I closed my eyes, tilted my head, and realized there were no other sounds besides those of the forest. It was a pure sound filled with the chirps of birds that I couldn't see, as well as other indigenous life. No cars racing down streets or beeping at each other No yelling or obscenities being thrown around. No sirens or gunshots. I became almost giddy, and yet sad at the same time. Everything I had ever known was gone. I was all that was left of my old life. I stood up and slapped my hands against my legs; I had to start somewhere.

I chose a direction and started moving forward into the forest. As I looked around, I realized it felt a lot like a game. I was seeing names of the different mushrooms and herbs along the path. I realized this was because my observation skill was activating. I grabbed a small mushroom and plucked it from the tree on which it was growing. I began to look it over. It had a small, rounded cap and a blue stalk; its name was blue-milk stalk. I sniffed it, and it smelled like a normal mushroom. I squeezed the cap, and a line of blue liquid started dripping from it.

"I guess I know why it's called blue milk," I said and then chuckled softly to myself. I looked at the name and saw a green letter *E* next to its name. "I really hope that means edible."

I took a bite of the cap, started chewing, and found its texture was incredibly different from that of a mushroom. It was almost like a banana in consistency. The sweet milk that flowed from the cap and the texture, when combined, tasted almost like a dessert. I looked at the stalk and threw it away. It actually had a toxic symbol next to it in the form of a skull and crossbones, and that was all I needed to know.

I kept walking along the forest path, sampling different items, and discovering their purposes. It really was like a game, and I was having a lot of fun with it. This new life was nothing short of amazing already.

"Hey, Eric!" the god called out loudly as he stepped out from behind a tree, smiling, which nearly led to my falling over from shock.

"Come on, man! That's not cool. You almost made my heart stop. Don't do that to me!" I yelled at him.

The god laughed and apologized to me while waving his hand around in a dismissive gesture. He pulled a book from behind him and handed it to me. "I forgot to give you your grimoire! It will keep track of any spells you create for yourself, as well as their recipes and effects. You can also record how the items you have seen and sampled looked and tasted. The book will never grow any larger than what you see here, no matter how many spells or recipes you gather. Part of the magic of this world," he said.

The god also handed me a leather pack in which to keep the grimoire. He taught me how to use my magic energy to pull out the book without physically touching it.

I smiled as I saw that the mushrooms and herbs I had sampled so far were already recorded, as was my custom magic that I had asked the god to create. I called it hard-light magic. It gave me the ability to take the energy as well as light from the sun and manipulate it into any shape. I could also use the energy and light of the stars and the moon; they just weren't as strong as the sun's.

The god waved his farewell, and just as quickly as he'd arrived, he was gone again.

I reached out and grabbed a streak of light that had broken through the dense canopy of the leaves above. The light looked almost like threads as it came into my hand. I pulled it slowly, guiding it into the shape that I desired. I formed a machete and then studied it. It seemed sharp. I let the machete go and canceled the spell.

It was going to be interesting to see what I would be able to build with my magic. I wondered how far the spell could be pushed and how much creativity it could handle. Was the sky the limit here? Only time would tell, and I planned on doing a lot of building with my hard light.

I started walking again, moving forward and forging a path into the unknown. I was full of excitement and ready for anything. After a few hours of walking, I groaned. My legs ached, and I was full from sampling the new plants and berries. I needed a nap. I looked around and made a mental picture for myself of where I should set up my shelter.

I grabbed a thread of light, pulled it into my hands, and shaped it into a golden axe that glowed with the light of the sun within it. It may have been due to my magic skills or something else, but the axe was not hard to look at, even though it was made from pure light. The axe itself was light and easy to swing. So I assumed a ready stance and swung the axe at the tree next to me, grunting as the axe bounced off the tree. Shocked, I looked down at the axe in my hand, confused as to why it wasn't working.

"Why won't this work? It's made from pure energy. It should have sliced through the tree like soft, warm butter," I said loudly.

I shook my head, took a more solid stance, and began slamming the axe into the tree as hard as I could. After a large number of strokes, I was able to cut a notch from the tree. *There has to be a better way than this.*

I took the axe and released the spell. It was time to come up with something new. I grabbed some strands of light and made an old-fashioned saw, placed it against the tree, and started getting to work. The saw worked better than the axe, slicing through the tree in less time than if I'd chopped it with the axe.

I had a smart idea—use the light to make a rotating hand-saw and start chewing my way through the trees. I'm glad the magic worked with my imagination; that made my job a whole lot easier.

I kept cutting trees down till I had a good-size pile, and then I gathered them together. I was going to make a house from those logs. It was not going to be a great house, but it was going to be mine. I took my time with the small golden handsaw and trimmed the branches from the logs. The next step involved cutting notches at the ends of all the logs and fitting them into each other until I had a large, but pretty shabby-looking, log cabin that I had purposefully built with one side taller than the other, so rain wouldn't sit on top of it. I used one of the logs to fashion a makeshift door. It was ugly, but it was home.

I looked around and scratched my chin. One more step, but what was it? I snapped my fingers and grinned. Take mud and moss and stuff them in between the logs, not only as insulation, but to keep the bugs from crawling inside the cabin.

Now that I had shelter for the night, which meant I wouldn't be preyed upon by any animals, I also needed something to sleep on or in. I reached into the leather sack that the god had given me and retrieved a sleeping roll, which contained something akin to a sleeping bag with a thicker end; I assume that could be used for a pillow. I also took out a small tarp, which I spread out on the ground inside the cabin, and tossed the bedroll on top of it. Home was all set up.

I felt accomplished and wanted to watch the sunset, so I stepped back out into the light of the day, which was quickly fading. The last rays of golden light glittered over the tops of the trees, illuminating the branches and leaves. This new world was beautiful; I was almost caught up in its beauty.

I looked up and gasped. As the sun was fading, a new wonder was springing to life above me, one I had never gotten to experience during my life on Earth. I watched the stars begin twinkling into existence and couldn't help but let out another gasp of excitement. Back on Earth, light pollution from large cities had long since erased the possibility of stargazing without the assistance of large, powerful tools called telescopes; even then, the light made it borderline impossible to view all but the most powerful of stars.

I was so enraptured with the stars that I wasn't keeping an eye on the tree line. I felt the hair start rising on the back of my neck; my stomach turned over. Something was watching me, and I could feel its bloodlust.

I reached out, curled my hand around a beam of waning light, and caressed it slowly into the shape of a sword. In the back of my mind, I felt the new sword's conjuring be added to the grimoire as a spell. Gripping the sword tightly, I started turning slowly and moving my eyes constantly in an attempt to spot what had me in its sights.

When it stepped forward from the tree line, I started shaking and felt my arms shivering along with the rest of my body. My heart started pounding in my chest, shooting adrenaline throughout my system, as I watched a creature move forward.

This is my first fight? This isn't even fair. What terrible luck I have, I thought to myself as I stumbled backwards, almost falling on my rear, and watched the ogre step into the clearing I had made from cutting down the trees.

"I smell fresh meat!" The ogre growled as it rubbed its muscled stomach and started looking around. "It's something new! Something sweet! A delicious and fresh treat!"

I groaned inwardly. *I am going to be eaten by this monster, and it is rhyming at me; life really is cruel.*

The ogre was easily twelve feet tall and covered by thick muscles that coiled and moved beneath his skin. Its skin was a pale and sickly gray. Its lower jaw jutted forward, exposing a set of lower canines that came up almost to his nostrils. It had beady-looking eyes that swiveled around in its head. I looked at its hands and swallowed dryly; its hands ended in claws that looked sharp enough to gut me.

I tried to slow my breathing, but I couldn't. How terrifying it was that I could feel my heart beating so hard in my chest that I thought it was going to burst. I clenched the sword harder as the ogre lifted its head and caught sight of me.

"Oh? What are you? Not an elf, that's for sure." The ogre shrugged and scratched at its thick forehead. "Makes no difference to me. You're made of meat, and I am hungry."

I staggered back, falling against the front of my cabin, and clenched my jaw so hard my teeth hurt. I had to do something, or I was screwed. This enormous monster was going to eat me, and my new, fun life was going to be over, just like that. I took a deep breath and readied my sword in front of me, standing in a basic pose I had really only ever seen on TV. The tip of my blade pointed towards the ogre. I was about as ready as I was ever going to be, but that wasn't really ready at all.

The ogre started running towards me, its arms outstretched, reaching for me. Its fingers splayed out to grab hold. I brought the sword down, slamming it against the ogre's hands, trying to deflect them. I was rewarded by the ogre's hands falling to the ground, smoking. I looked down at the ogre's smoking hands and back at the stumps with which the ogre was left.

I plastered a large smile across my face. I let out a laugh as relief flooded through my body. I had done it! In one slash, I had removed its hands. I could win this; I was going to live.

The ogre was staring at its stumps with an incredulous look. "What did you do to me?!" it screamed. The ogre began thrashing and lashing out, trying to strike me.

I danced backwards, out of reach, looking at the sword of light in my hands and wondering for a brief moment why my axe could not cut the tree, but it could tear through flesh as if it weren't even there. *I will just think about it later. I need to focus on the moment and not lose my possibly temporary advantage*, I whispered to myself, while initiating my next move. I lunged forward, swung my sword in a small arc, and cut more of the ogre's arms away. Then I ducked a blow aimed at my head and moved, dragging my sword through its belly, clean through to the other side.

The ogre groaned, dropped to its knees, fell over sideways, and died.

I collapsed on the ground, my adrenaline wearing off and leaving me feeling weak and exhausted. I dragged myself back into my cabin, slamming the door shut behind me, and collapsed on top of my sleep roll. I felt sick and worn out. I had just taken a life.

Even though it was in self-defense, I still felt shaken. Several thoughts went through my head. *Why had the sword cut through the ogre so easily, but not the trees? There is so little I know, but so many questions. Are there more of them out there? What am I going to do if there are? Sure, my sword can cut them, but will I stand a chance if there are more than one?*

I shuddered at the thought of many ogres coming for me at the same time. I was so tired and worn out; the adrenaline leaving my system was causing me to crash. My eyes felt as if there were lead blocks dragging their lids closed. I couldn't even bring myself to climb into the roll. I closed my eyes and let the sleep take me.

It was a fitful night of sleep for me as I lay in bed, tossing and turning, plagued by the foul visage of demons and monsters too terrifying for my own mind to comprehend. I took notice of how some of them had the face of my father. I woke up the next day, my body aching and feeling as if I had been mauled. Standing up from my bedroll, I stepped outside, saw the corpse of the monster that I had slain, and sighed while remembering the events of the preceding night. I needed to drag its body away from my home and then burn it; otherwise, monsters were sure to be attracted to my location by the smell of its decomposing corpse.

Using beams of light that I formed into strong pillars, I stuck one of them beneath the ogre's body and rolled it slowly away from my cabin. It was slow going as I had to keep moving the pillars to keep its body moving. When the body was a good distance away from my home, I took a large beam of light and bent it into a circle. Then I poured some of my magic into it, making it grow as I shaped it into a barrier. So now I had a barrier spell for defense and for one other thing I had in mind.

I canceled the spell and began gathering sticks, branches, and tinder and piled them on the ogre's body. When I judged I had enough, I bent a spot of light onto the pile and watched it take fire. I summoned the barrier around the ogre's body so that the fire wouldn't spread into the forest and cause a massive forest fire. One thing I hadn't considered, however, was the barrier causing the heat to build on itself and make it go wild. The fire was quickly turning into an inferno within the barrier.

The ogre was reduced to ashes within seconds. I released the spell and turned back towards my home, wrinkling my nose at the smell of the burning flesh and trying to keep from gagging, just thankful that it was over.

I needed to find a source of water as well as food. I was sitting back against the wall of my log cabin, trying to figure out exactly what my next step was going to be.

"Come on. All of this is just like a game, so where is my status menu?" I said loudly.

I almost screamed when the menu popped up in front of me like a status panel in a video game. Then I rolled my eyes, laughed, and gave myself a large facepalm. I had never even tried to say it out loud, or in my head, so how could it have opened? I scrolled the list of my different abilities.

I read through my light sword's description and saw that any weapon forged with light would create a high amount of heat, which could cause fire damage. I read more, and it said that, using light, I could create just about anything and then determine what led to the heat damage. I also learned that the sword I summoned would last as long as there was a light source; the same was true for anything I created with this magic, from barriers to pillars to my sword. As long as

I wasn't in a cave or away from the sun or the moon, my magic would last until I died. I could still use these spells in dark areas, but doing that would expend more than just my magic pool; it would steadily drain the item created by that magic. Another thing I saw was that it didn't matter if I used a sword or an axe, or any tool really, for cutting things. I couldn't have cut a tree quickly until I got this ability upgrade, apparently, which I fully intended to test.

I closed out my menu and lamented the lack of status-boosting levels. I could only level my abilities and the usefulness of them, which wasn't awful, but it was still not as cool as leveling up in strength or dexterity. I shrugged, summoned my saw, and walked up to a tree.

This hard-light ability was pretty sweet. The possibilities were endless as long as I had a good imagination. I felled a handful of trees and dragged them over to one side of the clearing. I grabbed a few beams of light, crafted a shovel, and started digging out the roots of the stumps before pulling them from the ground.

I licked my dry lips and groaned. I should really have done this step after finding a water source. I dropped the spell I was using and started walking in a straight line away from my home to find some water. I was fairly lucky in that regard, as there was a stream behind the cabin, some distance away. I grabbed a beam of light and fashioned it into a bucket to carry water from the stream up to my home. I should probably make a cistern as well to hold water. I shrugged and just made a larger bucket, to use as a hold for my water for the time being, and set it by the door. A few trips to and from the stream, and the bucket was full for the day.

I reached into my pack and pulled a few herbs from it. I munched on them, smiling as I felt my hunger physically melting away and being replaced by a sense of warmth radiating from my stomach. I summoned my grimoire and opened it to the page I wanted. Sunbloom herb was the name of the plant I had just eaten. It was a great plant that only grew in the sun and only grew while exposed to sunlight; it filled your hunger and helped to enhance healing capabilities. I could probably use it to make some healing potions or maybe a stamina enhancement. If there was anything like that in this world, that is.

I grinned and cracked my fingers. I just had a wonderful idea. I grabbed a nearby sunbeam, fashioned it into a trellis, and anchored it to the ground. I made sure it put out sunlight and no heat that would hurt the plants. I took the two remaining sunbloom herbs and planted their roots in the ground. My magic would help the plants grow quicker due to constant exposure to the sunlight provided.

Using a conjured saw, I began cutting a log down to size and fashioned several planks of wood into long rectangles, making them into raised garden boxes that I would put dirt into to grow other food items. I dragged the boxes I had made into four different spots where I soon planned to dig an irrigation tunnel. After the boxes were moved into position, I gathered some forest dirt and filled the boxes with it.

The sunbloom herb would replicate on its own. They actually grew fairly quickly if given enough sun. They were only rare because they grew in the forest where trees blocked most of the light; they needed a certain amount of time in the sunlight in order to grow. That's why they were only found in random sections of light beneath open patches in the leaf canopy.

"It's like I'm cheating," I mumbled.

As I watched, the plants slowly grew a centimeter every couple of minutes. Smiling, I turned from the growing plants and walked back to the stream. I grabbed a beam of light, rolled it into a tube, stuck it into the water, and guided the beam of light into my bucket. Water was pulled from the stream and fed into the bucket of light. The tube would pull water until it was full, then stop when my magic sensed it was close to the top. That was yet another benefit to using the light. Also, the ultraviolet rays given off by light purified the water, killing off the microorganisms in it.

I stood up from my task and decided I should find some meat for myself. I would need a weapon I could use from a distance. A spear was the best choice, as man had spent millennia honing his ability to throw a spear. I held my hand out, seeing the spear in my mind, and a nearby beam of sunlight gathered itself in my hand and formed a spear. I opened my menu to take a look and saw that my ability had leveled up. I wouldn't have to shape anything by hand anymore. I could just imagine it, and any nearby light would simply sense my will and build what I envisioned. But I would have to still fashion larger structures by hand until my abilities leveled higher.

I took out the heat effect, pulled my arm back, threw the spear at a nearby tree, and watched it pierce the tree. As the spear exited, it faded from existence. That was a successful test, and I felt safer and more secure about coming up with new weapons. If any more ogres wanted to try me, they would find themselves met with a constant stream of spears that could pierce the trees themselves.

Turning from the tree I had just speared, I realized that I should take a walk and start foraging for items that could be planted or used for food. What I really wanted was fresh meat that I could cook over a fire. I started my walk through the forest, listening, observing, and watching my feet to make sure that I would not trip over anything unseen while glancing around me for signs of life. I placed one foot in front of the other slowly, trying not to disturb the forest around me.

I winced as footstep after footstep resulted in branches cracking and dry leaves crunching. Every animal for miles around could probably hear my clumsy steps. I groaned loudly and winced, as they had probably heard that as well. I chuckled; this was going to take time to learn. I decided to just go back to foraging for more herbs and mushrooms, as well as fruits if I could find any.

I looked downward, scanning the floor of the forest. I spotted more of the blue-milk stalk mushrooms and began gathering them into my leather pack. I could take the toxic stalks and possibly make a poison from them or find another use. The forest floor was bountiful. I located nuts called maka that tasted like chocolate. The maka nut was small and round, its skin gritty; the outer shell was almost like leather—soft, stretchy, but very durable. The maka nut's properties were magic recovery and use as a fertilizer that sped up the growth of herbs and other plants.

Another nut I found was called a cala. The cala nut was shaped like a triangle. Its shell was hard and unyielding. I stood on it, trying to crack it open, but the only thing that could open the nut was a slash from my sword of light. The properties of the cala nut were outstanding. It had a high caloric content and could provide all the nutrients needed to survive. It was a very rare nut.

I pocketed the nuts I could find, smiling when thinking of the trees or bushes that these nuts would grow for me. I was going to start a farm and enjoy a nice, comfortable life making the things I wanted. If there was a winter in this world, I didn't need to worry. I could take the beams of light and use the heat from them to keep my plants and myself alive.

I was so lost in thought—thinking about the farm I was going to make and how it was going to look, as well as how many trees I would have to remove to gain more farmland—that I almost walked past a cave entrance. I stopped and turned to look at it and could almost feel a malicious aura emanating from the cave. I decided that I would come back to explore it the next day.

I needed to find more food items and prepare better for the cave exploration. I turned and walked away from the cave and made my way back towards camp. I made sure to cut notches in the trees as I passed, marking the way back to the cave. The cave practically screamed dungeon, and I was all for it.

After waiting an entire day and continuing to forage, I had gathered a nice stash of items I thought I could use. I walked back along the path towards the cave, and I was filled with a nervous wave of energy. I took deep slow breaths, trying to focus myself and keep calm. Running headfirst into a dungeon was a great way to get myself killed. I slowly followed the marks I had made on the trees, making sure I didn't get lost. I found the cave again, and before making my way in, I picked up a stick and made my way in. I conjured an orb of light on the end of the stick so that I could have a makeshift torch that would assist me as I explored.

The dark cave was illuminated by a soft, warm glow that reached all its corners; this made much easier what would have been a trial to navigate. Thanks to the light, I was able to see that there were actually quite a few pathways that split off from the main entrance. The main path that I chose was full of bones and tattered remains of what looked like strips of torn cloth. The smell of rancid and decomposing meat was thick in the air; it clogged my throat like a thick, wet fog. My skin crawled, and I felt my heart accelerating in my chest. Something was in this cave, and it was definitely not friendly. I felt it as keenly as an electric charge running through my skin.

I cautiously proceeded, moving my eyes side to side, warily scanning the corners of the cave. I stopped suddenly as I heard chittering followed by a loud scream of anger. The chittering almost seemed to increase, similar to cheering and goading. I canceled the light orb to avoid giving away my presence and noticed that there were torches along the walls; they cast more than enough light for me to make my way down the tunnel. I needed to be more aware; I had wasted magic when I assumed that the cave would be dark. It wasn't as bright as the ball of light I had created, but it was more than enough for my eyes. I could have just used the torchlight.

I approached the bend in the passageway and slowly peeked around the corner, trying to stay as hidden as possible to scope out the situation. The first thing I noticed were bodies, which were small and plump; the next thing, creatures. Then I saw the name highlighted in red above the goblins' heads. The creatures were goblins, and the red meant only one thing—definitely hostile. They were wearing loincloths, tied around their waists with corded string; I couldn't begin to guess what materials were used for them. The goblins were absolutely filthy and covered in nasty grime; they had daggers tucked into the strings at their waists. There were five creatures. Three of them were standing around the other two who were currently rolling around on the ground, fighting over a scrap of bone that still had a piece of meat hanging from it.

One of the fighting goblins rolled the other beneath him and began punching and scratching; the skirmish looked oddly as if it were a playground fight with no plan of attack, just a wild, scrabbling attack meant to cause harm. The disadvantaged goblin screamed in pain and dropped the bone fragment, which the winning goblin scooped up and started hopping around with, holding the bone above his head and letting out loud whoops of victory. He then tore the chunk of meat from the bone and smacked his lips while he chewed, making sure to utter sounds of ecstasy while it swallowed.

The loser grumbled and started dejectedly walking away. Part of me even felt bad for the little guy...till I noticed his depressed walk was leading him directly towards me. I clumsily moved back, falling on my butt, and let out a surprised gasp as my rump hit the ground. Horrified, I slapped my hand over my mouth.

The goblin let out a noise of surprise and began moving hurriedly around to find the source of the noise. He rounded the corner of the tunnel and spotted me. His mouth opened, revealing several rows of teeth that seemed to move independently in his mouth, and he let loose a loud hiss at me. Strands of saliva drip from his mouth.

I began crawling backwards quickly, grabbing stones off the cave floor and throwing them at the goblin as he waddled towards me at a rapid rate.

"Stay away from me! Stop! Go away!" I cried out. The horror and panic was thick in my voice.

The goblin lurched over to me and pulled its dagger free from his belt. With almost a grin smeared across his pale-green face, he scurried faster while making loud hooting noises. He chittered loudly and lunged with his dagger.

Screaming, I held my hand out, and a golden shield appeared in my hand. The goblin's dagger bounced off the shield, and the goblin was thrown backwards, firmly hitting the wall of the cave.

I looked at my hand and back at the goblin, a small smile creeping across my face. In my panic, I had forgotten I could use magic; a lifetime without magic had conditioned me to ignore its possibility. I held my hand out and conjured a sword.

The goblin seemed concussed; he was trying to rise to his feet, but stumbling awkwardly. I needed to do this quickly before his other friends showed up. I could hear them wad-dling towards us, having heard the screams of the goblin I was currently fighting.

I swung downward with my sword, and it easily cut through the goblin's neck and severed his head. I turned and started walking in the direction from which the other goblins were approaching. As I did, I conjured a spear, pulled my arm back, and threw it. The spear flew straight into the goblin in the front of the pack. It penetrated cleanly and dis-appeared immediately.

The goblin let out a horrible screech and clutched the burning wound in his gut. I ignored its death screech and focused instead on the final three goblins who were lurching around, trying to get close enough to stab at me with their small daggers.

I kicked out harshly, catching a goblin in his thigh and hearing a snap. I watched in surprise as the goblin was lifted and thrown back into the cave wall from the force of my kick. I was pretty strong, I guess, or they were very weak. I was focused on my feat of strength until I felt a stab of pain as a goblin plunged his dagger into the meat of my thigh. I let out a loud yelp of pain and turned back quickly, backhanding the goblin across its jaw.

He screamed as my fist broke the underlying bone where it landed and knocked the goblin off its feet; he lay writhing in pain and clutching his broken jaw.

I groaned, holding my wounded thigh, and finished the goblin off with another conjured spear. I turned to face the other goblin and saw him trying to waddle away quickly as he cast worried glances over his shoulder. I couldn't let him leave—what if he had more friends? He would raise the alarm, spelling doom for me.

I clenched my teeth and fought through the pain, limping towards the goblin. I tried conjuring a spear, but it appeared I had reached my magical limit. I remembered that, outside, I could almost limitlessly cast my light magic due to the source already being there; I just had to guide it as I wanted. Here in this dark space, the magic was all on me; I had to use my magic to summon the light and maintain it.

I groaned, felt dizzy, and almost fell, but I caught myself. I needed to do this without using magic. If I used any more, I was going to pass out; that was just not an option right now. I hurriedly limped after the goblin. I was slowly gaining on him, moving slightly faster than he could waddle.

It was almost comical. I lunged forward and grabbed the goblin by his ankle, dragging him back towards me. His chittering grew louder as he kicked at me with his other leg, trying to throw me off him. His kicks landed on my fingers, hurting and bruising them, but I used the pain and turned it into anger as I dragged the goblin towards me. I drew back my arm and slammed my fist into his head, repeatedly screaming all my fear and anger, till the goblin stopped moving under my blows. I let out long, rapid, ragged breaths, shuddering and trying to catch my breath as I sat there on my knees trying to breathe.

I rolled over onto my back, groaning, and tried to regain my stamina and some semblance of internal peace. I reached down into my pack and pulled a maka nut from my bag and ate it as I closed my eyes. I enjoyed chewing the nut and tasting the sweet flavor of chocolate. I could almost feel the energy slowly seeping into my body.

I sat up and dragged myself back onto my feet and walked slowly around the corner, to where the goblins had originally been scrabbling. There were no more goblins in that area, and as it turned out, it was the end of the cave. I rummaged through the things that the goblins had been hoarding.

I found a nice-looking sword and strapped it to my back as I thanked the loot gods for the nice sword. I had learned a great lesson about not relying completely on magic. I continued my search and found a chest that was emanating a soft glow. I walked over to it, popped the lid, and found a ring. I picked the ring up and looked at it. The ring's markings read, "Ring of light. Produces a glow that only the wielder can see." I smiled as I slipped the ring onto my finger.

I walked back into the dark area to test the ring; I could see everything easily. "What a great find."

I used a stone to mark the path that I had taken, with a large cross, to basically say that I had already gone that way. I walked through the rest of the cave, but found nothing useful. One mine had been used for excrement, unfortunately. I gagged heavily upon nearing it and decided to explore elsewhere. I made a large cross on the rock wall and turned back. Another mine held some shoddily made weapons and what I assumed were makeshift beds constructed from piles of nasty-looking reeds, grass, and horribly cut animal pelts, which were matted and still had blood on them from the animals from which they were cut. The rest of the cave was clear, so I decided to not waste any more of my time on it. I shook my head and left the cave, marking the outside with another cross.

Stepping back out into the light, I cracked my neck as I felt my energy returning to me. This felt great; I felt as if I were a recharging battery. I began walking in the forest with new-found energy. After a while, I headed back home after looking up and seeing that the sun was preparing to set. I must have been in that cave far longer than I thought; it had been early morning when I left my campsite.

I hadn't gone too far before my cabin came within sight, which was a little scary because that band of goblins had been very close. If they had found me unprepared, it would have been awful.

I checked on my sunblooms after making it back to camp; they had already split and begun growing. I took the two new sunblooms and placed them in the raised garden beds I had made. Then I strung a beam of light above the plants so they could continue growing.

After that, I had a little bit of time before the sun went completely down, so I conjured a shovel and began digging a four-foot-deep hole in the middle of my planting area. Then I dug trenches in four directions from the hole, so water could flow in them. The last trench I dug led back to the river, so the water wouldn't pool and drown my plants. I guided a beam of light from the river to the hole and watched it slowly fill. It was a pretty awful-looking irrigation channel, but it would work for the time being.

By then, the sun was sinking below the tree line. The only light keeping things visible was from the light beam I had used in building the irrigation system; that beam was still feeding off the fading sunlight, which would be replaced soon by the moon. I walked over to the irrigation tunnel and washed the dirt from my hands. I stood up and walked into my home to lie down on my roll. The day had been long, and I was ready to go to sleep.

I closed my eyes and felt as if I had accomplished a great deal during the day. I had learned to use my magic more freely and had realized I needed to learn to use a real sword. I didn't have enough magic yet on which to completely rely.

3 Meeting New Friends in Another World's Sun

When I woke up, I stretched and prepared myself for the day. I headed to the river, making sure I was downstream, and waded into the water to wash myself and soak. It felt wonderful being in nature. I closed my eyes to enjoy the sounds of nature. After a while, when I was finished bathing, I went back to shore, grabbed a ray of light from nearby, and spread it thin. I walked through it, watched the water dry off my skin, and smiled. Who needed a towel?

I returned to my cabin, picked up my satchel, and decided that it was a good day to do some planting. I stepped outside and looked for a good place to plant the nuts that I had foraged the previous day. I opened my skills tab and saw a foraging upgrade was available. It was a split path. Either I could find more of the same items, or I could find better and rarer items. I chose the better and rarer path because farming was my main goal; I'd be planting the items I found anyway and making more of them.

There was also an upgrade available for my farming. It made the plants grow faster, so I had the chance to produce two nuts, fruits, or herbs per harvest. I eagerly accepted the upgrade; these upgrades were amazing and would definitely help in the long run.

Smiling, I looked away from my menu and conjured an axe. I needed to make some more room for sowing. I cleared a few trees and planted the maka and cala nuts that I had found, making sure to space them several feet apart so that, as they grew, they wouldn't interfere with each other. From the data I read about the nuts, each plant had a growing cycle of one month and would produce around four to five nuts by the time it was ready to be harvested.

After having consumed a maka nut in the cave, I had two of them left and five of the cala nuts. I walked over to the water supply and, using light, constructed a pipe that led to the nut plants. I really needed a better way to irrigate and to get water for my personal water needs. There were way too many pipes leading here and there. But at the moment, I didn't have a better way of getting water uphill.

I needed a break, I realized, after I felt my backing growing stiff. I stretched and heard almost every vertebra down my back stretch and pop. I started walking in a different direction for foraging, hoping to find some fruit or more of the mushrooms. It was also a great chance to just stretch out and relax. I knew a basic fermenting method to make myself some good things. Besides that, I really liked fruit, and it was definitely beneficial for my diet.

As I walked, I found more of the same blue-milk mushrooms I had collected the day before; I tossed them into my bag. I heard a small chirp next to me and glanced down, hoping I hadn't been so careless as to walk close to a poisonous animal.

The creature I saw was about half a foot long and had six legs, each ending in little fingers, including a thumb, so it could grab things. The green fur along its back looked like grass and was mottled in a pattern that looked like leaves. Its face was similar to that of a hedgehog, and its nose seemed to be able to move in every direction, almost independent of its face.

I checked its name; it was called a deena and was an herbivore that ate only herbs and mushrooms. Its body naturally produced a spore that floated on the air and provided nutrients for the forest life around it. It wasn't poisonous.

I reached into my pocket slowly, pulled out a blue-milk mushroom, snapped off the poisonous base, and knelt down to offer the deena a bite.

It cocked its head at me and chirped again.

"It's good, bud," I said quietly.

I moved slowly so I wouldn't spook the little guy. It moved forward a few steps and reached out its little fingers to touch my hand. I felt my heart melt a little as I watched it. I wanted to pick it up and give it a big hug, but I knew that would be a mistake that could either harm or frighten it into never approaching me again. So I stayed still, not daring to move a muscle.

It leaned in, sniffed my hand and the mushroom, and then started eating from my hand.

My menu opened by itself, nearly causing me to fall back from surprise. A small script flew past my eyes; it notified me that due to my love of animals, I had been given the beast-tamer skill. It also came with its own skill tree that sat next to my own main skill tree. I was in awe at the detail of the menu that I had been given. The menu let me see my own skill tree, as well as how to progress. It allowed me to evolve and add on the beast-taming skill. The menu just kept growing bigger to accommodate my ever-growing skills. I didn't even have to talk for the menu to activate; I could just think about something, and it would do what I wanted. If there were any status changes or notifications, the menu read them to me. Looking at the beast-tamer tree, I learned that after I tamed fifteen more small animals, I would be given the ability to tame medium-sized animals.

I smiled and looked down. There was a suggestion that read, "Would you like to tame the small animal deena?"

"Tame deena," I whispered softly.

A small band of light appeared around the deena's neck; then it disappeared. "Taming complete," the menu read to me.

I smiled and willed the creature to jump up and ride on my shoulder. It skittered up my arm, chirped happily, and settled on my collarbone. I reached up and rubbed its little chin happily. *I have a new little friend now. How exciting.*

With the little deena curled happily on my shoulder, I turned and kept walking and foraging. Once in a while, the deena skittered down my body, ran off into the forest, chittering, and came back with a small nut or another mushroom in its mouth.

I checked the latest mushroom it brought me and grinned. This was a new mushroom—a chooka mushroom. It tasted like coffee and gave a small energy boost. It felt strange looking at this neon-blue mushroom with green streaks down the cap and a swirling red line down the stalks, which reminded me of a peppermint. I felt as if the mushroom should be brown, but with this world came all sorts of new rules. I would just have to deal with the fact that I was going to be slightly unsettled by all of the new things that I encountered. I placed it in my satchel, hoping I could plant it later and grow more of them. The energy spike was interesting, and I wondered if I could make a coffee from it, or even an energy drink to help boost my energy.

After about twenty minutes of walking, I came across what I had been hoping to find—a fruit-tree grove—just twenty minutes from my home. I walked up to a tree and plucked a large fruit from its branches. It looked just like a mango from Earth with its soft-green-and-red skin. It felt perfect—soft and juicy. I squeezed my hands firmly around it, and it fell apart, releasing juices that smelled almost similar to honey. After a quick check using my observation skill, I found that it was perfectly safe to eat. I drew the fruit to my mouth and took a large bite…just to choke and spit it out. It tasted as if I had just bitten into a mint. A minty mango that smelled of honey was almost too much for my senses.

I took another bite, now knowing what it tasted like, and swallowed. It tasted better than most mint ice creams I had eaten. If I could freeze this, it would probably be amazing. I grabbed a few of what I now referred to as mangoes and threw them into my bag.

I broke apart another one and offered it to the small deena on my shoulder and almost laughed as I watched it sink its teeth into the mango and try to stuff it all in its mouth at once. The deena swiveled its head and faced me with gooey mango dripping from its mouth; it almost seemed to smile in delight while it chittered at me excitedly. I reached a hand up, scratched its chin, and started walking back home.

When I got to the cabin, the deena hopped off my shoulder and began investigating its new territory, chirping softly after looking at my raised gardens and herb-growing area. It lowered its belly to the ground and shivered violently. I started forward to see if I could help the deena, but it stood up and shivered again, releasing from its body a soft, glowing green dust that the wind carried to each plant. I realized I was watching the deena use its special ability to fertilize and help the plants grow.

I turned from the deena and started walking towards the forest line. I wanted to clear about twenty feet around my cabin to increase my visibility. I conjured my saw and got to work. Trees were felled one at a time until I had knocked about twenty of them down. Using my hard-light ability, I maneuvered them into a pyramid behind my home and used some thick-cut wood to brace them so they wouldn't roll away.

Next, I thought of a mechanism to aid in the removal of stumps. The machine had a few arms that slid deep into the dirt and a slowly rotating pulley to wrench the stump from the ground. Using this method, I was able to quickly clear a rather large swathe of land.

I took a quick look around my land and appreciated how it was coming along. The herbs were growing at a steady pace, which was a good thing since they were my new pet's favorite food.

Smiling, I summoned the deena and rubbed its head. "I think you need a name, my little friend."

It chirped happily while staring at me. After thinking about it for a few minutes while looking at its little smiling face, I decided on a name. "I think you will be called Spot."

I smiled at the memory of my past-life's dog that bore the same name. He was a beautiful German shepherd, my so-called father's dog, and one of my best friends. He loved playing with me right up till the day he passed. He had already been old when I was a kid, but playing with him for the time he was around were some of my best memories.

I was pulled from my wonderful memories by Spot's happy chirping. It spun in circles before plopping down on the ground. I reached down, picked it up, and set it on my shoulder.

"Let's plant these mint mangoes. What do you say, Spot?"

Answered by a chirp, I proceeded to inspect the surrounding land and finally found a good spot. I dug a few shallow holes, dropped a mango in each hole, and covered them with dirt. I conjured a ball of light to produce sunlight and ran another hose from the water supply.

Chirping, Spot hurried over and let loose another dose of spores to settle into the earth to help the growth of the mangoes.

I rubbed its head again and walked down to the stream behind my home. I took note of the direction it was flowing and started walking up the bank. Every so often as I was following the stream, I notched a tree and cast a ball of light, which I fitted into the notch so I could find my way home—my version of a trail of breadcrumbs. The trees were beautiful with the balls of light stuck in them.

While I was walking, I noticed that the forest was alive with the calls of animals that were staying out of my line of sight—besides the birds, of course, that I could see flitting from tree to tree and chasing insects to pluck from the air. I followed the stream—making sure to keep placing orbs so I wouldn't become lost in the massive forest—until I found its end after walking for a long while. The lake was so large that I could barely see all the way to the other side. It was crystal blue and smelled amazing. I looked along the water line as I made my way closer to the water's edge and saw sand. Smiling, I knelt and ran my fingers through the sand; I had missed going to the beach.

I heard an odd noise and started walking in the direction of the noise. It was a weird plopping noise. I looked around for its source and found the most classic of all monsters, a slime. I used my observation skill and learned it was a water slime. They loved living in water and were harmless; unlike other slimes, these just wanted to swim, and they purified the water around them. I wanted one, for sure; purified water was great to have.

I slowly made my way over to the slime and tried to trigger my taming ability, but couldn't. I opened my menu and saw that slimes certainly counted as a small tame, but they had to be battled first. I rubbed my head and pulled out the stick I had been carrying since the cave. I reached out and bonked the slime on top of its sloshy body.

The slime turned to look at me, and I swear it looked as if it was crying. The tame ability became available, and I immediately tamed the slime. I pulled it into my arms and hugged it, rubbing my hands over its little form. "I'm so sorry, buddy. Don't cry."

It nuzzled into my chest, lying there for a while before bouncing away from me and landing back in the water.

I stood up, brushed the sand from my body, and bit my lip. I knew I should tame a few more. Just to filter more water. Three slimes later, I decided that I should head back to my campsite. While I walked along the path, the slimes followed my progress, swimming beside me, splashing, diving, and playing with each other. The slimes ended up swimming into the irrigation tunnel near my cabin, which was funny to watch; they used it like a slide. The pressure from the running water took them in circles, round and round again.

Watching them, I smiled and knelt to take a sip of the water. Thanks to the little guys, the taste was already so much better. My campsite was really coming together now, and I really couldn't be happier.

I turned from my new home and headed back to the dirt path so that I could continue exploring. As I walked, I saw another path that looked as if it had been crafted and wasn't actually part of the natural forest. I followed it and was led to what looked like ruins. Buildings made from stone and with holes that looked as if they could hold glass. I walked up to the first building I came across and stepped in through the doorway. Slowly, I began looking around the house and found remnants of broken bowls and plates, as well as cutlery so rusted parts of it turned to dust when I touched it. I wiped my hands against my pants and exited the house. I went from ruin to ruin, searching for anything I could use, but it appeared that the place was old and abandoned, and had been so for ages.

With only a few buildings left to explore, I stepped through a doorway and found boxes made from a peculiar material. I reached down, running my hands over the boxes. It was hard like metal and unyielding, but felt like plastic. I found a little dent on the back of a box and pressed it. The box hissed, which startled me. I jumped backwards, out of the building, and fell down the stairs. I landed with a grunt, all the air forced from my body. I groaned, coughed, clutched my chest, and tried to suck some air back into my body.

I slowly got back onto my feet, stumbled, and attempted to regain my balance. The box's hissing had reminded me of booby traps. For a moment, I thought the box was going to blow up and kill me.

I cautiously walked back into the building and saw that the box was now open, split from the top. I took a look inside the box and found rolled-up scrolls bound by cords. I reached in, grabbed the first scroll, and sat back while unwinding the cord.

"I wonder if everything is in English, or if I can just read this due to some magic ability."

I shrugged and started reading the scroll. It told of an encampment of a dwarflike race known as the Charulan. At the time the scroll was written, the encampment didn't have a name yet due to its being so new. It was simply known as "the camp," and it was located in the giantwood forest hundreds of miles from their original home. It told how the camp was in an area so rich in minerals and metals that the dwarfs had fallen in love with it.

"They *discovered* a love for mining? Aren't dwarfs all about smithing and mining?" I said aloud to myself.

Guess I showed up at some moment in time before the dwarfs had begun to discover their talents. I set that scroll down and began reading through the others. I searched for dates, but there were none. Not as if I could really see how long ago these were written; the scrolls in the box appeared to be just undated updates.

Scroll 1:

> We began building here in the early months. The air is still crisp and cool. The giantwood forest is a beautiful place, the flowers are in bloom, and the trees are all amazingly healthy. We pulled the stones from the earth to build our homes. There is a stream nearby that has the perfect sand to make glass. It flows from a lake located miles upstream. The water from it is pure and clean. The lake is deep and is full of little krakens.

Scroll 2:

> The buildings have been completed, and the windows have been placed. Our homes are complete now. The forest has grown hotter and hotter by day, causing irritation on our skin. We are from the mountains where the cool, damp air keeps us hydrated and our bodies cool. We need to get the buildings done during the early or later hours of the day while the sun is lower in the sky.

Scroll 3:

> We have finished our buildings of stone, each of us has taken one per family. There are five buildings now. My friend Gerad is expecting a child soon. He and his

wife are excited and full of happiness. Perhaps when more of my people relocate here, I will find a vreja of my own. Someone to fill the emptiness in my heart, who will give me a family to whom I can give my love.

Scroll 4:

The mines have been started. They go deep into the earth. We are pulling diamonds and sapphires and rubies from the earth, along with iron and silver and gold. The land here is rich with valuable resources. We will begin forging here and starting a trade path back to our home in the mountains. They will be happy and start a bargain with the elves in their own home city of Demane. Gerad had his child; sadly the boy cannot speak.

Scroll 5:

We have been mining here for the last few years, learning the lay of the underground. We have started hearing voices in the ground below. Motivating us to dig deeper and deeper. To find the source of the voices. It's eerie and unsettling, but with all the riches we have been finding, it's hard not to continue digging deeper in search of more of these veins of precious metals and jewels.

Scroll 6:

We made a mistake. We dug too deep into the earth and came upon a doorway. It was made from gold and silver and encrusted with jewels of every kind. It was beautiful. We opened the door, eager to find what was inside, and with that, we sealed our doom. It was a portal that brought with it all sorts of monsters and nasty things. It was like a whole other world in there. We had to retreat. The monsters were attacking us with swords and bows and lobbing magic at us. Somehow, we all made it out alive. We tried closing the door that we had opened, but it wouldn't budge. We ran back up the mines and blocked the entrance. I am selling my bojas now and leaving my things here. They wake during the night. We can hear them scrabbling at the boulder we left over the opening of the mine. We are leaving in the morning. Whoever finds this, please do not open the mines.

I shivered and looked up. *That took a sharp turn. How horrifying.* There could have been a bustling city, but instead it was abandoned ruins. No one had ever come back. There were two more boxes full of mining techniques and blueprints for making a forge. I pocketed them eagerly and thought about the two words I had learned. *Bojas* were probably the boxes from which I had retrieved the blueprints and scrolls. *Vreja* was most likely a soulmate or wife.

Groaning, I stretched out my legs and walked to the back of the ruins. I wanted to see the sealed-off mine. It was pretty close to the ruins, which was actually convenient. A large boulder covering the entrance did not appear to have been moved since however long ago it had been placed there. The boulder had a message etched into it that was almost faded:

D...p...n...mi...s...mon...r...i...s...e

It wasn't hard to guess what it said: "Don't open mines. Monsters inside." I was going to come back later and explore this mine. It was bound to have some amazing things in it.

I walked over to one of the remaining buildings and stepped through the open doorway. This must have been where the resources were brought for processing. There were loads of carts, each full of unprocessed ores and jewels. I went cart to cart, examining the contents and making mental notes. If only I had the knowledge to make something from all of this.

I was turning to leave when something caught my eye. It was a room I had somehow missed. I walked through the door and gasped. The room was full of jewelry, some pieces were small and simple, while others were extravagant. One of the simpler pieces was a gauntlet with sapphires on the back of the hand. It was a magical item that could store my energy almost like a battery, and I could draw on it when I needed to. I slipped it on and felt it start draining my magic. It was a low drag; if I had to quantify it, I'd say around five percent of my magic was being siphoned off by the gauntlet. It wouldn't weaken me any more than that, which would barely even be noticeable when I was outside, where my magic was replenished by the sun itself.

I could find no other magic items, so I walked out of the ruins and noticed the sun was going down. Nervously, I turned and looked at the boulder. I walked to it and stood quietly next to the sealed mine's entrance. After a few moments, I heard scrabbling followed by cries of anger and clawing against the surface of the boulder. The boulder rocked slightly, but held firm. I wondered how long that boulder had held securely, keeping the monsters trapped within the dwarfs' mines.

I placed my hand against the boulder and charged it with my own energy, turning the boulder into an excessively hot weapon. It would keep the mine sealed, and whoever touched it would not be happy.

"AHHHHhhhhh."

I flinched from the horrendous scream I heard. I pulled back as the scream started and retreated from the entrance; a wounded monster was apparently running from the boulder that had suddenly harmed it. I would have felt bad if I hadn't been so scared at that moment.

I turned and started walking away, back towards home, while rubbing my chin. There were several things to consider. There were definitely monsters in that mine. I would need herbs and mushrooms for healing, just in case I was injured or I started to run out of energy. While I was thinking of everything I needed on the walk home, nothing bothered me, not even the animals coming near me due to the light balls I had left along the path. That could be an issue for me because I wanted to find more animals—not only those that could be used as tames, but also animals that I could hunt and use for meat. I did not want to survive off mushrooms and herbs for the rest of my life, even if the god did give me the ability to not lose my physique for as long as I continued to eat. Meat was just too good to give up.

I reached my cabin and slipped inside. I yawned; it had been an exciting day, and I had a brand-new mine to explore. I undressed, down to my boxers, and stepped out of the cabin. I walked down to the stream and dipped my foot in it. Way too cold. I took a light ball and threw it in to heat the water before I submerging myself.

I sat in the stream and scrubbed at my skin barehanded. I would need to find some sort of cleaning agent at some point, but for right now, this felt amazing. I had gone days without cleaning myself. My clothing, however, was still clean somehow; the fabric was clean, it didn't smell, and it was as soft as if it were fresh out of the laundry.

After some time, I dragged myself from the stream and went home to lie down. Spot came running in chirping and lay down along my side, nuzzling into me. I stroked its head and smiled as I fell asleep.

Chapter 4

A dungeon in Another World's Sun

I woke up the following morning and stretched. Spot squeaked and chittered while leaving to spread spores on the growing plants. I stood up, grabbed the gauntlet, and strapped the sword to my side. Carrying my satchel, I strode from the building and started plucking herbs from the garden. I had plenty of them since they split so frequently, thanks to the combination of Spot's fertilization and the abundant sunlight. I still had a fairly decent stock of mushrooms.

I was going to open the mine and rid it of the monsters. I arrived at the ruins with the sun high in the sky. I envisioned a large rope around the boulder blocking the mine's entrance and watched as strands of light brought that vision to life. I started pulling the rope using a pulley made from hardlight, but the rock wouldn't budge. I frowned and conjured a few more ropes around the boulder, as well as a few more pulleys, and grinned as the ropes tightened.

The rock was pulled so fast and hard I had to dive out of the way as it was flung past me. I laughed and stood up, wiping the dust from my clothing. I walked into the mines with the help of ring I'd found; it was lighting the way like a nice pair of night-vision goggles. I grinned while making my way down the mine shaft, sword in hand. I looked from side to side and was able to see far down the tunnels. Oddly enough, there were no monsters in these tunnels; maybe they were just spawned from the abyss each night.

It took me about three hours of descent to get to the door mentioned in the scrolls. It was immaculate, and the door was covered in an absurd amount of wealth. I strode past the door, again looking from side to side, but there was nothing to be seen. The dwarfs had to seal the entrance to the mines because, once it was opened, it had to be cleared so that the monsters stopped showing up. That was similar to shows on Earth; I was finishing someone else's adventure. I began searching around the entrance and found a discarded pickaxe. It was rusted so badly I could see through some of the holes in it. I continued past the pickaxe and into the next room, which had stairs leading downward. I took the stairs and heard my heartbeat in my ears as I descended. I was glad I had found the ring because doing this in the dark with a torch would have been absolutely awful.

I finally found a landing with an open door and stepped through it, into an empty room with a single chest in the middle. *If that doesn't just scream trap!* I rolled my eyes and walked towards it. Was it a trap if you knew it was a trap? I grabbed the chest and flung it open, waiting for enemies to come flooding into the room. But all I found was an egg nestled in the soft fabric that lined the inside of the chest. I reached in, softly cupped it, and accessed my observation ability. It wouldn't tell me what kind of egg it was, just that it was an egg and that only something very hot would allow the egg to hatch.

I smirked, held a light orb to the egg, and channeled heat into it. The egg wiggled in my hand, but nothing happened. I frowned, sighed when nothing else happened, and stuffed the egg into my satchel. I would figure out how to hatch it later.

That was when the door slammed shut behind me. I spun around as I drew my sword and saw the door disappear into the wall as if it had never been there. A soft hiss behind me alerted me; I turned to see another pathway open behind me. I followed it and found myself in a bigger room. The walls were smooth and colored like steel. In the center of the room was a glowing orb; it pulsating a red light every few moments. I had just enough time to think about how that couldn't be good before the orb began growing from the size of a softball to around twenty feet in diameter.

I groaned, readying my sword as I watched the orb spit out a goblin. The goblin looked around, grunting and scratching his head in confusion, before he spotted me. This goblin was red in color and certainly didn't waddle like the last ones. He sprinted at me while readying his weapon, which was a small sickle. I jumped backwards as he swiped the air with blinding speed, cackling as he watched me barely dodge the blow. This thing was far more deadly than anything else I'd encountered.

I grunted and lunged forward, trying to catch the goblin with the tip of my sword. He casually swiped away the sword with his sickle, stepped forward, and tried to gut me. I dropped the sword and grabbed his arm with both hands, stopping him in its tracks. The goblin grunted, trying to pull away, but he couldn't budge. I squeezed harder and heard a snap. The goblin screamed in pain as he jerked away and cradled his broken arm.

Confused, I looked at my hands. *Am I really strong enough to break a monster's arm? What is going on here?*

I looked at the goblin; he was still grunting and squealing. I ran over to him, kicked his head, and watched it separate from the rest of the body. I pulled up my menu with a thought and scrolled a little till I found what I was looking for.

Combat strength — thanks to all of the continuous farming you have been doing, your strength has grown to superhuman levels.

So my strength was now off the charts, but I was trash with weapons, so hand-to-hand was my best bet. I sheathed my sword and looked at the glowing orb. It was still pulsating, but then it stopped as the bottom opened and released a golem. It was made of metal and had a soft-blue core that was glowing. It turned to look at me and released what sounded like a growl.

"Ah man, come on. How am I supposed to beat that?"

I groaned as it began to walking towards me. I noticed it was kind of slow, so I took a ready stance, my hands in a boxing form, and bent my knees so I was able to move at a moment's notice. As the golem took another step towards me, I did a quick kick at its right-knee joint. The knee jerked under the power of the kick, but other than that, there was no noticeable damage.

I jumped back as the golem took a swipe at me. I moved forward, swinging my hand, and hit its arm, pushing it out of the way. I pulled my other arm back, curled my hand into a fist, and punched it in its chest. As the power from the hit rocked the monster back, I punched it with my other hand, rocking it again. I moved back, breathing hard from the exertion as well as from the adrenaline coursing through my veins.

My hits were doing nothing to this monster. I would have to use my magic, which was definitely something I did not want to do. My magic pool was not large, and there was no sun underground that I could use to recharge my battery. I would have to be quick.

I conjured my sword and slashed downward roughly. The sword bounced off the monster's exterior, leaving a small dent in its body. I almost shouted with joy at the first sign of damage on the monster.

The golem looked down at its shoulder and reached up to touch the dent. The metal flowed like liquid, and the dent disappeared.

My smile disappeared. *It can heal itself. How am I supposed to deal with this?* I felt as if I had reached a boss fight too soon in the story.

Nervous, I studied the golem. It felt as if this thing had no weaknesses, and I was just scrambling. I noticed once again its core and bit my lip. *Maybe I can hit that soft-blue core hard enough to disrupt or turn off the golem.*

I bounced on the balls of my feet a few times and darted forward. The golem swung at me, but I dodged it by ducking under its arm at the last second. Then I leaned back, brought my leg up, and kicked the core harshly.

The core was ejected by the force of the hit and sent flying across the room, where it rebounded off the wall. The golem dropped like a sack of potatoes and clattered on the floor.

I turned to look at the orb, waiting for the next monster. I was surprised when it stopped glowing and simply dropped to the floor, bouncing a few times before coming to a rest. I sat down, catching my breath, and rubbed my face.

As the adrenaline faded from my system, I felt sick. I reached into my pack and ate a few herbs and blue-milk mushrooms. I sat there for a few moments to let the healing properties start taking effect and could even feel my energy returning.

I stood up, walked to the body of the golem, and studied it. It was made from a metal that had magic running through its very structure. I fed its leg into my satchel, and the bag did the rest, sucking the body into itself. I also looked at its core and found, with my observation ability, that it could be used as a magic battery; I could use it to power other golems. I placed that into my satchel as well. I could use that for a project later; magic batteries could have very interesting uses. The orb didn't have any information, other than a brief description of how it felt like a cold ball with ominous energy. I pocketed the orb as well. That was the first time my observation ability had been found lacking.

Turning, I glanced at the smooth walls surrounding me and noticed a doorway had opened in one of them. I strode towards the opening. The only way to go was forward from here. No looking back now.

The doorway opened to a long hallway. It was so long I couldn't see the end of it, but it was quite well lit. I reached out, running my hands over the walls. The stone beneath my fingers felt like brick, but it looked like marble. I started walking forward, my body tense and ready to strike or dodge should the need arise. I walked for around two hours, as best I could figure; the seemingly endless hallway went on and on until, just like that, it ended.

A doorway came into view. This door was just as beautiful as the last one. It looked as though it had been carved from gold and inlaid with jewels like sapphires, rubies, and emeralds. It was beautiful. I reached my hand out and pushed firmly, grunting as the door swung open and slammed into the wall with a loud crash. I strode through the opening, looking left and right; with my hands up. I was prepared to fend off an attack.

I heard a loud whirring, which was followed by lights—like the old electric kind back on Earth—flickering on. I winced; the powerful lights hurt my eyes as I looked around and waited for my eyes to adjust to the lights.

The room I was in was a small library. The shelves had books on a few subjects. Each shelf only had a few books on it. Some of them were so deteriorated that I couldn't even begin to guess what had been written in them. Others, due to their perfect condition, I had to assume were magic in nature. I read the titles, one after the other: *Using Your Aura to Find Precious Gems, Mining for Ores, Creating Your Own Home Forge, Creating Golems, Attracting Creatures to Your Home, Taming Methods, Using Monsters for Gardening*, and so on. It was a pretty good haul that I couldn't wait to start reading when I got back to my little home.

I pocketed the books and started looking for the next exit. I found it quickly. There was a handle extending from the wall. I grabbed it and turned it, pulling and opening a door. I walked through it and started down the stairs on the other side. I wondered how big this dungeon was; hopefully, my exploration would be over soon. I was starting to feel anxious in this place.

I reached the bottom of the stairs and saw another door. I opened it and covered my eyes while groaning as a blinding light made my eyes tear up painfully. I had stepped out into what looked like an open space. I looked around in wonder. I had been walking down the stairs for quite some time and knew that I had to be very deep underground. Yet here I was, surrounded by trees that swayed back and forth in the wind, and I saw birds hopping from tree to tree, sending a soft birdsong to each other.

I was in another dungeon. I started forward, heard the door closing behind me, and spun around and raced back to the door, which closed in my face and faded from existence, leaving me entrapped. I took a second to stop myself from screaming as a full round of anxiety flooded its way through my veins. I closed my eyes and breathed deeply to ground myself. *I can do this,* I thought to myself. Then I opened my eyes and chose a direction in which to begin walking.

I looked at the trees and realized they looked completely different from the trees in my own forest where my little log cabin was located. The observation skill tagged the tree as an ironwood tree. It grew like a normal tree and even looked like wood. I placed my hand on the tree and felt the cool, hard bark beneath my fingers. I rapped my knuckles against the tree and smiled as I heard the metallic clank. I looked around for a seed and ended up climbing the tree's branches to find one.

I climbed back down after searching the branches and was smiling happily. I had found two seeds to begin growing my own ironwood trees. I placed the seeds into my satchel and looked around for some sort of sign that would help me find my way out of this section of the dungeon.

I continued walking, waiting to either run into or see something that would give me a clue. I heard it a lot quicker than I thought I would. It came in the form of a great clamor.

I headed towards the noise of the fighting and came into a clearing where two great armies were fighting one another. One wore an armor colored a deep red with a picture of the sun on the chest. The other side wore deep, dark blue with rolling waves on it.

I started watching the armies' fighting from a distance, but couldn't tell which side was winning. A man fell, stabbed through his side with a spear; another, an arrow through his neck. A horse fell with a loud whinny; its rider, trapped beneath the horse, was slowly crushed to death.

My observation was cut short as I felt a sword pressed to my neck. "Don't move, or I will remove your head," the owner of the sword said.

I stood still, not sure what to do. I didn't speak either, afraid that it would be seen as a reason to remove my head from my shoulders.

The man told me to move forward, and I was guided to the left side of the battlefield, where the men in the red armor were based. Due to their sigil—a blazing sun—I hoped that my ability to use hard-light magic would give them a reason not to kill me. As I was led through the camp, I looked around and took note of the wounded men bound in blood-soaked bandages and lying on cots. Some were missing legs; others, arms. Still others, entire sides of their bodies.

There were no stops made as we wound our way through camp. A large tent came into view; it was decorated with several symbols, the most prevalent of which was the blazing sun. I was pushed through the entrance to the tent and shoved to my knees. I looked around quickly and saw several men, their eyes hard and mouths grim.

At the head of a table was seated a large man wearing a red suit of armor and a cloak of red scales that caught the light as it moved, making it appear as though the man were wrapped in fire from his shoulders down to his feet. His skin—and everyone else's here—was the color of obsidian. I was curious about their skin color; there were no differing shades amongst them. I continued observing the large man and saw that his eyes were as hard and cold as those of the rest of the men, but he felt more important than they. He had a regal aura that drew my eyes.

The man stood up, walked around the table, and gazed down at me with disdain. "Who have you brought before me, scout?" the large man asked. His voice was deep and smooth; it flowed out with all the authority of a king. "Is this man a spy from the Oceans Guild?"

I swallowed dryly and felt cold sweat drip down my back. This was horrifying. I knew I could use my magic to conjure my sword. But could I defeat an entire army if it came to that?

The scout cleared his throat and replied in a raspy voice, "He may be a spy. I can't confirm that, as he was just watching from the clearing. He was watching both sides as they fought and wasn't trying to make his way to either side, so it's hard to tell."

I chewed on my lip, still thinking about what I could do, but then the large man looked down at me.

"Who are you? Do not lie to me, or I will have your tongue ripped from your mouth and then fed to you," the man questioned and threatened in the same breath.

I met his gaze. "My name is Eric. I stepped through a door at the bottom of some stairs and found myself here. The door closed behind me and faded till it was no longer there. The sound drew me in, and I was found by your man here. I know nothing of your fight or your people. I am trying to find my way home and out of this mess," I replied slowly, making sure to speak clearly so they could understand what I was saying.

The large man ran his hand over his chin and scratched the stubble coating his face. "I believe you. But what is this nonsense of stepping through a door that is no longer there? How do you expect me to believe something like that? Do you take me for a child or a fool? Why are you spinning tales of magic like I am mentally deranged or insane?" he asked. His tone was harsh and beginning to sound angry.

I looked up at him, brought my hands to my chest, and conjured a ball of light into my hands while looking him in his eyes. I watched them widen as he stepped back, stumbled, and almost fell into the lap of the man behind him.

"You can use magic? That's just a fairy tale. The light is so bright. Like the sun," he said, almost mumbling in disbelief.

I nodded and watched as he rambled and fought an internal battle on whether or not he could believe the sight in front of him. I canceled the ball of light, and the man looked at me again. This time he had fear in his eyes as he regarded me now as someone who held power and was dangerous. The man held out his hand to me warily. "I believe you now. You have told me the truth and given me no lies. Would you join us? Help us to push back the Oceans Guild, which threatens our lands and our homes?"

I shook my head and explained again that my only wish was to return home.

The man sank down on his knees and sighed softly— thinking of some way to get me on his side, I'm sure. The man's eyes lit up with hope as he looked at me once more. "What if I could offer you a magic book?"

I hate to admit it, but that certainly piqued my interest. I loved the thought of adding more magic to my repertoire. "Let me see the book, and I shall consider helping you," I said slowly.

I couldn't believe he suddenly really had a magic book. Up until a moment ago, he hadn't even believed in magic.

The man turned and commanded a soldier standing nearby to run to his personal tent to retrieve the *Book of the Sun*.

The soldier replied with a sharp salute and a "Yes, My King." He then turned and ran from the command tent.

So this man is a king. I thought so, having seen how everyone defers to him and lets him speak alone and without interruption to me.

Within ten minutes, the squire returned from his retrieval errand, book in hand. The book was bound in what appeared to be the same scales as the man's cape. I reached out and took the book from his hands. It looked light, but was surprisingly heavy. An option to obtain the book's knowledge popped up in the menu. That was another function that I had seen from games on Earth, and I knew the only thing left to do was acquire the knowledge. I accepted the prompt mentally.

The book burst into flame in my hands. I gasped, dropped the book on the ground, and clutched my head as the book shoved all of its knowledge and secrets into my head. It felt as if my head were spinning; screaming, I fell to the ground as the world faded away.

I woke up what must have been hours later on a bed in a tent. My clothes had been removed, and I was in a white-cloth sleeping robe. Groaning, I sat up in bed and rubbed my head. *Finding the pain-medicine version of a plant is going to be a high priority for me in the near future,* I thought to myself. I conjured a light orb and cast it above me, where it hung suspended.

I opened my menu and scrolled till I found the fire magic I had just obtained. It was different from my hard-light magic. Hard light could make things to channel heat. This fire magic, however, was pure offense; I could use it as a fireball and flamethrower. It also gave me complete resistance to all types of fire attacks.

I smiled. *I am becoming one overpowered fire mage. I wonder if there's lava magic somewhere in this world for me.* I closed my menu and got out of bed, standing shakily. I needed some food to settle my stomach.

"Is there anyone there who can help me?" I called out.

The entrance to the tent was flung open, and the king's squire walked through the doorway and looked me over. "Are you well, mage? You collapsed so suddenly."

I nodded and explained what the book had done to me. I told him that I would help the king with his problems, But first I needed food and lots of it.

The squire gestured to the other side of the tent, where my clothes were. I had been unconscious for three days, and in that time, they had cleaned my clothes and provided under-garments since mine had some holes in them. The squire waited outside my tent patiently while I dressed.

I stepped out into the daylight and immediately felt better as the light from the sun was flowing into my body and recharging my cells. I opened my arms, receiving the sun, and stood there happily for a few moments. When I opened my eyes after basking in the light, I saw the squire standing there looking at me curiously. "The sun gives me energy and makes me feel better," I explained to him.

He accepted the information and turned to walk down the lines of tents to the cooks' area. The smell of cooking meat and vegetables hit my nose, and I felt my stomach start rumbling. I walked a little faster and came out into a clearing lined with benches, tables, and lots of men who were already eating. Again I noticed a lack of shades in skin color. Every man was the same shade of pure obsidian. Every one of them stopped talking and eating to look up at me as I followed the king's squire to the front of the line.

"Where is the head chef!" the squire yelled. "The fire mage is hungry and waiting!"

I groaned. I didn't feel important enough to be treated like this. I could just wait in line like the rest of the men. As I was having this internal struggle with myself and feeling very embarrassed, the head chef raced out, wiping his hands on an already-soiled white hand rag.

"I am here. No need to keep yelling, you ingrates!" the chef yelled in a harsh tone. And then he saw at whom he was yelling. When his eyes fell upon the king's squire, he paused for a moment and groaned. He didn't offer an apology; however, he did adopt a nicer tone when he asked, "Now what can I get for you?"

The king's squire issued an order for the king—a husk of bread, two pitchers of ale, slices of cattle, and a few pieces of roasted pork.

I stepped forward to place my order after the squire was finished. "Can I get a—" I started.

The chef wheeled on me, his face already red. "Who are you, brat? I didn't ask what I could get for you. This order is for the king. Who do you think you are?" he shouted.

Surprised, I took a step back. All feelings of embarrassment left me and were replaced with a warmth spreading throughout my chest—I was angry.

The squire looked at me and lifted an eyebrow, but did nothing to stop the stream of abuse coming from the chef's mouth. I could almost read his mind. *Are you going to let him talk to you like this? What are you going to do? If you can't handle this one chef, how are you going to help my king?*

I sighed and smiled as I stepped back. Time for a little shock and awe. Calling up my hard light with my imagination, I wrapped it around me like a shining cloak and started turning up the light. I commenced shimmering like the rays of the sun, and the chef's eyes started widening as he saw me appear to start wavering. Glaring, I moved towards the chef.

"Your King has made a deal with me to help save all of you from the Oceans Guild, and this is how you repay me?

Trying to bully me while I try to eat? Is this what the Men of the Sun are?" I yelled back at the chef.

The chef dropped to his knees and looked at me. To him, I probably appeared to be a golden god come to life. "No, my lord, I'm sorry; please forgive me. I'm sorry. Let me get you something to eat at once," he said apologetically.

Smiling, I canceled the spell and leaned towards him. "I'll take a few slices of the beef and pork, and some bread, please." Still smiling, I leaned back and folded my arms over my chest.

The squire looked away nervously. I realized that not only had I looked like a god to the chef, but I had looked like that to everyone else as well. I shook my head and waited as the chef hurried to get the food and drinks for the king's tent.

When ready, the food was handed to me on a large platter. I swallowed the saliva building up in my mouth, smiled, and thanked the chef for the food. I turned and followed the squire back to the king's tent. It was a short walk, and we arrived within a few minutes.

The tent flap was opened by one of the king's aides as we arrived; we entered, took seats, and began eating the food, which was amazing. The pork dripped fat and flavor as I bit into it. The bread was fluffy, crisp, and not at all what I thought it would be. It appeared to be closer to the naan that was served back in my home world—flat and flaky. I took a large bite and closed my eyes, enjoying the way it almost melted against my tongue.

The king began talking as we ate. "I take it you have agreed to help me with my war, mage?"

I nodded my agreement and asked him what he needed from me.

The king wiped his hands on a towel, stood up, crossed to a map, and pointed at a few areas. "These are the strongholds held by the Oceans Guild. They have been holding these spots uncontested for the last few hundred years."

I looked up sharply.

The king smiled. "This conflict is hundreds of years old. We have been fighting for so long."

I raised an eyebrow. *They have been fighting for hundreds of years, but magic is a fairy tale?*

The king saw my look and smiled again. "We are long-lived here, mage."

I just nodded and asked what he wanted me to do with the strongholds.

"Take them. Get rid of the guild members from them and help us push up and take more land. We have to reach the main base they hold farther inland to have any hope of winning this war. We have been in a stalemate for the entirety of the war, but with you now, we can finally gain the upper hand!" The king looked so excited he was almost bouncing on his feet.

I leaned back, crossing my arms. "I may have magic, but my power is not unlimited. I have no real combat experience."

The unlimited-magic part was kind of a lie; anytime I was in the sunlight, I received a constant bolster to my magic that kept me topped up. However, my bluff paid off as the king offered exactly what I was hoping he would.

"We can have a knight train you in the ways of swordplay as we travel. You won't be a match for most with the sword, but it may be enough to keep you alive."

I clapped my hands together and accepted the offer.

"William, come in, please," the king called.

The entrance to the tent was parted as William entered. He was tall, at least six foot seven; covered head to toe in thick, coiled muscle; bare-chested; and wearing only a pair of black pants and boots.

"Yes, My King? How may I be of service?" He smiled as he knelt and bowed his head to his king.

"Please stand. I can't stand it when you do that. I will never have the man who I shared my childhood with bowing to me. You know I can't stand that," the king said while smiling.

The king continued to smile and laugh with his friend as I stood there watching them converse. He finally waved his hands in front of his face to change the topic of conversation.

"Will, I need a big favor from you. I need you to train the mage here in swordsmanship. He is powerful, but it is not unlimited. Would you mind watching over him on the way to the next stronghold?"

Will walked over as he assessed me with his soft eyes. "You seem to be in excellent physical condition. Not a lot of fat on you. You're tall too. Usually, this kind of physique would be found on the soldiers using war hammers. Tell me, what do you normally do on a daily basis?"

I explained that I was just a farmer who liked to explore the forest and enjoyed taming animals.

"A farmer, you say! With a body like that? Amazing. I can hardly believe it," Will said.

Will and I talked for a bit and set our start for the next day. I was to meet him on the small field outside the camp to begin my training.

I yawned while walking back to my tent; it had been a long day, and I was ready to go to sleep. The next day was sure to be a good one. I would finally learn to use a sword and stop relying on my own brute strength. I lay down and closed my eyes, wondering when I would get out of this place.

Chapter 5

Warpath in
Another World's Sun

The next morning, my eyes opened, and I sat up in my bed, feeling tired and excited. Today I would begin my training with a sword and add to my abilities. I jumped out of bed and walked to where my clothes were folded on a chair. I quickly dressed and excitedly walked from my tent towards the training grounds.

When I arrived at the training grounds, I quickly found Will and walked over to him, waving a welcome. Will returned my smile and shook my hand. We walked over to a tent where the strong ring of a hammer could be heard echoing throughout the yard. We walked in and were smacked with the warmth of a forge.

Standing over the forge was a very large man named Mike. He was even more muscular than Will. The air seemed to shake with the force of the hammer hitting against the molten metal. I winced with each strike and watched as he took the metal he was striking and placed it back into the forge. Only then did he turn to us and welcome us into his tent, after which he walked over to a pitcher and poured himself some water before taking a long sip.

"Now, what can I do fer y'all?" Mike asked.

I looked at him, smiled, and introduced myself. Will took over the conversation from there and told Mike that we were there for me to get a weapon that would be good for me. I told him that I wanted a sword.

Mike looked me over, walked to the wall, and started reaching for a claymore, which I quickly declined. In the close space of a mine or the forest around my home, it would be a bad move to carry such a large weapon I couldn't even swing. After telling him my reasons, he grabbed a half-sword from the wall and handed it to me. I wrapped my hands around it, swung it a few times, and shook my head. I liked it, but it didn't feel as if it were meant for me, for some reason. I looked around for a while before my eyes landed on a blade with lines running horizontally along the blade. I reached for it and slid my hands around its handle, admiring the way it felt.

"Found something? Bring it over here for me," Mike called.

I grabbed the weapon's scabbard and sheathed it before I quickly covered the space to the front of the tent. I handed the weapon to Mike.

His face lit up happily. "You want this one? Amazing. You probably don't even know what you found, my friend." Continuing to smile, Mike led the way outside, unsheathed the blade, and gave it a few experimental swings.

"This blade is the love child between two weapons—the sword and the whip. It was found in some ruins a hundred or so years ago, and no one has even looked in its direction due to the unorthodox methods of the weapon." Mike swung it again and flexed his wrist quickly.

I watched as the blade seemed to lengthen and, like a whip, make fluid and sharp movements.

"The weapon will have a hard impact, like a whip, but will still cut like a blade," Mike said as he flexed his wrist again, and the sword shrank back to its original shape and size.

I reached for the blade happily; I spun it a few times and then flexed my wrist as I had seen Mike do. The blade lengthened and hit the ground with a classic crack noise I expected to hear from a whip. The ground released a puff of dirt and grass; a small crater was left in the ground where the sword had struck.

I looked up happily at Will and Mike. "I want this one, please. It suits me."

Mike signed the weapon out of the armory and gave it to me. As he waved us off, wishing me luck, I smiled as if I were a child who had received a new toy.

Will and I walked to an open area away from other trainers, and he unsheathed his own weapon, which was quite large.

The blade resembled a claymore, but was longer and wider. Will flourished his blade easily, whipping the blade around as if it weighed no more than a twig. He smiled at me and took a ready stance, both hands wrapped around the handle, the immense blade held in front of him.

"Now, tell me, Eric. If you saw a rather large, handsome warrior in front of you, holding a blade, how would you react? What would be your first move?" Will asked me.

I bit my lip, thinking, and then I held my hand over my head and conjured a fireball.

Will's eyes widened, and he took a step back while lowering his blade.

I canceled the spell, raced forward—covering the space between us faster than he could react—and held my blade to his stomach.

Will sighed and set down his blade. "For a moment there, Eric, I forgot you could use magic. But this is sword practice. No more magic during our fights, okay? This practice is to help you learn how to handle yourself when you can't use your power, or to help you save it for when you really need it."

I stepped back and nodded. "You are right, Will. I do need to learn more. I just can't figure out what else to do."

Will nodded and began my education. He taught me that since he was bigger, I should use a glancing blow—direct my opponent's blade away from my body with minimal movement to tire my opponent out till I could go in for the strike that would end the fight. I watched the smooth movement he made and held my sword out in front of me. Will swung his sword at me in exaggerated slow motion, and I brought my sword up and around in a slow circular movement, making sure to get the movement correct, and slapped the large blade away. It slammed into the ground next to me.

Will smiled. "Good! Now, again!" he yelled.

The training session lasted hours. By the time I was done, I could hardly raise my hands over my waist. I could almost feel every individual tear in my muscles. I groaned as I trudged back to my tent and pushed through its flap. As I sat on my cot, I received a notification through my menu, and I opened it.

> *Combat. Exotic weapons skills. Whip sword. The weapon of a true hero, from long ago, who led his people out of the darkness and into the light, creating an age of happiness and peace. Much to the despair of his people, the hero disappeared one day while exploring a dungeon.*

I rubbed my eyes. *Who is making this lore? Why does my system just know this information?* I shrugged and lay back, almost crying as every muscle in my body screamed in protest.

Will was a brutal taskmaster who made me do every drill till it was almost muscle memory at this point. Now, I could see why he was so muscular. I knew why the training was so important; I just wished it didn't have to hurt so much.

I rolled over and groaned, dragging myself from the bed. I walked from the tent and left the camp. I wandered around for a bit, looking for a river or stream. I closed my eyes and tilted my head, listening for the telltale burble of a nearby stream. I kept walking and every so often took a moment to listen.

I smirked as I caught a sound on the very edge of my hearing; I began walking towards the sound. I came upon the stream, smiled, and took a quick look around before I started disrobing till I was standing there in my drawers. I held my hand out, created a sun orb, and lowered it into the stream. I adjusted the temperature that the orb emitted till it was effortlessly heating the water—not enough to burn me, but enough to simulate a hot bath, which is exactly what I wanted.

I lowered myself into the water, groaning till the water started heating my muscles, relaxing them, and making me feel amazing. I missed taking baths; I missed the amazing smelling salts humanity had created. I laid my head back, closed my eyes, and reminisced about all the amazing things that I had taken for granted.

I jerked awake hours later and looked around warily. I was tired, and my body still ached. I dragged myself from the water and took note of the sun going down. I needed to make my way back to the camp and go to sleep. I stretched, found my clothes and new sword, and put them on. I slowly walked back to camp, enjoying the feel of the last rays of sun caressing my skin. It was easy to forget that this place wasn't real, that I was several miles beneath the surface of the earth, and that there was no way out. I groaned and slapped my hands across my face. *Great way to ruin the mood there, bud,* I said to myself.

The next thing to ruin that great mood was the man, in the Oceans Guild uniform, who stepped out from behind a tree and was swinging an axe at my neck. I threw myself backwards, letting out a scream that was cut short by my back slamming into the ground and driving the air from my lungs. I lay there groaning as the man ran at me with his axe raised over his head, ready to be planted in me.

I pointed the first two fingers on my right hand up and towards the man. A jet of flame shot out from my fingers and washed over the man. I inhaled the scent of burnt hair and flesh and retched while trying to stand up. The fight wasn't over yet though.

As the man writhed on the ground, he wrenched off his helmet, and I noticed he wasn't a man at all; he was a monster—like a jaguar in human form. I recoiled and then shook my head. I had fought monsters before; this was nothing new. I reached down to my side, unsheathed my sword, and held it in front of me in a ready stance.

The monster snarled at me and hissed. I flicked my wrist violently, turning the blade into a deadly whip that sailed through the air and cracked against the jaguar's chest, ripping out a chunk of its flesh. It staggered back, glaring at me, and let out a loud yowl that echoed throughout the forest.

I whistled slowly, twirling the whip in a slow back-and-forth motion, and waited. The monster turned to run, which was a mistake, as I took the opportunity to crack it across its back, causing it to fall and reach for its back while hissing and yowling loudly. I raced over, flicked my wrist to turn the sword back into a blade, and slammed it into the creature's back, severing its spine. It thrashed angrily and let out a slow groan as it passed.

I smiled as I pulled the sword from the monster's back and flicked the blood from the blade before sheathing it. I did it—that was a real fight, and I had won. The sword training was working. I could do this.

I looked down at the monster and was startled to realize it was gone. In its place was a small crystal. I knelt down, grabbed the crystal, and activated the observation skill—monster core. I looked at it closely and grinned. The core's description mentioned that it could be inserted in the bottom of a hero's sword. I grabbed the crystal and held it to the pommel of my blade. The bottom opened, and the crystal was absorbed. The blade's length flared then took on a dull pale-blue color. I held the blade to the tree, and the tree was soon covered by frost crystals. I couldn't help but laugh loudly. The monster cores held different attributes, from ice to light and electricity.

I re-sheathed my sword. Seeing the core brought up an important question. *Did they never experiment with the cores? Why didn't the monster use magic? Why don't these people think magic is real?* I had a lot of questions and absolutely no answers. I just sighed and started walking back to camp, where I made my way to the king's tent.

I walked in after the king's guard cleared me. The king was talking with some of his advisors. *Do these people ever sleep?* It certainly felt as if they were always at work.

The king looked up and smiled at me. "Hello, Eric! What brings you here to my council meeting?"

I took a deep breath and told him of the attack by the monster in the Oceans Guild uniform. I asked why I wasn't told that the Oceans Guild troops were not human.

"Eric, I apologize for not mentioning it, but you have to remember we have been fighting them for hundreds of years. There is not a single person in this entire camp who doesn't know what they look like or what they can do. Besides you, and for that I am sorry, but I assure you it was not withheld information for any other reason than it is such common knowledge."

I bit my lip firmly and nodded. "If they are all monsters, then why did you think that I was a spy when I was first brought before you?"

The king looked at me and nodded. "This is also another piece of common knowledge. People have defected from my army. Once they leave, a change comes over them, bleaching the color from their skin. I feared I had just caught someone in the middle of defecting."

I looked at him curiously. "In the middle of it? Are there not more traitors?"

The king shook his head and answered, "Not many betray the human race, Eric. Those who do, we go out of our way to find and put down. The last one was killed over twenty years ago."

That was a reasonable answer, and I accepted it. "I am tired, King. I need to sleep and regain my strength." I felt weary. The adrenaline was wearing off, and I was starting to crash.

The king nodded and wished me well. He also took a moment to remind me that I would be leaving with a force of men to begin my assault on the strongholds.

I made my way back to the tent and sat on the cot. I stared at the tent wall ahead of me for a little while, thinking about what my life was becoming. *What am I really doing here? Am I ready for this? Less than a week ago, I fell to my death for a loaf of bread, and now I am going to fight a war?* I lay back on my cot and closed my eyes, opting to fall asleep instead of focusing on the dilemma.

The next day was filled with grabbing rucksacks and packing a small caravan with food and supplies. Several soldiers, archers, and cavalry units joined us on our quest, as did William, who was to continue my training till we arrived at the final stronghold.

I was sitting on one of the wagons, watching the countryside go by and taking in all the beautiful sights. I took a few seeds from some plants whose petals looked as if they were fires dancing in the wind. Those would look beautiful outside my cabin. The trail we took passed over large hills, where I was able to gaze out upon the world.

Whoever built this dungeon was amazing, the amount of detail and craft that was sunk into this place was astounding. What truly won my heart, however, was the tree I found after going through a forested area. The trees were sitting there, slightly darker than the surrounding trees, but the bark looked like the planks and boards on a barrel.

I walked up to it and began examining it using the observation skill—rootsparilla tree, a mixture of root beer and sarsaparilla. I noticed a small tap that grew from the tree naturally; reaching up and turning the tap a few times produced root beer fizzing out of the tree slowly. I ran, grabbed a mug from the wagon, and held it under the tap in the tree to fill the mug. Then I closed the tap and sniffed the liquid, closing my eyes and feeling a rush of happiness from the nostalgia.

It was identical to a drink I would have purchased from a corner store in my home world—somehow just as fizzy and sweet. *How amazing.* I grabbed a few seeds from the tree and smiled after noticing that the seeds looked like mini root-beer barrels. I slid them into my satchel and returned to the wagons.

The caravan stopped later in the day. William, who was in charge, began barking orders to the others, and then he looked at me and smiled. "Time for more practice, my friend."

I smiled back; my muscles weren't quite so sore anymore. We headed to an area of the camp away from the other people and faced each other. I slid my sword from the sheath, flourished it, and held it up to my shoulder. I grinned at William, who was holding his sword out in front of him.

William charged me without saying a word, his sword flashing out at me in an overhead strike. I spun into the sword, using my left arm to push the blade out and away, and brought my own sword down against William, stopping before I hit him.

William smiled and said, "I guess that simple attacks with such a large blade won't be working on you after being attacked by that monster."

I shook my head and moved back, bringing my blade to my shoulder and letting it rest there. Then I watched something happen to William; he seemed to get a little taller and took another stance, his sword hanging loosely in one hand. William seemed to disappear with how fast he moved. I started cursing. *What in the anime-cartoon bologna is happening—?* But I didn't even have the time to finish the sentence in my head before William was standing over me and bringing his sword down on my head.

I flicked my blade out, tapping his sword over to the side as he'd taught me. I watched him spin around in the direction I had deflected him. He used the momentum of his large sword to swing himself around, cutting at me horizontally. I barely ducked under the blade before lunging forward and hitting him in the stomach with my shoulder, finding a load of resistance from his abs. William grunted at getting pushed back, and I cut at him with my sword vertically, barely missing him.

The fight went on for quite a while. It ended with my barely being able to breathe and William standing there as if nothing had even happened.

"Man! H...How are you... Just... Whew! Man, I can't breathe!" I wheezed out.

William laughed while sheathing his sword, and he gestured for me to follow him back to camp. "Eric, I have been fighting for a long time. If I was dying after a one-on-one fight, I wouldn't be a very capable knight for my king, would I? Your stamina will build over time, my friend. Soon you will be able to fight for hours at a time. You are improving at a remarkable rate, I must say," Will said encouragingly.

I smiled as I pulled my menu up to check my combat skill. It had leveled up during our fight. My stamina, recovery, and adrenaline output had increased to help me be faster and swing harder. The exotic-weapon skill had also leveled up, unlocking a better skill that my weapon had been hiding inside it—when it was in whip mode, the whip would grow blades like a saw; if it wrapped around something, it would cause additional sawing damage as it was pulled back, effectively cutting away whatever it was attached to. I grinned; I couldn't wait to test it.

After our sparring match, it was time to head out again. The men started packing up their gear. We climbed into the back of the wagons, and with the sound of snapping reins, the horses started moving us forward.

The day passed again slowly. The constant sound of the wheels crunching against the stones dug itself into my ears and made it easy to zone out; I found my thoughts drifting. I was back in my old home, watching an anime on my phone and snacking on zucchini chips I had made by sprinkling chili powder, pepper, salt, and some cayenne onto the thinly sliced vegetables before they were thrown into my air fryer. I smiled while I was rocking in my seat. I missed those days in which my biggest problem was waiting once a week for the newest issue of my favorite show to pop out a new episode. Instead, here I was, engaged in this battle between two forces. *I am living in an anime now.* I groaned as I wondered if I was on someone's screen at that moment, the boring in-between parts cut away as insignificant and unworthy of taking up the screen time on some network. I shook my head to clear the thoughts away. *Like that would ever happen.*

I must have drifted off to the music of wheels crunching against the stones slowly; it drifted to the back of my mind and pulled me away from the world and into a soft sleep. I didn't dream of anything. I didn't even think, but I could still feel the world around me. The soft, warm wind blew against me and through my hair. It was the most at peace I had felt since I had been brought to this world.

"Eric, wake up," Will said softly as I was jostled and gently shaken from my slumber by him. I looked at him, and he must have recognized the look on my face; I was questioning why I was being dragged from my sleep. "We are approaching the first stronghold on our journey. Its name is Locala. The enemy is unaware of our approach. This will be the first time any human has seen this side of the territory in hundreds of years."

William seemed to be very excited by this, and I could understand why. They were retaking territory that had been taken from them; they were getting their homes back. It was heartwarming, to say the least.

The wagon slowed to a stop after pulling up to a small group of trees. Around the path's bend was the stronghold. The plan was to sneak up in the middle of the night to go in through a back door that had been built there ages ago, and to fight our way through the hordes of monsters that would be within. I reached down and gripped the handle of my sword. I was nervous and anxious; I wanted to both go and not. I wanted to just do something, not sit here waiting. It was awful feeling that way—a slow buildup in my gut that was squeezing and wringing my insides.

I walked away from the group after our meeting was done and sat on the stump of a tree with rings so numerous they were almost impossible to count. The tree had been both massive and ancient. I looked around at its base and wondered what could have felled something so large. It reminded me of my old world's redwood trees that were so large you could have groups of people dancing on them all at once.

I looked up and noticed William approaching me with another man from the group. If I remembered correctly, I had heard him called Hector. He was a bright young man apprenticed to the blacksmith. Apparently, he was good enough at what he did to be trusted with us on this secret mission. So why not, right? Better to have someone who could repair arms than not.

The two approached me and began talking about some ruins that were located nearby and that may be worth checking out. I sighed inwardly, smelling a side quest and more danger. *How wonderful.*

I stood up and smiled at them. "Let's go check them out, guys."

That's how I ended up in another set of ruins, going through houses. It looked similar to the dwarfs' homes—carved from stone, with empty holes where the doors would be and the wood long ago rotted away and disintegrated. I stepped into them one by one, but found nothing of use or interest. I soon felt this venture was boring and kind of a waste; I had expected something more. Maybe I should count my blessings that nothing happened.

I stepped into another house that made me regret my thoughts. The house was enormous from the outside. I stepped through the hole and almost screamed at the multitude of people inside, all looking at me with their dead eyes. It took me a moment to get past my heart's thudding into my throat as I realized no one was moving. All of them were standing there, eyes forward, staring at me with such pale-gray skin and eyes that were…made from stone? I moved forward, looking around, wary of a trap being sprung or something jumping out at me. They were like mannequins—shaped like people, with eyes and everything, but they were not alive. I walked around one of them, looking it up and down, but there was really nothing to see. I shuddered.

It took me a moment to realize that they were arranged in a spiral with no apparent order. Some were small, and others were big, muscled, fat. I felt my mouth dry as I wondered if these people had been alive and then turned to stone by some form of magic or curse. That would be tragic. But what was the purpose of everyone having been arranged in a pattern like this, all of them in some different stances? Some were reaching out for the others; a few were huddled together with their hands held in front of their faces. Some looked as if they were in mid-run, sprinting away from something. I felt myself starting to sweat nervously as I walked the long, curving spiral.

I walked through the rows of them, getting closer to the center of the room, where I saw a pedestal. On the pedestal was a gauntlet. The fingers of it were pointed and tipped like talons. It was a solid-gold color and had a round disc of black on the back. It was beautiful and almost definitely a trap.

I sighed and activated my observation skill on it. The gauntlet was a long-forgotten hero's tool. It could take herbs and other items into itself and combine them for you, instead of having to do it yourself. It also upgraded the quality of whatever was put into it—making herbs even better, for example.

I ground my teeth, almost angry. The item was too good to pass up. I definitely could use this gauntlet; it would certainly be one of the most useful things I found.

I turned, used the observation skill again on the stone people, and groaned. They were definitely people at one point, a race long forgotten by both people and the god. Their hubris in creating tools and other items led to the anger of the very universe itself, causing it to turn them to stone, forcing them to live as stone for all eternity. Nothing could break the vessels; nothing could free them or kill them. They were aware of each passing moment and of everything said. They could not talk or move or see.

I shuddered at the fate of these beings. How awful that must be. I walked to the nearest one and reached out, caressing its face. "I know you are in there, people of stone. I see your fate and weep for you. It says you cannot be saved, and I do not know how to save you or end you. I am sorry."

I turned from them and walked to the gauntlet, picking it up and putting it on. I flexed my hand and marveled at how it felt almost as if it had been made for me. I turned, bit my lip, and felt like crying. There were tracks down the stone people's faces. Fresh tears dripped from the stone eyes. I dropped to me knees and let my tears fall freely.

I walked out of the temple after I regained my composure. My face was red, and my eyes were puffy from the tears. I met William, who noticed my gauntlet.

"Found a new toy, did you? It looks good on you."

I flexed the gauntlet and smiled as rays of light shimmered off it. "It will be very helpful to us and our mission. William, coming here was a great choice, and I am glad to have listened. Let's head back to camp and grab some food before we start our assault on the stronghold."

We turned, left the dead town, and made our way back to camp.

The fresh scent of pork hit my nose, and I closed my eyes as I breathed it in. How wonderful that smell was. I moved through the small rows of tents to the cooks' fire.

The man looked up at me and smiled as he pulled out a plate. He cut free a few pieces of meat from the roasting pork and piled them onto my plate, along with a husk of bread and some roasted veggies that had been found in the nearby forest. I had been worried we would be stuck eating cold rations and jerky, but thanks to the direction of the wind, the smells of the roasting meat and other foods would be carried away from the castle. We were safe to eat as we pleased. However, as night fell, we would have to put out the fire; it would attract far too much attention.

I sat on a stump and began digging in. The meat was tender and dripping grease. I bit into the juicy morsel and was rewarded with a crunch from the roasting skin. I rolled my eyes into the back of my head with a happy moan. I picked up a mushroom and bit into it, enjoying the flavors it had taken from the flames. I cleaned my plate, walked over to the pile of dirty dishes, and deposited it there. Then I walked to my tent and began gathering the gear I would need.

I peeked out of the tent and noticed the sun getting lower on the horizon. It was time to get a move on and join up with the group. I walked to the tree line, where I saw William leaning up against a small tree.

He nodded at me and looked away, using the last rays of light to keep a lookout at the stronghold. He smiled as he watched the enemy bring out torches and use small striking stones to light them.

"Why are you smiling, William?"

"Those torches they are lighting will only help us, my friend. They will mess with their natural night vision, as well as limit their line of sight."

I nodded as I listened to William explain the torches and go on further to explain the goals of the mission, which would commence once the other members of our party arrived. Our group was not large enough to do a main attack at the gates; it was just large enough to sneak in and catch them unaware. I asked why the cavalry wasn't going to be used, and William pointed out that there weren't enough of them for any sort of formation. They were more for hunting and, if need be, a final stand.

William also explained that there were different tiers of monsters that we would be facing. "There are cats, wolves, and bears," he said.

My mind flipped back to the cat I had fought in the woods. It was the fierce monster against which I had first tested my abilities when it ambushed me after my soak.

"The cats cannot speak; they are underlings and the most numerous of the monsters we will be fighting. Wolves are smarter and stronger; it would be safe to say that each wolf has the strength of ten cats. They fill the role of captains and can speak as clearly as you and I. They can plan and are good at tactics. Then there are the bears; they are large and powerful monsters covered in thick hair and muscle. They can talk and are incredibly smart and dangerous. They are the generals and leaders of the Oceans Guild," William explained.

He turned to me; his face was lined with nervous energy. "We are going to be clearing out this stronghold under the cover of night. These strongholds have many enemies within, and they provide backup for the main cities that our king will be fighting."

I grinned at him. "Taking out the trash, so our king can claim his glory without having to cover his rear," I said.

William smiled back. "You catch on fast, my friend. Now, let us be on our way; the time has come."

I pulled the hood up on my cloak and turned to the castle. I was ready to begin.

The slow movement killed me—crawling on our stomachs all the way from the tree line to the foot of the castle. We had wrapped our weapons in cloth rags to muffle the sound of the metals' clinking. I looked up at the castle that was looming overhead. It was tall and imposing; its sentries walked back and forth, waving the torches to try and see the surrounding landscape.

I made it to the castle first and pressed myself to the cool stone. From where I was standing, due to the overhang, they could look straight down without seeing me. William slid up next to me and drew himself up.

There was a door leading into the underbelly of the castle; that was our next goal. I slowly crept to the door and pulled on the latch slowly. I shook my head in disappointment as the door swung open with no noise. A well-oiled door was just asking for trouble. The buildup of rust would have left a squeak, which could have alerted whoever was near to the intruders. Nonetheless, good fortune for us as we all slunk in the back door.

The plan was to take out the men on the way to the main gate and have our allies outside be ready to join in on the fight as soon as we opened the gate. I retied the rags around my feet, making sure they wouldn't slip off after the long crawl outside. I nodded at William and slunk from the room, keeping low.

I cracked the first door I came across and peered inside the room, thankful for the ring I wore, which gave me the ability to produce a glowing light that only I could see. I saw a few bunks and some of the cats sleeping upright in the most ridiculous manner. *Who sleeps like that?*

I slowly drew my sword from its sheath, making sure to make no noise. I sliced through a cat's neck, killing it quickly, and held on to its body as it slumped backwards. The body only lasted a few seconds before it faded to nothing and left a small crystal on the bed. I picked it up and slid it into my bag. Moving from bed to bed, I repeated my actions. When all the cats were neutralized, I turned and walked from the room as William walked out of another, his sword dripping blood. I turned and moved down the hallway, looking for a way to the gate.

The castle's walls were stone blocks that had been almost meticulously laid. The stone was worn smooth from years of wear; the castle's hallways had a weird smell that made me wish for a can of air freshener, if there were such a thing in this world. What bothered me most was the lack of air movement; the castle was hot and stale. I felt sweat dripping down my back and soaking the undershirt; I shifted my shoulders with some irritation at the chafing that was starting.

William looked back at me. I nodded to indicate that I was fine and that we should keep going. Nothing was going to stop me from completing this mission; I didn't want him to think less of me. William's acknowledgment meant something to me; I couldn't let him down.

I took a slow breath and kept moving. I looked at pictures that were hanging on the walls and saw that the stronghold had definitely been in human possession at some point. I tilted my head and looked at the man posing with his family in the painting. He looked familiar to me, but I couldn't place him. I shook my head and kept feeling something nagging at me in the back of my mind. I inwardly groaned; that was going to eat at me for some time. I cleared it from my head and kept moving forward. There was a mission to focus on.

William passed a doorway as it was opening, and a wolf emerged, its teeth bared. It noticed him, stretched its mouth wide, and lunged. Without even thinking, I changed my sword into a whip and cracked it. My thoughts were on only one thing as I watched the wolf's teeth near William's neck—*Don't miss. Save him, please.*

Time seemed to slow down. The air felt thicker somehow as I watched the tip of my weapon; it felt as if I were cutting through a pool of water. William turned slowly and noticed the wolf was about to sink its teeth into him. I heard a gasp behind me, from the men who were not close enough to help their friend. I was angry and frustrated as I watched these events unfold. I felt rage burning inside me, and it was trying to burst forth.

I opened my mouth and screamed an enraged and wounded sound that was equal parts rage and fear as I watched the head of my whip slam into the side of the wolf's head. The force of the blow made the wolf's head jerk back and its mouth slam shut with a loud clack. The wolf burst into flames that were pure white; it screamed for a short while as the intense flames burned so fast that it was reduced to ashes faster than its body could disappear.

I stood there, breathing heavily, and looked at Will, who was walking towards me. "I'm sorry," I whispered.

I heard the castle coming alive around me. They had heard the scream I had loosed and now knew they were being raided.

Will shook his head at me and smiled reassuringly. "You saved me, Eric. What is there to apologize for? I'd be dead now or wounded if not for your quick thinking. Now we must be quick to the gate!"

We turned and sprinted throughout the castle halls. Will was in the lead, his sword over his shoulder, ready to fall on the first soul unfortunate enough to cross his path. I was close on his heels, my sword clenched tightly in hand. We turned a corner, and Will knocked a cat from his path with his arm; the cat screeched as it bounced against the wall and fell to the ground. I leapt over it, leaving it for the men behind me to finish off.

William barreled into a room that was massive. At the other end was a door with a wheel next to it. That had to be it! We began racing to the door just as a figure detached itself from the shadows. It was massive—had to be at least ten feet tall—and covered in thick fur; beneath that moved muscles that spoke of massive strength I couldn't even begin to guess at. It was a bear, something I was told wouldn't be this far from the main force. The bear was armed too, wielding a massive war axe that he held loosely at his side.

Will stopped and stood at the ready. I moved a few paces back, keeping my sword ready to attack.

"What do we have here? An intrusion in my home? My, oh my, aren't you humans BOLD," the bear said. The last word was spoken with such violence and hatred that I actually flinched and stepped back. It felt as if the bear were looking at us as though we were roaches he had found skittering across his kitchen floor.

My mouth dried and felt as if I had eaten sawdust. William just smirked.

"Your home? Like you filthy monsters could ever have made something like this. Humans made this, and humans should be living in it still. The best thing you could ever make is a new coat for the winter," Will said.

The bear growled and pulled his axe into both hands. The bear seemed to blur, and then he was suddenly looming over William, his axe hurtling down to kill him. William's sword batted the axe as he had taught me, not stopping it completely but redirecting it. But from the one hit and the look on William's face, I knew this would be a losing battle.

I ran to the back of the bear, switched my sword to a whip, and cracked it at the bear's back. Almost too smoothly, the bear's axe slammed into Will's sword and then was brought back around his head, slapping the whip away before it even hit him. I cracked the whip again as Will cut at the bear's feet.

The bear slammed the head of the axe into the ground, stopping the cut from landing, and he used the momentum to do a forward flip, bringing the axe with him to cut Will. The flip moved the bear out of the range of my whip, which cracked uselessly in the air.

I turned quickly; I had been too focused on the skirmish and had missed the cats approaching me from behind. I bit my lip, pointed my fingers like a gun, and whispered "bang" as a torrent of flame leapt from my hands, bathing the cats in fire. I cracked my whip, putting them down while they were distracted.

Turning back to William and the bear, I watched for a moment as the bear rained down blows on William, whose sword was as fluid as water as he deflected every blow. Spinning, jumping, and slashing, Will was doing everything he could to find some way to bring the bear down.

I sprinted for the door and pulled the lever next to the wheel, dropping the gate with an enormous thud. Men started streaming into the castle and through the doorways to begin the final part of the mission.

"Keep them away from Will and me! There's a bear here, and we can't have you in the way," I yelled.

I turned and sprinted back towards Will as I heard the soldier's call of acknowledgment from over my shoulder. William was cut in several places, his blood dripping slowly down his body. His movements were slowing down. He was a seasoned warrior who had fought in many campaigns in his king's name, but that was against enemies who had nothing on the bear.

I began cracking the whip furiously at the bear's back and feet. The bear looked back at me with disdain and moved from side to side, dodging the blows, and in a smooth movement, he threw a dagger at me. I coiled my blade quickly, knocking the dagger away from me, and missed the bear closing the distance on me. I looked up, my eyes opening wide as the bear lifted a leg and slammed it into my stomach and chest. I was thrown back from the force; I rolled across the floor, came to a stop, and threw up the contents of my stomach, all while trying to regain my breath through abused lungs.

We needed a plan and soon; otherwise, it wouldn't matter who we had in this castle; the bear would simply kill them all. I looked up and saw the bear slam his axe into Will's stomach before wrenching his axe back, grabbing Will by the neck, and tossing him against the wall as he laughed. I groaned, grabbed my stomach, and felt my bag clatter against my side.

My eyes opened wide, and I tore the bag open, reached in, and pulled the ice core out. I slotted it into the sword's hilt. Still laughing, the bear was now approaching me.

"Your friend's over there on the ground, like he belongs. His blood looks good on my floor. Maybe I should have the floors dyed with it," the bear called out.

I groaned weakly, feeling ill. I saw the corners of my vision going black, but held on. I needed to stay awake. I felt the bear's hands close around the back of my neck and lift me from the ground. He smirked in my face and opened his mouth wide, taking his eyes off me!

I slammed my sword into his side and was thrown against the wall for my efforts.

"You disgusting, filthy trash! You stabbed me! I'm going to tear the skin from your body and throw you into the sea!" he roared. He continued threatening me as he stomped over to me.

My eyes were locked on the blade still dangling from his side. *That's right; keep talking; keep threatening; give it more time to work.*

The bear reached down for me again and then stopped. He looked at the blade in his side and watched his fur falling out in an ever-widening circle around the wound. The hair was turning white and brittle before falling in clumps to the ground.

I smiled. It was working; his insides were turning to ice, freezing and solidifying.

The bear screamed and swiped at the blade, trying to pull it from his body, but his hands had become numb and clumsy. He dropped to his knees, continuing to watch the hair fall from his body, before he looked at me. The hate was gone from his eyes; all that was left was fear.

"I don't want to die, not from a human. Not like this," he said.

I stood up, groaning weakly, and stumbled over to the bear's axe. I picked it up and hefted it over my shoulder. "Shatter before me, you filthy beast. You killed my friend," I said sadly. I slammed the axe into his chest with all the strength I had left.

The axe passed through the bear, shattering his body into thousands of pieces. The force of the swing dragged the axe from my hands, and I stumbled, dropping onto my back. I breathed out raggedly and wanted to pass out.

Will! My eyes shot open, and I rolled onto my side, looking for him. I spotted him lying there, across the room, on his back.

I picked myself up, groaning and fighting a wave of nausea, as I trudged over to him. I fell next to him, but lifted myself enough to look at him. William's eyes were closed. I looked him over and saw the plate covering his chest was severely dented. I grabbed the straps, pulled the armor from his body, and saw the axe had never pierced his armor. The blood was from the slashes and cuts he had received.

William's eyes shot open, and he dragged in an enormous breath, his whole body shaking. The dented armor must have been preventing him from breathing. He sat up quickly, looking for the bear, and finally looked down at me.

"Where is the bear? Where has he gone, Eric?!" Will said hurriedly.

I gestured at the frozen shards on the ground. "I killed him, William; he will trouble us no longer," I said wearily.

William's relief was immediate, and he dropped onto his back. I watched his chest heaving from the effort and couldn't help but smile. I knew I was breathing just as raggedly. We had won by the skin of our teeth. Groaning, I fought a wave of nausea and vertigo.

"We have won then. The men can clear out the rest of the filth, and we can reclaim this stronghold," Will said with a smile.

I started to agree with him while standing up. But I was too tired from the battle. I passed out, happy we had won and happy that William was still alive. I don't think I could do this without him.

The last thing I heard as the world spun around me and the inky blackness swirled around me was Will. He was calling for me, worried because I had fallen.

6 Cats, Wolves, and Bears in Another World's Sun

I woke up later in a bed covered in furs. Groaning, I sat up and looked down at my body covered in bandages that, due to the lack of blood and filth on them, must have just recently been changed. I swung my feet off the bed and stumbled from the room. I had to find Will.

I walked the halls until I found one of the soldiers who could take me to Will. He led me back to the room where the bear had been killed. I walked over towards where I had gained victory. I knelt upon seeing the shiny core that had dropped from the bear's body. Before pocketing it, I used my observation skill—just a core from another monster.

That was a boss monster, if I've ever seen one. Should have gotten a new weapon or piece of armor for all that grief. I shook my head at my luck. "Trash loot in this game, I swear," I complained loudly to myself.

I almost laughed when a soldier walking past me looked in my direction as I was complaining. Good luck explaining that one if he had any questions. I turned and saw Will smiling and walking towards.

"You are awake! And so soon, my friend. I expected you to be out for a day at least after that fight."

I smiled as I clasped his arm and patted his shoulder. "I probably should be out. That bear absolutely wrecked me!"

William asked me how I had done it, and I told him about the power of the cores and how my sword could receive the cores and take on attributes from them. I reached down to grab my sword to show him and realized it was gone. Panicked, I looked up.

But it seemed Will had read my mind. Smiling he reached behind his back and brought out the sword. "My apologies, Eric, I had you sent straight to the infirmary after you passed out. I picked your sword up afterwards."

I thanked him for keeping an eye on the weapon. My skill activated and notified me the core was spent and should be removed from the blade. Taking it, I twisted the bottom of the pommel, ejected the core, and watched the blackened ball fall to the ground. Frowning, I reached down, picked up the core, and watched it start cracking. *Theres a limit to how many times you can use a core before it expends all of its energy.* I sheathed my sword, shrugged, and explained it to Will.

"Shame, we could have used it in the days to come, for sure," he said before bidding me farewell. He had more work to do in the reclamation of the castle, including checking to see if anything of value remained hidden anywhere within.

William tasked a man to guide me to get something to eat before I was put to bed. I needed to rest to regain my strength and to heal my wounded body.

Everywhere I went, I was given a hearty cheer from the other warriors and hailed as a hero. Taking a bear out was almost worthy of godhood, it seemed, and I understood that. From talking to some of the warriors, I found that there were only a few people who had ever killed a bear, and they had all been made kings after the feat; that included the current king. I was filled with a new level of respect for the man and couldn't help but wonder how strong he was. Will, who was considered one of the king's top warriors, had been beaten almost effortlessly by the bear. I had only won because of a cheap trick. Without that core, we would all be dead, and the king would be wide-open to a counterattack.

I accepted the bowl of stew from the cook and thanked him before tucking in and eating. When sated, I put my bowl to the side and grabbed my bag, opening it looking at the wolf's crystal I had picked up. Now that I had time to look at it, my skill activated and notified me that the crystal was used to increase the power of a hero's weapon. I held the crystal to my sword and watched it absorb the crystal and glow. I noticed nothing new or different; I used my observation skill, but found no new information. I shrugged. *Probably need multiple crystals before it can be upgraded.*

I groaned; the aches were spreading throughout my body. I started to stand; that was a mistake—pain tore its way throughout my body with such a force that I let out a bark of anguish.

Jake, one of the men near me, leapt to his feet, grabbed me, and held me steady.

"Please take me back to my room. I need to rest and sleep this off."

Jake picked me up as if I were a child and carried me to my room, navigating the castle hallways as though he had lived there all his life.

I passed out before I was placed in my bed. I dreamed of my home. It was not a good dream, as I remembered the man who claimed to have raised and saved me. He stood over me, yelling that I was worthless and a thorn in his side who just ate his food and took up space. I responded by looking up at him and angrily shouting that I'd saved myself and a friend today. His answering glare made me think he had actually heard me. When he accused me of leaving him alone as he was dying, I shook my head. He had been sick when I died, but that was his own fault. He had been a drunk and a smoker most of his life. It had finally caught up with him.

It was ironic that he blamed me for leaving him to die; I was the first to go. The only thing that I had wanted to do was help people. I didn't regret dying while trying to help that woman, and he would never make me feel guilty for being there for others.

I smiled at him and turned my back. I didn't need this anymore. I had friends, in a new life, who needed me, and I wouldn't let them down by being dragged down by the past. In the dream, I walked forward and kicked open the door to the bedroom. As it swung open, so did my eyes. I was greeted by the familiar sight of the castle's ceiling, followed by lances of pain shooting through my stomach.

I grabbed my side and massaged it slowly, trying to remove some of the stiffness that persisted. I finally gathered enough willpower to roll out of bed, and begin gathering my clothes. *I should find Will and find out what is next.* I left the room and started walking down the hall.

The castle had a faint stench to it, like that of a wet animal, which wasn't pleasant. I wrinkled my nose, shook my head, and kept walking. The sooner we left this place, the better. Honestly, it was starting to make my stomach feel unsettled.

I limped along the stone floors till I found my way outside and took a deep breath of the fresh air. Turning, I followed the wall of the castle, my mind replaying the fight with the bear and grimacing at how close it had been. There were things out there far stronger than I; if I was going to protect my friends and myself, I needed more power.

I had been zoned out for a while as I walked, so I didn't notice that I had found the castle gardens. The first thing that brought me back to awareness was the smell; then I looked around and started noticing all of the beautiful flowers. I made my way to the middle of the gardens, hobbling slowly, to lie down on a wooden bench. Lying there, I groaned as I massaged my sides and inhaled the crisp air filled with floral scents. I took time to really look at the flowers; there were blue flowers shaped like trumpets and red ones shaped like boxes. Yellow flowers were opening and closing like butterfly wings and fluttering in the wind. This place was beautiful and very relaxing; I even found a flower that looked like a DNA spiral. I closed my eyes, inhaled the scent of the flowers, and started nodding off again.

I woke up after some time had passed and felt much better, which was weird. The pain in my side had pretty much abated, and my hip felt much looser. However, it did feel as if there was something sitting on my chest. I opened my eyes to find a small creature doing exactly that. The creature resembled an axolotl covered in sparse downy fur; it had large black eyes, which followed mine and seemed to take up a good amount of its head, and small gill-like extensions on its head. I looked further and noticed it had six legs and a tail; its legs were splayed out and covered a good portion of my torso.

I used my observation skill—a bupo. They were healers and could sense bodily distress and come to aid those in pain, giving them good dreams and filling their bodies with warmth to aid the recovery process.

I smiled and whispered, "Tame."

The bupo shivered happily as the tame took effect, and he became connected to me.

"Hello, little guy, welcome to the party. Let's get along, okay?" I smiled and pet the soft fur along his head as he chirped happily, nuzzling against my hand. I stood up hesitantly and then breathed out a prayer of thanks to the god for the lack of pain. After taking a moment to look back and appreciate the garden once more, I headed to the infirmary to see if my little friend and I could help the other injured warriors.

I ran back through the grounds of the castle and enjoyed once more the pain-free movement. The little bupo chirped happily on my shoulder.

"Eric! Over here!" Will called.

I turned and saw him waving from nearby, so I changed my course to head his way. "What do you need from me, my friend?"

Will glanced over at me and noticed both my new friend and how I wasn't limping anymore. "My friend, you are whole once more! What glorious news! I am glad to see you are no longer suffering from our fight with that monster. However, we have little time to celebrate your recovery."

Will began telling me that there was no time to lose. We needed to head out immediately. I was to pack and meet up with the soldiers' caravan outside the wall in a half hour; they'd almost left me behind due to the severity of my injuries. Our mission was to destroy the enemy's nearby fort and then proceed along the route so the main force met no resistance. Will had received a letter from the king; they had taken out the city, but the fight had been horrendous. In the city, there had been three bears that the king took out by himself.

I did a double take and shook my head. *The king is insane.*

Will noticed my look and smiled. "Go pack. Hurry along now, Eric. We must move with haste, or we will bring my king shame."

I turned and sprinted to my room. While packing, I wondered, *When did I start considering Will's king mine as well? When did I start caring about bringing him shame?* I shook my head; it didn't matter at this point. I considered them my friends, and I would fight for them and their homes against the monsters that would take it all, including their lives, from them.

The caravan was slowly moving through the countryside, which was not a huge issue as we were still moving a good deal faster than the king's main army; they were still recovering from their siege on the city. I continued my training with Will and was pleased to find that after my battle with the bear, my skill with the blade had grown immensely. It was almost as if having your life on the line were just the thing to make your skills grow by leaps and bounds.

I also took the time to practice my flame-manipulation magic—casting fireballs and throwing them around, one after the other, and making them larger and smaller. I cast a flamethrower to practice generating a stream of fire that could go from a wide river of flame to a smaller, more concentrated beam of fire. Practicing my magic also made my internal battery grow larger to accommodate the amount of magic I was expending.

From what I could tell, there was an energy tier for magic. I had begun at miniscule and was now sitting at average. That was a pretty large upgrade from where I had been a while ago—almost dead from fighting goblins in a cave. I smiled and clenched my fist, covering a fireball. I was growing stronger, and I liked what I was seeing.

I turned from the crest of the hill on which I was standing and started walking through a clearing that interested me; I was curious about what was on the other side of it. I loved exploring places in this new world, but I looked around cautiously. Currently, this was still Oceans Guild territory, so I needed to be careful. I could fall victim to an ambush, and that would be less than satisfactory.

I made my way through the clearing and found myself standing at the entrance of a dark forest. I scratched my head slowly and considered—either go alone, or go back and get Will and some of the soldiers. I sighed and started walking into the forest alone. *This is probably a mistake, but nothing ventured, nothing gained, right?*

I smiled and started making my way through the trees. Spots like these radiated energy that screamed, "Dungeon," and any little bit of loot would help—maybe a new piece of armor or a weapon. Something that would help me fight off these monsters. Squinting, I looked around and raised my hand to conjure a hard-light ball that I set to stay above my head. That ring of light wasn't enough here; I needed more light than the hard-light ball could give me. Nonetheless, with the hard-light ball settled into its place above my head, enough of the darkness was pushed back so that the way ahead was revealed.

The path felt long, but that was probably due more to the internal anxiety I felt from traveling alone down the path. *What am I going to find down here?* I stepped out of the forest and into an abandoned city. There were a lot of those here in this world, I'd noticed. This, however, was different from the other abandoned places I had found; it was made from crystal. I walked up to the nearest building and then around it, looking up and down. I couldn't see through its exterior walls because of all the different shapes and facets of its unique shape.

I reached out, placed my hand on the structure, and felt how cool it was to the touch. I pulled my hand back and started looking for an entrance into the building so that I could start exploring. After a lot of touching and prodding, I finally found a slot built into the crystal structure. What looked like a card protruded from the slot; when pushed, the card-like device slid into the wall, and a door opened.

I walked into the crystal building and started looking around. There wasn't a lot inside, nothing to give away what the structure was. Maybe it was a house; maybe it was a storage building. I couldn't tell. So I exited the structure and walked from building to building, trying to find something that would give me an inkling as to what kind of place I had found, besides the fact that it was an abandoned crystal town.

After walking through the town for about an hour, I started getting tired. I wasn't finding anything worth writing home about. The buildings were empty crystal structures. The best things here were the structures themselves, and even that had lost its luster after the first half hour. I needed something that could help with the fight, not a tourist trap.

I ran my hands through my hair, groaned, turned my attention to the last few buildings, and started towards them. I already knew I wasn't going to find anything, but if I didn't at least look inside them, it would nag at me for the rest of my life. So I sighed and pulled open the door of one of the remaining unexplored buildings, walked inside, and started looking from corner to corner for anything useful.

I took a moment to at least be thankful that the buildings were empty; I didn't have to search through countless boxes or cargo, only to find nothing useful. I still stomped from building to building, right up to the final large building of the area.

I slammed open its door and started to enter…but froze, my hand still on the door, when I saw a crystal cyclops turning to look at me, its giant red eye glaring at me from its surrounding blue-crystal body. As it moved, its entire body creaked; it sounded as if glass were cracking. Its maw gaped and revealed a mouth full of shards of crystal and ropes of what I could only assume was liquid crystal.

I smiled softly and very slowly closed the door. Then, even slower, backed up a few steps, turned, and walked away. "Nope, I'm okay. That thing looks terrifying," I said aloud to myself as I continued to shake my head. *All these empty buildings, and the last one's holding that monstrosity? That's horrifying. The stuff of nightmares.*

The building behind me exploded as the cyclops screamed and destroyed the entrance in its clambering frenzy to pursue me.

I shuddered unhappily and reached for my sword. I didn't like this at all. I sighed and started running towards the cyclops just as its eye started glowing a deep crimson red. I feinted left and then jumped and rolled to my right as it shot off a beam of light. The beam left a crystal crater in the ground. I ground my teeth. *I definitely don't want to get hit by that.*

I swung my sword, flicking my wrist so that it turned into a whip and hurtled at the cyclops's eye; I watched it crack against its head.

The cyclops's head jerked back. It looked at me, screamed again, and ran at me with its arms outstretched, ready to grab me.

I groaned. *So that was completely ineffective.* I raised my other hand, cast a fireball, trying for offensive magic instead, and lobbed it against the cyclops's chest. I watched the fire wash over it and noticed its crystal belt was starting to slightly drip. I smiled. *Everything has a melting point.*

Rolling past the monster's outstretched hands, I sheathed my sword, stretched out my hands, and bathed them both in fire. I folded all but the first two fingers on each hand to concentrate the flames as much as possible; then I hurled two flamethrower streams directly at the cyclops's chest. The cyclops groaned and extended a hand in front of the flames, trying to block them, so I aimed one of my hands at its legs, which were thinner than its torso, and started severing the legs from its body.

I smiled as the beast fell to its knee. The crystal was melting slowly, however. I gasped for breath and started praying that the cyclops would melt before I ran out of magic. Fire was the only effective weapon against this thing; my sword wasn't able to deal with something as hard as the cyclops's crystal.

"Come on, die. Just die already, please!" I shouted. I pushed the last of my magic from my body and dropped to my knees in front of the crystal cyclops, watching as it dripped in small rivers in front of me. The cyclops groaned, reached for me with one of its arms, and hissed as its arm dropped from its body, the melted joints no longer able to support its weight.

I laughed wearily as its body continued melting. I had won...barely. I dropped onto my back as the cyclops became a puddle; the only thing left was its eye, which went from red to a dull brown, and then even it shut down and died.

Groaning, I sucked air back into my lungs and heard a small chirp as the little bupo climbed out of the back of my armor and settled on my chest, spreading himself out. I smiled as I reached up and petted him.

"I didn't get hurt, Just a little low on my magic, buddy. I'll be okay. Just need to recharge."

He chirped softly and seemed almost sad that he couldn't help me. He slunk off my chest and back into his hiding spot in my armor. I smiled; he was a cute little guy.

I rolled onto my side, pushed myself up slowly, and coughed, fighting off a wave of vertigo. I groaned as the magic sickness washed over me. Forcing myself to my feet, I made my way back into the building that the cyclops had been guarding and started looking around. *There's no way there isn't a piece of loot in here. Had a whole boss battle and everything.*

Searching the entire building from top to bottom resulted in finding two knives made from the same crystal from which the buildings were made. Using my observation skill, I found that the crystal knives had a unique ability—anytime I threw them, they used my mana and warped back to my hands. *Throwing knives I don't have to pick up after throwing them! Not bad loot.* I smiled as I wrapped the knife sheath around my waist, glad that the whole trip hadn't been a complete waste of my time.

I turned and started making my way back to the caravan. I had been gone for some time, and I bet Will would be wondering where I was. As I stepped out of the clearing, I met Will and a small search party; they were getting ready to start the search for me. I raised an eyebrow at him questioningly. I hadn't been gone that long—only about two hours, maybe three.

"Where have you been?! What happened to you, Eric?!" He sounded more than a little upset.

I gestured behind me and smiled. "I found a small dungeon. I cleared it and found some useful weapons that will help us in the fight against the Oceans Guild. What's wrong; why are you so upset with me? I was only gone for a few hours. We are supposed to spend the next two days here until we receive word from the main group to push the fort, aren't we?" I said, trying to calm him.

Will cocked his head at me and shook it a few times. "Eric, you have been gone for a week. The dungeon must have altered your sense of time. But, for us, you have been missing seven days. The main force has just started their move from the city; the toll they took was worse than we thought. Thankfully, that gave us more time than we had originally planned."

I couldn't believe it. A whole week? That was insane. I didn't know that dungeons could distort time like that. I sighed and rubbed my head; no wonder I was tired.

"Will, I'm sorry. I didn't mean to disappear on you like that. Next time I find a dungeon, I will let you know. I wasn't aware they could alter time like that."

Will accepted the apology, and we returned with the entire group to the main caravan. The next day was going to be busy.

***

I rolled from my cot and looked outside; the sun was starting to rise. I grabbed a small pale of water and a rag to wash the sweat from my body before I strapped on the armor and weapons. Today was the day that we took the fort. The last fort before the final city. I smiled; hopefully, this massive dungeon was coming to an end, and I would soon be able to go back to my farm and see how it was coming along. I also wanted to get the dwarven forge up and running again. Now that the dungeon would be cleared of any hostile creatures, I could learn how to smith and process some metals to ease my farming burdens.

I shook my head and focused. I had to survive this dungeon first; these monsters were nothing to scoff at. They were dangerous, and I was having a very hard time with them.

I walked from the tent to the cooks' area, sure they'd be preparing food. I was going to grab a quick meal for Will and me. We could eat as we planned the assault—by that, I meant he planned it, and I did as he asked. I smelled the cook station long before I got to it—the fresh loaves of bread being pulled from the ovens, the boar being roasted and spun over a spit. My stomach growled in anticipation. I strolled up, grabbed two metal plates, and gave to the chefs the orders for Will and me.

The chef looked up at me and smiled. He gave me large portions and said, "Good luck today, mage, and thank you for the help you have given us."

I smiled back, returned the thanks, and hurried to Will's tent. I set the food down on the table that was outside his tent and called out to him. His finely tuned warrior senses must have heard me approaching his tent because as I reached out to hit against a pole of his tent, he strode through the flap.

"I am awake, my friend. No need to knock."

We sat down, ate our food, and discussed what he and his advisors had already gone over while I had been missing. This fort was nowhere near as big as the castle had been, so there was no need for a stomach crawl in the middle of the night to gain a tactical advantage. His warriors were going to be approaching from the front on horses armored with heavy shields to ward off bolts and arrows. I was going to come in from the back; my only mission was taking people out stealthily and thinning the numbers of the enemy before the fighting actually started. When the fighting did start, I was free to fight as I wished. My only mission then was not to get killed.

I told William that was easier said than done. After wiping the grease from my hands, I reached out and grasped his forearm.

"Be well, my friend. I'll see you on the field," he said.

I stood, picked up our plates, and returned them to the cleaners before I went to the edge of the forest to start scouting out the enemy's fort. I squinted, trying to pick out a spot from which I could approach. The main army would be coming from the south. Directly behind the fort, the forest line came a bit close; I could approach from there and sneak up by climbing the wall and dropping in from there. That was the best course of action that I could think of.

I heard sticks cracking behind me, so I pulled my daggers from their sheaths, spun, and held them up in a ready-to-fight position. Turns out, I was the one who had been scouted. *What a clumsy mistake.* There were two cats, swords drawn and ready; they hissed at me, ready to pounce. I inhaled slowly, drawing a deep breath in preparation for the skirmish.

The cat to my left leapt forward, and I threw my blade quickly. Reaching down, I grabbed my sword and drew it before the dagger hit its mark, taking the beast by surprise as the knife sliced its thigh. The wound was shallow, though, and didn't do much damage. But it was enough to stop the cat in its tracks long enough for me to twist my sword into its whip form and send it cracking through the air at the other cat.

The cat leapt forward, grabbed the whip, and tried to pull it from my hands. I smirked as I activated the weapon's new ability; the whip spun to life like a chainsaw and quickly cut through the cat's hand. I jerked the whip back to my side and flung my dagger at the cat who was now staring at its stump. The dagger flew through the air swiftly and struck the cat in the side of its chest with a dull thump. The cat groaned and dropped to its knees.

I didn't stop to celebrate; there was one more cat left. I turned in time to see it charging towards me. I tried to dodge, but I couldn't move in time. The side of the cat's shoulder hit me, and I was flung several feet backwards; my sword was knocked from my hands. I rolled to my feet and looked up at the cat; it had its lips pulled back into a weird approximation of a smile.

I held my hands up in surrender, doing my best to look as if I were giving up. The cat growled softly as it stalked towards me. It circled me to be sure I was not concealing any weapons; then it faced me and started grabbing me. As I jumped and latched on to him in a bear hug, I repeatedly cast fireballs and flameflowers. I felt the cat beneath me; its muscles rippled as it tried to throw me off. I didn't stop until I felt the cat cease moving; then I let go and watched its withered body until it faded.

I shuddered. Of course, there would be scouts out here; we were near a fort. It was such a bad mistake on my part; I wanted to bang my head on a tree. I picked up my sword and sheathed it before flexing my hands and warping the daggers back into them. I did a quick glance at the forest floor and smiled—two upgrade crystals. I quickly scooped them up and pulled my sword back out. Leaning against the tree, I fed the two crystals into the whip sword and watched it start changing.

It was still a whip sword, but its appearance changed. It no longer looked like a normal sword; the blade took on a more glassy shine, to the point of being almost translucent, and the hilt turned blue. I used the observation skill. Information had been added to the original description of the whip sword.

> *Its evolved form comes from the grace of those who have given their lives for others. Its cutting ability is levels above all others, and its whip form produces greater impact damage.*

I put it away; that was just what I needed for the upcoming battle. This sword was going to help.

Now that I had chosen my hiding place, all I had to do was wait for the main assault to take place. I knelt in the brush to make sure I would remain unseen.

Watching Will and his battle group come around a hill in heavy armor was awe-inspiring. I smiled. My friend looked glorious in full armor, and threatening too; I wouldn't want to be those animals hiding in the fort right now.

I waited until the Oceans Guild began firing arrows before commencing my approach to the fort. A good deal of it was covered by the brush and trees that the beasts had grown too lazy to clear over the years. Even if I didn't have ground cover in which to hide, though, it wouldn't have mattered; everyone's attention was completely focused on the approaching army.

The fort's outer wall was made from wooden poles tied together and dug into the ground. I took out my daggers, wedged them in between the poles, and started climbing my way up and over the walls. When I got to the top, I took a moment to look around and check the area out. There was a cat below me, but other than that, it appeared that everyone else was on the other side of the fort, dealing with the approaching army.

I pulled my sword and dropped off the wall and onto the cat's back, driving my sword into its neck and dispatching it cleanly. I looked but found no crystal this time. Turning, I started making my way through the fort, searching for the Oceans Guild soldiers. The cats were everywhere. I looked around slowly before moving behind one of the cats and pushing my sword through its back. I watched it slump over and fall before fading from existence.

The new upgrade was really working wonders; even from behind, the blade was going right through the cats. I didn't even try to fool myself that bears would be easier to kill; those things were monsters, and I would gladly leave them to the king.

I cocked my head and heard footsteps running close by. I dove into a nearby building and peeked out of the doorway to see what was approaching. A wolf, probably the one running this show. I had killed wolves before; they were not that strong.

The wolf stopped its running on a dime and lifted its snout into the air, pausing to sniff. It growled low in its throat, looked around, and then bent low to the ground.

I rolled my eyes. Of course, it would have a great sense of smell, but how dare it use it right now while its whole fort was under attack.

The wolf started sniffing the ground and following my scent to the building. It pushed the door open, snout first. I saw its head coming through the door and had a great idea; I hoped it worked. I took my sword and drove it, tip first, downward into its skull, hoping I was strong enough to drive it through the skull and praying the upgrade was enough to provide the penetration needed.

As the blade drove clean through, pinning the wolf to the ground, I blew a whoosh of air from my lungs, breathing a sigh of relief. I watched the wolf fade; then I pulled the sword from the ground before leaning against the wall for a moment. I'd had visions of a boss battle; this was a relief.

Leaning out from the doorway, I took a peek around. No one was coming, so I closed the door and checked the ground where the wolf had been, looking for any materials that could have been dropped. There was a pair of pants on the ground. Armor made from wolf skin—the stats were better on it, and it was lighter than the actual armor I was wearing.

I took a moment to switch out my armor and stuffed the old armor into my inventory. Then I turned from the room and walked out of the building, towards where everyone had started running. I had a job to do, and Will was counting on me.

I had to take the enemy out from behind and start thinning their numbers. With no bears here at the moment, the fight would be a lot easier than the one in the castle. I palmed my daggers and looked around the corner. When my body shuddered, I realized I was holding my breath, so I forcibly exhaled and then pulled more air in. When I had regulated my airflow, I turned the corner and found a solo cat pulling on a cart of arrows and bolts; it seemed headed towards the main gate.

I dashed forward and jumped into the air, driving my daggers into the cat's back on my descent. One of the daggers went into its back and the other into its heart. The cat started writhing, which startled me; it should be dropping. I definitely pierced its heart. I charged the daggers with fire and poured it into the cat; that finally made it stop moving and drop.

I crouched, looked around, and sheathed the daggers before turning and spotting a bow. I smiled, grabbed it and a quiver for the arrows, and slung them on my back. I jumped up, pulled myself onto a nearby building, and started moving from rooftop to rooftop, thankful they were the square-top kind, not the angled ones.

Soon I found the rest of the fort's war party; they were busy fighting off Will's attack. I readied my bow, nocked an arrow onto the string, drew the arrow back, and pulled.

I channeled the hard light onto the head of the arrow, making it glow golden. The arrow now could cut through most things. I needed more though—more power—if I was going to be firing into the entire throng of creatures. I added a fireball onto the arrow and felt a new spell being made. I smiled. *An explosive sun arrow, this is going to be fun.*

I aimed at the cat in the middle of the pack and loosed the arrow, watching it move almost in slow motion, glowing like a beacon in the sun as it sailed over a row of houses before sinking into the back of a cat that had been loading another bolt into its crossbow. The cat had a moment to reach back for the arrow before it was consumed by a ball of fire over six feet across; that was both violent and ferocious.

My eyes went wide as I glanced at the bow; this was wild. I grabbed another arrow and started aiming for more knots of cats standing together, but after the first one went up in flames, they started taking cover and not standing together. I just started raining arrows down on the cats and watching the balls of fire spread. Even if I couldn't see the cats, I knew their general area, and I could still hit them from around a corner due to bow's area of effect.

I grinned ear to ear as I watched the fireballs. I reached for another arrow, only to find I was out. I sighed. *There goes my fun.* I stuck my bow into my inventory, along with the quiver, so it didn't get in my way while climbing down from my perch.

Will had noticed the lull in the arrows and bolts being fired at him and his men, so he charged the gate quickly; he was already there, battering at the gates. He had men climbing the walls and fighting back the cats who were slow, not to mention wary of going back to the gates, lest more of the fireballs rained down on them.

I joined Will's men and helped them in pushing the cats back. The gate was thrown open, and the rest of the men poured in. From there, it was a simple task to go from building to building and clear the cats out.

When I next saw Will, he was scratching his head and looking a little worried. "What's wrong, Will? This fight was pretty easy, wasn't it?"

Will nodded and was still looking around as if he were reluctant to take his eyes off the area. "Yes, it was, Eric. Too easy. There were only cats around here. Didn't you notice? Nothing of a higher intelligence to guide them and lead the way, nothing at all," he said warily.

I laughed and rubbed the back of my head. "Well, Will, that's because I killed the wolf before you got in here," I said with a smile.

Will looked over at me with his eyebrow raised, before tilting his head back and laughing. "Why am I not surprised, my friend? You are a one of a kind at killing bears, wolves, and cats."

"Oh my," I mumbled. I smiled to myself; he'd reminded me of a saying from an old movie back in my world.

Will clapped me on my back, turned, and walked away, calling over his shoulder that he was going to get washed up and get some food.

I smiled as I followed him. That was a great idea.

Sitting by the fire later that night, I was stretched out with a cup of mulled cider made from crushed apples. The drink warmed me, and I sighed happily, feeling the cider pool in the pit of my stomach. I grinned. This was a drink Will had made for me; it was a reward for having taken the wolf out; they weren't bears, but they definitely were nothing to scoff at either. Wolves were strong, smart, and cunning. Will had laughed at how easily I had killed it and how fortunate I had been in getting in a lucky blow. Usually, it took a whole squad to kill a wolf, or a strike from behind while it was distracted, as had happened in the castle. The strong could usually take them out one-on-one. Will could do it, and he reasoned that at this point, I could too, especially after how strong I had become—that and my advantage with magic.

I hadn't realized I was zoning out till Will sat next to me. He was holding a few plates piled high with skewers of bacon steaks. I took the plate, thanked him, and started eating happily while sipping my drink. I was eating too fast, though, and started choking, coughing harshly as the meat was caught at the back of my throat.

Will smacked my back a few times, helping me clear my throat. "Easy now, Eric; slow down. It's not going anywhere, my friend," he said with an easy smile.

He ripped a piece from his own skewer and chewed it slowly. "Be a shame if the great warrior who goes around killing the mighty wolves and bears was brought low by a simple bacon steak," he said with a smirk.

I laughed and turned away, grabbing some more cider. I hated choking on food; it made my chest hurt. I set my plate aside and looked at the fire, watching the flames dance and feeling its warmth. How wonderful it was to be able to camp in this place. I closed my eyes and watched the shapes of the flames' dance through my eyelids.

I opened my eyes, suddenly curious. "Will, do you have any family?"

Will stopped chewing, set his skewer down, and closed his eyes for a few moments.

I felt as if I had asked something I shouldn't have. "Look, I'm sorry. You don't have to answer that if it's too much trouble," I said quickly.

Will shook his head slowly and opened his eyes as he turned to me. "Eric…did you see any of the pictures hanging in the castle where we killed the bear?"

I thought back and remembered the familiar face. Understanding began to dawn; the familiar face was his. When he was younger. He had looked like a teenager in those pictures, but with how long they lived, who knew how old he really was. The Will in front of me looked around thirty, but he very well could be over a hundred years old.

"I did. That was you in those photos as a younger man?"

Will nodded and took a sip of his cider before he began. "That was before the war with the Oceans Guild started. I was actually eighteen in that picture when it was painted. I had my family young. My wife, her name was Nina. My two children, Joma and Prayla. They were everything to me. I was a duke to the king; I was appointed the title because of our friendship."

I sat there listening; my heart had already dropped. I had not missed his use of the past tense while he was talking. His family was dead. I was sad for my friend and felt an overwhelming desire to cause the Oceans Guild more harm than I had before. I'm sure his story was a common one among the humans fighting for their lives, and I hated that.

"Just five years later, the first bears began showing up and causing disturbances. They were few and far between and in far-off regions. The people who had survived the attacks sounded like madmen—'Bears attacked us. Huge monsters standing on two feet and holding weapons. They called us insects.' We didn't believe them, of course; we thought they had perhaps had too much to drink, or were eating hallucinatory plants they had found in the forest. When people kept showing up with that same story, though, we had to start considering the possibility that maybe there was some truth to it."

I was enraptured. I could only imagine what that had been like. It sounded like the beginning of a zombie invasion, one in which no one wanted to believe that the zombies were coming till it was too late.

"Word reached the king of these events, and he sent a war party to investigate the claims. I was not part of it, thank the heavens. Not a single one of them returned, and the king finally started taking the threat of these monsters seriously, as did the rest of us.

"The nobles gathered their armies and marched. I had never seen so many of us, Eric. Hundreds of thousands of us marching together under flags of every house and castle known to man. Going to face down this threat. But it was too late, Eric. The Oceans Guild had already formed and swept us aside.

"Some humans are born naturally talented and able to fight. Those of us born with those talents survived the next few weeks. The king died, and we were left without a leader as those animals marched through us. One bear goes down, and another takes his place. A king goes down, and it takes months for us to recover."

My eyes widened at hearing the king had died. I thought that the king I'd met had reigned all this time.

"The king you know now is the original's son. The original king was a natural-born champion who gained his valor on the field of battle. When his son showed up on the field, against the advisors' wishes, everyone rallied around him. He was a force of nature, Eric; he was everywhere on the field, it seemed, all at once. A bear rose in front of him, and it was struck down. No one had ever seen anything like it. He was humanity's hero.

"But he was only one man. He could never make enough headway for anything to work in our favor. Once he appeared, we entered into a deadlock, having skirmishes and yearly battles, testing the waters and seeing if one or the other could gain an advantage. You saw how far we had been pushed back. How far humanity had fallen before our savior took to the field." Will looked up at me, his eyes shining with the pain from a freshly opened wound.

"I was on the field with my king when I heard the news; we had been fighting for hours when a messenger rode beside us. We had just repelled a wave of the Oceans Guild forces. The messenger called out, 'My King, the castle at Locala has fallen.' The Oceans Guild had claimed it. Oh, Eric, I knew what it meant the moment it happened. The Oceans Guild spared no human who meant nothing to their victory. They killed my family," Will finished.

I exhaled slowly; not knowing what to say, I just stared into the fire. Poor Will, going through that must have been awful. I couldn't even imagine. I stood up and left Will to sit by the fire with his memories. It didn't seem as if he wanted to talk anymore.

I had already started to walk away when I heard his voice call out softly behind me, "Eric?"

"Yes, Will?"

"Would you take me with you? Take me from this world and back to yours? A world where I don't have to see the place where my family was murdered?" he asked in a small voice.

I felt my heart drop and turned to him. "Well, if it's in my power, I will take you with me. Even if I have to talk to the god himself for you."

Will looked up at me and nodded a few times before thanking me. He bade me good night and walked away, presumably to go to bed.

I walked to the building that had been given to me for sleep. It was going to be a long night. We had a few days left until the main army got here from wherever they were staying. That would give us time to rest and recover from the fighting. I lay in my bed and closed my eyes; sleep would be nice.

Sleep would have been nice. A lot of things would have been nice, really. But that was not to be. I was woken by the sound of my door crashing down, and a cat yowling as it barreled into my room. My heart clenched in my chest, and I thought I was in a nightmare for a moment. The cat's eyes latched on to me quickly, and it leapt at me. I pulled my hands up and used a hard-light barrier into which the cat slammed. I squinted, trying to shake off the drowsy feeling. I cast a fireball, and the cat died quickly. I must have gotten stronger from the fighting yesterday.

I ran outside with my sword in hand and looked around. It was chaos; there were flames in the street and animals running around with swords in their hands. Will's men were being cut down. I ran forward wielding my sword, which was in constant flux—sword, whip, swing, cut, slash, sting. I grunted angrily, as every animal I cut down just made me angrier.

Why are they here? Why now?

I looked around, trying to find Will. Trying to find anyone. All the men near me were dead; I couldn't save anyone. I started running through the streets, trying to find someone…anyone.

I grabbed a wolf from behind; it had stopped to bite into the throat of a naked man. I stabbed into its spine before throwing it to the side. I turned from the dead man, closing my eyes sadly. This man, I actually knew—not well, but I knew him enough. His name was Jake. He had helped me, had even carried me to my room after my first bear fight.

I ran from building to building, trying to find anyone I could. I was alone. I killed any animals I could find; most of them were cats. There were so many of them; I kept finding them in ones and twos. I finally walked out into a street slowly and found what must have been the main army of the attackers.

I also found Will. He was bloodied, but still fighting and working his way through the enemy. He was not wearing any armor. Like the rest of us, he had been caught unaware, probably while he was asleep.

I ran forward to join him, only to be met by cats. They slashed at me, and I parried, driving my blade forward into one's mouth. I pulled back and summoned a dagger before throwing it wildly, not aiming it, but just trying to cause any damage that I could. I moved forward quickly, slicing and slashing with my blade. The cats quickly realized that my blade was not normal. It was cutting too viciously. Before me, their blades were rent, dented, bent, and pushed away, all by the hero's blade.

I looked around and spotted Will. He was still doing his best, his enormous sword slashing wildly and taking out cats and wolves alike.

Men were coming from the houses—some covered in blood, some in armor, some in various stages of undress, some bandaged, some missing arms. All of them were pissed.

I grinned. These animals, who came in to drown the humans like an ocean, were now going to be scorched by the soul and the burning passion, like the burning sun, that we all had raging down inside.

I roared a war cry, pointed both hands at the approaching cats, and cast a flamethrower. From both hands, jets of flames bathed the opposing forces. The cats yowled, and the wolves let out a mixture of howling and screaming. A large number of them dropped.

The men who saw this smiled, roared with me, and charged in to do battle, swords drawn, ready to fight to the last to put these animals down where they belonged. I grinned wildly, running with them as they caught up with me and leapt back into the fight.

We raged against the animals for what felt like hours. Bodies piled up in the streets. Will had disappeared somewhere, leaving me with the men in the streets, but I could tell we were losing this fight. The animals kept pouring in from somewhere, and the men were being beaten back. I looked around, taking a moment to breath before leaping forward and slashing down harshly. The cut I let loose severed a cat in two. I turned, saw a cluster of cats, and pointed, casting fireballs. I saw them scatter while their bodies twisted under the intense flames.

I grunted in pain as a cat's claws slashed down my chest and left a bloody trail; I stabbed it in the chest as repayment. I wish I had my armor; that would have been nice. I sighed softly as I looked at the bloody marks on my chest and all around me. There were no men left now. Only the horde of animals, all looking at me.

I smiled at them with no small amount of insanity and giggled. I saw one of the wolves flinch and take a step back. *Good, fear me. In a second, you're going to have every reason to.*

I abandoned every thought of survival. Instead, I thought of Will, probably dead, on the ground somewhere beneath the press of bodies. I thought of Jake, his throat ripped out. I felt a tear roll down my face as I summoned a dagger into my off hand and looked at the animals who had surrounded me.

"Well, come along now. I don't have all night now, you ugly varmints. I'm going to show you how bright the sun burns in my world!" I yelled.

I leapt forward swinging my sword and catching a cat's jaw. Turning on a dime, I swung my sword wildly, expecting them to come closing in to try to stab at me. I extended my fingers, blasting them with a flamethrower as I spun, moving like a flame and spinning like a top. Animals caught fire and dropped to my left and right as I moved.

I felt myself growing weaker; my magic was being drained, and my arms were beginning to feel as if they were made of lead weights. A wolf grabbed my arm and stopped me from spinning; it opened its jaws to bite me, only to get kicked back. *I can use my feet, you know.* Using the room I had made with the kick, I lobbed a fireball into its chest and watched it drop to the ground and roll, trying to put itself out.

I felt a wave of dizziness wash over me and groaned, dropping to my knees. I couldn't even see now; everything was swimming. I grabbed my chest, groaned again, and saw the animals huffing—no, they were laughing at me. I smiled at them and laughed with them.

A wolf stomped closer, grabbed me, and slammed me against the wall. "What's so funny, human?" it growled. Its voice had a nasal tone, and it was annoying to my ears.

I smiled at it, took a deep breath, and leaned in. "Flamethrower," I whispered with a crazy smile on my face.

The wolf cocked its head in confusion and opened its mouth to demand an answer, but before it could get the words out, I grabbed its head, held its mouth open, and poured a flamethrower down its mouth from mine, looking to all the world like a dragon. The act was petty on my part, but I figured if I was going to die anyway, may as well take one more with me.

I collapsed as the wolf that had been supporting me fell, its mouth burned and its internal organs crisped away. It died in seconds. I passed out and welcomed the encompassing darkness.

7 Something Lost and Something Gained in Another World's Sun

When I woke up, I was in less than pleasant circumstances. I was chained to a post and wearing bandages and a pair of shorts. I looked around without moving my head and saw Will next to me. He was breathing, but barely; he had been beaten and cut pretty badly. I wanted to help him, but I couldn't. I had to find a way out of this mess.

I pulled against the chains slowly and softly, so they wouldn't make any noise, but they wouldn't budge. I couldn't use my sun powers on them, or the metal would heat and burn me long before the metal melted. I had heat protection, not melted-metal protection.

I heard footsteps falling heavily on hard steps, and then the door swung open. I involuntarily flinched as the bear walked in smirking; the double-headed war axe strapped to his back glistened in the light almost menacingly.

I looked at the bear, and he looked back. I glared at him angrily, remembering the hell that I had gone through the preceding night. The bear returned my glare with a smile as he walked around Will and me as if he was studying us.

"You must be the king's generals. I heard you killed my brother in the castle. I'd be lying if I said I was unimpressed," the bear said. His voice was deep and warm. Almost rich. I shuddered while listening to it.

He walked up to me and ran a hand over my chest, touching the cat scratches I had gotten the night before. "After all, you humans are so fragile. I'm surprised you can walk without breaking your legs half the time. But you do have your uses; you certainly do keep things entertaining. Tell me, human. How do you do what you do?" Looking directly at me, he made a gesture with his hands, extending and closing his large, thick fingers tipped with gnarled and heavy claws that could probably cut me to ribbons in a heartbeat.

I looked at him and smiled. I was already a dead man. Telling him the god owed me a favor for a trash hand in life was not going to do me any favors.

The bear shook his head, walked up to me, grabbed me by my throat, and started lifting. I was easily dragged off my feet and pulled against the chains till it felt as if my arms were going to be ripped off. I cried out in pain. I wasn't really a warrior; I was just trying to be a farmer. I wasn't raised to keep the pain inside, to never show fear in the face of the enemy. I wasn't prepared for how much pain there was in the world. I wanted to go home to my farm now. I wanted to lie in my bed and sow my fields. I teared up and let them flow to acknowledge my weakness. I wasn't a god here; I wasn't a hero. I was a man, and a weak one at that. I'd had my own advantages with magic and a weapon that upgraded itself and could confuse the enemy with how it moved. But now, in the face of this overwhelming violence, I was at a loss and at an overwhelming disadvantage.

The bear thought it was hilarious though. He saw my tears of pain and started laughing. In fact, he dropped me and grabbed his sides from laughing so hard. Then he turned and walked out of the room. I knew he would be back soon, so I laid my head down and kept crying.

I heard the chains next to me rustling and looked over. Will was looking at me through a swollen eye and smiling. For a moment, everything felt okay. This was Will, after all— strong, reliable, and indomitable. I saw it, though, in his eyes. I saw that we were going to die down here, and I nodded my understanding.

Will couldn't talk, not really; his jaw had been broken in several places and was swollen. I smiled at him and told him to rest. He didn't need to make me feel better; I'm sure that smile he gave me must have hurt like hell. Will was a good man and a brave friend; it was a shame it was going to end like this. Part of me hoped we were going to hear alarm bells soon, a last-minute assault by the king and his forces once he realized that the fort had been attacked and that we were no longer holed up there. But, truthfully, I realized that was probably not going to happen.

Will passed out again and went limp against his chains. I looked at the door and with a heavy heart braced myself and waited for that bear to come back and kill us. It wasn't a long time till he did return. I heard him coming from a way off—his footsteps pounding on the castle flagstones, the tips of his bear claws clicking on them as he walked.

The door swung open, and with an arrogant smile, he walked in. "I want to know how you can use fire, human, and you will tell me."

He walked over to Will and held out one of his massive claws. I knew exactly what he was going to say, and I immediately told him everything.

The bear stepped back while listening. He nodded, cupped his chin, and scratched his jaw. "You're lying to me, human," he growled.

I groaned loudly and strained against the chains. I heard them rattling and clanging as I pulled on them hard. I fought through the pain of them as they cut into my hands and dug into the bones on my hands. "I'm not lying; I'm telling you the truth. I come from Earth. I died and was given a chance to come here to live and be reborn. The god gave me these powers. That's it! I'm not lying to you!" I practically yelled. I could almost feel the frustration building in my system and bringing me closer to the brink of losing it.

The bear shook his head, walked over to Will, and dragged his claw down Will's chest, cutting him open. It wasn't deep, but the blood began running down Will's chest.

I cried out while watching this act of aggression, and the bear smiled.

"I suggest you tell me what you know, or I will bleed this man in front of you till he is a corpse on the ground. Then I'm going to eat him in front of you for dinner. I am undecided as to whether or not you will be eating him too. Depends on whether or not you want to keep pissing me off," the bear growled at me.

I clenched my jaw angrily and my fists so hard I'm sure I was digging holes into my palms with my nails. I shook my head. I knew he wasn't going to listen. I knew it. No one would believe that story. It was so farfetched.

The bear reached out for Will, and I started begging the bear not to hurt him. The bear asked for new information, so I told him about the pyromancy book that the king had given me. While holding on to Will's arm, the bear asked where the book was. I gulped then told him how the book had burned to a crisp after I read it. The bear sighed softly, grabbed Will's arm, wrenched it downward, and tore it from his body.

I screamed, not in horror but in rage. Will's arm was on the floor. The bear was wiping his hands on a rag, a disgusted look on his face, as if he could not bear to have the blood of a human on his hands.

Will had woken up and was gasping loudly, his body already going into shock as he looked at the bear and at me.

I looked at Will with tears flowing from my eyes. I lunged, trying to go to Will despite the cuffs. I felt them cutting me and digging into my wrists. Lines of blood were dripping down my arms from my struggles. The pain and my despair mingled together and left me crying as I looked at Will.

The bear shook his head as he watched the blood gushing from Will's body. Will was slipping in the blood under his feet; his breathing became shallower as the blood slowed. I watched him die and slump against the pole he was chained to, hanging by the cuff on his remaining wrist.

The bear walked around the puddle, taking care not to touch the blood. He smiled at me and said, "I'll have you know I didn't doubt you for a second."

My head whipped up, and I glared at him; the blood in my body boiled. "What?" I asked confusedly.

The bear said happily, "About the god. It was so unreal it has to be true. How else could it happen? I mean, you just watched your friend die right in front of you, and you didn't budge on your story one bit! Has to be true." He was almost gleeful as he smiled again and patted me on my head as I stood there.

Every cell in my body felt activated at that moment. Every fiber of rage was coursing through my body; I felt as if I were on fire. The bear turned from me and walked out of the room as I slowly went insane from the rage. I no longer cared about leaving here, I wanted to die with Will, but before I did,

I wanted to kill every single one of the animals in here with me. I was going to put them all in the dirt.

I started gathering all of my magic—every single magic particle—and focusing it around me. I was going to burn these shackles off me; I didn't care if the metal burned me to the bone. I didn't care about anything anymore. I watched the magic come from my body, but it didn't just heat the metal; it surrounded me. Encased my body in layers of orange and red magic, forming a suit of hard-light armor that snapped the chains and broke me free.

It was a new spell. The hard-light armor, made from the sun, radiates heat and grants the user enhanced speed and strength to double its usual rate.

I looked at Will and clenched my jaw. "I couldn't save you, my friend. I'm sorry for that. You were the best man I have ever known, and I truly mean that," I said to him softly.

I walked over, broke his chains, and picked him up. I almost gasped as I remembered the suit generated heat, yet it didn't seem to be harming Will. But something else was happening that I hadn't foreseen.

The hard-light armor was pulling light from Will. It was siphoning it from his body and shining it right in front of me. I set his body down and turned to look at the holographic Will made from pure light. I reached out for him, and he smiled at me brightly.

"Take me with you, Eric. We can beat them as one!" he said excitedly.

He grabbed my outstretched hand, and the light that made up his body poured into my hard-light suit and formed into an obsidian gem in the middle of the armor. I stopped for a moment to rest my hand over Will's and feel the warmth radiating from it. I also felt Will's love and compassion. With it came his power. The hard-light armor now said my speed and strength had experienced a massive increase.

I left the room, and started running down the stone path towards where the bear had gone. I would come back for his body after I was done. One way or another, Will and I would be leaving here together. These filthy animals needed to be put down. Will and I would do it together.

I was running, the stones cracking under my feet from the force as I slammed down on them. The doors flew by. I was looking for the bear, but it didn't matter whom I found; I just wanted to start fighting.

I found a wolf first; it was walking from a room, holding a platter. I pulled back my fist and threw a punch that caved in the side of its head. I tossed its body several feet down the hall, where it slammed into a wall before it slid down to the floor. I looked at my hand, grinning, before I walked into the room the wolf had exited.

It was a guardroom, and there were several wolves and cats in it. I grinned as I ran forward yelling; I was on them in an instant. I spun, kicked a cat in the arm, and felt it break; I threw that cat across the room. Then I jumped back as a wolf leapt into the space where I had been. I straightened my hand and chopped down on its neck, breaking its spine; I grabbed it by its neck and threw it at the other wolves so forcefully that they were staggered. I shoved my straightened hand through the chest of a cat and pulled its spine through the hole. I smiled mercilessly; that was for Will.

I was going to kill everyone here and avenge my friend. I just wished I had my sword. Almost as soon as I had the thought, my suit formed a sword in my hand. I looked at it and lunged forward, cutting a cat in two easily. I smiled; I missed the whip function, but beggars certainly can't be choosers.

The sword disappeared back into the suit, and I found that the suit could manifest the weapons I wanted on command. Since it was made from hard light, the suit was powered by the sunlight flowing in from the windows along the castle wall. So there was no time limit on the suit. I wanted to get out of this soon; I didn't want to be stranded here without the suit or the power that it gave me.

I also wanted to find that bear and feed him his own heart. He was going to pay for what he did to Will; I was going to make sure of it.

"Where are you?! Bear! Come out and play with me, you pile of sh—"

I was cut off by the bear grabbing me from behind. He was surprisingly quiet when he wanted to be. He grabbed me, picking me up, and slammed me so hard against the floor it broke, sending me down to the floor below. The floor below had vaulted ceilings, which meant the fall was from a lot higher than it should have been before I slammed into the open area below.

Laughing, the bear landed beside me and kicked me away. I skidded about twenty feet before I came to a stop and rolled to my feet in the suit. The attack had been aggressive, but in the suit, I had felt nothing. It was a nice touch for this boss battle.

The bear actually looked surprised that I was standing, but then he shrugged. "You are a surprising human; I will give you that. You have killed a good number of my royal guards, and above that, you even came looking for me without your friend that I killed. You could have escaped. You could have hidden. You could have done a good number of things, but instead you did something incredibly stupid."

I smiled. The bear was here, but I could barely hear him. My heart was hammering in my chest; that's how excited I was. I had my chance now; I couldn't waste it. I had to kill the bear.

I crouched and lunged forward explosively. The bear's eyes opened wide as I was in the blink of an eye in front of him. I spun around, kicking his leg harshly. He roared and with an open palm swiped at me; I watched it coming almost in slow motion. It was so exaggerated, as if it were going through heavy water or pudding. I grabbed his wrist and yanked down, kicking my leg out and against his ribs. The bear roared again, grabbed his ribs, and looked at me confusedly.

Grinning, I hopped up and down. The suit had greatly enhanced me, but really that made me just over a wolf in terms of raw power. The bear still could beat me. The suit had taken a good brunt of the damage he had dished out, but it was not invulnerable. The suit would fail if it took a few more hits like that. I needed more sunlight to strengthen the suit, but we were in an enclosed place. All I could do was hope that I could end the fight before either I or the suit ran out of power.

I leaned forward and lunged again, this time jumping, as I had seen him prepare for me to go low again. He apparently thought I was stupid enough to go for his feet again, so he'd left his head wide-open. I delivered a brutal kick to his head and grinned as I watched the bear's eyes shake in his head. He stumbled a few steps before he gathered himself and made sure he was steady.

Serves him right for what he did. I didn't even know how many humans he had killed, but he had killed the one who had mattered the most to me, and that sin was grave enough.

"You, human, how dare you do this to me?" the bear said as he reached back and pulled his axe from its scabbard. "You are going to make me use a weapon on some worthless little human. Do you know how long it's been since I have had to use a weapon on a human? I was a cub. Barely old enough to walk on my two legs the first time I killed one of you lowly worthless humans."

Snarling, he leapt at me; his snout pulled back and showed all of his sharp, long teeth. Saliva dripped from his mouth. His axe whistled through the air as it came straight towards my head. I ducked the blow that time, but he was speeding up as his rage grew. I was barely keeping up. This was insane.

I moved in and hit him in his stomach with three quick blows before I ducked behind him, through his legs, and heard the axe slam into the floor behind me. I jumped into the air and slammed both of my feet into the small of his back, sending him staggering forward. He whirled around, catching his balance. His mouth was wide-open and still dribbling saliva from his intense focus as he watched me.

I was being elevated; I was no longer just a lowly human in his eyes. Now I was a threat, something for him to regard as an enemy. He growled low in his throat and charged me again. At the same instant, I sprinted towards him, my suit speeding me up, and then I quickly dropped to the floor and slid between his legs. The axe again came down inches away from my head. I flinched.

I grabbed his ankle and pulled hard. The bear was pulled off-balance, and he fell. I grabbed his head by both of his small ears and started slamming his head, snout first, into the floor repeatedly. Over and over, he hit the stone floor. I heard him roar and push himself off the floor, so I danced backwards, away from him, and put myself into a slightly bent-knee stance, ready to move in any direction.

The bear stared at me; his face was bloodied, and some of his teeth were missing. I gave him a friendly smile and pointed a finger at my face, as though appraising him.

"You look way more beautiful like this, I gotta say," I said, taunting him.

The bear glared at me and clenched his battle axe angrily. He was ready to kill me, I could tell. But he was going to have to try harder, or I was going to kill him first. He had killed someone precious to me. I ran forward and almost caught the head of his axe with my face as I dodged and quickly jumped over it. I missed an attack on this pass, but the bear was learning quickly.

I needed more. I needed a whip. I tried to make the suit manifest, but it wouldn't. All it would give me was a sword. I would take it. Hopefully, it would cut through the bear as well as it had the cats and wolves.

Holding the sword in my hands, I started walking around the bear, looking for an opening. He was watching me more carefully now too. I had a golden weapon in my hands, and he was wondering what kind of magic it must possess to be that color, and what it could do to him if it touched him.

He let out a low, growling bear sound and cocked his head; brute force won out, though, as he decided to just charge me.

I breathed in slowly and watched his charge, trying to slow the situation down. I needed something—anything—to give me an opening. I moved to the side as he neared me and swung his axe. He grazed me, chipping the hard-light armor. I swung the sword at the same time, slashing at his thigh. The blade made contact and cut a groove into his leg, leaving a long, bloody gash that was steaming from the heat of the blade.

The bear watched me closely and definitely watched my blade. This was the first real damage he had taken; his leg had really suffered from that hit. I started walking forward, towards him, waiting for him to make a move. Suddenly, the axe came whistling in towards my head. I rolled forward and executed an upward slash, cutting his arm from his body. I grabbed it and moved back, smiling as I watched him drop his axe and cover the wound.

I held up the arm and looked at it. It was heavy and ugly. I looked back at him and waved at him, using the severed arm in a fake-friendly greeting before I dropped it on the ground and kicked it away. I was adding insult to injury with that. Trying to provoke him, to make him even angrier.

The bear snarled at me as he removed his remaining hand from the wound.

"That was for Will, you flea-bitten animal!" I yelled.

He seemed to realize the wound wasn't bleeding; after all, the blade was so hot the wound was cauterized. I flourished my blade and readied myself for the unarmed bear.

"Are you ready to die? Are you ready to pay for the sin of removing such a wonderful person from this world? You are going to die now, and I'm going to be the one who did it. Isn't that just embarrassing for you, bear? Tell me. Will you beg for your life like your brother did?"

I grinned as the bear went into a fit of rage. *Good, get mad; that leads to mistakes, and I can take advantage of those. Anger makes you sloppy, makes you rash. I am going to kill you, bear.*

I lunged forward towards his outstretched arm and sliced that from his body too. He tried to bite me with those gnarled teeth, but I moved and backhanded him in the mouth, breaking more of his teeth. He landed hard on the floor, not able to catch himself since he had no arms. I grabbed his head and started slamming it into the floor over and over again.

His head hit the floor so hard and for so long that when I was pulled away from the smear that was left, I was no longer in a suit; the magic had run out. I was covered in red. I was crying, I realized then, as I was pulled away from the bear's body. I felt myself shaking, and I fell to the floor, ready to be cut down by the animals remaining in the castle.

I looked around and found other humans looking at me with sadness in their eyes. The saddest was the king himself.

"Eric, what happened to you? Where is William? The fort was completely destroyed when we arrived," he said.

I teared up more while looking at the king, ran my hands through my hair, and told him slowly about how we had captured the fort, about the fight in the middle of the night, about the bear demanding the secret to my magic, and about my telling the bear everything in an attempt to save Will and myself. I told him about Will's death, and at that part, the knights and the king dropped their heads and whispered prayers for their fallen brother-in-arms. it was heartwarming. I finished by telling him that Will's death had unlocked in me a new ability, the hard-light suit, which allowed me to fight the bear and kill it.

Nodding, the king looked at the bear and back at me. He then grabbed my shoulder and said, "That bear you are so calmly talking about killing is the Oceans Guild's king. He is the strongest, most vile bear that has ever lived. I was not looking forward to fighting him. I was counting on you and Will for that. But you have done it by yourself. The kingdom cannot repay you for this, Eric. What do you want? Name it, and it's yours."

Looking around me, I felt empty.

"I want to give Will a funeral. Then I want to go home, My King."

8 Returning Home to Another World's Sun

The funeral was beautiful, to say the least. It was for everyone lost over all of the years fought against the Oceans Guild, for the nameless warriors who laid their lives down throughout all the past years, and for those who died in the last hours.

I stood there in ceremonial armor, which was pitch-black and had ruby eyes, the centers of which were missing, so I could see through them. I watched the funeral procession. Mostly empty caskets carried down the long street and lined up. Everyone said a few words about a warrior they knew or someone they had lost in the years of fighting. I was last.

I stood next to William's body. He looked very peaceful. I noticed they had reattached his arm and had placed a golden cuff over his arm to cover the stitching. I nodded approvingly; he managed to look impressive even in death.

"Will was a good man. I didn't know him long. I was brought into your world by accident really, and I never intended to stay. I made a few friends along the way, but they are all dead now."

I shook my head and placed a hand on Will. I felt my grief replacing the emptiness that had built itself inside of me. My eyes watered, and I steeled myself to do my best in eulogizing William.

"I...told myself I would die for this place because of the friends I had made, but I'm the only one that's still alive. How is that right? How is it that I'm a stranger, and I'm still standing here. But this man who lived, breathed, and loved his land died for it, gave everything for it, this man who lost his family and continued fighting for them for all this time?"

I looked around at all the faces lined with grief.

"I am happy I knew Will for the time I did. I shared food and drink with him, and he taught me many things. I wouldn't give those memories up for anything in this world...or the next...or the last."

I raised a golden cup full of a special drink and watched the crowd raise theirs. I made a small toast, and we all drank together. Setting down the cup, I looked out over the crowd and felt the tears start falling down my face. I wanted to go home now. I gave my friend in his coffin one last look, then turned and walked through the crowd of mourners.

***

I sighed as I walked through the halls of the castle. It had been three weeks since I had killed the bear. Since Will's funeral.

No one could find a door out of this place. No one could find a way to leave. I told them to scour the countryside for a doorway similar to the one I had entered months prior. So far, nothing. I slammed my head against the wall in frustration. I wanted to go home *now*. There was nothing left to do here. The Oceans Guild had been disbanded, and the animals had been rounded up and taken care of.

The humans were spreading across the land, retaking the old castles and forts that they had once inhabited. Meanwhile, I was given free rein to do as I pleased. The king made me an honorary noble, and I could do anything I wanted, go anywhere I desired, which was why I needed to find the door.

That's how I'd found myself back in the castle in which Will had died. Evidently, the last castle the enemy boss was in is always you will find the door. I just had to find the darn thing. I walked from door to door and touched every frame. I also touched all of the windowsills, trying my best to find something, anything, just some kind of clue to get me the hell out of here.

I sighed with aggravation, knowing there was nothing here; I had searched these doorways a hundred times. I started walking back the way I had come, but the hallway was gone; it had been replaced by a door. I smiled excitedly. *Finally, here it is!*

I grabbed the handle and threw the door open...then screamed and fell back on the floor as the god jumped out at me.

"Hey, Eric. You completed your first dungeon! And, hey, why are you on the floor? Get up; there's something cool for you in here."

He has to stop doing that. It is getting to be rude, the way he jumps out and scares me like this.

I stood up, cursing the god in my head, and groaned as I walked through the door and into a room. The first thing I noticed was the chest that the god was standing over.

"You beat the dungeon, Eric, so you earned a reward." He turned and kicked the chest open.

My menu flashed open automatically and scrolled to my upgrade trees. The existing trees moved closer together and made room for a new one—friend of nature. The tree grew several unnamed upgrade options, only one active—animals would be more likely to come near me without fearing me and would be less likely to attack me. It was a great skill to have if I could find more creatures to pollinate and fertilize my farmland. I closed out my menu and looked at the god.

"Completing these dungeons will result in new upgrades to your existing skill trees. Or completely new trees altogether. Pretty standard things you would see in the games back in your own world."

I closed the menu manually and looked at him. "Now, how do I get out of here? I don't see a doorway or a tunnel...or even a window."

"These places are all set up so that upon completing them, you will be teleported from them. I'll be on my way if there's nothing else," he said quickly.

I started to open my mouth to ask him about the locations of other dungeons, but in a flash of light, I was at the entrance to the mine, and the god was gone. I was once again alone. I sighed loudly. *What a rude way to leave me.*

I turned from the entrance, walked back through the ruins, and started making my way back home, stopping once to look at the entrance to the mine and thinking about Will and the king. I shook my head. It was a dungeon. Who knew if the people there were even real? I reached up, cupped my chest, and shook my head. They were real to me; that's all that mattered.

I walked along the path as I looked around. Everything looked so different after spending all that time in the other world. The colors looked brighter, more vibrant now that I was back. I smiled and inhaled the air. I stepped into the clearing of my ho—

Completely taken aback, I came to a dead stop. Everything looked different. My log cabin was now made from stone and looked like an actual house. My fields were no longer in raised beds, but actual fields, and they were a lot bigger; my hard-light structures had been situated a lot more efficiently. And leading from the river, there were underground pipes for crop irrigation.

Someone had modernized my home while I was gone, and based on the fire in the chimney, they were still there. I walking up the path to the front door, opened it, and saw a dwarf. He was sitting in a chair, reading a small scroll, and drinking from a small metal cup. He looked quite alarmed that someone had come into his home.

I looked at him and started yelling, "Who are you? What have you done to my fields and my home? What gives you the right? Where are my pets?"

I pulled out my whip sword, ready to use it if I had to, but the dwarf held out his hands and gestured for me to wait. I cocked my head to the side. *Wait for what?*

He ran to the back and came back with a small slate and started scribbling on it. I read on the slate that he was from a nearby settlement that had been overrun some time ago and that he had come back to collect some things and found my home, which appeared to have been abandoned.

Technically, he was correct. I didn't really know how long I was gone because time worked differently in the dungeon. I sighed and told him that it was my home and that I had just cleared the dungeon he was talking about. I generated a hard-light beam to prove it was mine, and he nodded. There was no denying it was mine.

I looked around and realized he was an amazing craftsman. I asked him if he would stay and work with me to keep making my home a better one.

He looked up excitedly and scribbled that he would be glad to. He also wrote that my slimes were still in the pond, making the water clean, and that my creature that pollinates was still around. He had brought several little friends with him to help with the expanding fields. I smiled happily at the news.

I was glad that everything had been going well in my absence. I walked outside and took a look at all the dwarf had done while I was gone; I definitely approved. I was glad I didn't have to do it myself, honestly.

I walked back inside and sat with the dwarf, who was making some fresh bread in his stone oven. I asked him about where he was from, and he told me all about the mountain from which he had come. There was a special city that was being built inside the mountain where the dwarfs lived, and in a few hundred years, they hoped to all be living underground, away from the oppressive light of the sun.

I looked at him and noticed that his skin was a very pale shade of white. I nodded a few times while he was telling me his story. I wanted to go to this city at some point. I had just gotten back from the other world's dungeon, though, so now was not the time for more exploring. Now was the time to rest. I smiled while lying back and took a slice of the bread that the dwarf had just made. I learned his name was Brama, and he was unable to speak.

I pulled a book from my inventory and read the title, which was about creating golems. The book asked if I wanted to absorb the information, and I did. It disappeared, and I felt all the information get pulled into me as if it were a data download. I grinned. I wanted a golem—not right now, but they could be useful later for heavy lifting.

I stood up, stretched, and wondered what I was going to do. "Maybe I'll go to the dwarven mines today and search for some gems and ores," I said to no one in particular.

The dwarf looked alarmed; he stood up quickly, ran in front of me, and made an X with his arms. He grabbed his little slate and scribbled a message. He wanted to tell me that there was a dungeon down in the mines and that I couldn't go there. I would be killed. The dwarfs were pushed out by the monsters a while ago and couldn't return, or they would be killed.

"I thought I told you I cleared the mine, Brama. It's empty now. That's where I have been all this time—clearing it out and making it safe."

Brama smiled widely and ran to a back room. He returned with a large bag that was almost the same size as his body; it contained a great number of tools. Brama gestured that we should be on our way. I smiled at him and let him lead the way.

Walking from my home to the mines was nice; seeing all the trees and the river again felt surreal in a way. I almost wanted to dance and jump with joy, but I held it in, considering that my new friend might become a little concerned about my mental state.

As we approached the village, I felt a queasiness in the pit of my stomach and grabbed it; I could feel an awful stomach-ache building. It reached an apex when we got to the mines.

We stood together at the entrance to the mines, and I was hit with a wave of nostalgia that was so strong I wanted to cry as I remembered Will and all the people with whom I had fought. It was almost too much. I could barely stand it. I shook my head, walked down the stairs, and kept going till I reached the bottom. Then I almost smiled. The door that led into the mine was gone. All that was there now was the cool, smooth earth. If I weren't so sure of myself, I would almost think that I was crazy for thinking there had ever been a doorway there.

I shook my head and turned to Brama, who was looking at me. I gestured at where the door used to be and grinned. "The door leading to the dwarfs' dungeon was right here; the problems that all your people had were right here. Not even a year ago, I walked right through that spot there and kicked that dungeon's butt," I bragged.

Brama nodded at me encouragingly, and I smiled. Brama reached behind him, pulled out a pickaxe, and handed it to me while smiling back at me. I got the message: "Get to digging, kid." I took the pickaxe and watched Brama. He just walked up to a wall and started digging. I scratched my head, wondering what I was looking for. Was I just supposed to start hitting the wall and pray, or was there something I was supposed to know? I remembered another book that I had found in the dungeon—*How to Find Gems and Ores*—and pulled it out.

I read the book, absorbing its knowledge quickly. I knew why they had picked this mine to work. In this world and this area, there had once been an ocean that was gone now. Oceans have lots of minerals that soak into the ground. Over time, the minerals come together in pockets and leave behind veins of ores and gems. I took the pickaxe and started hammering at the wall. It was just up to me now to find all the deposits that had been left behind. I was going to find lots of goodies down here. The lower the dwarfs went, the more good things they found.

Well, until they found the dungeon, that is. Hammering away at the wall was not the most exciting thing in the world, but I was highly motivated, especially after having absorbed the knowledge in the book. This world had all the same gemstones as Earth, as well as a couple more that were just from here. Rubies, which are red gems, are a good source for focusing mana; sapphires are good for being melted down and used in golems as mana conduits for charges; emeralds are good for storing information. All of them can be used like a battery, though; some are just better than others for certain things. Diamonds are really good as combat gems—you put one in the tip of your gloves, wand, or staff, and you can wallop on things because they're so hard, sharp, and virtually unbreakable; they also hold a large amount of energy, which makes them all-around great options. I was personally hoping to find some sapphires for my golem project; I wanted to melt them down.

Brama exclaimed happily behind me, and I turned to see him pulling a hunk of ruby from the wall. I smiled. *Good for him.* I turned and kept going—you never stop; you always keep going. I had my first find about two hours later and almost leapt with joy.

After that repetitive work, I felt as if I were going to lose my mind if I didn't find something soon. But then I found a chunk of gold ore, smiled, pulled it from the wall, and placed it in my inventory. I was so excited to find it; I started searching around, hoping that it was a vein. Gold was a good find because it was a great electricity conductor.

I didn't find anything else, so I decided to head back up for the day. The mine was going to be a great resource at some point, I was sure, but for right now, I had other things I wanted to do—for example, explore the dwarfs' town again. Maybe, with the abandoned materials, I could build a golem and have it do the mining for me. I grinned at the prospect of automating my work.

I headed back to the surface. I waved at Brama as I passed, and he waved me onward; he would see me later at home. Since I had cleared the mine, there was no longer anything to be worried about.

Exiting the mines, I looked up at the sky and noticed there was still a good amount of daylight left, so I headed to the buildings in search of metals. I found the carts full of unprocessed materials and started making my way through them, trying to find everything I needed.

I pulled a few blocks of uncut sapphires out of the carts and tossed them into a pile. When melted down, they would run through the golem like veins and hold magic that would be like command codes, basically giving it the information it needed to function. More advanced golems made from liquid metal could also hold information. After deeming I had sufficient sapphires, I looked for the metal I would use for the main body; I settled on iron because I didn't need anything too heavy. There were several carts of iron already, and I only needed one.

In my inventory, I had a core that I could use, so I pulled it out. I needed to rewrite it though. It was currently programmed to attack the first person it set its eyes on; I didn't need that. I sat down cross-legged, held the core in my hands, closed my eyes, slowed my breathing, and tapped into it using my magic and my willpower to put the core under my will. The core was very advanced; whoever made it was a genius. It was amazingly well put together; I saw line after line of magic defense all tangled together to try and keep whomever out. I smiled, feeling the sweat dripping down my brow. This test of endurance was probably the thought of whoever built this, but as I sat in the sunlight, my magic was kept full to the brim, which allowed me to keep going as I plucked string after string of the tangled defense.

Finally, it yielded to me, and I nearly let out a loud yelp with joy at my success. The core was glowing a cool blue in my hands, and I slid it back into my inventory. I would now need someone who could run a forge. I turned, looking back at the mines, and smiled.

I ran to the mines quickly to fetch Brama. Nearly dragging Brama from the mines around a half hour later, I pulled him through the doors. "Brama, come on. I need you to help me! I need help melting this iron and these gems, so I can make a cool golem to mine and do the work for us," I yelled.

Brama grabbed his slate, started scribbling furiously, and turned it to me.

I need fire for that. I had a kit before to make the pipes beneath our home that carry the water, but the fire-stone has gone out. I cannot make a fire hot enough to light the forge.

I rubbed my jaw. *Hot enough to light the forge?* "Brama, can't we just make a fire in the forge, like a campfire, and use bellows to make it hotter with air?"

Brama slowly shook his head and started scribbling again before turning the slate to me.

For a human forge, that would be fine, even if the process is probably more complicated than that. For a dwarf forge, you need a firestone. Or the equivalent of a small inferno. Otherwise, the internal machinery won't warm up and clear out the smog inside, and the equipment will stall out.

I nodded in understanding. I just wanted to see his reasoning. I held my hand out and generated a fireball. "Will this work?"

Brama's eyes widened, and he fell back after feeling the great heat coming from the orb. Brama had really only dealt with the structures that generated minimal heat; he hadn't realized that I could generate such heat. Nodding, he sat up quickly, motioned at the enormous forge, pulled me to a large gate on which he grabbed a lever, and tugged on it with his whole body. I saw the large muscles on his arms straining and the veins popping out. The gate slowly started opening, and he motioned for me to lob the ball inside. I threw it in, and he let go of the gate.

I heard a large *whoosh*, as if a furnace or a stove had been turned on; it was followed by a grinding noise that came from all around us. I turned my head in sync with the sound, following it around the workshop as the machinery came alive. The dwarven forge was back in action.

Brama ran over to the cart holding the iron and started grabbing hunks and throwing them into forge to get it heated up. He wanted to handle it; he was the first dwarf to use these mines in many years. I turned and walked away; I needed to come up with a design for the golem.

After sitting in the sun for a while, I decided on a golem that was a bit like a spider; it would have four legs for balance and two more in the front with drills that could turn into claws to pick up materials. I pulled the core out of my inventory and started programming it.

I wouldn't need a mold, thankfully, as I had no idea how to do any of that. All I had to do was take the core, program it with the design for the golem, and toss it into a pile of molten sapphire and metal. The core would do the rest. I smiled. *How convenient.* I was still going to watch it though. It was going to look awesome, I bet.

I walked over to a cart, pulled out a few uncut rubies, and set them on a table. I wanted to make a few batteries for the golem. I sat at the craftsmen's table and started going over the tools. I didn't want to actually start anything yet, and I was glad I didn't.

Brama came over, saw what I was doing, started showing me how to cut gems. He had a passion for this kind of thing. He showed me a drawer, in the craftsmen's chest, that held a special oil. I dribbled it slowly over the rubies and watched the debris slowly drop away. Next, I took a small tool to mark off areas that were damaged or not well formed. Those were the only parts I was going to remove. These materials were going to be melted down anyway, so it was not important that they be pretty or cut a certain way. As I used the final tool and slowly pared the ruby, I saw the beginnings of the red gem shining through. It looked beautiful now, but it was going to look even better shining on the golem.

I handed the gems over, thanking Brama for the lessons, and brushed the cut-gem parts into a disposal bin. Brama nodded and carried the rubies over to the fire and threw them into a special section of the forge. I grabbed the sapphires and made sure they were filed down and clean before passing them along.

I turned back and watched Brama taking his time while purifying the iron. He had a special tool he used to skim off the impurities that floated to the top of the iron as it heated up. Back on Earth there would be a certain amount of waste that came with this part of the process; here, with his tools, Brama wasted nothing. I was in awe of these craftsman.

Brama grabbed the shirt he was wearing, pulled it off, and tossed it to the side, showing his short, stocky upper body. I had seen his arms, which were covered in dense muscle, but I wasn't prepared for the body that looked like a professional bodybuilder's. I felt my eyebrows rising. *This guy is shredded!* I almost laughed; it was evident he was good-looking, but this was something else. *Man must be a killer with the dwarf ladies.*

Brama looked back at me as if he could read my thoughts. I almost looked away, but then I realized he was asking if I was ready to proceed.

I stood up and showed him the core in my hands. I ran to his side quickly and watched him tilt a lever and pour the melted iron into a bowl-like structure to the front of the forge. Thanks to the book I had absorbed, I knew exactly what to do after that.

I lobbed the orb into the melted iron and watched the process begin. The orb floated to the top for a few moments, flashing as the programmed magic within it began to take effect. I saw several magic circles flashing on its surface; they were as intricate as lace and as detailed as any design could be.

It was almost incomprehensible that I was the wielder of that magic. I had just imposed my will on the orb, and my magic had done the rest. I shook my head and focused as the orb dipped into the pool of molten metal, and the iron began swirling around it in a slow vortex. More magic circles, more shapes. The metal covered the ball suddenly, and I told Brama to release the melted gems. Brama reached out, hit a lever, and I watched two smaller kilns tilt and drip the red and blue liquids into the melted ore.

The orb went crazy, blinking with information as it absorbed the new material. The ore and gems mixed together, and shapes began forming within the swirling liquid. I saw a small spiderlike structure and smiled as I watched the product of my mind take shape.

This was exhilarating. The melted sapphire turned into thin blue lines and was pulled into the legs and body of the spider, sucked up like small lines of spaghetti. The rubies turned into the eyes of the golem. I walked up to the finished product, looking at it while rubbing my hands together. *A nice little piece of automation here.*

I generated a hard-light ball, slipped it into the back of the golem's head, and saw the rubies begin filling the spider's head. I watched the golem jerk to life once all of the rubies were absorbed; it looked around before standing up and testing its limbs. The spider walked around and bounced up and down, making sure everything was working. It looked at its hand and fired up its drills, making sure they spun correctly; then it split them apart into hands, opening and closing them. The golem seemed content because it scurried to the opening of the mines and down into them to begin its work.

I turned to Brama and gave him a thumbs-up that Brama returned happily. This was a good day's work for us. Turning from the forge and stretching, I started my walk home. I was losing daylight, and I needed to bathe.

As I headed home, I took a moment to thank the god that he had led Brama here. Brama had really done me a great favor by making my home so amazing. Before, it was improving very slowly, but this was like a time skip straight out of a TV show. Everything was so beautiful now. The fields were growing; Brama had recently learned from me that his crops wouldn't die during any season because I had placed a large sun sphere underground that generated heat year-round. The herbs on the sun trellis grew constantly and were a great source of food and stamina boosters; they had saved me a few times already.

I walked past my line of cala and maka nut bushes and saw they were growing nicely too; it brought back memories of how they helped me in the cave. I brushed the growing nuts with my hand and watched them swing on the branches. Turning away, I walked to the water-supply pond that Brama had made for the slimes; they seemed to like it. It had a direct line to the river for fresh water, when it went below a certain level, and a built-in block that stopped water from rising to a level too high; these safeguards ensured the water in the pond was always refreshed by the lovely slimes.

I reached my hand into the water and summoned the slime I had first tamed; I watched it climb out of the pond and into my hand. I smiled as I held it and gently rubbed its soft, gelatinous head. It made its normally round body grow two arms so that it could hold on to my hand.

I closed my eyes and gave it some of my magic as a little treat. I felt the slime growing, and I watched until it was large enough to hold in my arms. The slime had been around the size of a basketball before; now, it was the size of a water-melon. Its color was changing from a transparent blue to a golden color. As I watched, in a few places, its body seemed to sprout pale, ribbonlike appendages that fluttered in the breeze; it looked as though they were mimicking the sun.

I was shocked. *What did I just do?*

I used my observation skill and found that I had just acted as if I were the god. I had created a new evolutionary path for slimes. I blinked, looked around, and saw the god standing next to me. "Ack!" I screamed and almost jumped out of my own skin.

The god was staring at me and the slime in my arms, which was now radiating warmth. "Young Eric, what have you just done?" the god asked me. He scratched his head and held out his hands. The slime jumped into his arms, and the god smiled softly at it.

The name of the new species was sun slime. They generate warmth and happiness wherever they go; they can also produce a fair amount of light. It was a cute little slime, and if possible, one that I would definitely like to breed and make more of. *Have a bunch of the cute little slimes bouncing and lighting up the farm? Yes, please.* They were like plants—eating the rays of the sun and producing energy from that.

"I was just feeding the water slime some of my magic energy, and he turned into a sun slime. I'm sorry if I did something wrong. He was just holding on to me, and I wanted to do something nice. That's all. I wanted it to feel loved."

Hearing this, the slime turned to me and took the shape of a heart while still in the god's arms; then it turned back into the shape of a slime.

The god smiled at me, and I felt warmth radiating throughout my soul. I knew there was no anger in the god. Had there been a test, I would have passed it; more likely, the god was just curious about this turn of events. The god handed me the slime and nodded.

"Good work, Eric. Keep loving your pets and taking care of them, and they will take care of you," he said with a smile. He then turned from me and disappeared mid-turn, presumably to return to someplace like heaven to watch over everyone.

I looked at the slime and felt the warmth from its ability. I grinned and said, "You're coming in the house with me, buddy."

The slime wiggled happily in my arms as I walked to the house and passed through the doors. I set the slime on the bed and watched it bounce repeatedly and throw around its glowing aura.

Still smiling, I softly petted it. The slime was just way too cute for me. I loved making things. I wondered now what else I could make with my mana.

I strode from the house and walked out to the farming area. I wanted to see for myself what Brama was growing. I inspected the sprouts, and from what I could see, it was a grain of some kind. I walked to the next field, and there were vegetables, possibly gourds of some kind if the vines were any indication.

I looked everything over and tried to determine Brama's planting process. I wanted to be a farmer, but I knew next to nothing about farming. I would have to ask Brama to teach me.

Yawning, I walked from the farm back to the house. It was time for bed. I crawled in and yawned again. I was so tired that I closed my eyes and immediately fell asleep.

Chapter 9

Something Sinister in Another World's Sun

I woke up the next day and stretched in bed. I sat up and rubbed the sleep from my eyes. The sun slime bounced beside my bed, happily soaking up the sun's rays coming through the window. I opened the window and let it bounce outside, so it could move around. I walked into the kitchen area and ate the bread and pieces of meat Brama had prepared for me; he had already left for the mines. I smiled; he and the spider would no doubt be competing to see who was better.

I put on a cloak before heading to the woods nearby. I wanted to see if I could hunt down some boar or deer. I hadn't seen any large animals since I'd returned from the other world, but I was going to change that. I wanted some large game. So far, I knew there definitely were smaller animals, like rabbits and squirrels, which Brama hunted and prepared. As well as fish, which he also caught. Brama was a lifesaver and definitely someone I wanted to stay with me.

I stepped slowly foot over foot, making my way through the forest, looking from side to side for animals worth taking back. I still winced at the sounds of the breaking branches with every step and lamented not having had the chance to work with Marcus, the hunter of the war party. I stopped and closed my eyes to fight back the tears—he was dead too, along with the rest.

It happened in a dungeon. Were they even real? I leaned against a tree and took deep breaths. *Were those men real people in another universe, or were they made up by the unique magic of this world?* I shuddered and felt a heavy weight on my chest as I wondered if it had even been worth it. *Had I put myself in all that danger for nothing?*

I shook myself out of the funk and slapped myself on the face a few times. They were real to me, and that is all that mattered. It *had* been worth it. *They* had been worth it. I opened my eyes and steeled my heart to stop the grief. Will would have wanted me to carry on with laughter on my lips and joy in my heart, not all this grief. We had won, and his people were safe.

I continued moving and searching as I worked my way through the forest. I knew I was bumbling, and that didn't help; it just added to my frustration. I wish I could find a small animal to tame, at least; that would have made my trip a whole lot better. I looked up at the sky and found that the sun was starting to drop. In the interest of not being out in the dark with all sorts of animals, I started making my way back home. I also wanted to check on the progress of the golem, so I decided to check in on the abandoned village.

The walk took a few hours, which surprised me. I didn't think I had gone that far. Walking up the dirt path into the village, I saw Brama sitting on the steps of one of the houses. He was chewing on a rabbit roll when he noticed me. He waved and smiled, still chewing happily. I smiled, waved back, and walked over to him.

So far, he had found a few rubies and a vein of iron in the mines. He was eager to get back to work. He finished his roll, started walking to the mine, but after looking in the hole, he moved back quickly.

The spider came rushing out of the hole, its four metal legs whirring around. It rushed to a small pile of items and emptied its hands, dumping the contents on top of the pile. Turning from the pile, the spider rushed back down into the tunnel.

Grinning, I walked to the pile and looked at the loot. It didn't matter what it was—it was collected without effort, which was the main thing. I knelt and sifted. A few pieces of iron, two pieces of gold ore, a ruby, and…

My eyes opened wide. *What is this?* It was definitely metal and a deep-blue color. I didn't recognize it, but the golem definitely thought it was valuable. I used my observation skill and saw a name pop up. I read it out loud, tasting the name on my mouth, "Denthyl ore." It felt weird in my mouth.

But having heard it, Brama turned quickly, his eyes opened wide, and he sprinted over to me. He looked at the ore in my hands and started jumping up and down excitedly, like a child. He grabbed his slate and smiled as he wrote furiously. When he turned the slate around, it was clear just how excited he was—his usual clean handwriting was messy and almost illegible.

> *Denthyl ore is the strongest ore and can be made into the most powerful items around!*

Brama grinned and started scribbling again.

> *It takes a skilled master forgeman to be able to work this type of ore. Lucky for you, I am a master forgeman. It can absorb magic from its user and be transferred into attacks most efficiently.*

I nodded. I had heard of this kind of metal before, in shows and books. It was basically mithril or adamant from other places; it was just called denthyl here. Smiling, I put the rare ore right into my inventory, just in case. I didn't want the ore to get lost. Brama agreed with my decision; it was too important to just leave around.

In my inventory I once again saw the egg and frowned as I pulled it free. I didn't know what to do with the egg. It wouldn't hatch. I looked to Brama and showed him the egg.

His eyes lit up again, and he scribbled with blinding speed.

> *How did you get a magma wyrm egg! Where did you find it?*

I smiled. A magma wyrm, huh? That sounded dangerous. I licked my lips nervously.

Brama saw that, shook his head, and wrote more on his slate.

> *Magma wyrms are used to power our forges in the mountains. They are smart, sentient monsters. They gladly sign pacts with us. They let us use lava magic, although in a form not as powerful as theirs, and they feed on the castoffs from the forges and the metal and gem cutaways. They love them. It's perfect for us here. They grow very slowly over thousands of years. A hatchling will be perfect for just the two of us.*

I finished reading and smiled at Brama. "That would be great and all, but the wyrm won't hatch for me! I have tried."

Brama raised an eyebrow as he erased a few lines on his slate, wrote a few words, and smiled before turning the slate towards me.

> *You threw the egg into lava?*

Horrified, I shook my head before answering, "No! I'd never do that to the poor thing!"

Brama shook his head and wrote some more.

> *There are two ways for a magma wyrm to hatch. Being warmed by lava or being thrown into an active dwarf forge.*

I turned and looked first at the building that housed the forge and then at Brama.

We both ran into the forge excitedly. Neither of us had ever seen a magma wyrm before, but that was about to change. I cast a fireball as Brama ripped open the gate of the forge. I tossed in the sun orb, and we watched the forge come to life. Brama jumped into action, stirring the flames to life and driving the heat of the forge to greater heights. I watched admiringly this master forgeman at work.

Brama turned to me and nodded. It was time. I took the egg and tossed it into the fire. I would have set it in the forge, but the flames would have crisped me long before I got close enough. We both watched the red egg in the flames. Due to the heat distortions of the flames, it looked as if the egg were dancing in the flames. The apparition lasted until the egg began rocking back and forth wildly, and shell particles began dropping from the egg. As we watched, a small body slid from the egg and sat in the flames, basking in the heat and seemingly enjoying itself.

I used my observation skill, saw its name—baby magma wyrm—and smiled. I said, "Tame," and watched the spell take effect, after which I called to the baby wyrm through the magic in our blood.

The wyrm lifted its head, looked around, and then started crawling on its four little legs towards me. Smiling, I held out my arms and waited for it to climb into them.

Brama hadn't realized what I was doing until the wyrm climbed right into my arms even though it was still smoking and steaming from the intense heat. Brama grabbed me and tried to get me to drop the baby wyrm.

I looked at Brama curiously.

Brama cocked his head to the side and scribbled on his slate, *You aren't burning?*

Smiling, I shook my head. "I'm a sun mage. I have very good resistance to heat, as long as he isn't dripping metal on me. He's just really hot. I'll be fine."

Brama looked at me oddly, as if I were crazy, before turning his gaze to the little wyrm, who was still in my arms and looking from Brama to me. The wyrm was softly chirping and felt a little too cold. Brama walked over to the gate, opened it once more, and motioned for me to toss the wyrm inside.

I did as he indicated and immediately felt happiness flood through me from the bond that the wyrm and I shared. It was feeling snug and warm inside. The forge had a permanent power source in the wyrm, which was a great thing; we no longer needed a firestone…or me, for that matter.

Brama grabbed his things and started heading home. I followed him. It had been a nice little day; I hadn't hunted anything successfully, but it was cool that I had a new tame. I pulled open the menu and found that due to my other tames and the new skill tree I had gotten from beating the dungeon, I could now have medium-sized tames as well. I no longer needed a certain number of small-animal tames before unlocking that ability. That was nice.

Walking back along the river, following Brama, I watched the water's ripples as they danced past me. I saw a hand in the water as we passed by; it was small, delicate, and brown-skinned. I kept walking and stopped abruptly. *A hand?*

I turned, hopped the bank, and quickly ran back. This time, there was a hand coming from one of the bushes. It was a small hand. I pushed the bush's branches apart and found a small woman; she looked pretty badly beat-up. I pulled her from the bush slowly, making sure I didn't hurt her any worse.

As I looked around to see who could have harmed her, I noticed that Brama was watching me from across the river; he looked worried. Focusing my attention back on the woman, I saw that the wounds were still dripping blood. She had been attacked recently. I gently picked up the woman, hopped the stream, and started walking quickly back to the house; her wounds needed to be wrapped. I would also set my little tame on her, and it would aid in her healing.

Running up the path, Brama opened the door, and I walked inside. The sun slime bounced in happily, radiating light and warmth throughout the room. I set the woman on one of the beds, summoned a knife to my hand, and trimmed away her clothing. I wished for another female at that moment, but knew there was no time to be prudish. I had to take care of this now and make sure there were no injuries. As I cut away her clothes, I pulled a sheet over her body to keep her naked body covered.

I called the little bupo and set him on her chest. He stretched out his arms and legs, covered her body, and closed his eyes to start the healing process. I grabbed some sheets, started tearing them into strips, and set them to the side. I walked outside and picked some sunbloom herbs before walking back inside. I crushed the herbs into a paste; in this form, sunblooms aided healing more effectively, as the fluids were absorbed directly into her system. After applying the crushed herbs to the wounds, I bound them with the sheet strips.

Her color already looked better. From her ears, I could see she was an elf. Using my observation skill, I saw she was a dark elf and that she was healing slowly, thanks to the paste and the bupo. I went into the back room, grabbed a few items, and dressed her slowly, making sure not to disturb her and to respect her privacy. I was glad she was going to be okay.

Nervously, I looked out the windows and wondered what creature had done that to her. I grabbed a chair, pulled it next to her, and grabbed a book on smithing that Brama had brought with him from the mountains. I started reading it, thumbing through the pages by light generated by the sun slime; it was rocking from side to side, humming happily.

Brama tried to stay awake, but ended up falling asleep. I could have slept, but I wanted to be sure that she would be all right. I could always sleep later. The hours of the night slipped away as I turned the pages of the book. I learned about the tools needed at each stage when treating metal and turning ore into ingots.

I was stopped by the rustling of the elf. Groaning she turned over in her sleep. I watched her for a few moments, making sure she was all right. I used my observation skill on the bandages—they were still in good condition and didn't need to be changed.

I leaned back and ran my hands through my hair, noticing how long it had gotten. It was down to my shoulders now. I hadn't cut it since I had arrived in this world. Yawning, I crossed my arms and cracked my neck; it was going to be a long night.

I jerked awake and looked around. I must have fallen asleep at some point. The bed was vacant, except for the little bupo chirping at me. He must have just been tossed there—based on how upset he seemed, rather unceremoniously at that.

The door was open, so I jumped up and raced to it just in time to see the elf limping through the fields, back towards the forest from which I had carried her. I raced after her. Whatever had hurt her was still in there, and clearly, she was not yet at her best. Catching up to her was easy. I reached out and grabbed her shoulder gently to avoid hurting her.

She screamed, spun around, and struck me in my stomach.

I grunted loudly and grabbed my stomach. "Why would you do that, lady? After all my efforts to save you, you're gonna just punch me right in my gut?" I complained. I continued to hold my stomach and groan as I glared at her. She packed quite a punch in that small frame. Later, I was going to have a dark bruise there to show for it.

She frowned and without taking her eyes off me, crouched into a ready stance to fight me. "You won't get me. You're a monster. You're not going to eat me, you pale-skinned freak." Her voice was tinged with a bit of a Southern accent, but not enough for it to alter the words she was saying; her voice was easy to hear, and it projected well with her with confidence.

I looked at my tanned skin. "Hey, I have a tan! Should have seen me last year. I looked like a ghost." I laughed, trying to make a joke to lighten the mood. I saw her look scared for a moment, and I realized quickly that the joke had gone over her head; it had been a mistake.

"You looked like a ghost? I knew it. You are a monster," she said.

I sighed loudly and face-palmed. *That's what I get for trying humor here.* I took my hand down to try to explain further, but didn't get a chance. I was distracted by something moving behind her.

An ogre was standing there, a good ten feet away for the elf. It looked different from the one that I had beaten when I first arrived. This one looked like something out of a horror movie. In a shot, which could only be described as chilling, as I looked past her, I saw the ogre tilt its head back, open its mouth, and let out something between a howl and a scream; the sound was deafening, violent, and, worst of all, hungry.

The ogre was thin, gray, and wearing clothes that were in tatters and falling off its body. Both its clothes and its skin were dyed with the blood of its previous victims. I felt my skin crawl as I met its eyes and my stomach flipped. Its eyes were deep and sunken into its head like holes, its skin pitted and deeply lined, and its head spotted with tattered fragments of hair. Then I saw its teeth—jagged like arrowheads, sharp and dripping with saliva.

The girl had stopped moving and was hyperventilating, panicking at the worst time. I got it—this is what hurt her so badly.

I moved forward slowly. "Do you know the way back to the house?" I asked softly. "Nuh-uh, don't answer. Just barely move your head."

I saw her nod once.

Good. "On the count of three, you are going to turn and run. Do not worry about me or what I will be doing. You will be in my way if you hesitate or stay. Do you understand? I can't be worried about you while I do this. This thing looks dangerous, and I need to focus.

"I'm going to start counting now. Three…"

The girl tensed subtly and bent her knees, getting herself ready to run.

"Two..."

I flexed my hands, summoning into them the knives from my inventory, and readied myself to fight this monster. It seemed to know something was about to happen because it started leaning forward. I felt my heart begin accelerating, beating heavily, and pumping adrenaline into my system.

I inhaled deeply and yelled, "One! RUN, RUN, RUN!"

It all happened in slow motion. The girl turned to run, her arms coming up to start pumping and moving. The ogre stretched out its arms and started barreling towards me. Knives in my hands, I started walking forward, my eyes locked on the ogre and my brows furrowed, locked in focus. As soon as she passed me, I engaged my hard-light armor wrapped around me. I felt its magic enhance me; the world slowed down a little as the enhancements took over.

The ogre was probably weaker than a bear, but stronger than a cat, for sure. Perhaps somewhere around a wolf, but bigger than a wolf and with better reach. I placed a hand on the black gem sitting on my chest—a small homage to Will before battle—and crouched into a battle stance as the ogre got closer.

I ducked its first swing at my head and slashed the inside of its wrist. *Too shallow.* I hissed as I watched some of its blood splash onto the ground. I pivoted in between its legs and ended up behind it as I stabbed down viciously, digging a dagger into its calf. I let my momentum carry me a few paces away as I listened to the ogre scream.

I turned to look at it and held out my hand, summoning the blade back into my hand. Doing that caused the wound to leak blood at a faster rate. The ogre grabbed its leg and hissed while glaring at me. I hissed back, which made it flinch. Most creatures probably cowered in fear when they heard that noise, but here I was, hissing back.

I held my knives in front of me, ready again. Resorting to a little trickery, I drew my arms back and threw the knives. The knives flew end over end.

The ogre pulled its arms up and covered its face, which allowed the knives to sink into its stomach. The muscles there were so ripped the knives couldn't penetrate very deep.

"Oh no, I'm defenseless! Whatever will I do!" I said, making sure my voice trembled.

I watched the ogre pull the knives out and toss them aside while smirking. It charged me without seeing that I had stretched my arms toward it, closed my hands into fists, but left my two index fingers pointed directly at it. I walked forward and backhanded its outstretched hands, knocking them aside, and lunged forward digging my fingers into its open wound.

It screamed, grabbed my shoulder, and started lifting me. But not before I yelled, "Flamethrower," activating my very powerful, condensed stream of flame that was sent from my fingertips directly into the ogre's wound.

The ogre released me and screamed as flames streamed directly into its body, cooking it from within. Groaning, it dropped to its knees.

I pulled my hand free from the wound, noting how charred it was. I summoned a dagger and drove it into the ogre's thick skull, ending its misery quickly. Nothing should be left in pain like that for long. I exhaled a long breath, realizing I had been holding my it for a long time. This had not been a hard fight, but it had definitely put me on edge. The ogre had been creepy as hell.

I turned from the ogre to see the girl still standing there. I shook my head in disbelief. "Why are you still here?!" I yelled.

She looked nervous and wrung her hands in front of her for a few moments. "I'm sorry. I did run back to the house," she said softly. She pulled my whip sword from behind her. "I came back to give you this, but by the time I got here, you had already won."

I ran my hands through my hair slowly and thanked her. The whip sword would have been a great weapon to have in that fight, simply for its extra reach. I moved forward, took the whip sword from her hands, and attached it to my hip.

I looked down and into her eyes, for the first time noticing how deep a purple they were. I looked away and gestured back towards the house. "Come with me. I want to make sure your wounds didn't open while you were running."

She followed, hobbling behind me silently, as we made our way back towards the house at a walking pace. I didn't figure she would want me to carry her, so I didn't offer. The house wasn't too far away anyway.

I thought back to the ogre I had fought and grimaced; it was a lot stronger than the one I had fought originally when I first arrived in this world. Bigger, faster, and far more deadly. It smelled of death and despair. I was mulling this over in my head when we reached the house.

I pushed the door open and invited her in. "First off, what is your name?" I started as she walked past me.

She sat on the bed, and the bupo crawled into her lap and looked up at her curiously before spreading and attaching itself to her. She ran her hand over it slowly while listening to it purr softly.

"I am Mira Norfally of the settlement Narba," she introduced herself.

I leaned against the counter. That piqued my interest. Narba sounded like fun. "Why have you come out this way from your settlement? And alone, at that? I'm sure I don't have to tell you this, but the forest is deadly, especially at night."

Mira nodded her head a few times. "You are right about that. I started this journey with two others—skilled warriors, both of them my protectors. They were killed by the ogre you took care of; they were friends I had grown up with," she told me sadly. Mira looked down, gathered her strength, and tried not to cry as she remembered their being beaten to death by the ogre.

I sighed and looked away, almost regretting having said anything. When I turned my head back towards her, Mira was staring at me through tear-filled eyes. Watching them, I never saw a tear fall. *She is holding them back very well, poor thing.*

I sat down in the chair in which I had spent a good portion of my night. "You did not answer my other question, Mira Norfally. Why did you come here?"

She looked away, wiped her eyes, and breathed in, gathering herself. "The ogres are why we came here, if you must know. They came from the wastelands across the seas. Distorted by the pollutions there, they were changed. Altered. The ogres are normally carnivorous, but sane. They search for mates and fights and food, and that is how they live their lives—doing only those things. However, some time ago, they found out that there was land across the water. An enormous land filled with monsters and treasures and"—she paused for a moment—"other things."

Intrigued, I looked at her closely. I wanted to find this place; it sounded amazing.

"The ogres that sailed there in large numbers disappeared for years, going in search of things to fight and eat and mate with. They disappeared and were never heard from again. Then, about two years ago, an enormous ship landed on the coast, miles out from Narba. It was covered in gash marks and stained with blood splashes across the hull. When the ship beached, birds on the coast rose in a great storm to get away from it and to fly from the area. We should have followed suit.

"The ship was carrying those same ogres, but they returned carrying the plague and stronger and faster than before. They are killing my people. The only saving factor is that they are somehow dumber; they aren't able to plan as well. But whatever they are afflicted with is killing the lives of my people and polluting the lands around them, turning it into corrupted lands."

I felt my skin itching—a quest was coming on—and I was smiling. "Any chance you could use the sun mage to assist you and your people?"

Rather than going to the corrupted lands, I was more interested in the possibility of seeing Narba with my own eyes and learning some new magic. If taking some ogres out and putting them in the dirt was all it took, then sign me up.

Mira looked up with her eyes open wide. "You'll help us? Why? What's a sun mage?"

"I will help because I want to; it's my choice and mine alone." I held out my hand and made a hard-light ball of fire that glowed a dull orange in my hand; it seemed to waver in the tiny flames around it. I smiled at her.

"I am the sun mage. I can use the power of the sun and bend it to my will," I explained.

Mira was in awe at seeing the sun in my hand; she watched it slowly spin in my palm. "You must be powerful if you can hold the sun."

I shook my head, canceling the spell. "It's strong, but not all-powerful."

Frowning, Mira cocked her head to the side and gave me a weird look; her eyes seemed to go towards the side of my head repeatedly.

I thought that was pretty weird during our conversation, so I decided to question her on it because it was starting to get to me. "Why are you looking at me like that?"

I moved past her and started packing a go bag, placing underclothes and other necessities inside it—boxers; a brush for my teeth; a special paste Brama had given me, his version of deodorant; and socks he had made—they soaked up all forms of moisture and felt amazing.

"Your ears, they aren't pointed; they are rounded at the top. What did you do to them?" she asked me.

I looked at her with an eyebrow raised. "Never seen a human before, pointy ear?" I asked with a smirk.

"Pointy ear! Human? What's a human?" she asked, sounding slightly offended.

I stopped packing and looked at her closely to see if she was joking or messing with me. But her face was dead serious. I crossed my arms and leaned back. "I am a human. Have you never seen another like me? Really?"

She shook her head a few times, gazing at me up and down and leaving me feeling a little self-conscious. "I would definitely remember someone who looked like that," she stated matter-of-factly.

I rubbed my head a few times, then held my arms out wide in a "whatever" gesture. I dropped my arms as Brama walked in looking at me with his slate in his arms. I pointed at him so I could get his attention. "Brama, have you ever seen a human before?"

Brama shook his head.

I sighed. He must have just accepted I was a weird creature whose home he was sharing. I turned my attention back to Mira and decided to change the subject because the discussion about my being human wasn't going anywhere. "My offer still stands. I will help you if you'd like. I want to see this Narba and the ship these plague ogres come from."

Mira slid off the bed, holding the bupo in her arms carefully. She was starting to look excited; she had found the warrior she had been looking for. Someone or something that could help in the fight against this new menace. "I accept your offer…uh…"

Slowly, I held my hand out towards her. I didn't want to move too fast and risk spooking her, or have her think that I was going to attack her. "My name is Eric."

Mira shook my hand and thanked me for offering my strength to the cause of helping her people. We would be leaving the next day and making our way to the settlement of Narba.

***

I strode out of the doorway and looked back at my home, remembering the last time that I left. It had been months before I was able to return. I got the feeling it would be the same for this trip.

I looked for Brama and waved farewell. He would be taking care of the place while we were gone. I was taking bupo with me for his healing properties. I turned from my home with Mira in tow and began walking in the direction she was indicating. Time to go to the settlement and begin another journey.

I walked down the road, past the place where the rage ogre had been slain, and paused. The ground where its body had lain was gray and bruised as if it had been poisoned. If left unchecked, the ground and wildlife would be contaminated. I shuddered at the thought.

"The ground is infected; the forest is sick now," I whispered.

Casting a flamethrower, I burned the ground, purifying it just as those of old had done it—with fire. The ground seemed to resist the fire, though. I frowned as I pushed the magic harder, deeper into the ground. After a time, I felt it give way, the fire finally destroying the sickness. I shuddered; I hadn't expected that.

"The ogre's blood infected the ground and killed it. I need to burn all the spots touched by ogre's blood before it corrupts too much of the land."

Mira had been watching me. I turned from her as I started systematically burning the ground, tracing the ogre's blood, and killing all of the corrupted patches. When I was done, we kept moving along the forest path. I remained vigilant of everything in and around our path as we went along. The ogres' catching us by surprise was the last thing we needed.

After I let Mira take the lead, I started watching how she walked and realized I couldn't hear her footfalls. I strained my ears, trying to catch even the slightest crunch of leaves, but couldn't. I shook my head; creatures with magic in their blood were in a whole other league. I could just use magic; I wasn't born with it or made of it like Mira.

As the forest walk continued, I looked around and noticed the trees growing larger around me. The deeper we went, the older the trees were. I wondered at the age of them, *How many ages does it take for the trees to grow this large?* I had heard of a forest back on Earth where there were redwood trees large enough that when cut down, several couples could dance at the same time on them. Looking at these trees, they could probably hold hundreds of people; I knew these would dwarf the redwoods and make them look like saplings.

I reached out, placed my hand on a tree, and felt a little breathless. The forest was sick, and I knew the cause. The plague spread from the ogres—their blood was seeping into the earth, cursing and decaying it. Feeling sad, I took my hand from the tree and turned to see Mira looking at me.

"Can you speak to the trees, Eric? Can you feel them?"

I nodded and told her the trees and the forest were growing sicker; they needed help and soon.

Mira turned, shaking her head helplessly. She couldn't do anything for the forest. We needed to keep walking and get to Narba so we could talk to the people there and formulate a game plan.

Mira's head was always on swivel, so when she let out a squeak, I summoned my blades to my hands quickly, ready for battle as she sprinted ahead. I dashed behind her, only to see her stop at a bush and start plucking small berries from it.

I sighed. The squeak hadn't been a battle call; it was excitement at having found a treat. I shook my head as I used my observation skill—pentu berries. They were a dark-orange color, and smashing one released a smell similar to watermelon. They were edible and favored by elves for their flavor, which was light and delicious, close to that of a watermelon.

I popped one into my mouth and bit into it. It was harder than I thought it would be, but it was definitely tasty. The bush was stripped bare; we placed the berries into my bag after I explained to Mira that it was an inventory space that could hold many things.

So we were full of fruit as we kept walking. The sun shone as it slowly made its descent. Birds sang above us, chirping and tweeting as they danced branch to branch, playing and chasing each other. I inhaled and pulled the fresh smell of the forest into my lungs. I loved this smell. I would never miss the smells of my original home world or all the pollutants in its air, the cars honking or the roaring of trains and planes. I used to hate how loud it was all the time.

The hours whittled away, and finally it became time for us to set up camp. I reached into my bag, pulled out a tent, and began setting it up while Mira collected wood and other tinder for a fire. I pulled out two sleep rolls, setting them in the tent for us later, when it was time to sleep.

I backed out of the tent and saw Mira struggling with a flint. "Why don't you just use a fire spell?"

Mira turned to me with a small frown on her face. "All elves are born with the affinity for all magics, Eric. We just choose not to use them. I was born to mingle with the forest and life itself, not its killer."

I raised an eyebrow at her. "Little dramatic there."

I raised a finger, conjured a tiny fireball, tossed it into the fire, and watched flames jump to life. I sat by the fire and yawned; I was tired. I hadn't done a lot of walking lately, besides the back and forth to the village, which was not all that far from where I actually lived.

Mira reached into a bag at her side, pulled out a wrapped sandwich, and tossed it to me before pulling out her own.

Brama had made us traveling food. Good ole Brama, taking care of us. I took a few bites and chewed it, already feeling a little homesick for my friend's cooking.

Mira had her eyes closed, enjoying the food too.

"Mira, how can I get stronger? I have my base stats, but I can't make them go up. I have some abilities that I can make go up by completing tasks and doing things repeatedly, but other than that, I am at a standstill."

Mira looked at me closely. "Human Eric, all beings in this world are born with a base. It all starts at one, grows as you age, and stops when you turn sixteen. When you turn sixteen, that's it; what you've got at that point is what you get. It sounds like you have a very unusual circumstance—getting more power through an ability. It sounds like you are talking about gaining levels."

I smiled at her use of *levels*. That was exactly what I needed. "Yes, levels, that's exactly what I want!"

"No!" Mira yelled suddenly. She seemed very upset and angry with me rather suddenly.

"Mira, what's wrong? Why are you so mad?" I asked, startled.

She relaxed, shook her head at me, and waved her hand in front of her face. "Forget it; you know not what you are asking for. Remember this, and remember it well. Levels are for monsters...and only monsters. They can grow stronger, and that's to eat and take advantage of people. You don't want levels. Unless you want to lose your sense of self and soul, Eric. It's not worth it. Learn the sword; learn some magic. Gain experience; better yourself. Please, never become a monster. You will lose yourself and become the very thing you wish to destroy and be rid of. It will corrupt you. You will think you are in complete control, but all the while, the power will begin turning you into one of them, a monster. Someone as strong as you would break this world, Eric... break it right in two."

Frowning, I leaned back. *Only monsters, huh? Well, that sucks.* I was limited in my paths then. Mira still looked a little concerned, so I smiled at her. "Don't worry. I don't plan on becoming a monster or anything, I just wanted to know.

I feel very weak, especially against the monsters I have been fighting. I've been gaining weapons and spells that have been making my time here easier, but I wanted to see if I could make easier progress with it. I apologize if my questions frightened you or made you upset, Mira."

Based on how she seemed to relax a little, I could tell I had put her mind at ease. I wasn't going to go running off into the forest, chanting to the demons or gods to make me into a monster so I could gain power or anything.

I decided that was as good a point as any at which to turn in for the night. I crawled into the tent after waving good night to Mira; she was going to stay awake a bit longer. I slid into my roll, closed my eyes, and fell asleep quickly.

Chapter 10   A New Settlement in Another World's Sun

I stretched, yawned, and noticed that my chest felt heavy. I also noticed that I felt damp. I frowned, opened my eyes, and saw that Mira had somehow slipped out of her bedroll and managed to crawl half out of it and onto me. I raised an eyebrow at her sleeping body, but sighed after realizing that the damp feeling was her drooling on me.

Good grief, I thought to myself, *is this normal for elves? Are they cuddlers?*

I reached up and wrapped an arm around her, placing my hand on her shoulder. She seemed to relax more. Nuzzling into my chest, she let out small snores; it was almost enough to melt my heart. She seemed pretty adorable right now.

Feeling comfortable, I closed my eyes and started falling back asleep. The extra warmth from her body was very comforting and felt nice. Now that I was relaxing, I noticed something else—her scent. It was not a bad smell, more like the forest. An earthy smell that reminded me of the leaves and trees. If there was ever a natural smell to have, it was a good one. Better than the musty ones most humans had.

Miss one shower, and you could smell them from several feet away; it was terrible.

I felt Mira rustling around in the bedroll and opened my eyes to see her struggling out of it; her eyes were still closed though. Was she a sleepwalker? Once freed from her roll, she climbed on top of me, her body completely covering mine.

My eyes shot wide-open. *What is going on? Is she still asleep? Is she coming on to me? Oh god, what's happening to you, Eric?*

I was frozen, completely still, and couldn't move an inch. I was worried that if I woke her up, she would be upset that I interrupted her rest. Or, even worse, blame me for what was going on. Neither option was in my favor. I had to lie there as this small five-foot-nothing elf straddled me like a backpack and snored away softly. I closed my eyes and prayed this situation would resolve itself peacefully.

I felt her rustling around again and opened my eyes to see her start peeling off her shirt. I almost screamed. I peeled my arms free from my sleep roll and grabbed her arms. "Mira! Wake up, please!" I yelled.

Mira's eyes shot open. She looked down at where she was, on top of me, and then over at her bedroll. Then she looked angry.

I sighed. *Of course, here it comes. She is gonna get mad at me, and all I did was lay here trying to sleep.*

"I was sleepwalking again, wasn't I, Eric?"

My eyes lit up. She wasn't going to yell at me, after all. *Score one for the guys!*

"I think so, Mira. I'm still kind of waking up, so I'm not really sure what happened. I just saw you removing clothing and knew something wasn't right."

Mira looked at me closely. "What? You don't want to see me without clothes, Eric? That's not right, according to you?"

I choked as I looked at her and felt my face flush.

Mira only laughed at me and punched me in the shoulder. "I'm joking, Eric. Relax. I'm only trying to lighten the mood. You look like you have a dragon chasing you!" she said and then laughed at me again.

I snickered mockingly, ran my hands through my hair, and then sighed. *What am I getting myself into here? Plague ogres and an elf throwing mocking pickup lines at me?*

I rolled out of my sleep roll and crawled from the tent to stretch and look around. It was still fairly dark out, but I could see that telltale clue in the sky that meant the sun was coming up soon. Staying awake was probably best at this point. Looking around at the dark forest, I saw a sparkle out of the corner of my eye. I looked towards it, only to see whatever it was dance out of my line of sight. I felt uneasy.

"Hey, Mira," I called.

She crawled from the tent and stood next to me after almost falling when her foot got caught on the lip of the tent. I'd steadied her to make sure she regained her balance.

"Hey, I just saw something flash over there. It moved out of my field of view as soon as I looked at it," I said a little nervously.

Mira looked up excitedly and stared hard in the direction that I had pointed. Soon there was another flash and I saw her smile. "Those are pixies. They only mean one thing. We are near an oasis of the forest," she said excitedly.

I looked at her and cocked my head to the side.

She started explaining, "An oasis holds fresh water, herbs, and other goodies. We should go there right now and collect some fresh things!"

I couldn't help but smile at how excited she was, so I agreed to her request. We packed our bags and began heading in the direction of the lights. As Mira and I approached it, the flashes started coming more frequently. I saw the pixies up close—tiny male and female bodies dancing in the air. Once in a while, a body would glow as magic built up and was released in a puff of light.

Then there were more; they rushed around us. Mira smiled and laughed while dancing with the pixies as they giggled and shone. I, too, smiled as I watched her, and I started feeling something in my chest I couldn't quite place. It was a warm feeling that I enjoyed. A feeling of closeness I hadn't felt since I had traveled with Will. I was so caught up in these thoughts that I almost missed her dancing over to me with fluid movements and grabbing on to my hand as she tried to pull me into the middle of the floating fairies.

"Mira, I don't know how to dance. I can't. Let me watch, please," I begged.

Smiling at me, Mira shook her head, took my hands, and started spinning with me in a circle, slowly dancing to the beat of a song only she could hear. The wind in the trees, the swaying of the branches, the leaves brushing together—she danced to it all, and to nothing at all.

I was mesmerized by it—the movement of her body against mine as she used her hips, stomach, and legs to guide my body as she wanted it to move. I let myself go limp so I could be a puppet for her. I moved to her rhythm and fell into her world, and as I looked, I was enraptured by her purple eyes as they pulled me deeper into them. It was similar to going deaf in the middle of a whirlwind of sound created by the pixies as they swirled around us.

When the dance ended, I noticed I was breathless and sweating. The sweat dripped down my body in rivulets. I smiled at Mira. She smiled back and thanked me for the dance. A few of the pixies flew in front of her, and she held her hand out; I watched as they landed and started using her hand as a dance floor. I just laughed and felt as if it were something out of a cartoon. Sensing that I was making fun of her somehow, Mira looked over at me and stuck out her tongue.

I stood up, looked around, and saw a large pond surrounded by herbs. I used my observation skill and smiled—moonlit bloom. *Huh.* It was known to raise defenses and to have healing properties.

"Hey, Mira, can I harvest these?"

Mira gave the okay.

The forest can always regrow anything harvested from within it. We could take as much as we wanted and always come back for more. I pulled up moonlit blooms and started putting them into my bag.

Then I began looking for other things to harvest. I walked up to a tree, looked it over, and saw buds growing from it. *Sap cones—the nectar from within can be sipped and is highly nutrient dense.* I started plucking them from the trees and throwing them in my bag as well. *Gotta love the observation skill.*

I walked to the pond and used the observation skill again—the water was safe to drink, but had no added benefits. I refilled our water flasks.

I walked back over to Mira, who was smiling as she waved goodbye to the pixies. Walking from the oasis I, too, smiled. *I love little moments like these. They give me strength to keep going and enjoy my life.* I looked at Mira, who was still wearing a large smile, and got the feeling that she felt the same. Then I turned my attention back to the forest trail. *Time to keep moving on.*

Mira turned to me as we were walking. "Before we get there, I want to warn you. Outside the settlement of Narba, there is an elven mage whose name is Milan. He is a young, kind elf who is extraordinarily gifted in two forms of magic— soul judgment and barrier magic. When he turned sixteen, he erected a barrier around the entire settlement and became the guardian of Narba. He won't let pass into Narba anyone who can't pass the soul-judge spell. Do you think you will be okay?"

I nodded thoughtfully and wondered if the spell took into account past lives or not. I shrugged inwardly. Only time would tell the answer to that question. "Do you know what he judges? Any tips or anything I can use?" I asked her out of curiosity.

Mira shook her head as she explained that no one, except Milan himself, knew anything about the spell. He refused to tell even the elders of the settlement, which really got on their nerves. They knew he was only doing it to protect them, though, so they let it slide. Mira was still explaining when we heard a scuffling noise above us.

I looked up in time to see a young elf sliding backwards off a tree branch, doing a backflip, falling several feet before catching another branch, and using it as if it were a gymnast's pole to swing his way from branch to branch till he reached the ground.

When he landed in front of us, I brought my hands up and started clapping.

The young elf smiled and bowed for me. "Thank you, thank you. Welcome to the settlement of Narba."

I smiled back at him.

Then he seemed to realize it was Mira. He smiled brightly and jumped forward, picking her up and spinning her in a circle. "Oh, Mira, welcome back, my friend. I missed you!" he said excitedly. Still smiling, he set her down and started looking around. His smile dropped very slowly, but I knew why and felt my heart break inwardly.

"Mira…" he began softly.

"M-M-il-an…" she replied even fainter, choking on the word.

"Where's…" He stop to calm himself as he fought back his emotions.

"Where's my brother? Where is Bolan? And where is Hoffy?" he asked, holding back his tears.

Feeling Milan's grief rolling from him in palpable waves, I was forced to look away from him, and almost regretted it as I caught Mira's purple eyes leaking tears in a stream that ran down her face. Damning the ogres to whatever version of hell the god had made for this world, I clenched my fists so hard I dug grooves into my palms. I barely knew these elves, but even my emotionally damaged self could see the damage and pain caused here.

"They are dead. They were killed by a plague ogre. The same one almost killed me," Mira eventually said.

Milan staggered backwards. It was one thing to assume your friend and family were dead; it was another to hear it be confirmed. Milan grabbed his head, holding it so hard I saw the knuckles on his hands go white. He stood there for a few moments till he stopped and looked at her, his own eyes stained with more than a few tears.

"How did you get away? Did you avenge them? Did you get the ogre and put them to rest?" he questioned.

Mira shook her head, pointed to me, and told Milan how I had saved her, nursed her to health, and killed the ogre.

Nodding, Milan looked at me, and his jaw dropped at the part where he learned I was a new species to this world. Never before had anyone met a human—apparently that was a running theme.

"Listen, we need access to Narba. He's willing to do soul judge," Mira said.

Milan looked at me and rubbed his hands together. "Okay, I understand. Come on over, Eric. I will start the spell. Your head is going to feel weird for a moment."

I knelt in front of Milan, and he started chanting slowly and mumbling the opening chant to his magic. I watched as glowing words highlighted in blue started appearing one by one in the air until a circle was formed. Upon completion, the circle burst into flame, and I gasped loudly.

My question was answered—the soul judge included past lives. My soul was pulled from my body. It took the form of a glowing orange dragon; it was tiny, looked almost newborn, and was crying and whining.

Milan walked over, picked up the dragon, and cradled it gently.

"This is the first part of the spell—soul. Here's the second part—judge," he said.

Smiling, he held up his hand, smiled, and started chanting some more; this time, there were no glowing words. However, a scale did raise itself out of the ground. It was an old-fashioned scale with a weight on each side.

"Your soul will be measured against a feather. If the feather is heavier than your soul, you will be allowed to enter Narba."

I nodded and watched as he walked over and set the crying dragon onto the scale before conjuring a feather and setting it on the other side of the scale. The scale wiggled back and forth. My eyes locked on the dragon as I wondered what the color meant, why my soul was a dragon, and why it was crying.

I reached up, grabbed my chest, and closed my eyes, knowing it meant something inside me was still broken. There was something about seeing my soul take form and cry that really hurt me in a deep way. I opened my eyes and saw the feather was lower.

Milan was smiling. He grabbed the dragon, walked over to me with the soul in his arms, and handed it back to me.

I held my soul in my arms. Sniffling, the dragon looked up at me and then nuzzled its head against my chest. I cupped its head and held it until it turned back into pure light and disappeared within me once more.

Milan walked to an empty spot in the middle of the road and then smiled at Mira and me. "I welcome both of you to the settlement of Narba. Congratulations on passing the soul judge." Milan sounded proud of me for passing the test.

I nodded at him, not quite feeling up to talking just yet. Milan seemed to understand; he waved me past him, and I continued walking forward, not quite understanding into exactly what he was allowing me passage.

After a few more feet forward, the world spun on itself. I staggered a few times and felt waves of vertigo spinning my head round and round. I held my arms out, trying to grab hold of something to steady myself.

Milan grabbed my arm. He smiled at me and said, "There is no way to prepare someone for that. I am truly sorry. It will pass in a few moments. Just bear with it."

I gritted my teeth against the pain and groaned as waves of nausea rolled over me. My eyes were swimming in my head as light waves changed and rolled around me. When they settled, nothing was what it once was.

The empty forest around me was now filled with houses of all sizes. They were built into the trees and made from a mixture of tree roots and stones. They had taken the time to grow the roots around the stone to make the frame for the outside of the dwelling. I was very curious about what the insides looked like.

Mira grabbed my arm, wiped her face clear of any evidence of her tears, and smiled at me while pulling me forward. "Come on; we need to go farther into Narba and see the council. They will have a plan for us; they always do," she said, full of hope.

As we turned and walked forward, I looked around me at all the faces of the elves. I had expected the people to be livelier and happier. Instead, they looked gaunt, worn down, and ready to give up. I shook my head, wondering how hard life must be for them so close to the ogres. The settlement was not very large, so we made it to the council in little time.

Mira smiled at the passing elves and called them by name as she waved. They returned her greetings and wished her well on her return from her journey. Some looked at me suspiciously, and others greeted me as if I were another elf. I smiled at them gratefully, returning their hellos and waves with my own.

The ground was paved in the same mixture of stone and wood as the houses. I looked at the patchwork of wood and stone mixed intricately and wondered how long it had taken them to get the wood to grow like that; magic must have been involved in the process.

Looking up, I found we were in front of a tree that had been grown rounder, rather than in the square shape of the other buildings. I watched Mira walk up to the opening in the front and step through the leaves that acted as the makeshift door. Following suit, I walked through and barely felt the leaves as I passed. Mira was waiting for me on the other side, already talking to an elf who asked her a few questions before running off. Curious, I looked at Mira and hoped that it had been a good encounter.

"That was Milly. She is an assistant to the elders; they are being alerted to our presence. We just have to wait here for them to call us," she explained to me.

I leaned against a nearby wall and crossed my arms, hoping these were not like councilmen in my old world, the ones who would take ages to come to any decision and acted snooty, as if they were the hottest things around. Half the time, they had a thumb stuck up their rear end and knew nothing about the outside world. Last time, they'd had a coherent thought was probably eighty years before, when they got their college degrees, and twenty years after that, everything they knew was out-of-date. Yet they still ran everything the same way.

I shook my head. We should have just gone to the ship and started searching. I was standing up to voice my opinion when Milly came walking into the room and stopped in front of us. I noticed something odd about her; when she stopped, from the hips up, her body leaned at an angle to the right. I found it so odd I almost didn't hear her say that the council would see us.

Mira started forward, and I moved with her, following her into the back room and through a few hallways. I smelled the wood of the tree around me and stepped around a few puddles of sap that was dripping from the ceiling. They definitely needed some more janitors in this tree.

Mira stopped before a set of large doors that had been made from the tree; patterns in the form of leaves and vines had been carved into them. She placed her hands on the doors and shoved forcefully. I watched her arms strain against the weight of the doors as she struggled, putting her weight into it. I started forward to help her just as she grunted, and the doors swung open. She turned and smiled at me, flexing her small arm at me before turning back around.

We entered the large room where several older men were sitting around a table. They were all wearing robes that went down to their toes. I couldn't see much, but they did appear to be in their forties, so I guess they were not terribly old. Mira and I strode to the middle of the room, and the men stopped talking to acknowledge us.

"Mira! You've come back. I'm glad to see you well," a man at the table called.

The elder at the head of the table held his arms out and smiled with joy at her. His eyes radiated kindness and warmth that was hard to ignore. I hoped that the man's kindness was not fake; I truly enjoyed finding rare people who were just genuinely kind.

Mira returned his smile and stepped forward, grabbing his hands, pulling them to her face, and nuzzling them for a moment before stepping back and looking at me. "This is my father; his name is Prayde. He has been the head of the elders since the settlement was started."

I looked at him and smiled while greeting him. I stepped forward and extended my hand. "My name is Eric; it is nice to meet you, Prayde."

Prayde looked at my hand, smiled softly, and leaned forward, clasping my hand and shaking it a few times. "Well met, Eric."

Prayde turned his attention back to Mira, now that the introductions were done, and asked why she had returned alone.

Mira sighed and then explained everything once more to the entire council. She hated reliving the events over and over again, but she understood that it was important to give an accurate report.

When Mira finished, Prayde turned to me. His eyes were open a bit wider than normal. "You can dispatch these beasts fairly easily then?"

"I can. To me, they are not too much more difficult than normal ogres. One thing I do worry about, however, is that they are more resistant to pain and damage. After receiving damage, they go on for longer than other beings. Also, the blood that they carry is infectious. The ogre I put down, his blood was seeping into the forest floor and infecting it; it spread the plague that it carried within it. The only way I found to stop its spread was to burn it, and the ground surrounding it, until the contagion was completely dead. However, that means that if the ogres ever infect more than the few small pools that were in my area of the forest, it will be a huge disaster. The loss of life, including plant life, would be insane for the forest, all creatures, and surrounding wild-life," I explained.

Prayde nodded a few times while rubbing his chin; then he sighed, hit the table with his fist suddenly and started cursing. I had guessed at how he would react; that was why I had brought up the ramifications of the plague ogres' very existence. The elves had been fighting the ogres, so it followed that the ogres had already feasted and dripped blood in and around the elves' settlement, infecting everything.

I was willing to bet their forest was doomed. A full-on zombie invasion was taking place.

"Fire was the only way to stop its spread, you say? That does limit our options," Prayde said. He shook his head, stood up, and looked at me. "Are you a mage who can freely use fire?"

I smiled at him. "I am the sun mage, the first and only."

At hearing that, Prayde looked interested. "A sun mage, you say? How interesting," he said while rubbing his chin again.

Then Prayde stood up so abruptly he almost knocked his chair over. He hurriedly walked away while waving for me to follow him.

I looked at Mira, who looked a little concerned. We both followed after Prayde, chasing him through a few hallways built into the tree, till we were outside, in the settlement, once more. At this point, Mira and I were running to keep up with Prayde.

He called over his shoulder excitedly, "We chose this spot to build our settlement years ago for a few reasons, Eric, and I think one of them was you!"

I looked at Mira again and wondered where this was going and whether I should be following this elf. We went through the settlement's barrier; I felt its magic sliding over my skin and knew we were in the forest again. Running through the open forest after being in a safe area felt risky to me. Especially with the leader of a race with me. It felt as if I were on an escort mission from one of those old video games I used to play when I still lived on Earth.

Thankfully, this elf was running at a speed that wasn't slower than mine. I used to hate that. I cursed any game developer who designed an NPC who walked slower than the other characters' running speed, but faster than his walking speed, leaving you in that awkward hobble of a jog-run while he dribbled on about whatever, bleh.

While I ranted about video games in my head, we arrived at a set of ruins. I looked around at the sigils covering the stones and the grooves running through them. It looked as if they had been connected by something at some point. I turned to Prayde and waited for an explanation.

He turned to me and started telling me how he and his friends had been scouting the area for the settlement and had found the ruins. In the ruins had been several tablets talking about a way to cross the land swiftly by using the powered of the sun.

I looked at the ruins curiously. *Am I going to unlock fast travel too? Seriously? That would be amazing, honestly. I hate walking everywhere.* It sure sounded as if this was leading to my being able to travel to places by stepping through a portal.

Prayde walked me to the front of the ruins where a pedestal was standing. I looked at it and saw a round hole in the top of the pedestal. From the hole led lines of words running down the pedestal. I held up a finger, and made a hard-light ball. *If this doesn't work, I am going to be crushed. Please let me be far enough into this story for a cool way to travel,* I prayed to the god.

Prayde watched the ball appear and held his breath excitedly, as if he'd been waiting for this moment all his life.

I reached forward and slid the ball into the opening. I pulled my hand away and waited as sunlight filled the ball. I could have used my own magic, but I wanted to make sure the sun could power it enough by itself. The hard-light ball began glowing a deep golden, and the words that were written on the pedestal began glowing and flowing down its sides.

The grooves began to fill with light and expand as if it were a river flowing down into the ground and making it tremble. The ball generated the hard light that filled the grooves, similar to how the golem's core had reacted. It was making its own schematic that was probably held inside the pedestal. The magic knew what to do even if I didn't. I just had to stand back and watch the show. The hard light began picking up stone pillars and blocks lying nearby and underground, until a doorway was made. Some pieces had been broken and worn away by age, so the hard light filled in the missing pieces.

The result was very cool. I looked at the pedestal and found an orange stone almost like... I grinned, suited myself up in my hard-light armor, grabbed the stone, and placed it next to Will's soul stone. The orange stone fit in place as if it had always belonged there.

Immediately, my menu scrolled open by itself—*Gate travel has been unlocked. You can travel to other gate sites once they have been opened.* My map opened, and I found that I had actually passed one—the dwarven village. *This is getting interesting, to say the least.*

I smiled at Prayde and dropped my hard-light armor. "It's a gate spell only I can use. It's as if it was made for me."

Prayde grinned at me excitedly. "Will you use it for me? I'd love to see it," he almost begged.

I shook my head. "Sorry, I need to visit another spot to activate the gate there before I can travel from place to place," I explained.

He looked a little disappointed, but he didn't let it get him down; a great mystery had been unraveled for him. The ruins were renamed the Sun Gate. We walked back towards the settlement while excitedly talking about the discovery of the gate. I was eager to return to the dwarven ruins and open travel between the two areas.

We walked back across the border into the elven settlement, and I felt a disturbance in the air. I quickly stopped our excited chatter. We all looked around and saw Milly running up hurriedly; she had a panicked looked on her face.

Milan was fighting for his life in front of the settlement. I didn't stop to hear more; I sprinted from the group. My armor shone to life around my body; it flashed around me so forcefully it created a minor blinding effect on the populace, causing people to shout in fear as they moved away from me. Milan was important for many reasons—his soul judge made sure nothing foul got into the village, his barrier magic made sure no one found it, and he was very gifted. As he aged, he would become a genius, I was sure.

The settlement flashed around me as my feet pounded the ground so hard plumes of dust were left behind me. I could see it from up the street now. Milan was surrounded by the ogres. They were howling and slashing at him. His hands were contorted as he parried with barriers, causing the ogres' strikes to slide off the barriers and strike the ogres nearby. He was wearing a bright smile. Milan was enjoying the battle and the adrenaline brought on by fighting for his life. I took in the entire scene in the few seconds it took to clear the remaining distance.

A few elves must have joined Milan, trying to help him; they were dead, the bodies mangled with slashes across their chests and throats. I pulled my sword from its sheath and charged the first of the beasts. My shoulder connected with its hip, and I twisted harshly while shoving, which caused the ogre to be launched backwards. I grabbed my sword in a two-handed grip and did a quick downward slash that sliced an ogre from its shoulder down to its hip. It hissed at me and threw its arms out wide in an attempt to make itself look bigger. I wanted it to do that because that maneuver left it wide-open for the second part of my move as I brought the sword back up and slashed across its throat, beheading it. I immediately turned from the beast, no longer concerned about retaliation.

I saw Milan use his barriers to push the ogres back and into spikes; I watched as one was lodged into the chest of an ogre. *So the barriers aren't just for defense; they can be shaped and used for offense as well.* That was definitely good to know. I held my hand up, conjured a golden sun spear, and threw it, burning a hole through an ogre's stomach. It grabbed its side, groaning from the intense, burning pain. I jumped and used the forward momentum to cut its leg from under it, spinning and cutting its throat open immediately after the initial assault.

The ogres' numbers were dwindling, and we were winning. I looked around quickly; Milan and I were still the only ones fighting for the elves. *Is no one coming to help us? We are fighting for the settlement here.*

We were down to the last ogre. Milan used his barrier to sweep the monster's legs from under it, and I slammed my blade home into its head and ended its misery. I exhaled heavily while scanning the area—no more ogres.

I dropped my armor and smiled at Milan. "We did it. Are you okay?"

Milan was breathing heavily. His skin was flushed from the thrill of the fight. Grinning, he thrust his chest out. "I have never felt better. But this is definitely not good; they have never come this close to the settlement before. Somehow, they knew it was here. I think they can smell all the elves in there."

I nodded; it made sense. I wondered h— "Agh!" I yelled.

Blinding pain tore through my leg. Quickly, I turned, looked down, and saw a plague ogre with its teeth buried in my leg. I felt my heart drop while I summoned my dagger and stabbed the ogre through its eye. Its jaws went slack immediately, and it released me.

I fell to the ground, the pain in my leg excruciating. I used the dagger, cut my pant leg open to check the wound, and gasped. The leg looked bad. I used some water to wash the wound and felt my heartbeat in my throat; the teeth had left ragged holes in my leg. The area around the holes was red and bruised, and there were already red spiderweb veins extending from the holes.

Slowly I pulled the menu up. There was a flashing warning sign—INFECTED—scrawled across the entire menu. I cleared it. *Thanks a lot, I must have missed that happening,* I thought to myself. I was vaguely aware of Milan crying, trying to talk to me, looking at my wound, and falsely telling me it was going to be okay. I closed my eyes and kept reading the menu in my head.

You have been infected with the chona virus. The virus has three stages.

Stage one: Infection. There are multiple ways for the chona virus to begin its incubation within the chosen host.

A picture popped up of a cellular organism. It was disgusting—round, wriggling, tiny body covered in thousands of cilia-looking long hairs, and veinlike structure of purple that pulsed like neon. All of this in a cell so tiny you would need a microscope to see it.

The chona normally inhabited a plant called a chontatta. The plant itself was beautiful—a blue-and-purple plant closely resembling a lily—and it was indigenous to the wastelands across the seas. In the chontatta, the chona virus is neutral and remains dormant all its life. When the plant is disturbed, it releases the chona as a defensive mechanism to take the offender out.

At that point, the menu played a video of a small animal, one I had never seen before, sniffing the plant. The plant writhed and whacked the small rodent across its nose, releasing the chona spores onto it. The animal squeaked and ran away, upset that it had been disturbed from its meal. Meanwhile, the chona within the animal was already multiplying and taking over its internal systems. The animal returned to its burrow and lay there, its sides heaving until it finally stopped.

The chona had reproduces internally to the point that it takes over the infected host's internal systems and causes the host to perish. After the death of its host, the chona dies out naturally. With no life to feed on, it can't grow and replicate.

Stage two: Survival. Some larger animals are able to survive after being infected by the chontatta plant. That survival leads to stage two of the chona virus. The chona, realizing it cannot kill the host, switches sides and bolsters the host internally, giving it better protection and durability. The host becomes stronger and faster by great amounts; its pain receptors become dull, meaning it can receive more damage before it falls in battle.

I leaned forward. This sounded great actually; maybe my injury wasn't so bad. Maybe the ogres were just messed up because they had barely any brain function to begin with.

Stage three: Rage zombie. Once the host has become enhanced, the final stage begins. The chona virus attacks the brain, which results in enhanced aggression and unyielding rage. The host attacks anything nearby that is not itself. The chona virus will not attack others similarly infected.

Once the host has lost all of its faculties and only the rage remains, chona's stage three is completed, and a chontatta rage zombie is born. The rage zombies will work together to infect everything around them, even the very ground itself. Once an outbreak has begun, you must be quick to take the hive out. To learn more about the hive, please ask.

I quickly selected *Hive* from the menu.

The chontatta hive is made by the base-level zombies. The material can be made from wood, stone, mud, or even bodies, depending on what is most prevalent in the area. Once the infected number has grown high enough, a community forms and is centered around a chontatta chonker.

I almost giggled at the word *chonker*. The chonker was pictured; it looked similar to an ogre—large and fat—but surrounded by fleshy tentacles and large mounds of flesh, which was corrupted, decaying, and falling apart. *How disgusting.* I almost gagged when I saw it. It was clear the chonker was not meant to move around. Its purpose was to act as the chona's higher mind and to guide the chona further.

If we took the chontatta chonker out, we could stop the current spread. I looked for a cure—nothing. I opened my eyes and gritted my teeth. My last act was going to be fighting this chona and saving these people. I had just gotten to this new world, but I was already going to be killed. But before I died, I was going to blast this virus back into the ages if it was the last thing I did.

I stood up, looked around, and saw Milan sitting near me, crying. "You need to come with me. We need to talk to the council...and now," I said.

Milan looked up at me, nodded, and stood up while wiping his eyes. We headed back into the settlement and found Mira arguing with her father.

"Prayde, I have to go outside. What if Milan dies! Nothing will stop those things from finding us if that happens. Nothing will stop them from killing us all," she said.

"I told you no, Mira, and my answer is final; you are not going out there," Prayde said. He turned and saw me approaching with Milan in tow. "Oh good you made it. I'm glad you are all righ—" He stopped short when he saw the bite mark on my leg.

I narrowed my eyes at Prayde and opened my mouth to berate him for leaving us out there to die, but before I could get a word out, I was surrounded by elves with spears. My irritation launched so high I almost couldn't contain myself.

"For your own good, we are locking you in a cell. You will remain there until you pass," he said with such authority that I almost laughed.

"Prayde, I have information for you. There is a hive being built for the rage zombies, th—" I was cut off by a spear nudging me from behind.

I looked at Prayde and sneered. "If he pokes me again, you're gonna lose another elf. You can hear what I have to say, and then I'll be leaving. Or I can just leave."

Prayde looked irritated as he opened his mouth to speak, but I'd had enough of old men telling me what to do and bossing me around.

"Shut up. I changed my mind. If you speak, I will burn you. You've lost your vote on things. I can see you have no intention of listening. I'm leaving before I turn your settlement into a crater of cinders in the middle of this forest."

I turned and started walking down the path, feeling my rage burning bright within me; it was mixed with fear. *Is this me or the rage virus growing within me?*

I stopped at the entrance to the settlement and turned to see Milan and Mira standing there. "Hey, guys. I'm gonna head out. I have to do something about this virus. This isn't going to end well."

I told Mira what I had learned and asked her to pass the information along to the rest of the council. She promised she would and almost looked as if she was going to cry.

"It was nice meeting you both while I was here. I gotta say, place is beautiful. I'd have loved to spend more time here and visit. Turns out I'm gonna die soon."

Mira turned away, choking back a cough.

Milan was teary-eyed and stepped forward to hug me. "I'm sorry this happened, Eric. It's all my fault. If I had been sure to kill that ogre, you wouldn't have been bitten."

I shook my head and rubbed his back. "Hey, man, I let my guard down. Don't let that get to you. Things happen in and after battle; remember that."

Milan stepped back, nodded, turned, and walked away from me.

Mira looked at me and smiled through her tears. "Get it done, sun mage. Save our forest, please. If you need anything, please don't hesitate to ask. I will do whatever I can to help."

I smiled, waved, turned, and started walking away. As I made my way back home using my mini map as a guide, I was thankful the god had added that spell. I groaned and put my hands behind my head as I walked. The god was gonna give me a lot of flak for dying so soon.

I took a second to look down at my leg and made a face. The wound still looked pretty raw. The red spiderweb veins definitely didn't make me feel any better. I took a deep breath and started walking again. I wanted to get home and the sooner the better.

I need a plan.

Chapter 11

Changes in Another World's Sun

The hours passed as I walked. I made camp by climbing up a tree and wedging myself into a fork of the branches high up. I didn't need another ogre or animal coming upon me in the middle of the night. I closed my eyes and fell asleep, wishing my warm elf blanket were still with me. My sleep came quickly and passed uneventfully.

I woke up with the sun coming over the trees and shining into my eyes. I felt my heart jump just looking at the distance to the ground below me. I still didn't quite like heights. I gathered myself and began to shimmy my way down. Checking my mini map, I found I had covered a good distance the day before and started on my way once more. At this rate, I would be home before midday. I looked down, checked my leg, and saw that the red veins had spread farther.

I shook my head and tried to push it from my head; nothing I did was going to change the infection. I needed to do what I could now, or nothing would matter. I quickened my pace, just putting one foot in front of the other to get home.

Soon, I was back in familiar territory once more. I looked around, found the river that marked the area near my home, and crossed it. I walked past my home and up to the dwarven village. I still wanted to try the gate magic out.

Entering the village, I looked everywhere for the pedestal, but couldn't find one. I rubbed my head. *Where could it be?*

I heard a tapping noise behind me and nearly jumped out of my skin. Spinning around, I saw a smiling Brama standing behind me.

"Hello, my friend!" I said.

Brama smiled, waved, scribbled a "welcome back," and asked what I was looking for. I told him about the pedestal, and he scratched his head, thinking back to his early childhood. He finally shook his head and held his arms out to his sides. He couldn't remember any ruins or pedestals in the village. I rubbed my head, pulled out the gate map, and sighed. The mark clearly showed it was outside the village. I shook my head and waved at Brama to follow me.

"Sorry, Brama, I was so excited I forgot to check on the map for the exact location. It says that it's just outside the village, not in it."

Brama smiled and walked with me. The walk didn't take very long. We found a path that didn't appear to be man-made. I saw writing along its sides in a language I couldn't read, but I thought it looked like the language from the other sun gate. I smiled excitedly, ready to test it out. The path led us up to the top of a large hill that was flat on top, where we found what appeared to be several gates going in every direction. Was this the main hub for travel? I was pretty sure I could travel from here to any gate, anyplace I wanted.

I shrugged and walked into the middle of the stone formation, taking note that the pedestal here was a lot bigger than the one in the forest by the settlement. Maybe they just wanted this one to look cooler. The place for the sun core was also a lot larger; it was the size of a boulder at least. *It must take an amazing amount of power to get this place going.* I held my hands over my head and started building the massive hard-light sphere. I wanted this to be done correctly, so I took my time with it. I guided light strand by light strand into building it perfectly and continued until I was satisfied.

Using willpower, I built magic symbols into it; the magic did the rest. The sphere would gain energy from the sun, as usual, but instead of keeping the entire area powered, it would just power the gate I needed powered at the time. No energy waste here, that's for sure. I could change the design later if I wanted. But, for now, I only needed one active gate.

Smiling, I set the completed core into its slot and watched it start glowing as the orb pulled energy into itself from the sun. The orb went from its normal dull orange to a brilliant golden radiance. Words glowed, and the grooves filled with the hard light that would rebuild the sun gate and make it functional once again. The light strands extended from the grooves, grabbing stones and lifting them into the air to light their magic scripture. I following their progress.

Rebuilding took the better part of half an hour as the magic took effect. The result was a sun hub—the sun mages' mode of travel for traversing the world as needed. If I weren't going to die in a few days, this would have been the coolest thing I had ever seen. Unfortunately, though, I was just filled with regret that I wouldn't be able to complete the map. I shook my head. *What a waste.*

I looked at Brama and grinned. "Want to go see the settlement with me? We will have to be sneaky though."

Brama looked at me and raised an eyebrow.

I sighed and had to explain everything that had happened to me in the last few days. When I got to the part about my dying, he started tearing up. I shook my head at him and continued my story. He made a silent laugh when I got to the part about leaving the settlement a burning crater in the ground. He respected me for holding my boundaries and keeping my priorities straight, instead of letting them keep me locked up where I couldn't do anything.

When I finished the retelling, I activated my hard-light armor and held my hand over the pedestal. The hub registered me as the sun mage and told me I could now travel between areas. I wondered how it would feel. I activated the gate spell and watched as the orb began rapidly spinning in its socket; a lance of golden energy shot through the grooves, lighting up an archway. The archway shimmered a few times as the magic was activated for the first time in what must be thousands of years. I realized I was looking through the archway directly at the settlement's sun gate in their ruins. I looked around, making sure no one on their side was near, and then walked through holding Brama's hand.

The archway felt warm; it bathed us in heat like that of the forge in the dwarven village. Somehow, I knew that if I didn't hold his hand or some part of him, he wouldn't be able to cross with me. He would have been stuck on the other side. I checked my mini map and found that we were indeed back near the settlement. The gate spell had worked.

I cheered happily, looking at Brama, who was also excited for me.

"He's here!" I heard someone yell.

I spun quickly, fearing for Brama, and started pulling my sword from its sheath, only to find Milan standing there smiling happily.

"Eric, it's just me," he said.

I started moving towards the gate, but he held his hands up in a wait motion.

"Eric, please, I only called Mira. We have been here waiting for you. Please, we have something we need to tell you."

Laden with bags, Mira walked around the corner. "We are coming with you, Eric. We can't let you do this on your own. I mean, how selfish would that be? It's our forest too."

I couldn't help but find myself smiling. I wasn't full of enough bravado to turn down the help they were offering me. Quite frankly, I was glad to have them. Milan, for sure, could hold his own. Mira, I didn't know if she could fight; I had yet to see her in action. However, it was nice just to know she would be there.

"I only have one problem with that, Milan. What happens to the settlement if you are gone? Isn't your magic very important to the people and the settlement's defenses?"

Milan smiled, reached behind him, and pulled out a small piece of crystal that glowed a light neon blue.

I used my observation skill on it—*crystalized mana ore.*

"This helpful little piece of crystal is my own magic that I have crystalized. Placed in strategic positions, they cover the whole village in a barrier. They will have to fend for themselves otherwise. You are our first visitor in over sixty years, Eric, so I'm not terribly worried about having to use soul judge. When I turned sixteen, I went around using it on everyone. There is nothing to worry about there."

I nodded and turned to Mira. "What about your father? I don't need an angry father coming after me while we are busy trying to save the forest and everyone in it."

"My father no longer exists to me. I cut off all ties with him when he drove you away. You were our greatest hope in saving this place, and he ruined that in one fell swoop. When we are done, I will be coming back and challenging him for the leadership of this settlement. Sometimes, being the leader for the longest does not mean that you are the best choice for the role. I can see that now."

I nodded, thinking back to some leadership positions held by officials who were in my old world. Times change and things change. Sometimes people don't change with the times; that leads to stagnation and brings decay. The world needs change.

Smiling, I turned, looked at my new traveling party, then faced the gate. "Let's go save the forest, guys," I said.

I reached out, wrapped my arms around their clustered bodies, and stood up, lifting them all easily. I strode forward through the gate, back into the dwarven village. It was time to begin the planning phase.

We sat around a table near the forge. Serenaded by the snoring of the magma wyrm, we discussed once more all of the relevant information about the virus.

I tapped my lip a few times. "I think that we need to visit the ship. I need to see what they came back in."

"Why?" Mira asked.

"The virus strips them of mental faculties, right? How did they think to sail back? What if they brought something else with them, something worse that's telling them what to do? Or maybe there is a clue on board. Or did the elves burn the ship to stop the spread? I wouldn't be mad if they did; it would have been a good move."

Mira shook her head. "We haven't been able to go anywhere near that ship, Eric. Those things can almost sense when we go within a mile of it, and they come swarming."

Sighing loudly, I reached down and rubbed my leg. Everyone looked at me, and I smiled ruefully. "The information my ability gave me tells me that those infected with the virus won't be attacked by others that have it. Looks like it's up to me to do a little investigating."

Everyone, of course, immediately had a problem with that. They tried to dissuade me, telling me it was dangerous and foolish. Mira said that I could die.

I gave her a wry look, and she raised her hands to her mouth, shocked at what she had said. She already knew I was a dead man.

I smiled softly at her. "Either way, Mira. Either way." I stood up and walked from the room. I needed some fresh air.

I walked to the pond to watch the slimes squirming under the water. I watched a rat go running by and accidentally fall into the water. I reached out, intending to lift it from the pool. But a slime snatched it from the surface, eating it before I could get to it. I watched the rat be pulled down and dissolve in seconds. I shivered. *That was horrifying.*

I used my observation skill again on the slime. Scrolling past the information I already knew—it cleans and purifies water, eats anything, breaks down everything it put in its body, can't be poisoned, and can't be afflicted with disease. I kept scrolling, marveling at how amazing slimes wer—

But I then abruptly stopped. *Can't be afflicted with disease?*

I called the slime to the surface, picked it up, and smiled. "Can you save me, little slime?"

The slime wriggled in my arms, excitedly feeling my hope through our bond. I set it near my leg and watched it extend an appendage and probe my wound softly before pushing some of itself inside my leg.

I grunted in pain. The slime manifested a sad face as it felt me hurt. "Don't you worry, little guy. I've dealt with worse."

The slime looked as if it gave me a nod. I saw it pull some of my blood into its body, and the blood dissolved. The slime withdrew its appendage and sat there thinking. It shivered as it failed. I almost screamed in frustration, feeling my last bit of hope slipping through my fingers until—

My menu came to life, and a new tree opened—but not for me—for slimes. I opened the tree, my body shaking nervously. *What is this?*

> *Infectious-disease slime: New slime subclass. By feeding this slime an infectious disease, you have helped it gain a class. The slime can develop antibodies within its body if given enough infected material from several sources. Current possibility of curing disease: ten percent.*

The little slime shivered happily and twisted on itself; it felt my heart pounding with hope as I kept reading.

> *The slime will use the blood taken from you to work on a booster that will lessen some of the effects of the virus. It will inject you with the booster here and there.*
>
> *The booster will not prevent you from succumbing to the disease. It may not even come up with a cure, but your odds of survival are increased from zero.*

I almost felt as if I would cry. All I wanted was a chance. I had hope now. I had something to fight for.

I turned to the slime and smiled. "Thank you, my little friend."

The slime wiggled happily and slithered forward, climbing onto me and up to my back, finally perching on my shoulder. It would stay there to be safe and near me for my shots.

Feeling the best I had in days, I stood up. I walked back into the house and up to my circle of friends sitting at the table. I opened my map and asked exactly where the ship was. I was going to go and do a little searching.

Mira looked at me and sighed as she pointed on my map to where the ship would be along the coast. "It is going to be somewhere here, along this stretch of beach. I can't pinpoint it exactly because none of us has really seen it. We just know the direction that they have been coming from."

I nodded at her and studied the map. The best course of action would be to go through the settlement gate and walk from there. I closed my map and grabbed a go bag. I saw an alert pop up in my menu as I was getting ready and opened it.

The virus has settled in your body leading to stage two.

I felt the blood drain from my face. It had been a few days, but still. This was too fast.

A new message popped up.

The virus within your body has made your body grow stronger. You also feel less pain when taking damage. The virus has begun making changes to your body to make it more suitable.

I clenched my hands. I needed to go *now*. I almost ran from the house to tell my friends goodbye as I speed-walked to the sun gate past the village. I activated my gate magic, walked through the portal into the settlement area, and took a look around, making sure no one was there to ambush me.

I could almost feel the blood pounding in my head. *Why hasn't the slime done an injection yet? The virus is clearly spreading unchecked throughout my body.*

I shook my head. The slime was doing the best it could; I was sure of that.

I checked my mini map and started walking towards the area in which Mira had told me the ship would be. I had started early in the day, and I was glad I did; I did not want to be out here and doing this at nighttime. If I listened closely, I could hear the screams far off in the distance as the infected ogres fought or hunted something.

I kept my head on a swivel, moving it from side to side, checking around corners, and being wary of what might be lurking behind trees. After watching Mira, I had adopted some of her movements as my own—for example, brushing sticks to the side before completely stepping down, which eliminated the cracking noises that branches made when they broke, and stepping on the outside of my foot before rolling it flat, which made the footfall more silent. The going was slower, but I moved quietly through the forest and was able to finally start seeing some of the wildlife that otherwise would have disappeared before I got the chance to see them.

I checked the map frequently to make sure I was on the right path; I was making good progress. When I reached the halfway point, my skin started crawling; I couldn't really figure out why. I felt very unsettled and had to stop. I scanned the area, but everything looked normal.

What is wrong?

I finally realized what it was. The forest had gone silent— no bird noises or animal calls. It was as if someone had flipped a switch, and the world had been blanketed. I shuddered. It was unnatural, to say the least.

I saw a bird drop down to peck at the ground a few times. When I turned to look at it, I almost recoiled from the sight— the bird was in the final stages of the virus and was going to die soon. It was dripping red fluid from its beak.

I grabbed my slime and told it to catch the bird and eat it. I threw the slime as hard as I could at the bird and watched the slime expand. The bird tried to fly away, but it was too weak. The slime caught and ate the diseased body of the bird, processing the virus information within it.

The bird was already dissolved by the time the slime came slithering back and moved its way up to my shoulder. I checked the progress bar and sighed; the bird must not have had enough biomass to give the slime enough information with which to work. *What a shame.*

I started moving out once more and felt a sharp pain in the side of my neck. The slime had administered my first dose.

I almost cheered. I opened my menu and read the effects of the booster.

> *The booster shot will hold the virus at bay and help you survive longer. It will not save you; it will just buy some time.*

Even if the booster shot didn't end up saving me, receiving it felt like a positive thing. I closed out the menu and kept walking to the boat with a new spring in my step. I needed to find an ogre to give the little guy something with which to work.

While in the forest, I looked around and tried to find anything else that was infected. I didn't find any animals that were, but I did notice that the trees were all starting to look a little off. I walked up to one, placed my hand on it, and could tell from its internal magic that it was dying. The virus was killing the trees off. The forest was in great danger, but we already knew that.

Taking my hand from the tree, I kept walking. I reached into my bag, pulled out a sandwich Brama had made, and smiled; he always made the best food. I took a few bites and savored the flavor. *I hope I lived long enough to keep enjoying his food.* I really needed him to teach me some of his dwarven delicacies. I washed the food down with water from my bottle, sighed happily, and felt content.

I checked the map again and knew I was coming to the end of the forest. The beach should be just up ahead. I crept up to the forest line and peered through the tree line, making sure no one was on the beach. I looked up and down, and there was nothing, not a single person, monster, or beast to be found. I walked out onto the beach, right up to the ocean, looked up and down the stretch, and tried to locate the boat. To the right, I thought I saw a mass way down the beach. So I started heading that way. The sand was too slippery for me, and it made my footing too unsure, so I made my back to the tree line and walked along it. The soil provided much better footing.

While I was walking, I kept myself aware, waiting for an ambush. I knew the monsters weren't supposed to attack me, but I couldn't be sure. I didn't want to take the chance that they would just let me go. The closer I got to the mass, the surer I was that it was the ship. Sitting on the beach, it was massive; it must have carried hundreds of ogres. It really put into perspective what we were dealing with here. This was an outbreak of the highest level. This was something we were definitely not prepared for. This should have stayed over there in the wastelands.

This was just a rat killer to the monsters that lived there. To us, it was something that could potentially wipe us all out, down to the very last creature. Once I was parallel to the boat, I walked toward it to make my way to the ramp, which had been lowered onto the beach. The sand around the boat was beaten flat by the heavy feet that had stomped it down. The sand was also red. I was not a good enough tracker to tell if the tracks in the sand were recent. So, feeling my heart skipping beats in my chest, I took a deep breath and made my way up the ramp and onto the ship.

On the deck, there was more red fluid. I had the slime start sucking up the juice while I was exploring. I turned and made my way into what was possibly the captain's quarters. The poorly put-together hut was hastily made, and the inside was filled with scratches. I almost overlooked them, but then realized they were actually tick marks meant to mark the passage of time, possibly days. Six marks with one going through it; that was seven. Something was smart enough to have counted the time passing. I didn't think that a rage zombie could do that. I bit my lip; I knew something else was here. But what was it? What had they brought back with them from the wastelands?

I didn't have enough information. I'd have to ask Mira and Milan when I got back. I turned and made my way from the captain's area; there were no books or documents in there, nothing to give me any more information that I would need. When I got to the side of the ship, there was a latch open on a hatch. I sighed loudly. I really did not want to go down there. I activated my armor before hopping in. The fall wasn't very long, and I landed in a crouch on something soft. I looked around, checking to make sure I was alone.

The inside of the ship was entirely covered by slimes. The ground beneath me squelched as I moved along. I also noticed what looked like mounds of flesh on the walls; they were held in place by slime. I shivered. *What the hell is this?*

I was hoping it wasn't a biomass situation. *Are they gathering and building a hive mind? That would not be great.*

I called my slime to me. I had to wait a few moments till it came wading through the mounds of flesh and slime. I picked my slime up and held it to the piles of flesh.

The slime reached out with an appendage, touched the mound, and pulled some of the meat back, absorbing it. It shook slightly. Whatever this was, it wasn't corrupted with the infection enough for it to process into usable data. I set the slime down and watched it start absorbing one of the ship's slimes. It definitely held the corruption.

I moved farther into the ship and felt the hair on the back of my neck standing on end. There were slime cocoons hanging from the ceiling; I could see people and animals in the cocoons. Some were dead; others moved once in a while.

I used my observation skill.

> *slime cocoon. A new observation on the behavior of the rage zombies. They capture creatures, drag them back to quiet, dark places, and wrap them in paralysis, causing slime that they can naturally make in their own mouths. Once cocooned, the prey is hung from the ceilings and left until ready to be eaten. They are infected once they are in the cocoons; some are left in the cocoon until they are changed into rage zombies.*

I sighed. I had been hoping this would be a search and rescue mission. But this was a feeding station; there were no more clues here. I had learned something important from this journey though.

I started turning back towards the ladder when I heard a peculiar noise. Almost as if fabric were being stretching. I tilted my head, trying to hear it better. The noise was coming from the back. I started moving through the cocoons, pushing them to the side. One in the back was wriggling from side to side. The slime around it was stretching and tearing. This cocoon was enormous. Easily three times larger than any ogre.

I started backing up when my mind started swimming; it sent me to my knees. I grabbed my head, trying to hold in a scream. Something was wrong. My head hurt so bad it felt as if something were squeezing it.

My menu flashed open: *Warning! Infection spreading! Change occurring!*

I screamed, "No, not yet!"

I had to stop the infection before it was too late. I had to save the forest. I had to save Mira. My mind flashed to her smile and those soft-purple eyes before my head started swimming again, causing me to throw up on the floor. My body was racked with pain; it felt as if my stomach were going to tear itself apart. My hands hurt just as bad. I looked down at them and screamed; my nails were growing thicker and longer; my hands, larger and stronger. It was similar to watching a werewolf transformation in a movie.

The bones cracked under my skin, changing their shape, becoming bigger and stronger; my nails grew even longer and ended in pointed tips. I knew this change was happening down my entire body, making me larger and stronger. The virus was changing my body into a more effective killer for the transmission of the virus.

I slammed my eyes shut as they started burning as if someone were stabbing them with hot irons. I grabbed my head again, screaming, slamming myself onto my back, and flailing. There was so much pain. *Please, the god...anyone, please make it stop.*

I felt something stab my chest, and I looked down. It was my slime; it had a determined look on its face. It had grown six pale appendages that had turned into six needlelike arms; it was slamming them into my chest, distributing the booster throughout my body at different points for a more effective spread.

I felt the pain subsiding and waited for the change to start reversing itself, but it didn't. I still had the claws on my hands. I was still a large monster.

What am I becoming now? I rolled over, feeling weaker and yet stronger. The change had brought me so much pain. I almost understood the rage the ogres carried, why they lashed out at whoever was nearby. That pain was so bad I wanted to rip and tear myself apart.

I was still pulling myself up when I heard a thumping. I looked up and almost screamed again. I found out what they had captured and turned. Using my observation skill, I found it was called a forest troll, a normally passive and friendly creature that spent most of its time sleeping. It could often be mistaken for a small hill.

Yeah, but this small hill was stomping towards me. I was confused. Why was it after me? The virus was supposed to distinguish me as infected so that I would not be attacked.

I felt the slime hide on my back, and then I understood why. It wasn't after me. It wanted my slime.

I stood up and activated my armor...only to find it didn't. I tried again as I watched the small hill get closer.

"Come on!" I hissed.

I got nothing. Groaning, I put my fists up; there wasn't enough time to turn and run from this thing. It would be on me the second I tried to get up the ladder. I looked it up and down, and saw on it the same transformation I had just suffered. Its normally large hands had been given sharp claws. Its eyes were filled with a feverish hate so deep I almost flinched when its eyes locked with mine. It realized I was blocking it from its next meal; that made me an enemy, virus or not.

The troll roared a sound that started as a deep rumbling in its chest, but turned into a shallow, squealing, hateful scream.

I felt the skin on my body crawl. *This thing is scary as all hell.* I moved forward and almost fell. I was surprised by my own newfound speed. Stumbling, I collected myself and tried again, this time keeping my footing and stopping by its leg. I kicked out, slamming the bottom of my foot into its leg.

The monster groaned a little and reached down to grab at me.

I moved out of the way quickly. That was highly ineffective. I drew my sword and held it at the ready in a two-handed grip in front of me. This thing's skin looked thick enough to repel most things. I wished I could use my sun armor, and having that times-one bonus would have been really helpful right now.

The troll stomped over to me and tried again to grab me.

I danced to the side smoothly and sliced at its arm. The blade bounced off as if I hadn't even touched it. I sighed and looked around. *What do I do?* I needed something—

The troll lunged at me while I was in the midst of thinking and trying to plan.

I jumped to the side so aggressively that I cleared half the ship and hit one of the pillars that held the ship together. I gasped as the wind was blown from my body. *That defi-*

nitely didn't feel great. I shook it off and stood up, looking at the place I had been standing; I had jumped clear across the ship. *How?*

I almost smiled. I was a stronger killer now. I sheathed my blade and crouched, my arms outstretched. Time to test what I was given.

The troll roared as it charged me again.

I yelled back and ran forward.

The troll grabbed at me again, and I ducked its claws. I used my own to dig into the calf muscles on the backs of its legs and marveled at how easily my new claws sliced the skin that my sword couldn't even cut through. Now, I knew why the virus normally prevented them from fighting other infected creatures—they would tear each other apart like paper-mache.

I jumped back, making sure to not put too much into it; otherwise, I would be rocketed across the ship again. The troll turned easily; the monster was large, and it would surely take more than my one cut to do anything lasting to it. Smiling, I flicked my hand; blood flecks from my hand dotted the slime on the floor of the ship.

It seemed my speed had been upped by a few points as well. If, before, I had been able to move at twenty-seven miles per hour, about the peak for a human, I could now move closer to fifty. It wasn't blinding, but the upgrade was staggering to me. I felt as if this was what I needed to flip the tables on these zombies. I was going to save everyone.

I crouched, brought my legs under me, tensing them and building power before I launched myself at the troll as if I were coming off a springboard.

The troll growled, whirled, and slammed its fist up, around, and into me, crushing me into the deck.

I groaned as I felt the wood beneath me splinter; if it hadn't given, I knew my skeleton would have. I was a fool. If the change had enhanced me so much, what had it done to the troll? I was cocky and got myself wrecked for it.

I still had the connection to my slime. I sighed as I felt blood flow past my lips. At least, it was still alive; that was a good sign.

The troll growled again and spun, throwing me harshly against the side of the ship, so hard, in fact, that the hull splintered around me. I broke through the side of the ship and hit the sand fast, skidding like a stone skimmed across the surface of a lake. I landed on the far side of the beach and lay there on my side, groaning. I was lucky nothing was broken.

I looked up at the sun, feeling its warmth and the faint breeze bringing the salty smell of the ocean with it. I was finding that I loved this smell. I closed my eyes and felt the waves of pain rolling over me. I also felt through our bond the slime's concern for me. It was worried because of both the change that was overcoming me and the physical damage I was taking.

I held my arms out and soaked in the rays of the sun. I heard more cracking and opened my eyes to see the troll screaming as it tried to pry its way through the ship's hull to get to me. I could try and run. But that would mean this monster would be out running loose and could possibly hurt more people. I needed to get rid of him.

My menu flashed open and I almost gasped.

Infection tree unlocked. One ability. Boost infection. Mutation.

I scrolled the ability. It was dangerous. It was tempting too...almost too tempting.

The ability would let me for a brief time encourage the infection raging within me to mutate me further. I would gain more power, but I would also change more. *Is it worth it?*

I almost dismissed the idea and closed the menu, but just then I heard the troll screaming again. All I could see in my mind was Mira—her eyes so soft and caring—being ripped to shreds. Milan being pulled apart. Brama being eaten—silent screams no one could hear.

I stood up and roared back at the troll. It was a strange noise that escaped my throat. It was pain, grief, and fear, all mixed into one noise. It was all my courage and foolishness as I hit the Boost button. I felt the virus flare to life within me; the pain I had experienced earlier seemed like child's play next to this. If there was a comparison between the two, the first would have been a stubbed toe. This would have been surgery on every muscle at the same time with rusty, dull tools. I felt my bones shatter in my skin and fell, trying to catch myself with arms that were already shattered.

I watched the bones moving around as they rebuilt, the muscles growing larger around the bones. My arms were longer too. Once my arms had stopped rebuilding themselves, I pushed myself up off the sand. Feeling my teeth shifting around, I opened my mouth; the canines on the top and bottom were extending like fangs. Other teeth became sharper for biting and tearing through flesh. My jaw thickened and widened, which also increased my biting power.

I looked down, and my eyes opened wider. If I had been six feet before, I was closer to seven now. My legs were packed with muscles; my toes ended with the same tipped nails as my hands. I straightened my spine, grunting as my body shifted with loud, jostling crunching noises as things inside of me were moved around and placed more effectively. I twisted my neck to the side slowly and cracked it. My back was packed with more muscle for striking and slashing. I was truly a killing machine now. I was probably the apex of this virus.

The transformation ended, and I stood almost naked on the beach. The only thing left of my clothing was my boxers;

my other clothes were either stretched and torn to ribbons. I slowly extended my arms out, listening as the newly enhanced bones and muscles stretched and cracked as they were used for the first time.

The troll was finally breaking free from the boat, and it landed on the beach, grunting with simpleminded hunger.

I watched it coldly; it had caused me this mind-numbing pain. I had gone through hell just to make sure I could put this beast down. I wasn't even sure I was a human anymore. I was something else now. Changed because of some hell-spawn plant in a wasteland across the sea. I opened my mouth, inhaled, and let out a guttural growl at the approaching troll. The rage in my mind and heart took over.

***

The troll stopped and looked at thing it was pursuing. The thing it had thrown through the ship was now different. It was more dangerous, a challenge. The troll sniffed at the air and smelled the same virus that ran through its veins. It cocked its head and wondered why it wanted to fight. The troll was confused.

Then it smelled it again. It smelled so good. It wanted to eat...what was it again? The troll almost couldn't remember and groaned as its stomach growled with such intense hunger. Why couldn't it just eat the nice-smelling thing? It remembered a faint trace; it was a small ball, and it was on its back.

The troll looked up excitedly and growled. The thing wasn't wearing stuff anymore. Nowhere for it to hide!

The troll also saw the ball it wanted to eat bouncing away behind the thing. The troll started running after it, the hunger taking over its better senses once more.

***

I saw the troll start running after the little slime, and I moved forward, my arms still outstretched. My rage was burning red-hot; I could feel it as if it were a heat wave burning around me. As the troll stepped within range, I leaned back and slashed down heavily. I heard the wind whistling behind the strike, the very air parting behind the sharp nails.

The troll screamed as its flesh was torn by my claws. It started backing up, holding its wounds. I kept moving forward, keeping step with it. My arms and hands clawed here and stabbed there. It tried to hit me, but I ducked its blow.

I jumped onto it, biting its arm. I wrenched with my whole body and pulling out a chunk of its arm. It tasted so good I wanted to eat it. Instead, I spit it out in disgust, worried for my own mental state. If I thought it tasted good, that was not going to go over well.

The troll screamed, started throwing a tantrum, and rushed me, trying to windmill its arms to hit me. That was not going to work on me, not anymore. The blows were coming in quick, but I could see them; they were easy to read, and with my enhanced senses, I was able to dodge them. I moved behind the troll and kicked the back of its leg. The troll screamed as its leg folded. I made my hand into a flat shape and speared the troll through its back, severing its spine. The troll's scream was cut short, and it rolled over, hitting the sand.

I didn't stop there though. I had been bitten by one that had just suffered a chest wound. So I reached down, grabbed its head, and started jerking violently until it cracked. I had severed the spinal cord in two separate places. If that didn't put it down for good, I'd be surprised.

I lay down, grunting harshly. The two transformations had taken a lot out of me. I needed to rest. It felt as if my heart were going to beat its way out of my chest. I looked at the ship and remembered all of the cocoons. One more thing to do.

I stood up and tried the armor one more time. I smiled as it sprang to life around me, but I noticed it was different now. Before, it had looked like a thin version of knights' armor. Now, it looked thicker, like bruiser armor. I felt as if I were walking around in a powered exoskeleton.

I closed my eyes and breathed deeply. Then I raised my arms over my head and breathed in slowly. I started gathering the fire in my arms over my head. I felt it gathering, swirling, and raging. I roared and threw the fireball through the troll-sized hole in the hull of the ship.

Slimes must be combustible because the rate at which the ship was engulfed in flames was insane. I staggered back from the force of it and the heat. I turned away and moved back so I wasn't within range of the flames. I walked back to the troll, grabbed its legs, and dragged it to the forest line where the slime was waiting for me.

It jumped excitedly as it watched me. Dropping my armor and breathing heavily, I leaned against a tree, still recovering, and told my slime, "Go ahead, little buddy. Eat up. This is the freshest sample we will ever get."

The slime wriggled and started eating the troll. As I reclined against a tree and started falling asleep, I was jostled by the slime bouncing up and down on me. I looked for the troll's body, but it was gone; only a blood stain on the sand was left. Smiling, I petted the slime and picked it up. "Time to go home, little one."

I stood up, stretched, and opened my mini map back up, checking the direction I needed to go. Once I found it, I started running. The trees flew by me in a blur. I jumped up into a tree and started springing off branches. I covered a lot more ground that way. Instead of six hours, I was back at the settlement in an hour and a half.

I jumped from a tree, landed easily, and got ready to walk through the portal.

"Eric, stop there!" I heard called out to me.

Recognizing the voice, I turned and narrowed my eyes. It was Prayde. "What do you want, elf?"

Prayde walked up and looked at me. "What has happened to you? What have you become?"

I sighed and looked at my body. I looked great, honestly; my body was stronger and harder than it had ever been. But at what cost? "The virus changed my body and caused me to mutate. I turned into this." I didn't know why I was telling him this. Not like he had any right to know.

Prayde looked me over and sighed. "For the record, I *am* sorry. I panicked. I have to think of my people. I won't ask for you to understand. When you have people who will follow you, you'll understand. There's nothing you won't do to make sure that they are safe and sound."

I nodded at him. I understood that well enough already.

"Eric, are they okay? Mira? Milan? I know they went with you. I don't want any trouble. I just want to make sure my daughter is safe. Even if *she* did cut all her ties with *me*, nothing will *ever* sever the love a father has for his daughter."

"They are safe; do not worry. We are working to save the forest as we speak."

I then gave him an update on the ship that I had burned on the coastline and about the infected troll. I saw his heart drop. That meant that the virus not only infected terrifyingly vicious monsters, but also it infected poor docile monsters who just loved sleeping and were being killed as they did so.

Smiling sadly, I turned and walked to the gate, but not before I said, "Prayde, we really should be working together on this. I'll be back in a few days with some news if there is any. If I'm not dead, that is. If not me, it will be your daughter."

I walked through the gate before he responded and found myself back at the outskirts of the dwarven village. Brama was there, tinkering with something in his hands. He looked up at me and looked stunned.

I smiled kindly at him. "It's me, Brama. I promise. It's Eric. Gather our friends; I have news."

I took a step, and my body shook. I coughed, spitting up blood. I made sure to aim it away from Brama; I didn't want him getting sick. I fell to my knees; more blood came from my mouth, and I groaned. Something was wrong; everything was going dark. I flipped onto my back, away from the blood, and grabbed my chest. My heart was slowing down. I wasn't going to turn into a zombie. I was going to die of a heart attack.

I closed my eyes to the sound of Brama's retreating footsteps. He was going to get the rest of the party probably; he couldn't move me on his own. I faded out and found myself sitting with the god back in the same room in which I had met him.

The god was looking at me and smiling. "Back so soon, Eric? It hasn't even been a year yet!"

I smiled at him and held out my hands out. "I did what I could. Without that last boost, I think that troll was going to kill me. I couldn't bear the thought of my friends being killed or turned by those zombies."

The god nodded at me a few times and folded his arms over his chest. "Eric, you are going to survive this. I don't know if you are going to like what they are doing to you right now, but it's the only thing they could really think to do. That Brama is a smart cookie. I will give him that."

I nodded. Brama *was* very smart. It was crazy what he could come up with in that brain of his. "What are they doing? Something crazy, I hope," I said, only partially joking.

The god laughed and slapped his knee before pulling up a view of my large body inside of the house, surrounded by my friends. "It's crazy, all right. Right out of a horror movie, I would say."

I couldn't help but agree as I watched Brama take a knife and start slicing down the middle of my chest. I grabbed my own chest, watching in horror and fascination at the scene playing out before me. Brama reached behind him and pulled out a metal core lined with gems; it glowed from the magic that was poured into it.

"Is that a magic golem core of some kind?" I asked as the god and I watched Brama set the glowing orb into my chest.

The flesh of my chest started smoking, and then the core sank into me. I watched as magic runes spread out from the orb and throughout my body. The incision Brama had made was closing, sealing the orb within me. The orb was healing me from the inside. It was a last-ditch effort by Brama. No one had ever placed a golem core inside a person, so he had no clue what was going to happen.

"This is definitely going to open up some new doors for people down there," the god mumbled to himself and then chuckled. He rolled some dice a few times.

I looked over; the dice he was rolling were made from several kinds of crystal and possibly bone. I cocked my head to the side as I watched him. "What are you doing?"

The god looked at me and grinned. "I am rolling for your chance at survival, Eric. Anytime something new happens, I have to roll for its odds of success. After that, it's handled by the world itself. That's what makes being a creator so exciting. I never know what you people are going to come up with next; I can only modify the rules after I have seen it."

I nodded and continued watching. My body was shaking on the table. Brama had his hands on my chest, holding me down; his hands were stained with blood. I gasped. "Is Brama going to be infected now? Look at him; he is covered in my blood!"

The god shook his head. "When the slime you made started giving you the boosters, it may not have cured you, but it did stop the virus within you from being transmittable."

I let out a loud *whoosh* of breath, relieved I hadn't killed my friend.

The god grinned and jumped to his feet. "Success! You are now part golem, Eric. The surgery was a success, and I think you'll find that your magic has gained a nice bonus as well from it.

"There's something more with that core; it's only been partially written. It seems like there's another part to it that can be added on. I'm not sure how you'll be able to do that with it inside of you. I'm sure you'll be able to work that out later though."

Excited, I opened my menu to review my status and found that it had jumped an entire tier, from average to adept. I was growing stronger, and I think using my own magic would be a better move from here on out, rather than using the weapons I had been gathering. I could replicate my weapons through hard-light magic; now that my magic was strong enough, I could just fight by combining the spells I had learned with my enhanced physical form.

Smiling, I looked up at the god and was just about to say something when he reached out and pushed me.

I gasped and started falling backwards, not realizing there was no floor behind me. As I fell back to the other world from the heavens, I watched the platform I had been standing on grow smaller and smaller. I had a job to do anyway. No time to sit around and talk.

The fall ended, and my eyes opened. I was lying on my bed. It was time to find my friends and get the ball rolling.

Chapter 12
Another War in Another World's Sun

My bupo was lying on me and trying to heal me. He looked stressed that he couldn't remove the virus from my body and make me well again. I groaned softly and lifted my torso off the bed while holding the bupo. He chirped happily as he looked up at me. I hugged him tenderly.

"Trying to make me all better, little buddy?"

The bupo danced in a circle excitedly and jumped from my arms, landing on the bed in a little mound.

I slid off the bed and then stood up and stretched; I had rested long enough. I strode from the room and looked around; my friends were nowhere to be found. I walked outside, but they weren't there either. I summoned my little doctor slime and felt it quickly bouncing its way towards me. I felt it jump up and land on my shoulder. *Good, now to search the area. Maybe the dwarven village?*

I jumped into a tree and started going from tree to tree towards the village. Traveling sure had gotten easier since I'd gone through my mutation. I hope I lived long enough to enjoy this. I looked around from my perch in the tree and saw my friends huddled together and talking around the dwarven forge.

Smiling, I leapt from the tree and, with a hard thud, landed next to them in a crouch. "Hello there, guys. Guess who lived?"

All of them jumped back, screaming and gasping at the sight of me. I grinned and gave them a little wave hello.

Mira was the first to recover. She jumped forward, latched her arms around me, and hugged me. "Eric, you're alive again! How?"

I smiled and hugged her back, holding on to her for a moment before letting go. "I was up there"—I pointed to the sky—"watching you."

Milan arched an eyebrow.

I tapped my chest over the spot where there was no visible mark left from Brama's procedure. "Good call on the golem core, Brama. Without that, I would definitely be dead right now." I walked over to Brama, knelt, and pulled him into a hug.

Brama hugged me back hard.

"Thank you, my friend. You saved my life, and I owe you one."

Brama nodded and tapped his chest over his heart; it looked as if he was going to tear up.

I turned to Milan and smiled.

"I'm not hugging you, but I am glad you are alive, Eric," he told me.

I grinned and held up my fist to him. He smiled back and looked at my fist before finally raising his hand and touching my fist with his open palm. Fair enough. I guess it wasn't fair to assume fist-bumping was a common world-to-world occurrence. "On a more serious note, did anyone come up with a game plan while I was out?"

Mira looked at me with a good deal of concern. "Are you well enough to carry anything out?"

I closed my eyes. It was true; I felt a mixture of worn down and beat up, even though I also felt the most powerful I had ever been. I opened my eyes and nodded at her. "I will do what I can till I can do no more."

She seemed to take the answer well enough, but she kept that look of worry in her eyes. I didn't like it.

"We think we found the hive while you were out. Well, my dad did. Apparently, you told him someone would be stopping by, so when we didn't, he sent a party to come find us. He didn't know exactly where you lived, so they spread out pretty far. In doing so, they came upon another settlement that had been established by some gnomes. Unfortunately, they had been completely wiped out. The zombies were apparently exhibiting some odd behaviors that were uncommon. I think it's a good shot that they are holding the chonker within," Mira said.

Nodding, I rubbed my chin. "Just how far away is this settlement? I think we should go and kick this thing's ass."

Brama tapped my leg a few times, and I looked down at him. "Yes, my friend?"

Brama smiled and gestured me over to a table.

I followed him over and looked at him questioningly.

He grabbed his slate and started scribbling away.

> You need new clothes and new armor. I am going to make you some. Please give me some time to do so before you leave again. One day.

I nodded. It would be good to have some actual armor. I let Brama take his measurements. Shortly after that, I heard the forge start roaring to life. Brama had asked me for my chunk of denthyl ore, so I had pulled it from my inventory and handed it over. I was excited to see what the forge master would make for me. I asked him to leave the tips of the fingers and toes open; the nails on my hands and feet had been enhanced so much that they actually cut better than my sword and daggers.

Leaving Brama with all of this information, I started walking to the outskirts of the area; I wanted to get a little more air. I opened my menu and looked through my status and the new tree that had opened with my surgery. Most of the golem tree was blocked from my view. One interesting thing was unlocked though—I could now create a facility to make golems. It was hefty in regards to the materials it required—lots of gemstones and metals, a dwarven forge.

I smiled; this was gonna get interesting if I could start pumping out golems. I certainly loved the thought of getting some golem creations going; it would make my automation easier.

I closed my menu and turned back. It was time to head home and rest. Tomorrow, I would have new armor, and then our party would head out to fight the chonker. We were going to win and find a cure.

I was walking past the forge when I spotted Mira. I raised my hand in greeting and walked over to her.

She smiled at me. "Hey, Eric, how are you feeling?"

"Still not at a hundred, but I'm doing better than I was, which is good. But I do have a question for you, Mira. Where is your weapon?"

Mira sighed, looked at the ground, and kicked at it, sending a pebble flying. "When you found me after the ogre beat me down and nearly killed me, I didn't have one. I lost my weapons somewhere; I don't have any."

I nodded, reached into my inventory, and retrieved my whip sword. Pulling it free, I handed it to her.

Mira looked at me curiously after taking the sheathed sword from my hands. "Isn't this your sword, Eric? What will *you* use?"

I held out my hand and summoned the golden hard-light sword into my hand. It had been a while since I had used the weapon. It was going to be my main one now since my internal battery could support greater use of magic.

Mira's eyes opened wider. "Wow, that looks really impressive. It looks like it's made from sunlight."

I grinned and told her that was exactly what it was made of.

Impressed, Mira nodded and took the whip sword from its sheath. She looked it up and down. "This looks really sharp and deadly. Where did you get it?"

I sat down at a nearby table and told her the story of the dungeon in which I had been trapped. Mira sat down next to me and listened as I told her of the months I had spent training and fighting for my life against the monsters of the dungeon before I finally freed myself.

She then looked down at the sword in her hands. "This can turn into a whip too? That sounds pretty cool. Will you show me how?"

I took the sword from her hands and showed her the wrist-flick technique required to shift the weapon between forms. After handing it back, she practiced a few times and nodded.

"I had a whip when I was younger. It was made from a length of iron that was lengthened, rolled out, then braided together," she told me.

I raised an eyebrow. That sounded as if it would hurt if it hit you, but then again, so would mine.

Mira sheathed her new blade and smiled at me. "Thank you. I was worried I wouldn't be able to play much of a part tomorrow. But, thanks to this, I will be able to help you now."

Smiling, I reached out my hand and placed it on her shoulder. "I wouldn't want you anywhere else but at my side, Mira."

I saw her face flush as I stood and started walking away. I didn't quite understand for a moment. Then it hit me. *Oh man, I just told her I want her at my side and nowhere else. I just meant I trust her; she definitely did not take that the way I meant it.* I sighed and rubbed my forehead a few times. *What a pain.*

I jumped into a nearby tree and made my way home. The trees went by me in a blur as I jumped from branch to branch.

I wanted to test something out with the other slimes back at the house.

I landed on the dirt path leading towards my home, and I walked the rest of the way, taking the time to appreciate this beautiful world. I inhaled slowly, smelling the fresh air, the flowers, and the herbs; my gardens brought such sweet smells. I smiled. *What a beautiful and wonderful time to be alive.*

I headed to the slime pond, where I had two more slimes. I called them to the surface. As soon as they were next to me, I opened the slime menu. I wanted to see if I could breed the slimes to make more of them. I was eventually going to tame more monsters, so I figured starting with slimes was the easiest option.

I stared at them and willed them to mate. That did the trick. My menu opened to a new option—monster breeding. I looked down the options and saw there were a few available to me. The water slimes could breed and make another water slime; there was even a chance they'd make a regular slime. The water slimes could also breed with my sun slime to make an elemental slime. Lots of interesting things could be done.

I chose to start with breeding water slimes. My menu played a quick video.

> *Water slimes breed in any available, nearby water source; the water supply is not affected. Water slimes produce jellylike eggs quickly and attach them to ver-*

tical structures of their environment. The eggs hatch within three days. Each breeding results in fifteen eggs. This may seem like a lot, but slimes are very weak creatures; in the wild, animals and monsters eat them for quick and easy experience points. Out of every fifteen eggs, often only one slime will survive to adulthood, which takes one month.

Having absorbed the information, I nodded and hit the Breed button. There was an option for continuous breeding—as soon as the eggs were hatched, another batch would be laid. I clicked on that option and started my plan in motion.

I walked away as the two water slimes climbed back into the water. I didn't need to watch this part.

Back at the house, I sat down and grabbed a preserve pack that Brama left. I opened it and pulled out a sandwich, then closed the pack to keep the other food fresh. I bit into the sandwich and enjoyed, as always, how good Brama was at making food. After finishing the sandwich, I walked into our food-storage area and noticed we were low on meat. I resolved to go hunting; we were gonna need some provisions for the journey anyway.

I walked out of the house and to the forest line; then I jumped into a tree and set off in search of food. Before, when I went hunting, I worried about making too much noise and scaring the animals away before I even saw them. Now, I could move so fast that it didn't matter.

I hurtled through the trees effortlessly, searching for any animal I could find that would make for good meat. After about a half hour, I found a deer. Head low to the ground, it was munching away at the exposed grass and raising its head to chew and swallow. It looked pretty big to me, and that was all I needed to motivate me.

I gathered my legs under me and felt all the new muscles in my legs coiling and tensing. At high speed, with outstretched arms, I launched myself at the deer, tackled it, and broke its neck. I grinned, grabbed it by its head, and lifted the carcass to bring it to my open mouth so I could take a bite—

I stopped short and dropped the deer. Closing my eyes to gather my thoughts, I tried to ground myself. *This is not me. I don't eat raw meat. That is the virus trying to take hold, trying to bring out the killer out in me.* Kill, eat, rip, tear, take—I could feel it so deep in my bones I could almost hear it pounding in my head like a mantra. The sickness was just barely being kept at bay.

I cleared my thoughts, grabbed the deer, and threw it over my shoulder. I took a moment to marvel that I had just thrown this deer over my shoulder as if it weighed nothing at all, when in fact it probably weighed around two hundred pounds.

I shook my head again and started heading back to my house. The walk back was a lot slower; I wanted to jump through the trees again, but that required the use of my hands. Without my hands free, I was likely to slip and fall.

I got back to the house after about three hours of walking. I saw Milan sitting close to the house; he was looking at me and smiling. "Wow, Eric, that's a big deer. Good job catching him."

I smiled happily, enjoying the praise. "Thank you, it took me a while to find him. Do you know how to butcher a deer, by any chance?"

Milan shook his head; unfortunately, that was not in his repertoire of skills.

Mira, however, did know how to butcher the deer. She walked from the house in an outfit different from her usual. The only thing covered was her chest area, and her hair flowed down her shoulders and back. She was wearing shorts and a pair of what looked like flip-flops, which were made from a flexible tree bark and twine.

Smiling, she walked over to me and inspected the deer. "Great work, big guy. You caught a really decent-looking deer. Bring it over this way, towards the river, so I can cut it up."

Carrying the deer, I followed her and set it where she indicated. "You don't happen to have a hunting knife, or a dagger even, do you?"

I held out my hand and summoned one of my daggers.

"That's a neat little trick. How did you do that?"

Smiling, I tossed away the dagger and saw confusion written plainly across her face.

"Eric, why are you doing that? I just asked how you pulled the dagger out so fast." She looked more than a little annoyed with me.

"I'm showing you how, Mira. Be patient." I summoned the dagger again and felt it warp instantly back into my hand.

Mira gasped.

"It's a special power. When I found the daggers, I bonded with them, and they activated the ability to warp to my hands at the cost of a little magic." I wondered how I had forgotten to mention that when I told her the story of the dungeon earlier. *Oh well.*

When Mira took the dagger from my hand, it may have been my imagination, but I swear she brushed her hands against my skin for a little longer than was necessary. I felt myself beginning to flush. *Is this flirting?* I didn't want to make the wrong move. Mira was an outstanding person, but this mission was too important for feelings to get in the way. Especially when I was at death's door, whether from a heart attack or the virus overwriting me and turning me into a homicidal rage zombie.

Mira set the knife down beside her and turned to the task at hand. She seemed to struggle with her hair, which kept falling in her face. I looked in my inventory and found a strip of cloth. Pulling it out, I reached forward, grabbed her hair, and pulled it back into a ponytail so that it was out of her way.

I saw her pause for a moment before thanking me in a soft voice. I turned and walked away as she began the process of skinning and disemboweling the animal. That was not something I needed to see.

One more thing to handle. I jumped into the trees and started making my way to the sun hub. I needed to speak to Prayde and see if he could possibly provide reinforcements. I landed at the entrance to the dwarven village and made my way through it, waving to Brama, who was working hard on my armor.

I caught a peek of black-and-gray armor, with a line of blue running down its sides, before he waved me away and seemed to say I should come back when the job was done. *No sneak peeks in my forge.* I grinned a little sheepishly and kept walking. I couldn't wait to see what he was making. It was going to be epic; I just knew it.

Focusing on the task at hand, I walked up the pathway and activated the gate leading to the elves' settlement. Stepping through always brought me that amazing feeling of warmth and happiness. I stepped out to the other side of the gate and looked around; it felt quiet here now. Maybe because I had come so late in the day, but I doubted that. I didn't know what it was that I was sensing, but something was off.

I walked towards the settlement and, as always, kept an eye out. The elves' settlement was a lot closer to the outbreak than the dwarven village, so they were a lot more likely to get attacked by the infected. Walking down the forest path, I kept my head on a swivel till I passed into the settlement. I saw an elven guard do a double take, probably mistaking me for an ogre.

Before I could ask for Prayde, the guard rushed me spear first, and yelled. I sighed. I just wanted to talk; I didn't feel up to doing this right now. He tried to run me through with the spear, but at the last second, I reached out and grabbed the head of it in a solid grip. He slammed to a halt as though he had rammed into a wall. I lifted the spear, elf with it, and slammed him into the ground hard enough to make him let go, but not hard enough to hurt him.

"Go get me Prayde before I break this over your head." I held the spear and smiled as I twirled it between my fingers.

The elf, realizing I was not a zombie, hurriedly got to his feet and started running towards the council building. In the interest of not getting attacked by more weapon-hungry elves, I stayed where I was and waited for Prayde to arrive.

Within minutes, Prayde and the elf were running back down the path towards me. I handed the spear back to the elf and thanked him for retrieving the councilman. The guard nodded and still looked rather shaken as he retreated.

I turned my attention to Prayde, who was looking me up and down.

"Are you all right now, Eric? I heard some rather disturbing rumors. You know, you were dead."

"Yeah, I was, but I got better."

Prayde gave me a funny look and shook his head, probably figuring that it was just a human thing to do. "I am glad to see you are well again, Eric. But why are you here?"

I told Prayde that we planned to attack the ogres the next day around midday, and that we would be happy if the elves of the forest would be available to join us.

Prayde looked nervous. "Eric, so soon? Elves do not move so fast; it would take us months to come to an agreement."

I felt a wave of anger wash over me quickly; it was red-hot, and all I wanted to do was slam my hand through his head. I clenched my fist and slammed my hand against the tree next to me, denting the bark. Taking a step towards Prayde, I yelled, "We don't have months, Prayde! *I* don't have months. I'm not even sure I have till the end of this week!"

Prayde looked shocked at hearing this. "You look stronger and better than ever though. What do you mean?"

I told him about the stages of the virus; the better I looked, the worse it actually was for me. I was dying and losing myself, at the same time that I was in the best shape of my life.

Prayde rubbed the back of his neck; then he sighed and stood up straight. "I will send as many of my warriors as I can, Eric. It won't be a huge army; I want you to understand that. Look around; this isn't our grand city. That's too far away, and we can't use gate magic like you can. It would take the better part of a year for us to make our way there just to request help. We only have what's available at our little settlement."

I looked around and nodded.

"Any help you can offer will be greatly appreciated, Prayde. Thank you. Now I am going home. Remember to have everyone at the gnomes' settlement by midday tomorrow. That's when the attack will begin."

I turned and started walking back towards the sun gate. Back down the eerily quiet forest path. The sun gate was within sight when I stopped in my tracks. The skin on the back of my neck was crawling. I looked around quickly; something was watching me, and it was not friendly.

I heard a soft giggling coming from out of the forest; it sent chills down my spine. *Why is a giggle so terrifying to me?* I clenched my jaw and spun around, trying to pinpoint a direction from which the giggling was coming. I heard some twigs breaking to my left and turned in that direction, readying myself for the coming fight.

I was not ready for the horror on which I laid my eyes. It was pulling itself from between the trees, using its many arms and legs. A mixture of several races could be seen in this blob of mutilated and ruined flesh. I took a few steps back to see the zombie. It had the main upper body of three trolls; ogres made up the length of the body, their arms reaching and grabbing for anything they could. I saw elves with their eyes closed and hands clasped together. I even saw what must have been gnomes, slack-jawed and staring ahead. Dwarfs were there too. All of the races I had seen previously were conjoined here in this monster. The smell coming off it was terrible.

Nervous, I blew out a breath of air; the monster wouldn't attack me unless provoked. My menu gave a notification in my head.

Notice: Because you no longer transmit the disease, you are now considered a meal to any zombie you come across.

The zombie turned and looked at me. Its three heads pulled back and roared hungrily. The elves' eyes shot open and started rolling around in their skulls as they giggled. I felt my skin crawling a mile a minute; this was absolutely the most terrifying thing I had ever seen in my entire life. I didn't like this one bit.

Similar to someone who had just seen a large spider scurrying across their door, I was so upset and disturbed that I got angry. My armor flashed to life around me as I roared and charged forward. I jumped into the air, clenched my fists as I pulled my arms back, and then slammed my fists into the side of one of its three heads.

The troll was rocked backwards and screamed, its many legs kicking out as it tried to regain its balance. I saw a fireball go flying past me and was confused. I looked around for what had cast it, and was shocked to find it that elves inside the monster were casting spells. As their arms waved wildly, some spells were cast successfully, while others failed. It was just another thing for me to worry about.

Screaming, the beast got back on its feet and started charging me. I moved out of the way, conjured my light sword, and executed a quick chop, removing a few legs as it passed me by. I saw a few stray bolts of fire and lightning coming my way, so I held up my hand and created a barrier using my hard light. The magic crashed against my barrier and dispersed easily.

Dropping the shield and sword, I smiled and held up my hands. "Let me show you a real fireball, you freak."

I gathered the fire into my hands, jumped into the air, and slammed the ball into the monster's back. Several arms reached out and grabbed me with an iron grip. I dropped the ball of fire and started punching at the arms of the elves that had grabbed me.

"Let me go, you spindly little freaks!" I yelled at them.

In response, some hissed, while others giggled. Still others were trying to bite through my armor, their teeth gnawing at the edges of my boot.

I reached down, grabbed an elf by its neck, and pulled up roughly. With a sickening noise that was a mix between a plop and a slurping noise, the elf was wrenched from its place in the monster. I snapped its neck with a quick tightening of my hand and watched its body go limp. I tossed it from where I was standing.

I conjured more fireballs. One after the other, I started slamming them into the monster's back. "Die, die, die," I repeated like a mantra as I kept conjuring fireballs and throwing them into its back as fast as I could.

I was cut short after seven, though, as a troll arm reached back, grabbed me, and pried me loose with a few elves who wouldn't let go of me. It looked as if the monster's body parts definitely were not working together. I was tossed roughly against a tree.

Grunting, I stood up quickly and felt the ground shaking as the monster charged me, intent on running me down and stomping the life out of me. I suddenly remembered reading about something a while back. Humans had a way of dealing with charging animals in warfare; I had read about it in a library once. Anti-cavalry spikes—archers used them to stop the cavalry from running them down on the battlefield, or at least slow them down.

I smiled as I came up with the hard-light spell on the spot. I raised my hands, and a few rows of hard-light spears grew from the ground in a crossed pattern. I was going to call that spell the ground spear; it would be useful for quick kills.

The beast impaled itself on the spears and screamed. Though they snapped and shattered beneath its weight, they held. The zombie was riddled with holes from the spears. I could tell the monster was wearing down; it had taken too much damage way too quickly. I wasn't going to let it go, though; this was way too much fresh material for my slime.

I conjured the ground spear again, this time directly under the monster, and increased the size of it so it would make larger holes. The force of the spell actually lifted the monster off the ground. Its scream filled the air. I rushed forward as I conjured a light sword and started quickly hacking away the legs of the beast. I wanted to destroy its mobility before it freed itself from the spears. I batted away stray spells, not letting them distract me from my goal. After I'd finished on the left side, I jumped into the air and landed on the monster's back, sword still in hand. The elves started reaching for me again, but I stomped on them till their arms stopped reaching.

"Enough spells from you annoying monsters; I am sick of you," I said.

The elves were limp; none moved, which meant no more spells would come flying at me. The trolls reached back to throw me off again, but I lashed out with my sword, cutting their hands and removing a few of their fingers.

"Don't touch me with those filthy, disgusting hands, you monster!" I screamed.

I lunged forward and sliced three times, cutting their arm in a few places before removing them completely. I made a slash at the bottoms of the trolls' stomachs and dragged the blade as I ran until I had separated the trolls from the rest of the monster's body and watched as it was dying.

They looked up at me with oddly curious eyes, as if something else entirely was looking at me.

"Oh, he-hello there," a troll said softly.

The voice gave me chills, but I walked over and sat down in front of it. I knew somehow that I was talking to the main baddie.

"Hello there, to you too. Can I presume you are the chonk?" I asked. I laid a hand on my knee, feigned relaxation and wondered if I could fool it into thinking I wasn't taking this seriously.

The troll looked at me and smiled, which sent chills down my spine. "I can see you; you're my child. A product of me and my will."

"I am nothing of yours. I am of me and me alone. You are a plant that grew a little too far. A weed's root that found its way into my yard. I am the gardener, here to snip you back down to size."

The troll looked a little angry. "You would be nothing without me inside of you. You would be weak; you'd be nothing. Worthless. I made you stronger, faster. I made you better!" it yelled.

I stood up, sensing this talk was just going to go in circles. "You took away my life and are killing this forest. You are going down, weed."

With that, I brought my foot down and crushed the troll's skull. I called the slime to start doing its thing and watched it happily bounce over to start eating away at the zombie amalgamation.

I lay back, relaxing and thinking about the fight. How nice it had been to fight all-out with my magic and not run out. I had fought smartly and not abused my spells. I had found, if I focused, I could actually feel how much magic I had left.

Looking over, I watched doctor slime go to town pulling the monster in, eating it whole, consuming and disintegrating it. It was actually pretty wild to watch him go. There were easily two thousand pounds of monster there, and this slime that weighed less than a pound was just polishing it off.

When the slime was finished, it bounced over to me, landed in my lap, and nuzzled into me. The slime let me know it had enough raw data to make a cure, but it was missing something it needed. Without that, it wouldn't be able to produce the cure.

I knew exactly what it needed—the data from the chonker, of course. How could you make a cure without the boss item?

I smiled, stood up, put the slime on my shoulder, and felt it administer another booster. I shuddered, feeling it sink into my body. That felt so weird I couldn't get over it.

I walked to the sun gate, activated it, and stepped through.

Chapter 13   The Final Battle in Another World's Sun

The virus had certainly mutated from what my menu described. The creatures infected and fully transformed were learning; they could talk. They could join their biomass too. That was certainly not good. We had to beat this thing, and do it soon, or this whole world may be in danger.

I walked back into the village and saw that Brama had left; the armor was gone too. That must mean he had finished his work and taken it back to the house. I hopped into a nearby tree and headed home quickly.

When I landed close to the house, I felt my slime shuddering, bubbling, and shifting. It jumped off me and started rolling around; panic rolled through our bond.

I knelt next to it. "What's wrong, little buddy? What's happening?!" I said worriedly.

The slime, of course, couldn't answer me, but its panic was enough to let me know that it didn't know what was happening, just that it was scared. I hoped it wasn't dying; maybe the infected flesh was too much for the poor guy.

Maybe the virus had mutated and proved too much. I got ready to put down my only hope of survival. I wasn't going to let my friend turn into a bloodthirsty monster; he would die with some dignity.

The doctor slime started expanding and growing as it rolled from side to side. I watched closely, still not understanding what I was seeing, but wishing I could help my little friend. It didn't stop until it had grown from the size of a small cat to that of a grizzly bear.

I used my observation skill. Apparently, my slime had evolved from a simple doctor slime into a slime lord. I rubbed my eyes. *A slime lord? What the hell is that?*

I scrolled its definition and continued reading.

> *slime lord. Born in a time of need. Stronger than other slimes and more resourceful. Can command other slimes to do its will. Those who bond with a slime lord find few better companions.*

I scrolled from that to its new subclass, praying its transformation hadn't destroyed the progress with my cure. I almost cried when I read that a slime lord was a commander slime. It could give orders, create new doctor slimes, and hand over its progress; nothing would be lost in the transfer.

I reached out and petted my friend and watched it shift under my hand. It had evolved in response to sensing my need for a savior.

The slimes had finished breeding already, and I could see the slime eggs lining the pond wall. *That was fast.* In three days, there would be a lot of slime babies moving around. I couldn't wait to see the little cuties.

Through our bond, I felt the commander slime call a water slime and assign it to be a doctor. It transferred all the information it contained and the progress it had made toward a cure. The new doctor slime crawled up to my shoulder and settled in.

I petted it and smiled. "Welcome to the team, little guy."

I turned and staggered into the house almost blindly. I felt drowsy; I needed to lie down and sleep, which I did as soon as my head hit the pillow.

The night passed without any dreams, and the next day came quickly. My eyes opened wide. Pushing myself out of bed, I smiled and strode from the room. It was time.

Emerging from the house, I saw Brama loading bolts into a few holders and checking his crossbow. He also had a war hammer. I wouldn't want to be on the other end of that. Turning, I saw Mira running a cloth up and down the length of her new sword, making sure it was clean and ready to go. Milan used his barrier magic as his weapon, so he was checking everyone's armor, making sure it was solid and ready to go. I saw him find a hole in Mira's robe and start patching it immediately with the spare material he had on hand.

Brama finished what he was doing and saw me standing there. Hopping up, he smiled, reached, and pulled a black-and-blue ball from behind him. He tossed the ball to me.

I looked at it curiously. Then a message popped up: *Would you like to equip master-forged armor?*

This was gonna be great, I could tell. I hit Yes and watched the ball open, start flowing up my hands, and finally cover me in armor from head to toe. The armor was made in shades of black and gray; the tips of my fingers and toes were exposed as requested. A blue line ran along the forearms and stopped at my elbows. There was also a blue line on my chest, down my stomach. Another, on my feet, that extended up my legs, and Brama told me there was also one that started on my forehead and went down my back. These blue lines were made from denthyl and could enhance my magical attacks. Armor paired with denthyl could be repaired using magic, as long as the armor had some in it.

I didn't need a lot of denthyl ore. But if I got my hands on more, it could be added to the armor later without affecting the integrity of the armor at all. From what Brama wrote on his slate, it sounded as if the pairing of the denthyl and armor resulted in a kind of smart armor; it would learn as I fought and automatically apply new armor where it was needed. For example if I were a boxer, it would start applying it to my fists, but if I used my legs a lot during a bout, it would reinforce my ankles, knees, and shins.

The rest of the armor was made from a dwarven metal composed of a combination of several kinds of ores, with gem-stones thrown in. The fists had been reinforced; the knuckles pointed forward and were sharpened to increase the damage to an opponent. The waist had what looked like belts wrapped around my torso; they extended down my legs and turned into armor if needed. It was an interesting look, to say the least.

The armor was amazing. It looked great and fit like a glove that was made specifically for my body. It was going to be a great asset during the coming battles. I grinned widely, looked up from studying myself, and nodded my thanks to Brama.

Milan looked up and jokingly complained, "Where's my fancy armor? Guy's over here looking like the giant Black Death himself, and I'm here in a fancy elven bathrobe!"

I grinned as I watched Mira sheathe her sword and walk up behind Milan. She hit him on the arm and said, "That's the finest bathrobe in all the elven settlements, Milan. You better be happy."

Milan sighed and rubbed his arm playfully, feigning pain from the blow.

I looked at all of them and felt a wave roll over me; I was happy now. The happiest I had been in a very long time. I had a group I could call my friends, and we were going to do this together. Strapping on the rest of our weapons, we prepared to meet our fate.

The gnome settlement was actually closer to where I lived than going through the sun gates on the other side of the dwarven village. But it was still a solid three hours away; we had a way to go. So we set out on our quest to save the forest, and hopefully me in the process.

I had looked at my skin before we left. Over the rippling muscles and under the skin, the red veins were growing and moving. They were like worms under my skin. The flesh around the bite on my leg was an ashen gray and looked as if it was dead, the way the ogres' skin looked. It really made my resolve grow. I was going to take these monsters down. I was going to do everything I could before I succumbed to this disease.

Mira must have sensed what I was feeling because she reached out and grabbed my arm. When I turned to look at her, she gave me a warm, reassuring smile. I couldn't help but smile back at her, glad I had someone who was so kind at my side.

I turned my eyes to the road on which we were walking, held my head high, and led the group as we marched towards the fight that would decide everything. We kept a steady walking pace to conserve our energy, even though every part of me wanted to run there, to jump into the tree and speed along. I could be there in minutes, thanks to my viral enhancements, but the rest of my party would be left behind if I did that; I would have to face the threat by myself.

I chewed my lip and started thinking to myself, *There is really no guarantee the slime will be able to do it. What if Mira and Milan get infected too?* I shook my head; I couldn't bear the thought. *What if my new family gets infected and they die? What if a cure is found, and it only works on me? What if I have to be the one to put them down?*

I made up my mind right there. I couldn't let them be there for this. I had to do this alone. With my speed, I could be there in minutes and have this handled well before they arrived. So I jumped into a tree and looked down at them.

They were horrified. They knew exactly what I was doing. I didn't even have to say it, but I did. "I'm sorry, guys, I'm gonna go on ahead, okay? I'll have it all sorted out by the time you get there."

I turned, ignoring their cries. I felt something wrap around me and hold me in place—Milan. He was trying to stop me with his barrier magic. I sighed softly and broke through the barrier easily using my own strength. I didn't stop to look back as I leapt off through the trees at a breakneck pace to get away from them. I knew that if I looked back one more time, I wouldn't be able to leave them; I would stay, and it would risk everything.

They would possibly hate me for this, and I was okay with that. Their deaths were unacceptable risks I was unwilling to take. They were some of my first friends in this new world; I would do anything to make sure they were never in harm's way ever again.

The trees went past me in a blur; branches and trunks swept past. I checked my mini map and watched the gnome settlement approaching. I launched myself from the tree in a black blur and saw there were several infected shambling around, looking for something to kill and eat.

They turned towards me, growling and ready. They weren't aware of the danger they were in. The sun was in the sky, and I was fighting for my new family. My golden-knight armor wrapped around me and settled in place as I stared down the infected.

Trolls and ogres raced to eat me. Elves chanted spells and held magic circles over their heads. I looked at them all and wondered where the dwarfs were. I leaned forward, held my right hand out, and conjured the hard-light sword.

I lunged at the nearest ogre, cutting in a hard slash at its outstretched hands. The ogre screamed as it dropped to the ground and flailed around. I pointed the sword at its head, and the sword extended rapidly, right through the ogre's head, silencing it before it retracted back into a normal length. I grabbed the sword in both of my hands and readied myself as I watched the approaching horde. I was going to need more. I wanted to try something.

I breathed in slowly and cast a flamethrower. The spell burst forth, flowing out in front of me. I pulled the spell back, directing it to flow over the weapon I had made. I watched the flames coat the sword and turn from golden orange to red. I grinned when I saw the new spell I had made—flame augment.

I looked at the nearest monster, a troll, and jumped forward, slashing downward. The troll moved back, dodging the first slash, but got hit by the second as I spun around. I witnessed my blade make contact and the troll's chest burst into bright flames. My eyes opened wide; the spell was working better than I dared hope. In everything I'd ever heard, read, or seen, fire was the way to go when zombies and infections were spreading; it purified and stopped the spread. I was hoping that was still the case here in this fantasy world.

The fight was going by in a blur—slashes here, a stab there. An ogre grabbed me and threw me through a building covered in vines. I grunted as I went through the wall. I rolled to a stop as the ogre came running in, ready to finish the job and kill me off. I held my hands up and launched a wave of flame at the approaching ogre. I listened to its scream as I ran forward and tackled it back through the wall to the other side, making a brand-new hole in the process. I stood up from the ogre, now dead beneath me, and looked around me. I was surrounded by the infected.

I conjured my sword back into my right hand and lit my left on fire. Being surrounded just meant I could keep swinging in all directions, certain to hit something. I heard something move behind me, and I turned while throwing a fireball. It splashed against the ogre's chest, exploded, and hit two of the ogres around it. I turned back to face the others and was tackled by another. I was too slow to deal with them all, it seemed.

I grunted as my back hit the ground, but I used the momentum to throw the beast over and off me. I put my hand up, cast a ground spear, and watched as a group of three infected was caught in the rising golden spears coming from the ground. As the spell ended, the three dropped to the ground; I ran over and dispatched each. The monsters' pain resistance was supposed to be high, but the burning wounds must be doing a number on the nerves in their bodies; they seemed to be in a lot more pain than they were really equipped to deal with.

"I see you there," I heard from somewhere. I didn't see which had spoken.

I turned quickly, trying to find the source, trying to find those eyes that didn't have that rage or hunger in them. I felt the skin rising on the back of my neck as I looked around. There, the eyes of an ogre no longer consumed by rage and hunger. I knew it had been taken over by the chonker, possessed in some way so that it could speak to me.

Still in my armor, I sneered. "I see you too, chonker. I'm coming for you."

I held my hands and cast fireball that melted the ogre. I turned around and searched for more of them. I was going to wipe them out and clear the way for my party. I didn't want any surprises when they got here. I moved farther into the settlement while keeping my head on a swivel. It seemed abandoned; maybe the horde had been its only occupants. I tried to find some clue to follow.

Where are you, chonker? I closed my eyes, trying to focus, and heard a far-off sound. The sound of clinking and clanking. I tilted my head, trying to pinpoint the noise, but it was difficult. It sounded so far away it was weird.

I slowly walked towards the noise while looking around. I felt as if it was getting closer, but I couldn't see the source. I reached the back of the settlement, but was disappointed to find only the mountain. The noise was loudest here, yet I could find nothing.

Suddenly, I was slammed into the mountain. I grunted heavily; the blow hadn't hurt, but I had been surprised. *What snuck up on me like that? It didn't even make my skin crawl.* Again, I was picked up and slammed into the ground. Just as I was about to start fighting aggressively, something small jumped on my chest and peered down at me angrily. I had never been so afraid of small purple eyes before as when I saw they were Mira's.

I took a moment to appreciate that she looked positively stunning while she was enraged; the blood flowing through her skin made the brown of her skin flush, and the color it made was beautiful. I would have said something, but I feared doing so would result in getting a boot in my mouth. I focused my blue eyes and looked deep into her purple ones as I waited for her to say something. Waited for her to scream at me for leaving them behind, for her to call me selfish, which I deserved.

I finally decided I would talk first. "How are you here, Mira? You couldn't have gotten here that fast." She wasn't the only one angry; I was upset too. Why were they already here? I hadn't taken that long to get to the settlement; I should have had at least another hour and a half before Mira and Milan arrived. How had they gotten here so quickly? It shouldn't have been possible.

Mira smirked and looked over at Milan.

"That's on me. I can ride my barriers, fly on them," he said. "It's draining on me, but we were worried about you, Eric. I'd do it again in a heartbeat."

I shook my head. Trying to get here, they had wasted energy and made themselves tired. "Now, you don't have enough energy to fight the rest of the battle, do you, Milan? This isn't some monster you can half-ass! This thing will eat you. Or, even worse, take you for itself and corrupt you. I can feel it in me, trying to take control. It wants what I have, Milan. Your barrier magic? Must be enticing to it as well. Anything that it can get its hands on to make itself even stronger, it will go after with a single-minded purpose that is even more important than eating. We cannot underestimate how dangerous this thing is. This is the single most dangerous thing that this world has ever seen. If we fail now, this world is doomed."

Mira looked at me and cocked an eyebrow. "Oh, it's *we* now?"

I rolled my eyes, broke the barrier magic, and easily sat up. "You're here now, aren't you? I didn't leave you behind because you aren't capable. I left you behind because I didn't want to take the chance that you could possibly be infected."

Mira looked away suddenly, as if she hadn't even thought about the possibility of being infected.

I sighed and rubbed my head. "I can't even find my way to the thing. I hear clinking, but it's like it's behind the mountain itself. I have no idea what to do."

Brama stepped forward and pointed at the mountain behind me. I nodded. Brama looked at the mountain and ran his hands over the coarse rock, slowly pulling at pieces of stone here and there. Then he grinned excitedly and pushed firmly as a portion of the mountain sank in on itself and started swinging inwards, opening a way into the mountains. Smiling, Brama turned, gestured into the mountain, and bowed as if to say, "After you."

Smiling back, I clapped him on the shoulder. I'd never have figured that out without him. I walked into the mountain and noticed it was almost pitch-black. I conjured a light orb and put it in the air above us; it would follow us and light the way. Now that the mountain was open, we could hear the pinging a lot clearer; I was wondering exactly what it was coming from. It sounded a little familiar, but I wasn't exactly sure till Brama tapped my arm. I looked at him, cocking my head to the side, and wondered what he wanted exactly.

Brama mimed a pickaxe.

My eyes widened. *Of course. That's why the noise is so familiar.* The sound was a pickaxe; they were digging. *Where are they going? What are they doing?* I moved forward, eager to find the answers.

We kept moving forward. I was in the lead, Brama was just behind me, Mira was next to him, and Milan was covering our backs. I kept the light spell going to make sure we could see a good distance in every direction.

I didn't like what I was seeing though. There were small plants growing on the ground, their tendrils starting to slowly spread up the walls. These were the beginning stages of the chontatta plants. I bit my lip and looked around; this wasn't good at all. They were making a breeding ground for the plant to spread.

We kept walking onward into the mountain. The path opened into a mine. Looking around, I saw them. Infected dwarfs, pickaxes in each hand. One at a time in overhanded swings, they jerked their arms forward and hit the stone in front of them, chipping away at it. The shafts of the pickaxes were coated in blood from the hands of the zombies, long since worn down to the bone, but still they worked on, driven to the task by the chonker, not able to stop because they had no will of their own.

I looked around for a creature that looked intelligent. It was time to stop this thing and end this game. The final boss was here somewhere, and I was going to kill it.

One of the dwarfs dropped his pickaxes and turned to me. I watched him closely, saw the change come over him, and felt myself shuddering as the hunger and anger slowly started melting away to be replaced by a cunning intelligence and cold gleam in his eyes.

"Hello there. Seems to me you have found your way in uninvited. Would you mind leaving? I'm quite busy, you know," it said.

I looked at the dwarf and shook my head. I knew I was not speaking to the dwarf as I said, "I'm sorry. I don't think I can do that. We need to meet face-to-face. I suggest you come to me before I start trying to find you."

The dwarf peeled his lips back in what I could only assume was a smile. "I have a lot of my kind down here, you know. Who knows what will happen? I think it will not go the way you want it to," it threatened.

It was my turn to smile. "Tell me, what's the most dangerous thing, no matter where you come from? The dragons? The trolls? Giants? ogres?" I stopped to give it a moment to respond.

The dwarf smirked as he answered, "The chona virus."

I tilted my head back and laughed, remembering the run-down the menu had given me. "You may be a deadly little virus; I'll give you that. But, let's be honest, you're a rodent killer where you come from. Pest control. Anything bigger, all you can do is make us stronger. After that, the best you have is to make us insane. Can't even kill us properly."

I leaned in, my smile slowly disappearing until I was stone-faced. "The answer is the sun. It will burn you, dehydrate you, and do countless other things that will put you into an early grave. You managed to piss off the one man who controls it. I'm coming for you, chonker. Not one of you is getting out of here alive."

The dwarf hissed and lunged at me. I reached out, grabbed his head, and spun around, pulling him with me. I drove his head into the ground unit it crushed on the unyielding stone.

"That's one down," I said. I heard a roar as a horde began building. "Thousand or so more to go, guys. Let's get cracking." I strode towards the monsters confidently, fire streams flickering in my hands and between my fingers, ready to be cast.

Mira looked at Milan and shrugged as she smiled and turned to follow me. Milan grinned at my back. Brama took out his crossbow and racked the bolt loader home with a small grin building on his lips. The final battle was coming near, and we were ready.

The dwarfs turned to us and, holding the pickaxes, advanced steadily, hissing and ready to kill. Bolts slammed into the heads of the two nearest dwarfs, and I kept walking past them. Brama was an amazing shot with his crossbow. There were only a few dwarfs at the start of this area, but I could see more farther on and heading our way. In the mix were ogres, trolls, and dwarfs. I didn't see any elves at the moment though.

I saw Brama turn to fire another round of bolts. Smiling, I held my hand out; I hadn't used this spell since I was in the dungeon. I cast the explosive sun-bolt spell as Brama fired and watched as the heads of the bolts turning a bright orange when the flames merged with them. The bolts slammed home and exploded, taking chunks out of the infected.

Mira ran forward with the sword in its whip mode. She began moving lithely; every turn of her body resulted in the crack of the whip as it struck out and hit its target. The air was alive with the sound of it, and I realized into what good the hands I had entrusted my blade. She was amazing; I could have watched her all day.

I conjured my sword, lighting it with fire, and ran forward. I began slashing my way through the horde; with every strike, I saw the blade was still lighting them on fire and cutting them cleanly. They dropped to the ground, dying quickly, as we fought our way through the horde.

I almost got hit and flinched as a blow came too close, but it stopped short—Milan's barrier. I stabbed the ogre through its stomach and dragged the blade sideways, cutting it neatly.

Turning to Milan quickly, I nodded my thanks and activated my hard-light armor.

I wanted to wait longer, but looking at all the infected, I figured we needed every advantage we had to keep the tide rolling in our favor. I watched the armor crawl over my body and grinned. I loved this armor; it was beautiful. I placed a hand over Will's soul stone and held it there for a moment. *I wish Will were here with me now.* I took my hand away and smiled as I remembered how he had moved in battle with his greatsword. A force of nature in his own right.

The black stone glowed in my chest, and I looked down with my eyes open wide. *What is going on?*

"Eric?" I heard Will call.

That is Will's voice! I looked around for it; I couldn't believe what I was hearing.

I parried an ogre's outstretched hand and cut it off, driving my blade through its heart.

"Did anyone hear that? Someone saying my name?" I asked, looking around.

Mira looked at me concernedly; maybe she was right to be. She shook her head and kept fighting on through the infected.

"Eric, call me!" Will yelled.

I looked around anxiously. *What is going on here? That was definitely Will's voice.* I could feel my heart beating a million miles an hour in my chest.

I looked down. The obsidian stone was shining like a sun in my chest, but casting no rays. I reached up, grabbed it, and held it in my hands. I felt searing and something like a heart-beat in my hands. I felt lightheaded and winded. I tasted iron on my lips and staggered a few steps backwards.

Milan grabbed me and drew a barrier around us. He looked at me; worry was clearly in his eyes. He grabbed the helmet of my hard-light armor and tried to drag it off. The armor wasn't normal though; he couldn't take it off like that.

I wasn't really there. I couldn't hear him. My heart was in my ears; everything felt so distant. The stone seemed to vibrate at a high pitch, calling to me. Flooding out everything else.

"Eric, I am here. Bring me out with you so I can fight with you again," Will called.

I grabbed the stone again, and instinct took over. Guided by a source that was not my own, I flung my hand out and yelled, "Will, guardian of kings and warrior of the sun, I call on you to aid me!"

Magic surged within me, gathered in my palm, and flooded from my hand out, into a pool next to me. When the magic stopped, my hand dropped, and I was breathing heavily as I watched the pool. It was smooth and calm at first; then it started rippling and surging wildly. A hand dark as night reached out and dragged itself from the orange pool.

I felt my heart catch in my throat as I watched Will drag himself from the pool. Clad in his old armor, his enormous greatsword strapped to his back, he looked at me and grinned. "Hello again, my old friend, it is good to see you once more," he said.

I smiled broadly, dropped my armor, and grabbed him, pulling him into a hug. I felt close to tears.

Our reunion was cut short, though, by Milan, who had been watching us. "Guys, I don't know what's happening, but we need to get back to it."

I looked up at him and then around us. He was right; we needed to get this moving along. "Sorry, Milan, you are right. We just gained a massive ally though. This fight will be a lot easier now, believe me. Will is a god on the battlefield."

Milan looked Will over and nodded, dropping the barrier.

Will reached up and grabbed his greatsword, unsheathing it. His grin was wide, just happy to hold his sword once more. I activated my armor and stood next to him. I took a second to glance at him before we both moved forward with blinding speed. Will moved with all the grace of a large cat given human form, swinging his greatsword as if it were as light as a blade of grass. He cut the infected down left and right as if he were performing some intricate dance.

I moved through the ranks, stabbing and slicing the infected, grabbing arms and breaking them, using the hot blade to slice the bodies apart easily and carve them into pieces. The others in our group were astonished by the movements that Will and I made together. Working our way as a destructive force, we were embodiments of death.

Thanks to Will, the fight was rapidly changing in our favor; the infected fell quickly. I grinned, dropped my armor, and walked over to my group.

"I think all that's left is the last big baddie," I said as I turned to Will, who was off to the side. I waved him over.

Will smiled at me softly as he walked over.

"I'm glad you are back, Will! And you are here in my world now!"

I started telling him what had happened after he had passed away, but he held his hand up, smiled sadly, and tapped me on the chest where his soul stone usually sat on my armor. "I have seen and heard everything, Eric. That's how I knew of your need for me."

Smiling, I nodded and just gazed at him...but my smile dropped when I realized Will wasn't smiling so much as he looked at me.

"Eric, I'm not alive still. You know that, right?"

I felt my heart drop.

"I am part of some other magic you haven't fully gained control over yet. My soul and your magic reacted to a need and your innate ability. Soon, I will go back to being a stone on your chest. I am here until then. I suggest we move it, Eric. So I can help you one more time."

I felt myself holding back a choked sob as I nodded. That was not something I expected. I really thought that I had brought him back to life and that he was going to be here in this world with me. I turned from him and squeezed my eyes shut for a few moments.

Resigned, I nodded. "Let's go, guys. We have a job to do. Let's get this done."

The party turned and started walking towards the back of the mountain, where the horde had come from. The walk was not long, and the footprints left from the advancing horde were easy to follow.

The chonker, once it came into view, was unsettling, to say the least. It took up a large portion of the excavated area. Its accumulated flesh was naked, red, and covered in a layer of slimes and blood that shimmered in the light provided by the orb I had conjured. The mass of flesh quivered as it turned to look at us. Its arms looked as if they were made from several trolls' arms that had been twisted together to make one arm. The head was that of an elf. The body was made from ogres and trolls that seemed to have been melted together. I didn't see any legs on the mess of a body. Maybe it had once possessed legs, but no longer.

"Ah, you have made it," it said. The chonker looked around wearily at all of us and sighed. "Tell me, what is so wrong with wanting to live?"

I was taken aback with the question and simultaneously angered. "Did you ask the things that make up your body that question too? Were they given the choice to live before you infected them, absorbed them, and turned them into that monstrosity?"

Hissing, the chonker turned to me and narrowed its eyes. "I am just trying to live. I want my children to live, like any parent, and I am doing what I can to ensure that. I wanted a home to give my little ones so that we could live and grow and flourish. I wanted numbers so that we could protect ourselves."

I shook my head and pointed my hand at it accusingly. "You have wiped out settlements and killed populations and infected entire areas of forest. Just to try and do that? If we let you go, you will be a danger to the entire world, not just the forest. We cannot let you go now; it just would not be the right choice, chonker."

The chonker closed its eyes, sighed softly, and nodded. "There was never a chance for peace then, was there?"

I almost felt bad for it. I didn't know if there was something that could have been done. "I don't think so. I'm sorry, chonker. Your species will not die out though; your flower is plentiful across the sea. Take heart that you are not the last of your kind."

The chonker looked at me and gathered itself upright, balancing itself on tentacles. Tentacles came up from behind it. "Kill me then, if you can." The tentacles flew at me then, and at my entire party, ready to kill us.

Will moved first, his large sword swinging overhead and cutting a tentacle in half. I started after that; with my sword, I slashed and removed sections of the tentacles as they came close. Brama was losing more of his bolts, firing past the appendages, going for its head and body.

The tentacles sprouted weird-looking bumps along the flatter sides of them, which burst and shot spiky-looking spines. I realized that they would infect whomever they hit.

"Milan!" I yelled loudly.

The spines stopped in midair before dropping to the ground. Milan was moving his hands around in the air and blocking the spines as they were shot. He was on blocking duty, and that was now his only job.

I lunged in past everyone, slashing at the main bulk of the body. The thing was so massive that I couldn't quite tell if the damage was even getting me anywhere.

Will took a big hit when he got tossed backwards. I had to ignore it even though I'd felt it as a heavy weight in my heart. I still wasn't completely over his loss, and seeing him get tossed like that opened a fresh wound in my soul.

I turned away, attacking the monster more aggressively. I channeled more fire through my weapons. Instead of looking as if fire were running along the blade, it appeared that the blade was made of fire. The flames were swirling like crazy, blazing as they hit the chonker and left char marks and furrows of gouged flesh.

Will was back on his feet, his greatsword cutting more of the tentacles down to the ground.

I looked at the chonker and groaned softly. I was starting to tire; this battle of endurance was going poorly. I was tiring myself out. Looking at the rest of my party—aside from Will, who wasn't even alive—apparently, I wasn't the only one who was losing their wind.

I grunted as I got hit by a tentacle and was driven to my knee. I looked at the mountain of flesh in front of me and groaned. I had been cutting and stabbing for a while, yet the flesh in front of me was nowhere near as damaged as I would have liked. I got hit hard again and was thrown far. I rolled several times before I came to a stop groaning.

Man, that thing hits hard. It felt as if I had just gotten slammed by a truck. I shook my head, stood up slowly, and checked on the slime. It was gone. Probably dead from the hit, smushed inside my armor from the impact. That was not a good thing, it would take a while for the new slime to get here, and by then, it would be too late.

I sighed and moved, running back into the battle. I groaned in frustration as I swung the stingers faster and harder at the mass. Mira was cutting and stabbing at the body too, having found that the whip was wholly ineffective against it. Brama was out of bolts and had started using his war hammer against the chonker. The sound was awful; it made my skin crawl with each strike.

The battle raged for an hour, and finally it was over. I dropped to my knees and was grabbed by a tentacle, lifted, and thrown to the ground viciously; my armor had long since stopped working. Mira lay in a heap on the floor, blood dripping from a head wound. Brama had been thrown against a wall and had not moved since. Milan had tried to help Mira and had been struck by four tentacles at the same time; then he was hit repeatedly until his barriers gave out, leaving him defenseless. Will had been grabbed and slammed against the floor; his body turned back into magic and flowed back into the hard-light armor, settling back into his soul-stone form.

I lay there groaning. We had failed, and the chonker had won. I clenched my fists and looked up at it as I rolled onto my back and smiled.

"Smiling when you have lost? What is the meaning of this?" it asked me.

I shrugged and lay there feeling every inch of my body in pain. "We lost. We gave it our all. You are just way too strong. I mean, god, how can anything be that strong?"

The chonker seemed to smirk a little. "Well, I'm glad you aren't a sore loser. Although, I was hoping you would cry a little."

I closed my eyes and just let myself start slipping into unconsciousness.

"Hey! Oh, what is that? What did you do? No!" it yelled.

I cracked open my eyes and saw the chonker trying to slam its tentacles at something on the ground.

"Sit still! You must pay, you little pest!" it screamed.

Groaning, I rolled onto my side and peered through my swollen eyes. It was the slime! How was it still alive? Not that it mattered really. We had failed, and now the whole world was going to perish because of us.

The slime wriggled over to me and jumped onto my chest, bouncing a few times and seeming almost as if it were smiling.

"Why are you so happy, bud?" I asked.

I was almost cut short by it stabbing me with its booster ability. And then I almost flinched as my menu flashed a notification across my menu: *You have been cured. The virus is being purged from your system.* I looked at the doctor slime incredulously.

"You little pest! Come over here!" it yelled again.

I looked over nervously and saw that the chonker seemed to be sweating profusely; it didn't look as if it was doing so well.

What is going on —? I gasped then looked at the slime. *The chonker said the slime bit him! The slime gave the chonker the cure!*

I held the slime close as I closely observed what was going on with the chonker. It seemed to be melting in on itself, The virus was the glue holding everything together, and without that, everything was falling apart.

"No! It's not fair! I won! You cheated!" it shrieked.

I watched the chonker die and agreed with him—he *had* won. We were beaten fair and square. I rubbed the slime on the head and wondered how it had done it. I thought the boss would have needed to be beaten in order for me to get enough material for the cure to be made.

I looked around and gasped. All the tentacles we had cut off were falling on the ground. Sometime during the fight, the slime had separated from me and had eaten the falling biomaterial to make more of the booster for me. Instead of the booster, it had found all of the necessary ingredients for the cure.

The chonker was wheezing as it melted internally, its breaths bubbling in its saliva. It coughed around the fluid inside of it.

I walked over and looked at it once more, feeling sorry for something that was only trying to do what nature had told it to do. I shook my head.

Am I doing what humanity has always done? Deciding what the best course for everything is, only to change it because I didn't agree with it? Was I making the right call for the betterment of the entire world?

I rubbed my head and set the slime down. It started eating the rest of the monster. I almost stopped it, but I realized that the monster was dead. I walked away and started gathering my team, positioning them to lie side by side.

I heard footsteps approaching and looked up. It was the elven army arriving on time to help; too bad we hadn't waited. Probably could have used their help in the final battle.

Prayde walked up, saw Mira on the ground, and ran over to her, dropping to the ground, grabbing her, and tearing up.

"Prayde, she just got knocked out; the slime there can help heal her. Let him take a look at her, okay?" I said.

Prayde looked a little hesitant to let a slime touch his daughter, but he relented and let it crawl around on her. The slime injected her with a form of painkiller. Mira seemed to relax in her unconscious state, and that put Prayde at ease a little bit.

I reached my hand up and pushed it through my hair, feeling every ache and pain in my body. I wanted to crash. The threat was not over yet; I may be cured, but the plants were still here.

I turned to the slime and issued an order for it to start giving shots to those present after I told them what was going on. It started bouncing up and down excitedly.

"Everyone gather round, please. The slime here has the cure for the disease. I myself have been cured of the virus, so I can guarantee that it works. Line up in front of the slime here, so he can give you a shot that will prevent the virus from taking hold inside of you," I said.

The elves all looked to Prayde for guidance, and he looked at me. I met his eyes with a strong connection, hoping he believed me and would go along with what I was saying. He nodded, walked over to the slime, and knelt before it, raising the cuff of his sleeve. The slime extended itself and pressed against the flesh of his arm. Prayde winced as the shot went into his body. I smiled, silently thanking him for believing me. Prayde nodded a few times before walking back to Mira and sitting beside her, holding her head.

I closed my eyes as the elves made a line in front of the slime, waiting to get the shots. The slime lord at home was busy making more of the slime breeds and assigning roles.

I tasked him with making more doctors and to have them start spreading through the forest. They were to spread the cure around till the virus was wiped from the continent completely. I got a small form of acknowledgment from the slime.

I opened my eyes. I was feeling worse and worse as time went on. I checked my status again, and it said cured. I breathed a sigh of relief, happy it hadn't reversed itself. I was out of danger now.

"Eric, come over quickly!" I heard and recognized Prayde's voice.

I hurried to him. Mira was waking up. Her head was still cradled in her father's lap as she looked up. She appeared dazed and not all there, which I understood. Smiling, I sat down next to them.

Mira looked at me, and a small smile slid across her face. "Did we get it, Eric? Did we win and save our home?"

I nodded and realized she couldn't quite see me. "We won, Mira. We beat him down, and we even found a cure."

I saw tears start springing into her eyes slowly. "You aren't going to die?" she asked happily.

Feeling touched, I smiled and reached down to cup her hand softly. "No, Mira, I'm going to be around to annoy you for a while longer yet if you'd like."

She nodded a few times, unable to speak past the lump in her throat.

Prayde was smiling softly as he looked at me. "I think she would like that a lot, Eric."

I looked at him and reached out to pat his shoulder. I was going to tell him about the slimes being bred on my farm, but just then I felt a savage pain ripping through my stomach. I screamed and grabbed it.

Mira turned to look at me as Prayde's face registered that he, too, was very alarmed.

The pain stopped. But then returned with a vengeance, even worse than before. It felt as if someone were taking a hot knife and digging it into my stomach, sawing away at the abdominal muscles there, severing them. I looked at them concernedly. Something on an instinctual level told me that the pain was not the cure doing this to me. I needed to get out of the dark; my magic was gone here.

I turned to Prayde. "Someone car—"

I was cut off by my mouth filling with blood. I gagged, throwing up on the ground in front of Prayde. I reached for him, but I couldn't speak; the blood was choking me. I wrapped my arms around myself, my body aches feeling as if daggers were stabbing into me from every angle.

Mira grabbed her father's arm, looked at him, and yelled, "He needs the sun, Dad! Take him outside!"

Prayde looked at me nervously, unsure if what was happening was from the virus or not. I felt strong hands grabbing me and pulling me slowly. My eyes opened a crack, and I saw Brama. His head was dripping blood, and his face was furled into a snarl as he pulled me with all his strength one step at a time towards the exit. If no one would help me, he would do it and die of exhaustion—such was the loyalty of a dwarf whom I called a friend.

I felt tears in my eyes and tried to fight them. I realized to my horror that the tears were blood and that I had no control of them anyway. And then I felt many hands grab me; I was lifted onto the shoulders of elves and was run towards the exit. Prayde evidently had overcome his worries and wrangled the nearby elves to come to my aid. I tried to looked at him in thanks, but had to close my eyes; the pain was making me nauseous, and all the jostling around me was making it even worse.

I felt myself passing from consciousness as I was carried outside. I was in the sun finally, and I felt it sinking into my skin. The elves left me there and watched. Brama took a few steps back and watched, worry etched deep in every line of his face. Prayde was also nearby with Mira, holding her in his arms. Milan was pulling himself from the cave slowly, shielding his eyes from the sun and looking for me.

I groaned and heaved, blood coming from my mouth in a jet. I rolled onto my side and looked into the spreading pool. There were several teeth in the pool. I felt around my mouth with my tongue and realized my teeth were indeed falling out. I was falling apart, literally.

What is going on? I looked around for help. *Why is no one helping me?! Someone please help me,* I thought to myself. *I'm too weak to even say anything out loud.*

I reached out for someone, but no one would come near. I tried to activate my armor; it flickered to life for a moment, on and off again, stuttering and failing several times. I couldn't hold the concentration or power needed to keep the spell going. I felt another fresh wave of pain and clenched my fist in the grass, almost screaming as the effort pulled the nails from my hands, leaving bloodied stumps. I looked at my hands incredulously.

After all this, I was going to die, and I didn't even know why. I looked at the sun and felt the rays soaking into my body. I didn't want to die. I reached up to the sun, grabbing at the rays and pulling them towards me. I pulled and pulled until I was covered in them; as they piled on my chest, they slid down towards my feet. I was covered in the rays of the sun, all the way around, like a giant cocoon.

I felt myself falling asleep; the pain was fading away, which felt nice. It also felt as if my body had finally stopped falling apart. *I wish someone would help me.* I tried to move, but found I couldn't. I tried to open my eyes, but found they were unresponsive. I tried to activate my magic, but found that wouldn't work either. The cocoon had saved my life, but it had also trapped me within it; I was a prisoner unable to move or escape.

Mira, Milan, Brama. Someone. Help me, please!

I felt it then, just as I had felt it several times before—an inky blackness, a loss of consciousness. I was about to lose myself. I closed my eyes and drifted away.

Chapter 14

Awakening in Another World's Sun

Mira

I watched over him for days at a time. After Eric and our small group won the fight against the infection spreading throughout the forest, he succumbed to something in the depths of the mountain. He didn't deserve to go like that. I didn't even get to tell him the things I wanted to say. How I felt things for him that went beyond the group we shared. I tried a few times to tell him things, but I think he was a little too dense to pick up on them.

I am going to have to be a little more forward. I had planned on telling him after we won. I was so certain he would be cured, and he was. Everything was going so well that I thought I might be in the middle of the old stories my mother, Faiyla, told about the elven princesses and their green knights who would battle throughout the wastelands for their beloved. That was not to be. This was the giantwood forest, and I had just lost someone I considered a friend.

I sat against one of the buildings in the gnomes' settlement, looking at the glowing orange crystal that had been erected there as a monument to my friend's death more than two weeks ago. As he lay dying, he had grabbed the rays of the sun, pulled them together, and sealed himself inside. Away from anyone who could help him, although I don't think that anyone really could have helped him at that point.

Looking at the crystal, I hugged my knees to my chest and felt my grief welling up in my heart again. I reached over, grabbed a small flask of water, and drank from it, sipping slowly and washing away the grit that was building up in my throat.

The watches that we set up were not necessary, but we felt as if we owed it to Eric. He had died giving everything up for us, saving us and our forest, and giving us a cure to help us survive.

I heard the sound of crunching rocks as someone approached, along with the smell of cooking food. I looked up from where I was sitting. Milan was walking over with a sad smile on his face. He had been trying to cheer me up for a while, but had realized it was a hopeless situation. I wasn't going to be happy for a while now. Milan sat next to me and offered me a plate of food, which I accepted gratefully. There was a good deal of it on the plate—vegetables that had been sliced into disks and cooked slowly in the fat of a large, slow-moving herd beast we raised in the forest.

It was called a mupkral and was good for its meat and the milk it produced. Though technically more of a mushroom than a real animal, it reproduced by spore production and grew on the side of a tree till it was the size of an actual mushroom. From there, after it fell to the ground, it grew to the size of a large bush. They were peaceful and docile creatures and very easy to take down. They grew quickly, which led to their being great animals to raise and eat.

Focusing on the meal, I took several bites and realized how hungry I was. I heard my stomach growl aggressively and looked away from Milan's judging eyes. I knew he was going to say something. He said something every time he came here. He was always trying to be more caring and to be there for everyone.

"Mira, your poor stomach—" He stopped and shook his head. He knew it wouldn't get him anywhere. So, instead, he sat down next to me, grabbed his legs, and pressed his head to his knees. He then shuddered forcefully.

I looked at him worriedly. "Milan, are you okay, man?"

Milan looked up at me, his eyes already stained and lined with tracks from the tears he had shed. "No, I'm not okay," he said. Breathing deeply, he looked up at the sky and sniffled. "I'm not doing all right at all. Eric is dead; our group is gone. You are depressed. We both lost an amazing friend whom we'd only just started getting to know."

He looked at me closely, saw the tears, and nodded a few times. "You started loving him too, didn't you? Or at least started feeling *something* for him."

I looked away, set the plate down, and folded my arms.

Milan sighed softly. "I get it; he was special. He always seemed like he knew what he was doing. He had a go plan. A very capable man."

I nodded. I couldn't exactly put a name on what had made me feel this way, but spending time in Eric's presence had simply made me feel that things were good in my life again, as if everything was going to be all right again. Feeling that way had been almost intoxicating.

I leaned against Milan and felt him lay his head on top of mine. I was feeling sleepy all of a sudden. I hadn't been sleeping well lately. "Milan, would you mind staying awhile? I would like someone to be here while I sleep."

Milan agreed.

I closed my eyes and passed out quickly; I hadn't realized I was so tired.

Milan

I watched Mira fall asleep, felt a heavy weight in my heart, and sighed. She had always felt as if she were missing something from her life, and I thought she had finally found that missing thing when she met Eric. I had held his soul in my hands, felt the sins of his past weighing heavily on him, and then felt the light of his virtues sweeping them aside. He was a good man and someone I would have gladly followed into battle again any day. Yet here I was, looking at the monument to his death, crafted by his own hands in the midst of his death throes.

I sighed sadly again and stood up, walking to the orange crystal that pulsed faintly. I placed my hands on it while examining it. It was warm, and I fondly remembered the orange dragon, the shape his soul had taken. Dragons were a fierce race, but one of the most emotionally complex and deep races to inhabit this world. The fact that his soul had chosen that shape meant there was so much more going on inside of him than anyone realized. I couldn't see the insides of anyone's soul, but by touching them, I could get the gist.

Eric would be someone whom I would regret losing; his magic had been very unique and was possibly the key to unlocking many of the unique lands across the world. I shuddered at the thought, but knew of several in the wastelands alone that could possibly be accessed with his powers. Prayde had a small collection of scrolls that held the locations of several such areas.

I heard a small bounce and turned to see a small slime marked with a green plus sign on its body. It was one of Eric's doctor slimes; they had been spotted all over the giantwood forest lately, spreading themselves around. I watched the slime stop and spot a small area of corruption. It extended a portion of itself and released a fine mist; the effect was immediate—the corruption shriveled, died away, and left nothing behind. The original doctor slime had made the cure and given it to everyone; now more doctor slimes had arrived to begin the process of purging the surrounding land.

Eric had told us of the varying stages of the virus, and we had tried to cure those creatures and areas affected, but once it hit stage three, there was no going back. The virus completely killed whatever was left of your mind if it got that far, leaving only hunger and hate. So far, there were no new bosses, only the rage-afflicted.

I had learned that term from Eric, a boss. I had asked him why he kept calling the chonker a boss. He just smiled and then laughed, shaking his head as he explained, "*Well, you see, it's when there's a main bad guy we have to fight; we have to fight past all the trash mobs to get to the main baddie, which is generally dubbed the boss.*"

I had cocked my head, looked at him, and asked what a trash mob was. Eric had rolled his eyes, rubbed his head, and slowly tried to explain everything to me as he would a child, which I felt to be a little insulting, but I never told him that.

I took my hand from the crystal and felt its warmth fade away immediately. I rubbed my hands together and turned back to where Mira was lying. *I wish there were more that I could do, but now we just have to see where we go from here.*

I looked up the road, away from the gnome settlement, and saw Brama making his way down the road. I was pleasantly surprised to see him. He hadn't been back in weeks.

Last time I saw him, he was crying and walking back home alone, having refused to communicate with anyone.

I also saw that the ground next to Brama was bouncing and glowing. *Ah! He brought Eric's sun slime with him.* I went out to greet him.

Brama made his way up to me as I stood on the path. He grabbed his slate and started scribbling. The writing started to slow.

I looked up, surprised to see tears flowing down Brama's face. "Oh, Brama, you poor thing. Come here, man," I said. I grabbed Brama and hugged him close.

Mira and I had each other, at least, to deal with our grief. Brama had been alone all this time, locked away in his home. "You didn't have to go, Brama. You could have stayed with us, you know! You didn't have to bear losing a friend alone!"

Brama moved back, wiped his face angrily, and shook his head.

I looked at him questioningly. "What's wrong?" I asked.

Brama grabbed his slate and started scribbling quickly: *Eric's not dead. Sleeping. Healing.*

I looked up at him in surprise. "How do you know he isn't dead, Brama? You watched what I watched, what we all saw!

You can't tell me he's not dead in there, Brama." I regretted being that curt, but I had started feeling angry with him.

Brama shook his head and looked down as he scribbled more on the slate: *The god told me to bring the slime here; slime will do the rest.*

I looked at the bouncing slime curiously, but shook my head. "No, Brama, There is nothing that a slime can do for a dead man. There's just no way."

Brama looked at me, sighed, and started scribbling about what had happened since Eric sealed himself away within the cocoon.

Brama

I watched him, my friend. Bleeding on the ground, lying there. I could do nothing for him, but watch as he writhed in agony. I felt my heart breaking in my chest, watching the pain that the young man was going through. We had just won, and barely at that. I had woken to find Eric choking on his own blood, the elves hesitating to touch him.

I barely understood what was happening, but some part of me knew I had to get him out into the sun. I knew that the sun would help him; it was the basis of all his magic. He had told me on many occasions that outside he was basically always at full capacity as long as the sun was in the sky. So I grabbed him and started dragging him, not caring if his blood was on my skin. My friend was not going to lie in a pool of his own blood while I could do something about it.

After they saw my efforts, the elves jumped in to help, which was appreciated. If they hadn't, he would surely have died in that mountain. I was not strong enough to manage more than a few tugs of a few inches each; his body had grown so large and solid from the virus.

Once outside, I saw Eric reach for the sun and felt hope in my heart. *That's right, boy; go for the sun!* I said to myself as I watched him grab hold of the surrounding rays and start pulling them in, wrapping himself in them. They turned a solid-orange, like the rest of his magic; hard light, he called it. He disappeared from view, and the magic stopped moving around him, leaving him encased in the solid shell.

I felt my heart drop from my chest down to my stomach as nothing else happened. It was too late; Eric was dead. I felt the tears stinging my face and dropped to my knees. I started hitting my hands against my face and my chest, wishing I could be like Mira and Milan in the corner; they were holding each other, crying, and screaming their loss.

My voice had never been. I dragged myself to a settlement house, laid my back against it, and cried my grief until I was strong enough to hold my eyes open without shedding my tears.

I then stood. I needed to go home. I would tend the mine and Eric's home until the end of days. I turned and started walking down the path. I heard Milan calling my name, but I didn't stop; I was glad when he didn't try to stop me.

The return home only took a few hours, but it felt like ages. I had expected to take this walk while listening to them laugh and talk like children. Listening to them was the most fun I'd had in ages. I reached up and clutched my chest as the grief rolled through me in fresh waves. We had won, but at what cost?

I think Eric would have been okay with this outcome—his life for the world. He had a pure heart; I'd known that since he had told me of his time spent in the dungeons, of his friend Will, of his time spent fighting a war. He had cared for those people, not knowing if they were real or not, and still had trouble with that.

I walked until I found my way to the dirt path leading to our—my—home. Taking it, I walked to the house and then into the kitchen, where I pulled down an earthenware jug that I hadn't opened in years. Its contents was an old beverage made by my grandfather. A single sip could make you feel it to the tips of your ears.

I popped open the container, looked at the liquid, and repeated, *A single sip*, in my head. Then I tilted the jug, took a large mouthful, and swallowed. After closing the jar and setting it down, I walked over to my bed and sat down. The tears came down again as I looked at Eric's empty bed.

I could feel the heat crawling up my neck, flushing my cheeks and forehead. I had been foolish drinking so much. I hadn't done something like that since I was a young lad. After I settled into my bed, I was startled by a noise. I looked over and saw the sun slime bouncing into the house. It saw me and hopping over to get into my bed and lie next to me. I held out my arms, and it crawled in. I hugged the slime close, enjoying having something of Eric's to hold on to while he was gone.

I felt the room start spinning, and I groaned. The jar's beverage was going to put me out for a while. It was a strange drink. If you drank enough of it, it would place you into a coma for a while. I had a small feeling I had passed the limit and hoped I would wake up, not pass on. I fell back and passed out.

When I came to, I was sitting in a white room, across a table from an older man. I think he's an elf, but his ears are round, just as Eric's were. I leaned forward and peered at him.

The strange man looked up and smiled. "Hello, Brama, it's nice to meet you. I'm happy to meet someone who added something new to my world. I love it when you folk do something like that."

I stared at the old man curiously, not sure what he was talking about, and looked around the room, trying to see if there was a way out of this place. I had no idea where the house was or if I was even still in the giantwood forest. I certainly didn't have the telltale ache in the back of my head that came with drinking the brew, the pain that lasted a full month if you drank enough to hit a coma. I shuddered. I didn't even want to think about how my head would have felt from drinking that much of it.

"Brama, I need you to look at me now, okay? What I am going to say is important," the man said.

I turned back to him. *How does he know my name? Does he know Eric?*

"I know Eric, and that's why you are here. He is in danger right now; he just barely was able to keep himself alive with that little stunt he pulled, cocooning himself in the rays of the sun. You are once again going to be responsible for saving that man's life, Brama. I hope you are up for the task. As soon as you wake up, you are going to head back to Eric with that sun slime."

The man reached behind and pulled out a pure-black knife that shimmered against the light. He leaned forward and handed it to me. "Brama, this knife is made out of space and time; it's a one-time-only use. You are going to make a cut in the light that is surrounding Eric so that the slime can make its way in. After that, the knife will lose its luster and become a regular knife. Feel free to keep it."

I kept looking at the man and wondering if he was insane. Eric was dead, nothing was going to bring him back.

The man nodded as if he'd heard my thoughts. "You are going to wake up soon, Brama. The choice is yours. Remember—only you can save him from dying." He then turned around and picked up a scroll as the room around me faded away once more.

I woke up lying on my bed and couldn't really remember anything. I knew a lot of time had passed because my body ached wildly from lying in the bed for so long. I sat up and walked into the kitchen, rubbing my aching head and regretting having drunk the brew the night before. I put the jug back up, rummaged through a drawer, and pulled out a sandwich that I had prepared some time ago. I glanced over to make sure it was still edible and decided to just eat it. Biting into it, I nodded. *I am the best meal maker around, that was for sure. Weeks later and my food still tastes this good.* I smiled, reached down to scratch my side, and felt something move around in my pocket. I frowned, took another bite of my sandwich, and reached into my pocket to pull the object out.

I saw the black knife and dropped what remained of my sandwich onto the floor. I started coughing and choking. I remembered everything. I looked around and started gathering my things. I ran outside, looking for the slime, and saw it bouncing towards me. It had no reason to listen to me, but I was really hoping that it would anyway. I waved for it to follow me, and after checking a few times to make sure that it was following, I made my way back towards the settlement.

I looked up at Milan, who was still looking at me skeptically.

"You want me to believe that you are here because a mystical man came to you in your drunken stupor, telling you to save Eric with a slime?" he asked.

I nodded at him, knowing it sounded off. I reached into my pocket and pulled out the knife that the man had left me. I offered it to him.

Milan took the knife, pulled it from its scabbard, and looked the blade up and down, after which he raised his eyebrow. "This is a really good knife. I think that it can cut through anything honestly."

I looked at him pleadingly and saw him thinking it over.

Milan took a while going through the information in his head before making a decision. "Okay, let's try it out. At worst, it just confirms everything we thought anyway, and we know for certain Eric is dead. Best case, he is alive, and we can have him back again," he said sounding hopeful.

I walked past Milan quickly and made my way to Eric's cocoon with the sun slime. I looked at the little guy and reached down to pet it one more time. It looked happy and ready to go; it definitely had a mission.

I pulled the knife free of the scabbard and pushed the blade firmly into the cocoon before pushing downward, carving a hole into the side of it. When I made a decent-enough slice, I stepped back and watched as the slime wriggled up the shell and started sliding into the hole. Once the slime disappeared from sight, the hole closed up behind it as if I had never opened it to begin with.

I stepped back, looked at Milan, and waited. Milan walked up behind me and laid a hand on my shoulder; his breathing was heavy. Mine probably was too as we watched the shell for any signs.

Milan turned to look at me. "Did the guy tell you to look for anything? How long to wait? Anything?"

I shook my head. He hadn't told me much of anything really, besides what to do and where to go.

Ba-dump...

I looked at Milan and smiled. What sounded like a heartbeat was now coming from inside the shell.

Ba-dump...

Milan smiled back, and we both turned to watch the shell. The orange was glowing brighter and starting to turn golden. Within, we could see the shape of a standing body.

Ba-dump-adum...

The sound was getting faster now, and the shell was glowing brighter.

Crack!

The top of the shell split, and the crack ran like a jagged line down the middle.

"What's happening?!" Mira yelled.

Surprised, I turned back and saw Mira running towards us; her eyes were lit with panic.

I gestured to the shell Eric was in.

"Eric is waking up, I think, Mira. I think he was really alive!" Milan was yelling excitedly.

We all stood together, watching and waiting, as the glow grew so bright we had to shield our eyes and turn away.

Eric

I floated. There was nothingness all around me, all-consuming and all-enveloping. I didn't know where I was anymore. The shell I had built for myself was a last-ditch effort to save myself, and now I couldn't get out. My magic was gone; I couldn't break free from the spell I had wrapped myself in. I couldn't let them know I was alive. *How long have I been here? Has it been months? Years? Time is skewed in here.*

I was asleep and awake, all at the same time. Once in a while, I could feel a presence nearby. Mainly, it was Mira—waiting for me, I think. I didn't know though.

Now, I feel Milan, his hand on the shell. I tried to reach for his hand, but I couldn't move; it was so frustrating, not being able to do anything. I felt his hand pull away, and he left. He didn't go far though, and now he is here with Brama. The whole group is here; it feels almost nostalgic.

The feeling was short-lived as I started losing consciousness again. I wanted to call out for help, but I was slipping away too fast.

I was woken up rather abruptly with a searing pain in my leg. I tried to look down to see what happened, but I couldn't move. Then I felt warmth and happiness for the first time in a while. *What is radiating such happy feelings?* I basked in them for a moment, till I felt whatever had come into the shell start entering the wound in my leg.

I screamed as the pain grew worse; something was now inside me, spreading as the virus had. *What is that?!* I shuddered. *That feels awful.* Whatever it was, it was in me now, a part of me so completely I didn't even know where it had gone inside of me. What I did know was that, whatever it was, it had a lot of magic in it, and it gave it all to me. I held my hands out and moved through the shell easily with my magic restored.

I felt the shell cracking around me as I moved. Normally, the spell would just fade away, but with all of the magic I had poured into it when I made this cocoon, I guess the structure was a lot more solid, the magic more powerful. With another push, a large jagged crack opened in front of me. I grabbed the edges, pulled them apart, and emerged from the shell, back out into the world.

Groaning, I fell onto the ground. The first thing I noticed was how weak I felt. My muscles were shaking and twitching; turns out, not moving for long lengths of time was not a great muscle-strength program. I started to push myself up, but instead I was grabbed by a set of strong arms that I recognized.

Brama's arms engulfed me. *Did they look this large before?* I gasped as I was lifted and slammed onto my back, all the air pushed from my body. I looked up into his eyes and saw anger there. *Why is he so mad at me?* I wanted to ask him, but I couldn't pull the air into my lungs to try. I tried to breathe but was finding it difficult.

I saw Mira stepping into view and looking down at me. I looked up at her to ask for her help, but I saw the anger in her eyes too. *Why are they so angry at me? What happened while I was gone?*

"Who are you? Where is he?" she asked.

I shook my head. I didn't understand what they were asking me. I didn't know what was going on.

"Brama, hit him," she said.

I looked at her and back to Brama, who was raising his hand that was clenched in a fist. I furrowed my brow. *I just got out, and this is my warm welcome from my friends? A beating as soon as I am released?* I glared at them and triggered my hard-light armor; it pushed Brama off me.

I rolled backwards into a squat and held my hands out. The armor felt different to me; a quick glance over and I saw that the armor was less of the orange hard light and more solid, flexible fire.

I looked at my friends. I saw Milan moving to the side slowly, pulling a barrier between his hands, *Why is this happening?* I pulled in a large lungful of air and coughed while hitting my chest a few times. "Why are you attacking me?" I finally yelled at them. I was confused and hurt.

Mira looked angry. "Where is our friend?! He went in there and you came out!" she yelled. She reached down, pulled out her whip sword, flicked her wrist and let the links separate so the whip was extended down to her feet.

"I *am* your friend! I am Eric!"

That seemed to make Brama pause for a moment and look at Mira.

"You are not Eric," she said.

I cocked my head to the side. "How the hell are you gonna tell me who I am, you pointy-eared brat."

Milan started dropping his hands. "Pointy-eared" was a comment that had been brought here solely by Eric. "Eric? Is that you? Truly?" he asked.

I turned to look at Milan as I dropped my arms to my sides. "Yes, Milan, it's me. Please trust me. I don't know what has happened since I've been gone, or even how long it's been, but I don't know what I could have done to make you all hate me or be so angry at me. I tried so hard to save everyone!"

Milan looked as if he was going to cry, and Brama dropped his hands. Mira still glared at me, refusing to believe I was who I said I was, for some reason.

I looked at her and dropped my armor, hoping that I could pull it back fast enough if they tried anything. "Why won't you believe me?"

Mira turned, stalked back to a campfire, grabbed one of the metal plates that had been lying there, walked back, and held it up.

I looked at it and had to do a double take. I looked almost like a kid again, definitely closer to a teen than I had when I was basically juiced up by the virus. My hair was orange and red; it flowed to my shoulders and resembled flowing fire when it moved in the wind. My ears were slightly tipped now, just like everyone else's, meaning I was no longer completely human, which was kind of cool.

My armor had fallen from my body and gone to my inventory while I had been in the state between life and death. So I looked at my body now and saw the hard lines of toned muscle that had replaced the large muscles from before. I almost liked this look more; it didn't take up so much space. I was going to miss the height though. Before, I had gone from my original height of six feet, when all of this started, to around six foot seven inches. Now, I was back down to five foot six. Standing just a little taller than my friends here. Now, we were magical creatures—all of us, I guess.

I looked closer and saw that my eyes had a soft-red glow in them, and the pupils had turned a mix of red and yellow, like the sun. My teeth had grown back in, my canines on the top and bottom still longer than they were as a human, but not as pronounced as with the virus. I looked at my hands, and, thankfully, they still looked normal; the nails had grown slightly longer and ended in points. My skin color had also deepened and looked as if I had tanned in the sun, which had turned me a nice bronze.

I could see now why they thought I was someone else. Gone was the old Eric. Now, I was this new person entirely, changed by my time within the shell. I sighed and looked down.

"I see. I am Eric. I rescued you when you were beaten by the infected ogres by my home, Mira. Brama, I met you when I finished the dungeon, and you had taken over my home. Milan, you held my soul in your hands. It was an orange dragon that was crying. Better yet, do the spell again. You will see it's still me."

Milan shook his head slightly. "There's no need. I can tell it's you. Welcome back home." He moved towards me, opening his arms, and I moved in to hug him, grateful that someone was finally believing me and giving me a chance.

Brama was next. I felt him wrapping his powerful arms around Milan and me, pulling us in tight and hugging us close. I smiled happily and laughed for no reason other than I was finally with my friends again.

I looked up and saw Mira standing there looking at me. I smiled softly and held out my arm, waiting for her to come join us. She walked forward and wrapped her arms around us, leaning in and closely pressing her head into my side.

I closed my eyes, enjoying the feel of our whole group finally together again. The group hug broke, and I stepped back while smiling at everyone. "Guys, I don't know about you, but I am tired. Let's go home and lay down. How's that sound?"

Everyone looked around at each other and back at me.

"Don't tell me we are gonna disband the group now just because the threats are over. There's a whole world out there for us to see. We can go exploring and cave searching. There's so much for us to do!"

Milan shook his head slightly. "I'm sorry. I'm glad you are well again, but my place is at the settlement, making sure it is kept safe and hidden from the dangers out there. They need me."

I nodded. I understood. I looked to Brama, who was smiling and already writing.

Of course, I'm going home with you, but my fighting days are over. I want to stay home and spend my time forging and creating.

I turned to Mira last, clenching my fists loosely. "Mira, what about you?" I was hoping she was going to come with us. I know she had attacked me because she thought I was someone else, but that didn't change the fact that I still felt something for her.

Smiling, Mira stepped forward. "Of course, I'm going with you. You think I'd give up a life of adventure to sit around in a settlement, doing nothing, when you get yourself into trouble almost every day? As if."

I smiled brightly, happy to have someone with whom to explore the world. I pulled my armor back out, reactivated it, leaving the helmet part off, and started saying my goodbye to Milan. When he returned to the elves, he would tell Prayde that I had woken and that Mira was going to be staying with me for now.

Heading back home was great. Mira told me how my slimes had proceeded to produce the cure and pretty much eradicate the infection from the forest. The parts of the forest that had been desolate and empty were starting to show signs of small animal life again and would hopefully show signs of deer and larger animals again in the coming years.

I was intensely proud of my slime lord; he had done well in keeping things going while I had been incapacitated. *Good going, little man.*

I looked up from talking and noticed that it was starting to get pretty dark out. I reached out and cast a sun orb. The surrounding forest was lit up for over a hundred feet in every direction, and my eyes went wide.

Mira turned to me in surprise. "Why so much light, Eric. We don't need it to be that bright."

I pulled back on the power I put into the spell until it was the right amount of light; it felt as if it had taken no effort at all. I pushed the orb above our heads, once again taking note that the magic I was using looked more like actual fire now, rather than the solid orange and gold hard light that I had been using previously. I wondered if it was just an aesthetic upgrade or an actual tactical and powerful upgrade. I couldn't wait to test that out, maybe tomorrow.

While I was thinking about my magic, we finally found ourselves back on familiar ground in the form of the dirt path leading back to the house. Brama scribbled that he was going to start a large fire for us to relax around.

I smiled at the thought. I had always wanted to go to a bonfire back on Earth, but had never gotten around to it. *This is my time*, I thought. I walked into the house, took the armor off, and started rummaging for some clothes. All the clothes I'd worn before no longer fit me. I was shorter and thinner now. I sighed in frustration, pulled on the clothes anyway, looking as if I was wearing very baggy clothing, which I was, and shuffled back out of the house.

Mira, who had already changed and was wearing her shorts and a shirt that exposed her midsection, turned to look at me and giggled. "Whose clothes are those?"

I sighed and looked down in defeat. "Oh, hush your mouth, Mira. I have shrunk. I need new clothes. Only reason my armor fit is because the denthyl in it shapes the surrounding armor to my body perfectly, no matter what."

I shuffled over and sat down on a bench that had been carved from a tree by Brama at some point while I had been in the dungeons. It had special cushions that were made from a large goat that was native to the mountains he had come from; they never lost their volume, apparently, and could last for generations. Content, I leaned back, relaxed, and sighed; they felt great. I could use some of the gems I had found while mining to buy some more when I went to the mountains with Brama at some point.

I felt the cushions flexing next to me and opened my eyes to see Mira sitting next to me. There were three benches surrounding the fire that Brama had constructed, and Brama was sitting across from us. He was reading a book by firelight; I noticed he had opened it almost as soon as Mira sat next to me.

I looked into Mira's eyes; she had sat kind of close to me, and I didn't know how to deal with that. I felt myself flushing and was thankful the new darker complexion I had received would cover it up.

"I'm glad you are back, Eric. I didn't know what I was going to do without you," she said.

I smiled and reached out to place my hand on hers. "I didn't want to go, you know. I still don't know what happened to me." I closed my eyes and recalled the pain followed by the loss of consciousness in the shell. "I lost a lot of time in there, Mira. I was unable to move or keep hold of myself. I would wake up once in a while and know when you or Milan were there."

Mira was looking deep into my eyes while I spoke, and when my voice caught in my throat while talking about being alone and trapped forever, she changed the position of our hands so that she was holding my hand in hers, comforting me.

I looked into the fire for a moment and enjoyed the warmth and the breeze on my face as the wind blew them over me. I turned to look at Mira, who was still watching me to make sure I was okay.

"I'm glad I am back here with you, Mira. I am even more glad you decided to stay here with me."

I saw her smile and look away. I realized I had said something more than flirty, but I didn't take it back or explain it. I meant it this time. I wanted her here, with me, where we could be together.

"So we can go on adventures together? See the world and hang out?" Mira asked as she looking back at me, still wearing that smile of hers.

I reached out, cupped her face, ran my hand down the side of it, and looked into her eyes, once again noting the depth and color in the purple eyes that seemed to peer into my soul. "If I said I wanted more than hanging out, Mira? If I said I felt more about you than I felt about Milan or Brama?"

Mira's eyes opened wider, and she seemed at a loss for words, so I pressed on, "Mira, I can't tell you all of what I feel because I haven't felt like this before. But in the time I have spent with you—traveling between my home and the settlement and fighting with you and the time we spent at the fairy spring—my feelings for you have grown stronger."

Mira closed her eyes, leaned her head into my hand, and smiled softly. "Eric, it's so nice to hear you say those things to me."

I smiled at her and allowed her the time she needed to speak.

"I feel the same for you, Eric. Our time together hasn't been all that long, and, honestly, none of it was even romantic. Even still, I feel my heart beating for you."

She moved forward slowly until she was sitting on my lap and looking up into my eyes. She reached up, cupped my cheek, and pulled me down into a slow kiss. As our lips met, I felt something similar to a surge of electricity passing through me. I closed my eyes, leaned into the kiss, and wrapped my arms around her as I slowly pulled her against me and held on to her, enjoying the moment and loving the feeling of my first kiss.

Mira pulled away and smiled as she looked at me. "That was nice, Eric."

I smiled in agreement and leaned in to kiss her on the cheek.

I looked up into Brama's eyes and saw him grinning widely. He was in a great mood at seeing two of his young friends together. He stood up, faked a yawn, waved good night, and hurried inside.

I smiled after him and turned my attention back to Mira. The fire was crackling and snapping behind her, illuminating her body and making her look like a goddess in my arms. Mira smiled at me and leaned in, kissing me again as she pushed me back against the bench. I closed my eyes and let myself go with the moment, knowing it would be time to go to bed soon. We stayed like that for another hour, basking in the glow of the fire until it died and was nothing more than embers in the pit.

I stood up with Mira in my arms. I carried her inside with her arms wrapped around my neck; she was all smiles. I set her down once we were in the house and told her good night before going into my room to sleep.

I crawled into bed, smiling and knowing that tomorrow was going to be a new day, a better day. What I wasn't ready for was the sound of shuffling feet. I opened my eyes to see Mira standing in front of me with a blanket and a pillow in her arms.

Smiling, she said, "Move over, would you? I need some room."

I was looking at her as I moved back. "What are you doing here, Mira?"

She looked at me as she crawled into bed and snuggled in close. "Are you upset I'm in bed with you? I thought we were having a good night."

I wrapped a hand around her waist and pulled her close against me. Smiling back at her, I said, "We were. I just didn't think you would start sharing my bed so soon, is all. Thought that would be a bit later on."

Mira laughed. "I'm already basically living in your house, Eric. Might as well sleep in your bed."

I shrugged and laid my head down. "May as well."

Mira giggled, scooted back, and spooned me. I closed my eyes and fell asleep with Mira in my arms.

Chapter 15

The Last Day in Another World's Sun

I woke the next day with Mira snoring in my arms and smiled gratefully; part of me had worried I was going to wake up and find that she was not there anymore, which would have been a tragedy. I kissed her softly on her cheek and slid from the bed slowly. I didn't want to wake her.

I looked for some clothes that I could put on and found that Brama had slipped in a pair of altered clothes along with a note.

Here are some clothes for you, Eric. You look just a little bigger than the elves, so hopefully the clothes fit well enough till we get you a few things made. I didn't want you wandering around in those old clothes, shuffling around anymore. You could trip and fall, and then you'd have the pretty lady laughing at you. Can't have that, can we?

I smiled and slipped on the clothes. The sleeves were a little long, but that was no problem. The pants were perfect. *Great job, my friend.*

I turned to look at Mira one last time before I slipped through the doorway and made my way to the living room. Brama had already headed to the dwarven village. I think he had plans to get rid of some of the buildings there and expand on the forge. I was definitely okay with that. I wanted a large forge nearby, especially for the add-on for creating golems.

I smiled, walked outside, and looked at the trees, wondering if I could still do it. I crouched, jumped, and found myself hurtling towards the trees at a fast pace. I grinned. *So I've got that.*

I grabbed the trunk of the tree, my nails digging in to keep me there as I looked past it and targeted the next one, and so I started my journey from the house to the dwarven forge. The trip didn't take long; I found myself landing at the dirt path going up to it in no time. I heard a loud hammering off in the distance and knew that Brama was hard at work, as always. He loved making new things, like the bolt thrower, which had served him so well in the fight in the mines; he had been great at crowd control. The weapon had done wonders right up until we had gotten to the main bad guy. After that, no one had done very well at all.

When I reached him, Brama was standing over a fresh batch of molten ore, guiding it into some molds and then pouring it out. He was making some ingots, iron from the looks of it. I walked up and waited for him to finish pouring as I leaned against the wall. Brama finished, set his crucible down, and turned to look at me.

I smiled at him and waved. "Hello there, Brama, I have come to talk to you about something that I found out a little while back."

Brama came over and sat down on a seat next to me; he gestured for me to continue while he grabbed a small container and took a sip. I told him about the machine that I could make. It would add itself as a part of the forge and could make golems; they wouldn't be as good or complex as the golem I had already made, but they would be easier to make. I told Brama how to make the machine, grabbing some nearby parchment and scratching out some guidelines and blueprints.

Brama took them from me and was reading them over one by one as I finished them. He was nodding and smiling. Brama loved inventions, and here was something new before his very eyes. He hopped up and looked as if he had a new fire lit in his soul. It was go time for the dwarf.

I smiled and stood up. Time to make this thing. Brama and I started grabbing the materials that were needed—three carts each of copper and iron ingots, one cart of assorted gemstones, and the power from the dwarven forge. Thanks to Brama, who had been smelting the ore almost religiously, we already had most of the ore ready to go.

That reminded me—I hadn't checked in who knows how long the golem I already had. I turned and jogged past the line of buildings to where the dump area had been designated for the golem. My eyes opened wide. It must have been a while since I had last been here. There was a pretty large pile now of ores and gems, and to the side was an even larger pile of denthyl ore.

I grinned, pocketed some denthyl, and went back for one of the carts. I grabbed a smaller pull cart that I could handle and started tugging it towards the pile of ore. I started loading unprocessed ore by the handfuls. When done, I pushed the cart's handles down and started back towards the forge. The cart wasn't too heavy.

I was happy that I had kept the strength from when I had the virus. I was getting stronger all the time. I was going to protect my newfound love and my friends. And in the meantime, build some really cool things.

I dumped the cart beside the smithy. Brama looked up and smiled from where he was throwing the ore into the fire so it could melt down to be used. I was there to be helpful and aid in any way Brama needed me. I was lifting a large portion of metal that Brama had connected together, pulling it to the side so we would have more room, when I heard some footsteps moving along the path.

I turned to see Mira walking towards us. I smiled at her, released the metal, and moved to greet her. Brama waved at her and turned back to continue his forging. I moved up to her and pulled her in for a slow kiss that she returned happily.

She reached up with her hands, placed them on my arms, and looked into my eyes. "Tell me, Eric, what is the plan from here on out?"

I turned and looked at the place we were building. Smiling, I said, "Mira, when I came here, all I wanted to do was build a great farm and live in peace. Now I have traveled to other dimensions. Fought in wars. Cured a plague and almost died around four times. I think I want to get back to farming and living peacefully for now. I want to build what I have just found with you."

I turned and looked at Brama. "I want to go see the mountains that Brama came from and see more of the lands that surround the forest. The real answer, I guess, Mira, is I don't really know. Let's see where the world takes us. Because as long as I have you by my side, I will be happy, and I know I can face anything."

Mira smiled and seemed happy with the answer. She pulled back and looked as if she wanted to ask me something. "Eric, could you do me a favor, please!"

I raised an eyebrow at her and watched as she slapped her hands together and raised them in front of her in a pleading manner. I smiled at the sight and thought it was ridiculously cute. "Mira, go ahead and ask. If it's within reason, I am sure I can work it out for you."

Mira's face broke into a grin, and she explained that she wanted to go back to the settlement for a quick visit so she could purchase from her friend Pina a few beasts that she could raise on the farm. They were called mupkral and could be grown on trees, they grew quickly, and once they were off the trees, the flesh went from a mushroom consistency to that of meat and was quite tasty.

I was intrigued and told her to hold on a moment. Brama, who was still working away, looked up at me and stopped his work for a moment.

"Brama, Mira and I are paying a visit to the elven settlement for a little bit to acquire some new animals for our farm. You can spare me for a bit, right?"

Brama nodded and waved me off, not bothering to take the time to even scribble out his response.

I turned from him and started making my way to the sun hub, pausing only long enough to take Mira's hand in my own. We made it to the gateways, and I walked to the elven portal. With a flick of my hand, the gateway activated, and I strode right through with Mira in tow. I shivered as I felt the amazing warmth from the gateway as it passed over me, the heat going down into my bones and leaving me feeling rejuvenated and happy. I checked my mini map and oriented us towards the village.

Mira looked around and smiled happily; the forest had come a long way in the past few weeks. The birds were singing again, a sign that the wildlife was healing and prospering in the face of the infection that just a little time earlier had been running rampant. *Life will go on,* I thought to myself as I too looked around.

As we walked, occasionally I would see from the corner of my eye a slime bouncing to and fro. Each one had a green plus sign on its round body, which marked it as one of my slimes under the direct control of the slime lord. I wasn't bonded to them directly, but they were mine all the same.

Mira dropped my hand and wrapped herself around my arm as we walked. I kept my head moving from side to side, making sure to keep an eye out for anything. The infection had left me a very cautious person, always on the lookout for a threat.

Soon, the settlement came within view, and we crossed the barrier without incident. I looked around for familiar faces, but I couldn't find any. I let Mira take the lead; she grabbed me by the hand and took me down the main road towards the eastern end of the settlement.

No one stopped us or gave us any problems. It would have been weird, unless you factored in the fact that everyone was screened by Milan before they even got past the barrier. Continuing on, we exited past the rows of houses and found some small plots of farmland that were growing grain crops; they looked as if they were not getting enough light due to the overhang of the trees.

I looked around and found an elf who was pulling weeds and tending to the grounds. I told Mira to give me a moment and walked over to her. "Hello there. My name is Eric. Can I ask you something?"

The elf stopped what she was doing and turned to look at me. She looked pale and stood around the same height as Mira. Her eyes were a pale green, and her lips were a pale pink. She smiled at me, showing her teeth, and I couldn't help but notice how straight and white they were.

"Hi there! My name is Pina. Who are you?" she asked.

I introduced myself and asked her if she was the farmer of the crops that were here. She admitted that she was indeed the one.

"Pina, these crops are not getting anywhere near enough sunlight on them. They are going to wither soon, and you will lose the whole field."

Pina looked taken aback and then saddened as she nodded.

"I know that, Eric. The settlement here has been having a rough time growing their own food lately, and there seems to be nothing that we can do about it."

I nodded and rubbed my chin as I thought about what she'd said. As I did so, I saw Mira approaching us.

"Oh, Pina, how are you? It's so nice to see you again! You are actually just the woman I was looking for."

Pina saw Mira and moved forward to give her a big hug. Smiling, she said, "Mira, it is so nice to see you. I have missed you since you started staying at the stranger's house. What was his name again?"

"I think it was Eric," I said as I raised an eyebrow and waited for Pina to realize she was talking about me.

Mira sighed and rubbed her head.

"Yeah, that strange guy Eric. I heard he was pretty we—" Pina cut herself off as she realized I was the guy she was talking about. I watched her pale skin turn red as she slowly turned to me and squeaked in embarrassment.

I feigned being wounded and grabbed my heart. "Pina, your words, they wound me to my very soul." I turned, placed my hand on my forehead, and groaned loudly, making it seem as if I were upset.

"Oh, Eric, I'm so sorry. I didn't mean anything by it," Pina said.

I walked over to a tree and leaned on it, groaning louder. I'm sure Mira was rolling her eyes at this point.

"Pina, don't listen to him; he's pulling on your ears," Mira said.

I peeked at them and saw Pina looking from an exasperated Mira to me, back and forth, and sighing. "Well, it's not like I don't deserve it. Wouldn't be the first time my big mouth got me in trouble."

I dropped my arm and turned to Pina with a big smile on my face. "No worries, Pina. I couldn't resist getting a little jab in after you called me weird while I was standing right here in front of you."

Pina sighed as she nodded and turned to Mira. "Why are you back here?"

Mira clapped her hands excitedly. "We are here to purchase some of your mupkrals. I know you have been growing quite a few of them lately, Would you mind?"

Pina smiled and waved for us to follow her. "Come this way, and take a look. I have quite a few of them right now."

We followed Pina through a clearing to a grove of trees.

"If you are planning on raising your own, I recommend separating their patch of trees by at least six feet, all around them. And when they get to be the size of a regular mushroom, you should move them to a pen with bare dirt and very little light. Under the trees should be good if you haven't cleared them all away. You want the trees to be separated because they are easy to lose track of and very tiny when they are growing. Separating the trees makes it easy to know exactly where they are."

Pina walked us up to a tree and gestured for Mira and me to take a look. "They are all on the trees at this stage, so don't worry about treading on any of them."

I nodded and moved forward, wondering what I was looking for. Mira gasped happily as she reached out and grabbed something. She turned to me, her face twisted into a cute smile. She opened her hands and showed me a strange little beast.

It had little vine-like appendages that moved back and forth over her hands, searching for the bark that it had been gripping. Its back was covered in tiny leaves that were emerald green and seemed to move with the sun, trying to pull in its rays. Beneath the leaves was what appeared to be a small shell that they were sitting on.

Looking closer, I realized it was a mushroom cap. I reached out, flipped the little thing over, and saw actual legs beneath it; they were like little crocodile legs. Its head bore a resemblance to a lizard, angled and long, covered in green scales. Its eyes were little slits.

It was an interesting little monster that I was almost instantly fond of, a mixture of a crocodile and a mushroom. I picked it up by the nape of its neck and watched it wiggle in my hand.

Mira smiled and took it from me, putting it back on the tree before turning to look back at Pina. "How much do you want for them, Pina?" Mira asked.

Pina smiled at us. "For the heroes who saved the whole forest and everyone's lives? I'll give you six of them for free. They will make more from there, and you should have a good supply of them before you know it."

I looked at Pina closely. "Are you sure? You want nothing in return?"

Pina shook her head. "Go ahead and pick out your little creatures. Come see me when you have them."

I turned with Mira to start looking over the trees, the game of hide-and-seek beginning. Mira was way better at this than I was. She found four of them almost immediately; meanwhile, it took me a while to find even one. Mira was holding the little lizards in her hand, grinning like a child with her first pet.

We walked over to Pina, who was holding a small cage that was made from wood. The sides had been made from dark wood. The panels that were on the sides were a lighter wood that had been twisted together and fit into place inside the sides, so they wouldn't move. Pina grabbed a latch, pulled the front panel open, and started loading the little lizards into the box slowly, making sure she didn't hurt them. Once they were all inside, she re-latched the door and handed the box over to me.

I grabbed it carefully, making sure I didn't shake them too much. "What do they eat? Anything special?" I asked.

Pina shook her head in response. "Those leaves on their backs pick up the rays of the sun in a form of sustenance. That's all they ever eat, no matter how big they get."

That was easy enough—little plants that were made of meat.

"Thank you again, Pina. We really appreciate the gift and will take great care of the little guys," I said.

Pina smiled at me happily and told me I was welcome.

Mira and I waved to Pina as we left smiling with our new little monster babies in hand. I was excited to start the area that would house them. I also wanted to see how Brama was getting along. The add-on wasn't huge; it just felt that way due to all the materials required.

A dumb golem had to be given instructions and be updated constantly. A smart golem had a core inside of it that could adapt; it could think for itself once given a goal. One such smart golem was the golem that I had already built, constantly digging below ground, finding gems and ore for me to use. A dumb golem would be terrible for a job like that because of all the different materials.

I was planning on having the dumb golems start cutting wood and clearing portions of the forest so the farm could be expanded. They could also harvest things like stone from the nearby mountains that could be cut by more skillful hands into things like bricks for pathways and homes.

I was lost in thought on the walk back to the sun gates when I felt the skin on the back of my neck start tingling. I was feeling something that wasn't a threatening presence nearby. I smiled softly as I recognized who was watching me. I turned to see Milan lounging on a tree limb and looking at me with a large smile on his face.

I tapped Mira on her arm and pointed a finger in Milan's direction. "I see our friend over there. Let's go say hello before we head out."

We changed our course and started walking towards him. I watched Milan slide from the tree and land on his feet before heading in our direction. Milan took in the two of us walking arm in arm, and his smile got even bigger.

"I see you two have finally found each other. I am glad you did," he said as he turned to Mira and took her hand. "You look so good together. I can't wait to see where you two go together."

I stepped forward and patted Milan on his shoulder a few times in a friendly way. "Thank you for your kind words, Milan. I hope you know this already, but you are always more than welcome to come by my home whenever you want."

Milan turned to me. "Thank you, I appreciate that you are still so kind even though our quest together has ended."

I grinned and decided to let him know one more little piece of information I had been feeling since I met him. "Milan, you are like a little brother to me. I want you to know, if you ever need me, I will be there for you and will stand at your side."

Milan seemed a bit surprised by this and looked away as if a little embarrassed. He ran his hands through his hair and smiled at me. "Thank you, Eric, that really means a lot to me, especially when it's from a hero like you."

I waved his last comment away. "I'm no hero, Milan. I just did what I could to help everyone..." I trailed off as I realized that was basically what a hero did, so I mumbled to myself, under my breath, the rest of the spiel I had been about to say.

Milan just shook his head and started telling us goodbye before he climbed back into his tree so he could continue keeping watch over the settlement.

I took Mira's hand, and together we made our way home through the sun gates. Stepping out of the sun hub, we made our way down towards the dwarven village, making sure to stop in and check on Brama.

He was pouring more molten metal into molds and setting them to the side; the factory that looked a lot like a hut add-on was already being attached to the end of the forge. I nodded my appreciation; Brama was doing a spectacular job. Brama still didn't require any help from me, so I walked back home with Mira to find a place where we could start settling the mupkral shroomlings. Once home, I put the little ones inside before coming back out and surveying the area.

I decided to use the area on the other side of the bushes. There were plenty of trees there, and it was near an outcropping of rocks, so I wouldn't have to clear so many trees for the mupkrals. I held out my hand, conjured a sword into my hand, and started my work. I walked from tree to tree, slicing through them almost casually and watching them fall. I decided on leaving twenty trees and clearing a six-foot range around them.

The mupkrals would grow here till they were around the size of a regular mushroom; then they would dislodge themselves and fall to the ground. They wouldn't be on trees from then on; they'd live the rest of their lives on the ground and feed on the rays of the sun. Thinking about that, I walked some distance down and started clearing more land, more trees falling and hitting the ground with large crashes. I used my own hands and grabbed the stumps. It was almost fun, watching as the stump was slowly pulled, and the roots released their hold on the earth.

I dragged all of the wood off to the side and started piling everything in the fire area. Brama would cut everything down to size or use the wood for other projects. After I walked back to the area I had cleared, I conjured up a hoe made from hard light and took away any of the fire effect that it had. I put both hands on it and started tilling the soil. Once it was turned, I started grabbing wood from the pile and carving it. I made fence posts and started driving them into the ground, several feet deep. I slowly constructed a fence that the mupkrals could not get out of.

I moved back, looked at my work, and grinned; it really was nice when it felt as if everything was starting to come together. I spun on my heels and made my way back home. When I opened the doors and walked in, Mira was reading a book.

She looked up at me as I strode in smiling. "Is everything ready to go, Eric? I think the little ones are eager to return to the trees so they can soak up some sunlight."

I grabbed the cage, making sure I didn't jostle them, and grinned at her. "Come on, Mira; I just finished it all up."

Mira hopped off the bed and tossed her book to the side, following me from the house. We walked along the dirt path, back to the tree grove I had finished making a little while ago. Mira stopped in front of me and turned.

"Lift the cage up for me, Eric. I am going to take them out and put them on the trees now. All right?"

I nodded and lifted the cage so that she could start reaching inside. Smiling, I watched as she grabbed them one at a time and put them on the trees. I closed the cage after she had retrieved the last one and stepped back to watch them skitter around on the tree till they settled in patches of sunlight. The tiny leaves on their backs moved slightly as they adjusted themselves to catch the most amount of sunlight.

What fun little monsters. I couldn't wait to find out how they tasted. I bet they would be amazing.

I turned and headed back with Mira, who was practically bouncing next to me. "Why are you all happy?" I asked her.

"Because now we have some of my favorite food growing. In a few weeks, we will be able to start eating them!"

I looked at her quickly. "A few weeks? Are you sure they will be ready that soon?"

Mira nodded enthusiastically at me. "They are like mushrooms, Eric. They grow faster than average beasts and plants. They are the best of both worlds! Fast growing as a mushroom and all the sweet delicious meat of an actual animal."

I nodded a few times; that definitely sounded as if it was a great thing. I was lost in thought while I looked around. I stopped and scratched my head a few times. Something was missing, but I couldn't think of what. I put my hands on my hips and kicked the ground a few times.

"Eric, what's going on?" Mira asked once she realized that I had stopped moving and that something was bothering me.

"Something is missing, I can't really put my finger on it. There used to be something that was here, and now it is not."

Mira giggled. "That's what it means when something is missing. Come along into the house now, and we can think about it from there."

I listened to her and followed her home, knowing that whatever was missing was going to bother me greatly for the time being; it was as if something was on the tip of my tongue, just a push away. I sighed as I sat down.

"Are you hungry?" she asked.

I looked up at her as she started pulling some meat out of the preserving drawer. She took one of Brama's knives and began to slice the meat into strips and put it to the side. After that, she picked out a few vegetables and started slicing them into small chunks that would be added to the pan.

Mira asked me to start a fire in the stove so that she could cook. I lit it for her with a smile, and she started cooking the meat, reaching for a few herbs that were hanging above the kitchen and throwing them into the pan. She also reached for a small container that had some cooking oil in it. The pan sizzled as the oil was drizzled over it.

The smell of meat was wafting into the air. I closed my eyes and inhaled, pulling the scent into my nose. This girl really could cook. I warmly smiled at her as she finished up and put a plate full of vegetables and meat in front of me. I started digging in.

Mira sat across from me and started eating from her own plate. She could eat just as much as I could. I loved watching her eat. I'd heard that some women liked to act in front of their boyfriends as if they didn't eat a lot. I was glad Mira wasn't like that.

She started to get up and collect the dishes after we each finished, but I took them from her and told her to sit down. "Thank you for the meal, hon; now sit back and relax. I will wash the dishes and be back soon, okay?"

Mira started to argue, but I ignored her, grabbed everything, and walked out smiling. *Like I was gonna let her just handle everything? What kind of man would I be?* I walked to the river's edge and started cleaning the pans and plates using the sand to scour them clean. When the dishes were free of grease and oil, I pulled them into my arms and carried them back inside.

Mira walked over to me, grabbed everything out of my hands with a huff, and started putting them away.

"Hey now, why all the huffing, lady?" I asked with a small smile.

"I started something and I wanted to finish it. Whether its preparing our armor or making a meal, let me finish my tasks."

I raised an eyebrow at her. "What if I want to take care of you, Mira?"

She stopped and looked at me. "Oh. Well, I guess that would be nice."

I moved to her, smiled, and gave her a quick kiss on the cheek. "I am going to see Brama. I want to see if he has finished that project yet. Or if he needs any help from me. Would you like to come with me?"

Mira shook her head; she wanted to stay at the house till I returned.

I walked outside, a little thankful she wasn't coming. That meant I could travel through the trees at a high speed, the way I liked. I walked from my house to the tree line and leapt into the trees, moving quickly. I hurtled through the trees, launching my way over the houses of the abandoned village, and pulled a forward flip, landing in the area of the forge.

Brama was just stepping back from fitting a panel into place. He turned to me and grabbed his slate from where he had laid it down.

Hey, it's all finished. How do you like it?

Smiling, I gave him a thumbs-up and told him, "Nice work there. It looks just like the blueprint in my head."

As I stepped closer to examine the hut, a notice popped up in my menu.

Would you like to activate the golem factory? Current level can produce one golem per month.

Only one per month! That's terrible efficiency. I tried to look at an upgrade list, but I needed another skill to make upgrades to things. *Of course!*

I sighed and activated it. There was enough metal left over to start the process for the very first golem. I grinned as the bar in my menu started going and the forge rolled to life.

Brama looked at the hut that was now glowing and then at me.

"Don't worry. I just started the factory. Sadly, it can only make one golem per month. So it will take a while till we see the fruits of your labor."

Brama just smiled at me and started gathering his things. The sun was starting to go down. It was time to head home and get ready for bed. We walked home together. I didn't say anything, just enjoyed his company and thought of all the things that I had been through since coming to this world.

I smiled as I remembered how I had started with nothing, made my way in an unfamiliar land, and built my very first cabin. Explored my brand-new powers and learned how to protect myself. Found my first actual dungeon that had taken me to another world. Met Will, who had taught me how to use a sword so that I didn't have to rely on my almost-non-existent level of magic. Watched Will die. Found my freedom from the dungeon. Met Brama. Made a golem. Met Mira, whom we rescued from the infected, and with whom I am in a relationship now. Met Milan, another elven friend, who is the protector of the elven settlement, judged my soul, and helped us defeat the chonker. Discovered the virus that we bested and removed from the face of the continent.

Almost died from the virus that changed me and made me into a killer with anger issues. Almost died again and changed into what I am now.

It seemed both a long time since I had come to this world, and none at all. Not even a year had passed since then, and here I was, living the best life I had ever known. Reminiscing had taken a large portion of my mind off the walk, and I found myself at home already. Brama opened the door for me, letting me walk in first, and I thanked him as he closed the door behind me.

Mira was reading next to the window since the sunlight was fading. I conjured an orb and let it hang over her head. She beamed at me, as she could read at a more leisurely pace now that she didn't have to worry about the sun going away.

Brama made his own meal since Mira and I had eaten already.

I sat down next to Mira at the table and yawned. It was getting close to bedtime, and I was ready to go lie down. "Mira, I think I am going to head to bed."

Smiling, she looked up at me and set her book down. "Okay, let's go to bed then. I can finish what I am reading tomorrow."

I stood up, and bid Brama a good night. I walked into the bedroom, changed into my nightclothes, and waited for Mira. She came in from her room, wearing a large shirt that went down past her knees, and smiled at me. I crawled into bed and opened my arms, waiting for her to crawl into them. I didn't have to wait long, as she practically threw herself into my arms and snuggled into me.

She moved up, placing a few kisses on my lips, and I held on to her, smiling. She rolled over to spoon me, and I wrapped my arms around her. As my eyes closed, my menu went off behind my eyes.

End-of-day experience. Gained Level 15.

I smiled and nuzzled Mira. *Awesome. I gained a new level.*

My eyes shot open, and I sat up in bed, my heart hammering in my chest. I opened my menu as everything faded behind me, including Mira, who was asking me what was wrong. I felt my breath shuddering from my chest as I looked at my status.

Eric. Monster. Spirit of the Sun. Level 15.

I grabbed my head as I felt the room spin. Mira's words from when I first traveled with her were ringing in my ears. *"Only a monster can level up."*

I am a monster now? How could this happen to me?

Mira grabbed my arm and shook me. "Eric, talk to me. What's going on?!" she yelled.

I looked at her as I felt sweat dripping down my face. "Mira...I leveled up."

Confused, Mira just looked at me, not quite understanding what I was trying to tell her.

Scared, I said, "Mira, I'm a monster," as my heart hammered in my chest.

I watched the blood drain from her face as we looked at each other. Things had just taken a turn in another world's sun.

The End